DAWN COMES EARLY

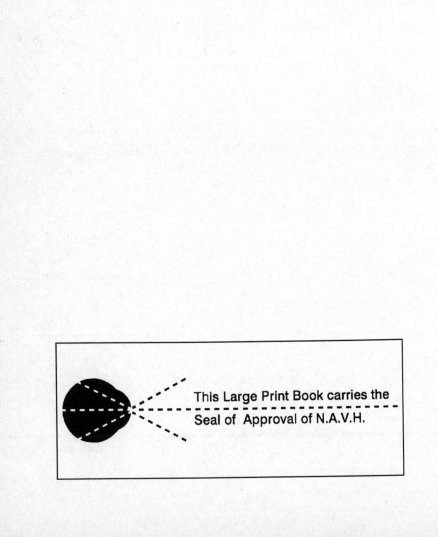

This Large Print Book carries the
Seal of Approval of N.A.V.H.

DAWN COMES EARLY

MARGARET BROWNLEY

THORNDIKE PRESS
A part of Gale, Cengage Learning

GALE
CENGAGE Learning·

Detroit • New York • San Francisco • New Haven, Conn • Waterville, Maine • London

GALE
CENGAGE Learning®

LIBRARY OF CONGRESS CATALOGING-IN-PUBLICATION DATA

Brownley, Margaret.
   Dawn comes early / by Margaret Brownley.
      pages ; cm. — (Thorndike Press large print Christian
   historical fiction) (A brides of last chance ranch novel ; #1)
      ISBN 978-1-4104-4583-4 (hardcover) — ISBN 1-4104-4583-6 (hardcover)
   1. Large type books. I. Title.
   PS3602.R745D39 2012b
   813'.6—dc23   2012007991

Published in 2012 by arrangement with Thomas Nelson, Inc.

Printed in Mexico
1 2 3 4 5 6 7 16 15 14 13 12

To my daughter-in-law Natsuko,
whose name means "summer."
Your loving heart and gentle spirit have
brought our family so much joy.

HEIRESS WANTED

Looking for hardworking, professional woman of good character and pleasant disposition willing to learn the ranching business in Arizona Territory. Must be single and prepared to remain so now and forevermore.

CHAPTER 1

Arizona Territory 1895

"Cactus Paaaaaaaaaatch!"

Whistle piercing the air, the wheels of the Southern Pacific ground against the metal rails, jerking passengers back and forth before coming to a screeching stop.

Kate Tenney was the only traveler to rise from her seat. Ignoring the curious gazes of the mostly male passengers, she walked along the narrow aisle and down the steps to the deserted open-air station. Steam puffed across the wooden platform like a hissing dragon. She clutched at her skirt with one damp hand and shaded her brow against the bright noon sun with the other.

The steamer trunk filled with her precious belongings landed with a thud by her side. It had been delivered by the dark-skinned, uniformed porter who then grabbed hold of the handrail and swung his bulky frame back onto the train. He leaned out just far

9

enough to signal the engineer with a wave of his hand and to afford Kate one last pitying look before vanishing inside. He wasn't the first to take pity on her, but if things worked out as she hoped, he would most certainly be the last.

The train slithered away, picking up speed until all that remained of the Tucson-bound express was the sound of a distant whistle and a line of black curling smoke.

Hands on her waist, Kate glanced around with a growing sense of dismay. This couldn't be Cactus Patch. *Please don't let it be so.* Never in all her twenty-nine years had she imagined such a desolate place.

Finding the nearby baggage room, ticket counter, and telegraph office empty, she turned a complete circle, squinting against the sun's white glare. Other than the cluster of sand-colored buildings in the distance, the flat, arid land stretched all the way to the purple-hued mountains on the horizon with only an occasional cactus to break the monotony in between. Heat waves shimmered from the desert floor and sweat trickled down her temples.

She removed her feathered hat and wiped away the dampness on her forehead with the back of her hand. The hat was more fashionable than practical and had to be tilted in an unappealing way before it offered any real protection from the sun, but the last thing she needed was freckles or a red nose. She was determined to look presentable, if not altogether professional. Her future depended on it.

She pulled a tattered telegram from the pocket of her blue traveling suit. It had taken six days to travel to Arizona Territory from Boston, and she longed for a bath and cool drink.

The telegram clearly stated that a ranch hand would pick her up. It was signed by Miss Eleanor Walker, owner of the Last Chance Ranch. The advertisement for a professional woman to be "heiress" to a cattle ranch had stoked Kate's imagination. She responded partly out of curiosity, but also out of desperation. She needed work, but more than that she wanted the respectability that came with owning land.

She sighed and tucked the telegram back into her pocket. So where was her driver? Where, for that matter, was anyone? The town — if indeed it was a town — showed no sign of life. She couldn't even make out a horse or carriage. Had someone played a trick on her? Was this, in actuality, a ghost town?

Shuddering, she shook away the thought,

but riding herd on her imagination was not so easy. What if she had to spend the night stranded in this deserted place? Or was attacked by Indians, bandits, or a pack of hungry, snarling wolves?

She groaned. Her vivid imagination never failed to make a bad situation worse. It was a writer's curse, and the only solution was a course of action that would keep her mind from going off on one of its flights of fancy.

Spotting a rope coiled on the platform, she gathered it in hand and tied it to a handle of her trunk. She wasn't about to leave her clothes and precious books unattended, though she couldn't imagine who would steal them.

She yanked the trunk off the wooden platform, stirring up a cloud of dust, and started toward town. Dragging the trunk was like dragging a dead mule. She moistened her cracked lips, but grit filled her nose and mouth. Her eyes burned and her throat was parched.

The going was slow. At that rate she would be lucky to reach town before dusk.

She stopped from time to time to catch her breath, but the closer she got to Cactus Patch, the harder it was to control her overactive mind.

It wasn't much of a town. Indeed, by

Boston's standard it was little more than a whistle-stop. Adobe false-front buildings lined the narrow dirt road, with only a narrow wooden boardwalk separating the two. The sun directly overhead failed to cast so much as a shadow, let alone a spot of shade.

She passed several buildings, the scraping sound of her trunk breaking the silence. According to the handwritten signs in the windows, all businesses were closed, even the barbershop, gunsmith, and Cactus Patch Gazette. A breeze had picked up and a tumbleweed rolled down the middle of the street. The wind felt like the gush of a hot furnace bringing no relief. A loose shutter on a two-story building banged like a slow-beating drum. A saloon's batwing doors moved and squeaked.

The town looked abandoned but oddly, she felt the weight of a thousand eyes upon her. Her imagination playing tricks on her, no doubt. Had to be. Still . . .

"Hello," she called. The word felt like a rock in her dry mouth. She cleared her throat and tried again, this time louder. "Anyone there?"

She came to a side street and breathed in relief. Horses were tied to wooden rails, their tails swishing back and forth like pendulums measuring the passing of time.

A buckboard wagon was parked on the side of the street along with a buggy.

Never did she think to see a more welcome sight. Horses and wagons meant people. This apparently was the heart of town. It had a bank, a hotel, and a sign that read Marshal — but all appeared to be deserted. At the far end of the street stood a windmill and water tank. Anticipating the feel of cool water in her dry mouth, she quickened her step.

"Hello," she called again, but her call was met with silence. She narrowed her gaze to the doors of the Blue Rooster Saloon. Where was everyone? Had she miscounted the days? Was this in reality the Sabbath instead of Tuesday like she supposed?

"Shhh." Bessie Adams hunkered behind a pickle barrel in Green's General Merchandise Store. A shadow inched its way across the floor indicating someone outside walking past the store window. The shadow stilled and Bessie's heart thudded.

Finger to her lips, she signaled for her sister not to move. Lula-Belle peered from behind the potbellied stove, her rounded, fear-stricken eyes staring from a well-worn face.

Bessie's joints ached from kneeling on the

14

hardwood floor. At age sixty she was too old for such calisthenics. Was it too much to ask that a woman come to town to do her weekly marketing without having to fear for her life?

As the town's resident outlaw, Cactus Joe had long worn out his welcome. Now he stood outside the shop, and only a pane of glass and a barrel of pickles separated her from him. It was enough to give a person heart failure.

If only she hadn't worn her flowery skirt and yellow shirtwaist. It would be easier to hide an elephant amid the store's adobe walls than her brightly colored garments.

At the first round of gunfire, Mr. Green had bolted the door and locked himself into the stockroom in back with absolutely no regard for the safety of his customers. Bessie hadn't seen hide nor hair of the store owner since. Just wait till she got her hands on the scoundrel. It would serve him right if she took her business elsewhere.

The doorknob jiggled and Bessie's stomach lurched. Gaze riveted on the dark form standing outside the door, she looked around for a weapon but the tools were kept at the back of the store. Only dry goods, sewing notions, and groceries were displayed in front. She eyed the bin of onions

15

and potatoes but settled instead on a can of VanCamp's beans on a nearby shelf. It wasn't much of a weapon, but it was the closest at hand. Let the outlaw raise one finger toward her or her sister and she wouldn't be responsible for her actions. She lifted her gaze to the ceiling. God forgive her.

Something caught her eye and she practically fainted. The peacock feather on Lula-Belle's ridiculous hat waved like an engineer trying to stop a train. Bessie reached across the aisle and snatched her sister's hat off her head.

"Ouch!" Lula-Belle hissed, glaring at her. She grabbed the hat in Bessie's hand, and the two struggled for a moment before the boater shot up and caught on a ceiling hook used to hang meat.

"Now look what you've done!" Lula-Belle rubbed her head, her tightly wound curls bobbing up and down like tiny springs. "That hurt," she mouthed.

"A bullet will hurt more," Bessie mouthed back.

The doorknob jiggled again and Bessie ducked out of sight. Despite her frazzled nerves, she thought up a plan. Unfortunately, the plan required her sister's cooperation — never a good thing.

Mercy, it was the same old story. Nothing would get done if it wasn't for her. Her husband, Sam, would starve to death if she wasn't around to feed him. As for her two grown nephews, their lack of domestic skills was the least of it. Neither one of them had the slightest idea how to find a wife. This meant she had no choice but to put her considerable matchmaking skills to work yet again. Now it looked as if she would even have to do the marshal's job and catch Cactus Joe herself.

Heart pounding, she forced herself to calm down. It was no time to panic. Lula-Belle would panic enough for both of them. "I'll hide on the other side," she whispered, pointing to the cracker barrel. "When he comes inside you distract him. Make a lot of noise."

Lula-Belle's already-pale face turned as white as the shawl around her shoulders. "What . . . what are you going to do?"

"While he's looking at you, I'll sneak up behind him and hit him over the head." She held up the can of beans. "I'll hold him down while you get the marshal."

Lula-Belle stared at the tin can in Bessie's hand, her face suffused with doubt. "I don't think . . ."

The sound of breaking glass sent Bessie

scurrying across the floor on hands and knees and ducking behind the cracker barrel. She grimaced. Her knees and back would never be the same. Too late she realized her sister had followed her and was now hunkered down by her side.

"You were supposed to stay on the other side."

"You didn't tell me that," Lula-Belle argued.

Bessie rolled her eyes and tried to think how to salvage the situation. The cracker barrel wasn't wide enough to provide adequate protection for both of them. Before she could think of a solution, the door flew open and Lula-Belle grabbed her arm.

Cactus Joe stepped inside the shop, glass crunching beneath his boots. Holding his gun aloft, he was dressed in his customary black trousers and shirt. He had dark, greasy-looking hair, a thin mustache, and an eye patch. It was the patch that saved them as he obviously couldn't see to his left.

It was now or never. After prying Lula-Belle's fingers from her arm, Bessie shot up quick as a jack-in-the-box and threw the beans hard. The can sailed past the outlaw, knocked over a stack of Log Cabin syrup cans, and bounced off the wall before ricocheting back to hit Cactus Joe on the shoulder.

Startled, the bandit fired his gun. The bullet whizzed straight up to the ceiling whereupon Lula-Belle's prized hat fell atop his head.

Blinded by feathers, Cactus Joe yelped and danced around the store, knocking over canned and soft goods alike in an effort to rid himself of the felt confection.

Lula-Belle let out a bloodcurdling scream. "Save the hat!"

Just as the outlaw freed himself, a woman stepped into the shop — a stranger.

Looking straight at Bessie, she said, "Thank goodness. I thought I heard a gun —" She spotted Cactus Joe and froze, her rounded eyes riveted on his weapon.

Cactus Joe swung around, grabbed the stranger with one arm, and dragged her outside.

"Quick, lock the door," Bessie yelled, even though the broken glass wouldn't keep out a fly. At the sound of gunfire, she and her sister dived behind the counter, cracking their heads together in their haste to hide. Never in all her born days did Bessie pray so hard.

Kate's captor dragged her along the deserted boardwalk. "Let me go!" she cried.

Her ears still ringing from the deafening report, she hit him hard with her fist and kicked him in the shin.

"Ow, that hurt." Sounding annoyed, he jerked her back and waved his gun.

She gasped. *This is my imagination. Please, please, let it be so.* Only it wasn't. His fingers digging into the flesh of her arm convinced her of that. She glared up at him and shuddered. The formidable black-clad figure glared with one good eye. He had a thin, slightly crooked mustache, shoulder-length black hair, and pockmarked skin.

He pointed the gun at some distant target and fired again. Kate flinched. The man shot at the trunk she'd left in the middle of the dirt-packed street, and her clothes and books were now scattered on the ground.

"You didn't have to do that," she cried. "You didn't have to shoot my trunk."

"It's this blasted eye patch," he muttered. He sounded almost apologetic, but the steel-like grip on her arm remained. "Can't see worth a plugged nickel. I was actually aiming for that saloon."

Another shot sounded, this time from a distance away. A chip of wood flew off a nearby sign. Fearing that the distant shooter would fire again, she screamed, "Help, help!"

The outlaw yanked her closer, slamming her against his chest. "Shut up."

"Let her go, Cactus Joe," someone called from atop the Golden Star Saloon.

"Come and get her, Marshal," her captor hollered back. He fired another shot, this time aiming at the roof.

Mercy. If she was writing this scene, her heroine would have a weapon in her boot and the courage to use it, but at the moment she lacked both. Since her high-button shoes contained nothing more than two sore feet, the man named Cactus Joe had little to fear from her.

Pointing his gun at the saloon, he moved backward to the opposite side of the street, pulling her with him. He reeked of whiskey, tobacco, and sweat. Fear knotted inside her. Her body shook so hard that at first she thought the jingling sound was her rattling bones instead of his spurs.

He walked faster now, dragging her along with him.

"You . . . you have no right to make me a party to your n-nefarious ways," she stammered.

"I hate to disappoint you, lady, but we ain't goin' to no party."

He forced her down an alley and behind the buildings toward two horses. No — one horse. Her eyes were playing tricks on her. She felt dizzy, faint, her legs weightless. Her head began to swim and she swayed. With a muttered curse the outlaw shoved her away. She fell forward, hitting the ground hard.

Momentarily stunned, she fought her way through the thickening fog. Confusion surrounded her. Running feet. Shouts. The pounding of horses' hooves. She raised herself up on both hands but was blinded by the sun.

She had no idea how long she lay there, unable to move. Finally a shadow swept over her, mercifully blocking out the relentless dazzling light.

"Ma'am?"

CHAPTER 2

The woman wasn't injured as far as Luke Adams could tell, but she was definitely dry as a bone. He helped her to her feet, but she started to crumble to the ground again. One hand behind her back, he slid an arm beneath her legs and lifted her off the ground with a quick swoop. She felt light, almost weightless in his arms, as he carried her into his blacksmith shop.

His wolf dog, Homer, greeted him at the door, tail between his legs. Part Mexican gray wolf, the dog had pointed ears and long legs and tail. Homer had dived for cover during the initial round of gunfire and that's where he'd pretty much stayed. Now he regarded Luke as if seeking reassurance, the dim light turning his amber eyes almost yellow.

"It's all right, boy. She's not going to hurt you."

A quick glance toward the darkened forge

told him his younger brother, Michael, had taken off the moment Luke stepped outside. His brother hadn't completed the simplest task Luke had assigned him. The unopened can of Neatsfoot oil meant the leather bellows had not been lubricated. Michael hadn't even calked the wood to keep the bellows from losing pressure.

Luke shook his head. The boy would be the death of him yet. Twenty years old and his brother still acted like a kid, taking no responsibility for himself or anything else. Biting back annoyance, Luke eased the woman onto the wooden workbench. First things first. He'd deal with Michael later.

He held her up with one arm while pushing away a broken wagon wheel with the other. He then laid her down gently, cushioning her head with a folded leather apron.

He gave her a quick once-over, his lips pursed in an appreciative though silent whistle.

Even with her alarmingly pale skin, she was a pretty woman. Mighty pretty. Her oval face came to a dainty point beneath a soft-curving mouth. She had a perfectly straight nose, lush eyelashes that swept across soft rounded cheekbones, and a smooth forehead.

Pulling his gaze away from her arresting

features, he glanced down the length of her slender figure. Still no sign of injuries. Quickly drawing his attention back to her face, he was alarmed by her shallow breathing. He wasn't a doctor, but he knew heat sickness when he saw it. He also knew he needed to cool her down, quick.

Tugging at the ribbons beneath her chin, he removed the hatpin from the felt crown of her hat. In his haste, he dislodged the pins holding her bun in place and a cascade of damp blond curls fell across his bench.

He held her upward so as to remove her capelike jacket. Working her arms out of the sleeves, he tossed it aside. Fumbling with the tiny pearl buttons at her throat, he undid the top of her bodice and eased her down again. Now to cool her off.

In his haste to reach the water pump, he kicked a newly minted horseshoe across the floor, and Homer dived beneath the workbench.

Some protector. "Chicken."

The dog responded with a halfhearted bark and Luke chuckled. "You sound like a burro with a bad cold."

Quickly priming the pump, he filled a clean drinking glass and metal basin.

Setting both on the workbench next to the woman's side, he soaked a cloth and trickled

water along her forehead. Pushing her golden hair away from her face, he dabbed the cloth across her pale, smooth skin.

Worried that she still hadn't responded, he dumped the basin of water onto her chest, soaking her lace-trimmed shirtwaist. Her eyes fluttered for a moment and she moaned.

"There you go," he said in relief. Cooling her down was only the first step. He now had to get water into her, pronto.

He slid his arm beneath her neck and lifted her head. He raised the glass to her lips and she took a sip.

"Come on," he urged. This time her lashes flew up, revealing eyes the same color as her bright blue jacket that he'd tossed aside. She drank a little — nowhere near enough — but he didn't want to force too much down at first.

A quick glance into her eyes was like diving into a pool of cool water. Yep. She was mighty pretty. Something stirred inside.

Her very presence made the blackened walls of his shop seem less dingy and dark. It was as if the second floor of the building had suddenly blown off, letting in streams of bright sunlight to the first floor.

Other than his two aunts, women didn't generally step foot in his establishment.

Certainly no one dressed as fancy as this one. Her garments told him she was from back east somewhere, Boston maybe, or New York. One of those big cities.

So what was a lady like her doing in a place like Cactus Patch? The town had settled down in the last few years, but the recent discovery of silver in the nearby mountains had stirred things up again, bringing all sorts of travelers to town.

He made her drink little sips at a time. After she'd emptied the glass, he hastened to refill it. She drank the second and third glass with little prodding. She murmured something and he leaned closer.

"Brandon," she said, looking straight at him. A shadow of a smile touched her lips. "Brandon."

He was still wondering who Brandon was when she shook her head and blinked. "Are . . . are you real?"

He pulled back. No one had ever asked him that before. She appeared lucid but looks could be deceiving. "Yep, I'm real," he said for want of another answer. "How do you feel?"

She frowned for a moment before answering. "My . . . my head . . . I feel discombobulated."

He scratched his head. Discom— what?

Sounded like something a man hanging from a gallows might say. "I reckon too much sun will do that to you."

He left her side to refill her glass. She cried out and he swung around, spilling water all over his leather apron. "Ma'am?"

She sat upright, eyes rounded. Color had returned to her face and her cheeks flamed red.

She clutched the gap at her neckline like she was protecting a bank vault or cash box. Yep, she was an easterner, all right.

"My clothes are wet."

"Sorry, ma'am. Had to cool you down fast."

Her gaze darted around before settling on him. "Thank you. I'm sorry to be so much trouble."

"No trouble, ma'am." Truth was he felt sorry for her. She looked scared half out of her wits. Not that he could blame her. She had probably never before encountered the likes of Cactus Joe. *Welcome to Arizona, lady.*

"Name's Luke Adams, but you can call me Luke." He gestured toward his gray-white dog. "That there is Homer."

Upon hearing his name, the wolf dog flicked his ears but his head remained on crossed paws. The woman let down her guard just enough to give Luke the faintest smile, but she still protected her neckline.

"Homer, after the Greek philosopher and poet?" She pronounced his dog's name as Hom*ah*.

"I don't know nothin' about a Greek philosopher," he said. "I call him Homer 'cause he can find his way home no matter where he's at. I was once lost in the desert but Homer got me back safely." He paused for a moment. "You haven't told me your name."

She observed him through lowered lashes. "Miss Tenney. Miss Kate Tenney." She glanced toward the door as if measuring the distance before turning her gaze back to him, her face shadowed with wary regard.

"Mighty pleased to meet you, Miss Tenney," he said, as gently as his deep baritone voice would allow. "You gave me a scare there. It might not be a bad idea to check in with Doc Masterson."

"Th-That won't be necessary," she stammered. She moistened her trembling lips. "I feel much improved. Thank you. I'm most grateful for your help." She studied him with rounded eyes before adding, "That man shot my trunk and my belongings are scattered all over the street."

He couldn't help but sympathize. He only wished she'd stop looking at him like some-

29

thing that should be locked up or buried. Not that he blamed her. After what she'd gone through it was only natural she would distrust him. Still, it bothered him, took him back to another time and place. He was only twelve when his childhood friend had drowned in the rain-swollen Gila River. "Trust me," Luke had yelled, tossing his friend a rope. But Jamie hadn't trusted Luke enough to let go of the tree trunk and grab hold of the lifeline.

Surprised to find himself suddenly face-to-face with a memory he'd sooner forget, he shook his head. Not the same thing. Miss Tenney wasn't drowning and the only lifeline he offered was water and sympathy. Still, he had the strangest feeling that the lady was caught up in floodwaters of another kind. Startled by the image, he shook his head. It wasn't like him to have such dark thoughts. The argument with his brother that morning must have upset him more than he knew.

"M-My belongings . . ."

"I'll get your things," he said, hoping that if he left her alone for a moment she would settle down a mite, relax even. "Give you a chance to rest a bit."

"No!"

The strength of her voice surprised him.

She still looked fragile but nothing, apparently, was wrong with her lungs. "No need to fret yourself, ma'am. I've already seen a lady's" — what do women call those things? — "under-riggin's."

She gave him an unflinching stare. "Please accept my apologies." She took a deep breath. "It's been a horrendous day. And then to be assailed by that abominable man . . . I'm sure you can understand that . . . that I'm not quite myself."

That explained why she had mistaken him for someone else. That Brandon fellow sure was a lucky guy, though not particularly smart. No man in his right mind would allow a lady like Miss Tenney to travel to Arizona Territory by herself.

"There were two women in the mercantile," she said. "They weren't hurt, but they must be terribly upset."

"If they're locals they'll get over it." Since Miss Tenney still looked anxious or nervous or both, he added, "If it makes you feel any better I don't think Cactus Joe meant to do you any harm, ma'am. He just wanted to use you to escape."

Her eyes widened. "He had a gun. He could have dragged me away, kept me hostage, and had his way with me. He could have used me for his reprehensible purposes, or left me in the desert without food or water. I could have ended up dead or . . . or worse."

He planted his hands on hips, not sure what to say. What could be worse than death? Whatever it was he didn't want to know.

"That man's as slippery as a greased hog, that's for sure," he said at last. "But he's more of a nuisance than a threat. Maybe this time his luck will run out and the marshal will capture him."

If he was a betting man he'd put his money on Cactus Joe. The desert favored outlaws, and most local lawmen knew little if anything about tracking criminals through rugged terrain. Some, like Marshal Morris, didn't even try. Not like John Slaughter, former sheriff of Cochise County, known as the meanest good guy who ever lived. The man brought law and order to the area during his two terms. What a pity he'd retired.

Miss Tenney pinned up her hair and reached for her hat. "The man should be incarcerated for the rest of his life."

"Here in Arizona Territory, the worse that can happen to him is a good hangin'."

She gave him an odd look. "Yes, well . . ."

"I'll go and get your things." He backed toward the door. "If there's anything else you need, just holler."

"Wait. There is one more thing. Could you tell me how to get to the Last Chance Ranch?"

"Last Chance —"

He should have known. A parade of women had passed through Cactus Patch in recent months, hoping to be chosen as Eleanor Walker's heiress in the unlikely event she should die. So far none of the applicants had lasted more than a few days — a week tops. Ranching was hard work. Judging by Miss Tenney's lily-white hands and delicate frame, she knew little if anything about manual labor. He gave her maybe twenty-four hours before the old lady sent her packing as she had the others.

"So you're another one," he said. The idea of women traipsing across the country in hopes of convincing an old lady to turn over her spread to them struck him as odd, maybe even distasteful.

She looked momentarily confused. "Another what?"

"Another woman who thinks runnin' a cattle ranch is as easy as making a pie."

She stiffened as if donning a suit of invisible armor. "I know that ranching is hard work."

Hard didn't even begin to describe it, but

he wasn't about to argue with her. Cactus Joe was no match for what awaited her on that ranch. "Is Miss Walker expectin' you?"

"She is. Someone was supposed to pick me up from the train station."

"Most everyone took off when the shootin' began," he said. "That probably includes your driver."

She tilted her head. "But not you."

He shrugged. "I have work to do." He indicated a wagon with a missing wheel. It belonged to Old Travis, a local farmer who couldn't afford to be without his only means of driving produce to the market for very long. "Like I said, Cactus Joe is a nuisance but not much else."

She looked unconvinced. "If that's true, then where is everyone? Except for the two women I told you about, the town looks deserted."

"Around here folks jump at the chance not to work on a hot day. Whenever Cactus Joe comes to town it's kinda like a holiday."

Her eyes widened. "I never heard anything so ridiculous in my life. Does . . . does he come to town often?"

"Often enough to wear out his welcome," he said.

She gave her head a slight toss, buttoned her shirtwaist, and put on her hat. Her bodice was still wet and the feathers on her hat drooped, but she sure did look business-like all of a sudden.

"How do I arrange transportation to the ranch?" she asked.

"Normally I would tell you to rent a rig from the livery, but Hopper — that's the owner — took off when he heard the first shot. I'm sure someone will come and get you. Eventually. Meanwhile, you can stay at the hotel." No sooner had he said it than he changed his mind. The hotel was no place for a lady, especially one as pretty as this one.

"Tell you what. I'll drive you to the ranch myself."

"That's very kind of you to offer, but I don't want to cause you further inconvenience," she said.

"You won't. My wagon's out back. All I have to do is hitch my horse to it and we can be on our way." If his lazy, good-for-nothing brother hadn't taken off, Luke would have made him drive her to the ranch.

She shivered. "You don't think we'll run into that awful man, do you?"

"Cactus Joe?" He shook his head. "He's probably in the next county by now, if not the next territory."

35

A shadow of relief crossed her face. "Thank you. I appreciate your kindness."

"It's my pleasure, ma'am." The moment he grabbed his leather hat, Homer lifted his head, ears forward. "Come on, boy. Let's give the lady some privacy."

Homer jumped to his feet, wagging his tail, but made no move toward the door.

"The dog's a chicken," he said, and Miss Tenney laughed. It was a tight little sound, but it was still the nicest sound he'd heard in a week of Sundays. He clapped his hands twice and this time Homer followed him outside.

The sun dazzled him as he walked up the alley, but no more than the sight that greeted him when he turned the corner and spotted the lady's fancy under-riggin's strewn upon the dirt-packed road.

CHAPTER 3

She stared into Brandon's velvet brown eyes and her heart gave a wild flutter . . . "You saved me, you saved me . . ."

Kate chased away the words running through her head. The man sitting on the wagon seat next to her had blue eyes, not brown, though he certainly was every bit as handsome as Brandon, the hero in her latest novel. Mr. Adams had a rugged square face, an indented chin, and a straight, narrow nose. Brown hair curled from beneath his leather hat, and a wayward lock swept across his forehead.

He had wide shoulders that tapered down to a trim waist. The rolled-up sleeves of his boiled shirt revealed the full length of his powerful arms.

Even more disconcerting than his likeness to her fictional character was the womanly way he made her feel each time he turned his blue eyes in her direction. Between her encounter with the outlaw and her imminent meeting with Miss Walker, she didn't need Luke Adams to add to her anxiety. But add he did.

The air practically sizzled with the strength and virility of him. Much to her alarm her racing pulse brought a flush to her face. She could not, would not trust him, not for a single moment. No man could be trusted. Not even one as handsome and seemingly kindhearted as Mr. Luke Adams.

The wagon jolted over a rut in the road and her arm inadvertently rubbed against his. Inching as close to the outer edge of the seat as possible, she measured the distance between them and it was still alarmingly close.

As much as possible she kept her gaze straight ahead. The long, narrow road seemed to stretch to the horizon. "Are you sure we won't run into that horrible man?"

"Cactus Joe? I doubt it. If you ask me the man's short a hat size or two but he's harmless. Not like the Texas Kid or the Tucson Kid. Drat, he's not even like Billy the Kid. Now *those* are outlaws."

His assurances did little to calm her nerves. Apparently the only bandits he took seriously were the ones belonging to a society of human goats.

Seemingly oblivious to her anxiety, he whistled softly but she didn't recognize the tune. He sat tall and straight, his shoulders wide, his hands firm on the reins. From time to time he pointed out various landmarks. He was extremely knowledgeable and described the history of the territory going all the way back to Spanish rule.

He indicated a building with a tall steeple and small cemetery. "That's the church. We don't have a regular preacher, but a circuit rider whizzes through every other week or so."

Homer trotted a short distance ahead, sniffing the ground like a hound trailing a fox.

About a mile or two out of town, Mr. Adams pointed to a small adobe house with a corrugated steel gable roof. "My Aunt Bessie and Uncle Sam live there," he said with obvious fondness. Homer stopped in front of the house and barked.

"Not now, boy," he said. "We'll pop in for a visit on the way back." For Kate's benefit he added, "Homer has a fondness for gingersnaps and Aunt Bessie makes the best."

About a mile farther down the road he tossed a nod toward another house almost identical to the first. "Aunt Lula-Belle and Uncle Murphy live there."

"How many relatives do you have?" she asked.

"Not many. I have a brother named Michael and another aunt who lives in Tucson. That's about it. I was born in Texas, but my parents died when I was eleven. My pa was killed in an Indian uprising and my ma died soon after, in childbirth."

"I'm so sorry," Kate said.

"I went to live with my aunt and uncle in Houston, but when a second smithy came to town my uncle decided Texas was gettin' too crowded, so we moved here."

A smile broke through her guarded countenance.

He grinned back at her. "What's so funny?"

"I can't tell you how many blacksmiths are in Boston. At least a dozen or more."

He grimaced. "Don't sound like there's enough room between the hammer and the anvil with that many people."

She couldn't imagine Luke Adams on the crowded streets of Boston. He was definitely a man who needed wide-open spaces.

"What do residents do here?" she asked. Boston with its libraries, museums, and theaters offered a rich cultural life she thoroughly enjoyed.

He gave her a cockeyed look. "What do we do?"

"For entertainment?" she said to clarify.

"There're more than a dozen saloons in town. I reckon that's about as entertainin' as it gets around here."

At first she thought he was joking, but he looked perfectly serious. She bit her lip and said nothing. She didn't know what to say.

He glanced at her. "I prefer it out here in the desert."

"There's nothing out here."

"It'll grow on you." After a while he said, "In the Bible God used the desert to test men."

She fanned herself furiously with her hand. "Is that what he's doing now? Testing us?"

"Could be." He clicked his tongue and his horse picked up speed. "Could be."

He stopped from time to time to offer the dog a drink. He also insisted Kate drink from his canteen, wiping the top with a clean bandanna before handing it to her.

They drove through what seemed like miles of high desert, ringed by steep-cliff mesas and littered with angry black rocks pitted with holes.

"Volcanic rock," he explained.

The rocks looked as inhospitable as the rest of the land, and she shuddered. "Everything looks so dry."

"We don't get a lot of rain out here," he said. "About ten, twelve inches a year if we're lucky. June and July are our rainy months."

Boston got at least four times that much rain. "Anyone saving for a rainy day around here could probably get rich."

"He'd be more likely to be robbed," he said.

She blew out her breath. Never had she met anyone with a more casual regard for crime. "How much longer?" she asked. She didn't mean to sound impatient or ungrateful, but the air was still warm and her body ached with weariness. The drive seemed interminable.

He guided the buckboard through a wire gap fence. "Here she is," he announced as one might introduce royalty. "The Last Chance Ranch. You won't find a better ranch in all of Cochise County."

She hadn't known what to expect, but certainly not this. A tumbleweed rested against a rock, but no sign. Just a barbed wire fence and more arid, flat desert dotted with rocks black as coal. The gate leading to the ranch was so different from anything she'd imagined, she would have laughed out loud had she had the energy.

"How ostentatious," she said in jest.

He glanced at her and frowned. Obviously, the man lacked a sense of humor. What a pity.

"Do you know the owner?" she asked, anxious to fill in the sudden awkward silence.

"Miss Walker?" He shrugged his massive shoulders. "I reckon everyone knows her," he said. "At least well enough to stay out of her way."

It wasn't what she wanted to hear. "Are you implying the woman is difficult?"

"I'm not implyin' anything, ma'am. I'm statin' it as fact. She's more like a runaway locomotive coming straight at you."

The picture he drew in her mind only added to her anxiety. It worried her that he used such strong words for the lady ranch owner, but described Cactus Joe as a mere nuisance. Could Miss Walker really be that bad?

In an effort to calm her nerves she rearranged her hat, wiggling the hatpin in place, and straightened her travel suit jacket. Her shirtwaist was now dry, but her skirt was wrinkled and covered in dust and smudged with train cinders. She neither looked nor felt her best.

She craned her neck looking for a ranch house or something — anything. Nothing stirred. Even the muted horse hooves and rattling buckboard failed to disturb the stark panorama that stretched all the way to the mountains.

She had taken him at his word when he said they had reached the ranch. So where was it? Maybe once she sighted civilization — if there was such a thing out here — the butterflies in her stomach would settle down.

"I thought you said this was the Last Chance."

"It is, ma'am, acres of deeded property surrounded by thousands of acres of free range. The ranch house is just a mile or so up the road."

"A mile?"

He glanced at her. "The entire area covers around two hundred and fifty square miles."

She stared at him, openmouthed. "That much?" Westerners sure did think a lot bigger than their eastern counterparts.

She already doubted the wisdom of coming to Cactus Patch, and the size of the ranch only added to her apprehension. Had she not been so hot and exhausted she would have been tempted to ask Mr. Adams to turn the wagon around and drive back to town and . . . go where? As forbidding and inhospitable as this land was, she had no desire to return to Boston and the terrible memories left behind.

She shook her thoughts away. "So where are the cattle?"

He pointed to the right. "Over there."

Shading her eyes against the midafternoon sun, she followed his pointing finger. The air shimmered with heat and the landscape was blurred. At first she didn't see anything but saguaro cacti rising from the desert floor. Some of the cacti stood twenty feet high, arms branching out from a rounded pole — a strange plant, indeed.

Finally she spotted little black dots of grazing cattle next to a body of water. She hadn't expected to see a lake in the middle of the desert and the sight offered a measure of comfort, however tenuous.

Spying the cattle too, Homer barked as if in greeting and raced ahead of the wagon.

"What I would give to dive into that lake," she said, fanning herself with her hand.

He grinned at her. "I wouldn't advise it, ma'am. That's a mirage. All that's out there is sand, rattlers, and burro grass."

She blinked. "It certainly looks real."

"The desert is deceivin'." He glanced at

her. "You just never know what you're gonna find."

"What about that up ahead? Is that a mirage too?" She pointed to a carpet of green that offered a pleasing contrast to the miles of arid land they'd passed.

"Nope, that's real. Two hundred acres of alfalfa and red-top clover. Up ahead is the ranch house." He clicked his tongue and flapped the reins, and his horse picked up speed.

At the first building they reached, he brought the wagon to a stop and set the brake. Jumping from his seat he hurried to Kate's side. Hands around her waist, he lifted her to the ground as if she were weightless.

His horse drank from the water trough next to the largest windmill Kate had ever seen. The sucker rods made a swishing noise as they rose and fell in the well casing. The metal teeth of the gears scraped and grated as the windmill drew water from the depths of the earth.

Homer stuck his long nose in the trough and drank with loud lapping sounds. Mr. Adams filled his canteen directly from the wooden tank that no animal could reach and handed it to her. Next to the hot air, the water tasted cool and sweet.

"Miss Tenney, I want you to meet your new friend, Adam," he said, introducing her to the windmill.

She tilted her head back to look up. "I didn't know windmills had names."

"There're more than fifty windmills on this here property and they all have names. If one gets into trouble you just yell out its name and everyone knows where to go. This here was the first windmill on the ranch."

"Is Adam named after your family?" she asked.

He laughed. "Nope, the first man in the Bible gets that honor. We had nothin' to do with it."

"It's huge." At least twenty feet wide, it was much larger than any windmill in Boston.

He nodded. "It has to be. It's pullin' water from hundreds of feet down. We don't get much rain so we have to depend on wind for water."

"I always liked Longfellow's 'Windmill.' I can't remember the words exactly, but he wrote that the windmill faced the wind as bravely as a man meets his foe."

"Never heard of a Longfellow windmill. Most of the ones around here were made by the Wolcott Union Windmill Company."

"Oh, but Longfellow's not a . . . a very

47

well-known company."

"Probably why I never heard of it."

"Yes . . . well." She raised her voice. "I'm pleased to meet you, Adam."

In response, the spinning sails turned toward the wind with a creaking sound. Homer, wanting to play, barked and wagged his fluffy tail.

"Come on, we're almost at the ranch house," Mr. Adams said.

She stopped to run her hand along his horse's slick neck. It was a reddish horse with white markings. "What's his name?" she asked.

"Bacon."

She smiled. "I wrote an essay on Bacon in college."

"Seems like a strange subject to write about," he said.

"A strange . . . oh." She blushed. "I was referring to Sir Francis Bacon, the English philosopher."

His mouth quirked but only briefly. "Named him Bacon because that's what he looks like." He raised an inquiring eyebrow. "Do you easterners name animals after philosophers?"

"Not always," she said, and because she wanted to return to their earlier rapport added, "Neither do we name our animals after breakfast fare."

His serious expression disappeared, but the smile she hoped for failed to materialize. "Come on, we better get you to the ranch house."

He walked by her without another word and climbed into the driver's seat. Had she offended him or had she only imagined his sudden curt manner? She watched him warily as she took her seat by his side.

Not that his abrupt change of mood surprised her. Men were unpredictable. It was part of their nature. One moment they could seem all friendly and kind, and the next . . . She shuddered and pushed the thought away but remained circumspect. If she'd learned nothing else in her twenty-nine years, it was never to let down her guard where men were concerned.

From early childhood people had drifted out of her life, never to return. Her father walked out on her and Mama when she was only five, but others had deserted her as well, including her grandfather, who had disapproved of her mother's fondness for alcohol and men. For that reason Kate had conditioned herself not to get too close to anyone, so she'd never had many friends.

Protecting herself had come with a price, of course, requiring her to trade hurt for loneliness, but it was the best she could do. Between the harsh desert land and the uncertainties that lay ahead she welcomed the blacksmith's acquaintance, however tenuous.

After passing a horse corral, large barn, bunkhouse, and various outbuildings, Mr. Adams pulled up in front of a two-story U-shaped adobe ranch house with a low-hip tile roof. The covered porch was supported by wooden columns and ran the length of the house. It provided the only shade Kate had seen since arriving in town, a pleasing sight.

A brick courtyard was hugged on three sides by the house and protected in front by a low adobe wall. An ornate metal gate stood open and looked surprisingly inviting.

Mr. Adams helped her down from the wagon, his work-hardened hands strangely comforting around her small waist. Nonetheless, she moved away the moment her feet touched ground and stared at the ranch house. It was larger than she'd imagined, larger even than the grand houses in Boston's south end, and perfectly maintained.

She brushed off her skirt, threw back her shoulders, and swallowed hard to brace herself. She hadn't come all this way to let a few quivering nerves get the best of her.

Mr. Adams leaned against the wagon with folded arms. "I can take you back to town now, ma'am. It would save you from havin' to hitch a ride back tomorrow or the next day."

It took her a moment to understand his meaning. "Are you saying that I'm not going to make it here?"

"None of the others have. The longest anyone stayed was a week, but that woman was a workhorse."

Irritated that he so easily assumed she'd fail without knowing anything about her, she tossed back her head. He wasn't the first man to underestimate her, but if she had anything to say about it, he would be the last.

"I won't be needing a ride back to town, but thank you for your concern."

He shrugged. "Suit yourself, ma'am." He nodded his head toward the back of the wagon. "I'll bring in your trunk."

Something in his voice reminded her that he had been obliged to pick her intimate garments off the street. Blushing, she turned quickly to hide her face and walked to the open gate.

Knowing he watched, she moved with quick, confident steps that belied her shaking knees, tightly clenched stomach, and dry mouth. Reaching the oversized carved wood door, she tugged on the bellpull with damp hands and glanced back. He stood where she left him, doubt written all over his handsome square face. Gritting her teeth, she gave the bellpull another tug.

From deep inside came the sound of chimes, and after a short wait, a Mexican girl flung open the door.

"I'm Kate Tenney," Kate said by way of introduction. "Miss Walker is expecting me."

"My name Rosita," the girl replied in halting English. Kate guessed that she was probably in her late teens. She wore a gray dress and white apron, her black hair tucked beneath a white ruffled cap. "Miz Walker back soon. Hurry, hurry." She motioned Kate inside and slammed the door shut.

"Flies," she explained.

"Oh." Relieved at not having to face the ranch owner immediately, Kate glanced around the large entry hall, which was as cool as it was dim. Adobe brick walls, partly covered by a colorful Indian rug, rose from a red tile floor. The house smelled of furniture polish, old wood, brass, and just a hint of freshly baked bread. The bread reminded Kate that she hadn't had a bite to eat since breakfast, and her stomach growled.

A sweeping staircase led to the second

floor, and Rosita was halfway up before Kate realized she was expected to follow.

Upon reaching the second-floor landing she couldn't resist glancing over the polished wood banister to the huge foyer below. Mr. Adams had not yet brought in her trunk. Was he really so certain that she wouldn't last? That she would quit before she'd even begun?

Something — a movement, perhaps a shadow — made her lean forward for a better look, but all remained still. Whoever it was had quickly stepped out of sight. No doubt a curious resident or employee.

Rosita led her down a long narrow hall past a small room with a toilet but no tub.

She opened a door toward the end of the hall and motioned Kate inside. The room was light and airy and surprisingly cool. A four-poster bed piled high with pillows and spread with a colorful quilt promised a good night's sleep, the first since leaving Boston. A mahogany lift-top desk stood in a corner next to a tall wardrobe. An oak washstand containing a porcelain basin and water pitcher was centered on the wall opposite the bed, next to a freestanding gilded mirror. The town, ranch, and surrounding area fell far short of her expectations, but the room was everything she could hope for and more.

"When you ready Señorita Walker meet you downstairs."

"Thank you," Kate said. "Is there a bath —"

The rest of her sentence was met by a closed door. Pulling off her jacket she stepped through the glass door that led to the balcony. Shaded by an overhang, the balcony stretched the length of the building, providing a panoramic view of the ranch and distant mountains.

She grabbed hold of the iron railing, surprised to spot Mr. Adams already driving away, his dog sitting in the seat she had moments before occupied. She had assumed he would bring her trunk upstairs himself.

Disappointed that he'd left before she had a chance to thank him, she watched until only a cloud of dust made by his wagon wheels was visible. Loneliness descended upon her like nightfall and she shuddered. The view outside her window looked every bit as forlorn as her future.

Someone knocked on the door and she hurried to open it. A slender Mexican man dressed in white shirt and pants carried her trunk inside and set it on the floor.

"José," he said with a grin, pointing to himself. She wondered if this was the person spying on her earlier.

"Pleased to meet you, José. Thank you for bringing my trunk." When he made no move to leave, she added, "I need to unpack my things."

"Better wait to talk to Miss Walker. The last one vamoosed before she unpacked." He grinned and left.

Refusing to be discouraged and anxious to change out of her traveling clothes, she knelt on the floor and opened her trunk. The instant the lid sprung up, her mouth dropped open and she sat back on her heels. Not only had Mr. Adams fetched her belongings off the street, he had neatly folded every last garment.

She picked up a corset and pair of lacy bloomers and held them to her bosom. She imagined his large, capable hands on the satiny fabric and delicate lace. A strange warm and worrisome current flowed through her.

Shaken, she stood and quickly stuffed her garments in a drawer.

Little more than an hour later, Kate walked downstairs mustering every bit of confidence she could manage. After vigorously sponging off dust and train soot, she'd changed into a plain but stylish brown skirt and tailored shirtwaist, then pinned her hair securely into a neat bun. Her appearance would pass muster for a job interview in Boston, but what was acceptable attire for being interrogated as a possible heiress?

Rosita greeted her at the foot of the stairs and showed her to a sitting room. "Wait here."

The housekeeper left and Kate walked through the open archway, her footsteps bouncing off the clay tile floor. Outside, the house had looked larger than it actually was, probably because of its clean, sweeping lines.

The room had none of the overblown fussiness of Boston parlors. A steer head with wide horns hung over the stone fireplace and seemed to gaze at her as if she were an unwelcome intruder. The walls were adorned with Indian rugs, the bold geometrical designs woven in vivid red and bright turquoise wools. The furniture, which included leather chairs and a matching davenport, was spare but substantial, more intimidating than inviting. Dark wood beams crossed the ceiling.

Beyond a second archway was a dining room with a polished table that could easily seat twelve. Two paneled doors stood open, revealing an office complete with a large oak desk and filing cabinets. The typing machine centered on the desk surprised her. She'd sold her own typewriter to pay for travel expenses. Though she had no further use for such a machine, already she missed it.

One parlor wall was covered with shelves holding leather-bound books. She ran her fingers along the rigid spines hoping to find a Twain, Brontë, or even a James, but every book was about cattle or the cattle business and she couldn't help but feel disappointed.

It wasn't that long ago that writing was her life, but after her last book was banned for "immoral content," her publisher quickly and firmly showed her the door. Immoral, indeed! Boston's Watch and Ward Society deemed her love story a detriment to society and accused her of putting wanton ideas into the heads of young readers. Maybe she did go a bit overboard in taking two pages to describe a kiss, but for the most part the society's critiques were unfair and unfounded.

Books had helped her through an unstable and unhappy childhood. Now as then, she looked for a means of escape. She was so engrossed in reading the titles that she failed to notice the open coffin partly hidden by a potted cactus until she practically bumped into it. The body of a pale-faced man sporting a waxed mustache and dressed in a dark suit lay in the satin-lined interior, a coin on each eye, hands folded across his middle.

Startled, she jumped back, hand on her chest. "Oh dear!"

CHAPTER 4

The lips of the dying man moved and Brandon leaned closer. "For God and country," the man said before taking his very last breath.

Kate gaped at the dead man, the pungent smell of formaldehyde making her eyes water. Nerves taut, she jumped when a cheery voice sounded from behind.

"I see you met my ex-husband, Ralph."

Kate whirled about to face the tall, stately woman with steady gray eyes standing in the doorway. Kate stared at her speechless. Not only did the woman's cavalier attitude regarding the dead man stun Kate, but never had she heard anyone so boldly admit to a failed marriage. Certainly not to a stranger. In Boston a divorce was considered shocking, if not altogether scandalous.

"Burying him on the ranch is more than he deserves, but no one else will claim him," the woman continued. "So what is one to do?"

Not sure whether she was expected to answer the question or simply offer condolences, Kate inched away from the corpse with a murmured, "I'm sorry."

Ignoring Kate's commiseration, the woman introduced herself. "I'm Eleanor Walker. Owner of this ranch."

Dressed in a divided skirt, heavy boots, and a man's plaid shirt, she wore her gray hair pulled into a tight bun with not a single loose strand. Her wide-brimmed hat dangled between her shoulder blades, the stampede string around her neck. The huge room seemed to shrink in response to her commanding presence.

"You must be Kate." She held out her hand and Kate shook it. The woman's grip was as firm as a man's. "Or do you prefer I call you Miss Tenney?" She spoke in a brisk no-nonsense manner, her gray eyes seeming to penetrate rather than regard.

"Kate will do."

"Very well, and you may call me Miss Walker."

It struck Kate as strange to call a previously married woman *miss*, but she would of course comply.

"Do sit down," her hostess said. "I trust

you found your accommodations satisfactory."

"Yes, thank you. My room is lovely." Miss Walker was every bit as intimidating as Cactus Joe, even without a weapon.

Miss Walker took a seat and Kate sat down on a chair opposite. She held her knees together, hands tightly clasped on her lap. Keenly aware that others had come before her and failed, she met Miss Walker's probing stare with chin held high.

As if on cue, Rosita appeared carrying a silver tray with a pitcher of lemonade and two glasses. She set the tray on the low table and looked at Miss Walker as if waiting for permission to pour. The younger woman's quiet, demure manner offered a striking contrast next to Miss Walker's broad movements and deep, vibrant voice, both of which would have been frowned upon in more civilized social circles.

"Thank you, Rosita," Miss Walker said. She waved the young woman away and filled both glasses herself. She handed one to Kate.

"Thank you." The lemonade was both cold and sweet and Kate gulped it down — something she would normally not do in polite company, but then she'd never been so thirsty nor so nervous. Miss Walker made

61

no mention of her ill manners. Instead, she refilled Kate's glass without comment.

Setting the pitcher on the tray, the ranch owner sat back. "I heard you had a little excitement in town."

A little? "The man grabbed me and shot at my trunk," Kate said, shuddering at the memory. When this failed to draw any kind of sympathetic response, she added, "I'm lucky to be alive."

"Aren't we all?" Miss Walker glanced at the coffin. "Or at least some of us are." She fell silent for a moment before adding, "I apologize that no one was at the station to greet you. When my driver heard that Cactus Joe was up to his old tricks, he turned around and came back."

"I don't blame him," Kate said. "Mr. Adams was good enough to give me a ride."

"Then I am in his debt." Miss Walker took a sip of her own lemonade before setting the glass on the tray, ice clinking. She looked Kate up and down, her expression registering neither approval nor disapproval.

"You stated in your letter that you were a professional woman familiar with ranching."

"Yes . . ." Kate had rehearsed this interview in front of a looking glass numerous times, but Miss Walker was even more intimidating than Kate's former editor, Mr.

Conner, and everything she'd practiced went out of her head.

"You wrote that you're a college-educated woman, but I'm not clear as to your profession."

"I'm a writer."

"Yes, you do write lovely letters."

"A *professional* writer," she said to clarify, though it was no longer entirely accurate. After the scathing review of her last book and its subsequent ban in Boston, she was currently unemployed.

"I've published several novels under my pseudonym, K. Mattson." She hesitated. "Some people have a rather jaundiced eye toward certain . . . literary endeavors." *Especially when they involve affairs of the heart.* "For that reason I prefer to keep my former occupation confidential."

Miss Walker's gaze sharpened. "Are you saying that you write . . . *wrote* potboilers?"

The question was pointed enough to raise the dead, but a quick glance at the coffin assured Kate that it hadn't.

"I prefer to call them novels," Kate explained. "Dime novels."

The woman had looked unflappable until that moment. Now she looked downright appalled. "And you think writing these . . . dime novels makes you knowledgeable about running a ranch?"

"Most of my stories take place on a cattle ranch," Kate explained. "That's because I . . . grew up listening to tales about the West. I enjoyed hearing the stories one man told about working on the King Ranch in Texas. He helped drive cattle to Kansas."

What she failed to say, didn't want to say, was that the stories were told by tramps gathered around a bonfire behind the apartment where she lived with her mama. Some were war veterans, others failed gold miners — all were society dropouts. As a child, she liked to climb out onto the roof and hide behind the chimney to listen. Their lively stories fired Kate's imagination like nothing else ever did.

"You heard these tales in *Boston?*" Miss Walker made it sound like Boston was located somewhere in the Boer Republics rather than the States. "I hope you don't believe everything you heard. It's my experience that most people have no idea about life in the West. As for cattle drives . . ." She made a dismissing gesture. "Long and costly drives have gone the way of hoop skirts. Now we simply drive the cattle a short distance to the Willcox stockades and train depot."

"I know ranching has changed, but it was

those stories that inspired me to write my books."

"So why *aren't* you writing?" Miss Walker asked.

"It's difficult for a woman to earn her living by writing," Kate said. At least that much was true. "That's why I'm here."

After her publisher refused to publish more of her books, she applied for a job at both the *Boston Evening Globe* and *Traveler,* but no one was willing to hire a disgraced writer.

Anxious to prove her competence, Kate hastened to add, "I'm quite good at bookkeeping and budgeting and —"

Miss Walker interrupted her with a wave of her hand. "We'll get to all that. First things first. We're in the middle of calving season and it will soon be April. How are you at calving and branding?"

Kate blinked. *Branding.* It never occurred to her that she would actually have to *work* with the animals. "Don't you employ cowhands to do that?"

"Of course I do. But how do you expect to know if the job is done right if you don't know how to do it yourself?"

Kate moistened her lips. "I've never actually *worked* with cattle but like I told you, I do know a little something about the workings of a ranch."

Miss Walker frowned. "The only way to learn ranching is through tenacity and hands-on experience. You can't learn ranching secondhand. Nor can you learn it from books." She waved toward her extensive library. "But even experience isn't enough if you don't have a real passion for the land. It must be in your blood. Do you have anything that qualifies you to run a ranch?"

"I . . . I believe so."

"Believe, Miss Tenney, or know?"

Miss Tenney. If the sudden formality hadn't already convinced Kate that she was about to be dismissed, the railroad watch Miss Walker pulled out of her pocket most certainly did.

"I'm extremely tenacious," Kate said, determined to rise to the challenge. She would never have survived her childhood had she not been strong-willed.

"I'm a fast learner and I'm trustworthy. I'm also honest and hardworking." She continued to recite her qualities as one might recite a list of groceries to a clerk in a mercantile store, but nothing she said pried the skeptical look off Miss Walker's face.

Miss Walker stared at her watch for a moment before pocketing it. "This is all very well and good and you do write a persuasive letter. But so far you've failed to convince me that a privileged upbringing such as yours qualifies you for ranching."

Kate jumped to her feet. "Privileged! *Privileged?* I've worked for everything I have. I earned my education by scrubbing floors, cleaning privies, and —"

Mortified, she covered her mouth with her hand. All her weeks of careful planning had been wasted in one careless, unguarded moment.

Expecting Miss Walker to order her out of the house, she was surprised when the woman gestured for her to sit down.

"I see there's more to you than meets the eye," Miss Walker said, and this time her face reflected the first signs of approval. "That's good. I don't know if mucking out stables is comparable to cleaning privies, but we'll know soon enough. We can't let you around cattle until we get the city smell off you, and nothing accomplishes that faster than a good mucking. I'll also ask Ruckus to find a horse for you. You do ride, of course?"

"Yes, but —"

"Excellent. What about work clothes?"

Kate glanced down at her skirt. These were her work clothes. "I'm afraid these are all I have."

"Hmm." Miss Walker tapped her chin with her finger. "You're about my size. Not quite as tall but I think I have some garments that will fit. I'll have Rosita bring them to your room."

Miss Walker rubbed her hands together. She had large calloused hands the color of leather. It was hard to know how old she was. She had a timeless quality that seemed to make age irrelevant. Her lively eyes, more blue now than gray, watched from a well-lined and well-tanned face, but her body was as supple as that of a young girl.

As if to guess her thoughts, Eleanor said, "I'm sixty-five years old. That's young for a saguaro, which can live for 150 years, but as far as I know no ranch owner could last that long. Nor would anyone want to."

Her actual age surprised Kate. In Boston, people — especially women — tended to look old in their forties.

"You do understand that if I decide to make you my heiress you will be required to sign a document stating that you will forever remain single."

"Yes, you explained that quite thoroughly in your letter."

Miss Walker regarded her with narrowed eyes. "You're young and attractive. Why would you agree to forego marriage? Do

68

you not wish to raise a family?"

"It's a bit late for that, I'm afraid. I'm twenty-nine." Far past the marrying age deemed proper by Boston society.

The older woman rolled her eyes. "Ancient," she said, her voice edged with irony.

Kate folded her hands on her lap and debated how much or how little to say. She sensed the ranch owner would see right through the vague answers she had prepared.

"Back in the States an educated woman is thought to be a liability in the home." Some critics had even gone so far as to say that educated women were not "real" women, and therefore incapable of loving a man, let alone bearing his children.

"You won't find things any different outside the States, I'm afraid," Miss Walker said. "Some men around here don't know what to do with a woman who has an intelligent thought of her own. And that includes you, Ralph," she added, addressing the dead man.

"But that's the least of it," the ranch owner continued. "You will work hard, harder than you've ever worked in your life. You and the land must become one. Its pulse will be your pulse, its heart yours. It will require everything you have to give —

69

and then some. No man alive can compete with such a demanding lover."

Kate flushed. Never had she heard anyone refer to land as a lover. In Boston most men were happy with a mere couple of acres, just enough to raise a milk cow or two and cultivate a vegetable garden.

"I'm not afraid of hard work," she said, hiding her soft hands in the folds of her skirt. She often put in twelve or more hours a day working on her stories. True, it wasn't physical labor, but writing a book was hard work and, at times, even grueling.

"If that does indeed turn out to be true, you'll be greatly rewarded for your efforts. Nothing in this world is permanent except for land. It will always be there for you. The question is, will you always be here for the ranch? If things go wrong — as they always do — will you walk away? Abandon ship, so to speak?"

"I'm fully prepared to prove myself worthy of your trust and generosity," Kate said. She would do anything — crawl to the ends of the world if necessary — for stability and permanence in her life. "I'll work hard and learn everything I can about ranching. I'll . . . I'll do whatever you ask of me."

"Hmm." Miss Walker studied her with cool appraisal. "You have three months . . .

no, let's make it four. That will take you to the end of our busiest season. During that time I will expect you to prove your sincerity and capability in learning the business. I will, of course, pay you a minimum salary. If you manage to last until the end of the trial period in July, you will then be required to sign a document that, among other things, will forbid you to marry. Do you have any questions?"

Up until that moment the whole idea had seemed so far-fetched Kate hardly considered the enormity of becoming a ranch owner. In Boston, property owners enjoyed more respect and privilege than non–property owners. It was a class distinction evident even during her school years. Though she despised being treated as a second-rate citizen she never thought property ownership possible. She still couldn't believe it.

"No questions," she murmured. No doubt later she'd think up plenty, but for now her mind was filled with the sheer wonder of it all.

"Very well. You have a hundred and twenty days to convince me of your trustworthiness, after which I shall then teach you the *business* side of ranching. In five years, *if* I deem you're ready, I will turn the ranch over to you. However, the deed shall remain in my name until the day I die, at which time the ranch will be yours and yours alone."

"That is exceedingly generous," Kate said. She still couldn't believe such good fortune. Her mama often said that nothing good ever happened to their kind because God favored the rich, but maybe, just maybe, she was wrong. Maybe God did on occasion favor the less fortunate.

"I'm not being generous, simply practical. Speaking of which, supper will be served at six in the dining room." Miss Walker indicated the adjacent room. "But you look exhausted, so it might be best if I have Rosita bring a tray to your room. I'll also ask her to heat water for your bath." She set her glass on the tray and stood.

"Breakfast is served between four and five. It's essential that we get the work done early before the heat kicks in. I'll see you in the morning." Without another word, she crossed the room, turning at the doorway.

"In case you were wondering, I don't plan on meeting my maker anytime soon. Until that day, the spinster pact is binding. Marry and you forfeit everything."

With that she hastened from the room, leaving Kate alone with only poor dead Ralph for company.

CHAPTER 5

A weaker or gentler woman would have swooned upon finding herself the recipient of such good fortune. But now that her destiny was secured, she had no use for feminine wiles.

Kate couldn't believe her luck. Just think, one day all this could be hers. Granted, the arid desert ranch was a far cry from the lush, tree-filled property she dreamed of owning, but land was land.

She had just finished arranging the last of her books on the back of the desk when a knock sounded at the door.

It was Rosita carrying her supper on a tray.

Kate stared at the large dinner plate piled high with generous portions of roast beef, gravy, mashed potatoes, and green beans.

"It's so much," she said. It would feed a family of four with enough left over for seconds.

"You must eat to be strong," Rosita said. She brushed past Kate and set the tray on the desk. "Steer strong." She lifted her arm and squeezed a muscle, and stared at Kate's slender frame. "Workers no be weak."

"I don't plan on carrying a steer or even wrestling with one," Kate said.

"That's what last señorita said." The housekeeper walked out of the room, leaving the door ajar, and Kate sat at her desk to eat. The meal was delicious, the meat so tender she could practically cut it with a fork. Though she hadn't eaten since morning, she could only finish half of what was on the plate. Even that was twice as much as she normally ate.

Rosita lugged a tin washtub into the room containing a stack of clothing, a pair of well-worn boots, and a wide-brimmed hat. She set the clothing on the bed and left, returning moments later with a kettle of hot water.

"Could you tell me who else lives here in the ranch house?" Kate asked, curious about the rooms she passed on the way to her own.

"You and Miss Walker," Rosita replied.

"That's all?" Kate asked, surprised.

"Me and my brother José live downstairs," Rosita said. "Sometimes señores come to buy cattle and Miss Walker let them stay overnight."

"I see."

Before Kate could ask any more questions, Rosita left the room, then made several trips back and forth before putting a clean towel and a bar of lye soap next to the bath.

"Ready," she announced.

"But there's not enough water," Kate said. Barely three inches covered the bottom of the tin tub.

"Water valuable," Rosita said. "More valuable than silver or copper. Tonight you guest, you get three inches. Next time you get two." She turned to leave, muttering beneath her breath, "If there is next time."

Alone again, Kate undressed and stepped into the tub, determined to make the most of what little water she had. She washed her hair and scrubbed herself from head to toe until her normally white skin was pink. She then reached for the pitcher of fresh water on her sink and rinsed away the soap.

Later she stood on the dark balcony brushing her damp hair and braiding it into a single plait down her back. It was a moonless night but the sky was bright with stars. The only visible light on land came from the window of the bunkhouse.

The wind had died down and the land lay

still, though by no means silent. A coyote howled from the distance, calling its pack. In response a chorus of lowing cattle rumbled from within a fenced pen. Not to be outdone, a horse nickered from an adjacent corral and dogs barked. Then all was quiet. Disturbingly so.

Kate missed the city, missed the sound of clopping hooves on cobblestones, the clanging bells of horse-drawn streetcars, the mournful toot of a distant foghorn. She even missed the cries of peddlers selling their wares and the rumbling of wagon wheels. Would she ever get used to the relative silence of this strange new land?

A sudden burst of laughter rippled through the night air, followed by the whiney sound of a fiddle. The gaiety of cowhands in the bunkhouse offered a stark contrast to the silence of the main house. She cast an anxious glance at the glass doors that led to other rooms, but all were dark.

Loneliness was not new to her and had dogged her all through childhood. Thinking her mother loose, neighbors treated Kate like an outcast, refusing to let their children play with her. Even in school she was considered an outsider — a nobody. Her family owned no property and therefore had no status in life.

A strange yearning for which she had no name rose up inside. Sighing, she withdrew from the balcony and sat at the desk. She opened her leather-bound notebook and dipped her pen into the inkwell.

The scratching sound of her pen against paper soothed and comforted her as she wrote.

Hidden in the darkness, Brandon hunkered beneath the window and watched her. She stood perfectly still but he could sense her distress, sense her loneliness, and he longed to go to her, but to do so would put her life in danger . . .

She stared down at what she had written before ripping the page from her notebook. Balling it, she tossed the paper into the wastepaper basket next to the desk. After the fiasco with her last book, her career as a writer was over. The respect she'd hoped to gain from the literary world eluded her, but that no longer mattered.

She stood to look at herself in the mirror, extending her hand as if greeting a rich cattle buyer from the east. "How do you do. I'm Miss Tenney, owner of the Last Chance Ranch."

She smiled. She liked the sound of that. If only those judgmental neighbors and snobbish classmates could see her now.

■ ■ ■ ■

She woke to the sound of a crowing rooster and buried her head under her pillow. Moments later she reluctantly rolled out of bed to the tinny hammering of the mechanical alarm clock. Yawning, she quickly dressed in Miss Walker's divided skirt and a plain white shirtwaist. The denim skirt was a tad too long but the peg-heeled boots were a perfect fit, though they took a little getting used to.

The dining room empty, she helped herself to coffee and bacon, eggs, biscuits, and gravy from the buffet. Worried that she might be late, she hardly tasted her food as she gobbled it down.

She had barely opened the front door before Rosita chased her outside, shaking a feather duster at her. "Hurry, flies." Kate stumbled onto the porch, the door slamming behind her.

Outside the sky was silver with streaks of yellow, pink, and red. The sun had yet to rise and it was surprisingly cold. Never had she experienced such a wide temperature swing between day and night as she did here in the desert. She should have donned a wrap.

With no one around, she circled the ranch house to the back, wanting to explore. A rooster eyed her from its perch on a white wooden fence before throwing back its head and letting out a loud crow.

A screened-in area directly behind the house held a clothesline strung with pieces of drying meat. A series of small boxy buildings were located off the southernmost U of the main house, which she guessed contained the kitchen and maybe even José's and Rosita's quarters. One building was a washhouse, complete with large metal tubs, ironing tables, and sadirons. She followed a well-worn dirt path to an icehouse. A short distance away was a granary and a smokehouse with stone chimney.

A vegetable garden spread between the buildings like a carpet, a scarecrow rising from its midst. She walked over for a closer look. A series of irrigation ditches crisscrossed the garden and the soil looked wet. Little signs read Lettuce, Carrots, Peas, and Onions.

Impressed with everything she had seen so far, she turned to watch two men lift caged chickens and a goat into the back of a wagon. The goat butted its head against a wooden side. The chickens clucked furiously, feathers flying about like snow flurries. A third man appeared from behind a barn leading a steer by a rope. Kate had never seen such a huge beast. It took both men to tie the animal to the back of the wagon. Once the animals were secured, the men drove off pulling the steer behind.

José walked out of the milk house carrying a bucket in both hands. Seeing her, he frowned and shook his head. "You better hurry," he said. He tossed a nod toward the front of the house. "Late not good."

Nervous about meeting the others, she ignored his warning. "You have milk cows too?" she asked, glancing at the milk sloshing over the sides of the buckets.

He grinned. "Last ranch I worked at had no milk cows. We had beef but no milk. Señorita Walker has everything."

"Where are they taking those animals?" she asked, pointing to the back of the departing wagon.

José put his finger to his lips. "That secret," he said.

"Why can't you tell me?" she asked.

"Señorita Walker said no tell. Now go. You be late."

This time she ran, her feet wobbling in her unfamiliar boots. Chickens clucked and scattered out of her path as she made her way to the front of the house and hurried to the main barn. The hem of her divided skirt flapped against her boots with a slapping sound.

She rounded a corner of the main barn and was surprised to see a group of men standing in a circle. All had lean, well-muscled frames, their faces weathered from countless hours in the saddle beneath the hot Arizona sun. All but one wore dark pants rolled at the cuffs, unbuttoned vests, and bright red bandannas. The sleeves of the collarless shirts were rolled up and held in place with twisted wire garters.

Gun holsters looped with cartridges sagged loosely down each man's side. Each wore peg-heeled boots similar to hers, but with silver spurs.

One of the men motioned to her and she hurried over to the circle.

He lifted his hat in greeting. "You must be Miss Tennis," he drawled.

"Tenney," she said.

"They call me Ruckus." A crooked nose matched his crooked grin and his horseshoe mustache drooped below his chin.

"That's 'cause he raises the roof with his snoring," one man added. "Been that way ever since he met up with a fist coming the other way."

His comment was followed by a round of

laughter. It seemed like a jovial group, and Kate found herself relaxing for the first time since arriving in Cactus Patch.

"That there is Stretch," Ruckus said, pointing to the tallest man of the lot.

Stretch raised a hand in greeting, his tan hat contrasting with his dark eyes, black curly hair, and pencil-thin mustache.

"Don't take anythin' he says seriously as his tales are as tall as he is." Ruckus pointed to the man next to Stretch. "And that funny-looking man behind the bush is Feedbag."

The "bush" was a square black beard that did indeed look like it belonged on a horse's muzzle.

"Howdy, ma'am," Feedbag said in a froggy croak, followed by a well-aimed stream of tobacco.

Ruckus went around the circle introducing each man in turn by his "barn" name. The names provided an astute, even comical description of the men, making them easy to remember. Wishbone's legs curved outward from the knee down. Moose's ears stood out like the handles of a sugar bowl. Upbeat grinned at her, his white teeth flashing against his ebony skin.

Mexican Pete whipped off his straw hat and bowed. "Señorita." While the other men were beltless, he wore a red sash tied around his middle.

The man in the odd short pants was called Dook. Since he spoke with a thick British accent, Kate assumed his name was the western version of Duke.

The last man Ruckus introduced was the ranch foreman named O.T., short for Old Timer. The man was probably in his forties, but he was clearly the oldest of the bunch. He stood straight as a soldier, his gaze never seeming to settle on any one person or thing, yet Kate was certain he missed nothing.

"Listen up, men," O.T. said. "In case you haven't noticed, Miss Tenney here is what you call a lady. Put a lid on your can of cuss words and keep it there. Is that clear?"

Feedbag lifted his hat and ran a finger though his jet-black hair. "How long we gotta watch our language this time?"

"For as long as she's here," O.T. replied.

"Ah, shucks," Feedbag groaned, putting his hat back on. "She could be here as long as a day or two."

"Don't forget one lasted as long as a week," one of the other men added.

Wishbone nodded. "Yeah, and I can't work as fast when I have to watch what comes out of my mouth."

"That's your problem," O.T. said. He removed his hat and held it to his chest. "And since you're the one with the problem, you can do the honors."

Much to Kate's surprise, the men all took off their hats and bowed their heads in prayer. Head lowered, she allowed her gaze to travel from man to man. The last thing she expected to see was a bunch of rough men praying.

Wishbone held his hat in both hands. "God, the Father, thank you for your many blessings and don't forgit to send rain. And if you ain't sendin' rain to us, don't go sendin' it to no other ranches neither."

Kate covered her mouth with the tips of her fingers. She'd never heard anyone speak to God with such informality. It was nothing like the stuffy, drawn-out prayers she was forced to endure while attending Miss Newcomb's Academy for Young Women.

An "amen" chorus went around the circle and the men stomped away in different directions.

Ruckus remained, regarding her with a frown. "You all right, ma'am?"

"Yes, I'm fine." And because he continued to study her, she added, "He prayed for rain."

He arched his eyebrows as if surprised by

the comment. "Every day. That's part of our job. Part of your job too."

Her gaze wandered across the dry land. "It looks like your prayers haven't been answered in a while."

He shrugged. "Sometimes God answers our prayers slow as wet gunpowder, but sooner or later he gets around to it." Ruckus made a face. "Some chuckleheaded politicians don't wanna wait on God. One got a crazy notion to explode dynamite over Texas to make rain. Nine thousand dollars went up in smoke just like that." He snapped his fingers to demonstrate. "They shot the feathers off a bunch of startled birds but they didn't make no rain. Only the Forever Man can do that."

"The Forever Man?" she asked.

He grinned. "We all have our barn names. So why not God?" He signaled the end of the conversation with a nod of his head. "The boss lady says I'm to make a rancher out of you." He looked her up and down and shook his head, his mustache seeming to droop another notch lower. "I reckon we'll see a whole lotta rain before I succeed." He turned and walked away. "Time to get to work."

Not knowing what else to do, she followed him. He spoke slowly, drawing out each

85

word like one would draw out a sigh, but he walked with quick, long strides and it was all she could do to keep up.

He led her to the side of the barn. "Mexican or Western?" he asked.

She glanced at his profile. Was he joking? Mexican? With her blond hair? "I'm American," she said with more than a little patriotic pride. "Born and raised in Boston."

"God, give me strength," he muttered. He yanked a door open and led her into a dim room. "I'm talkin' about saddles."

"Oh," she said, cheeks flaming. Biting her lower lip she glanced around. Never had she seen so many saddles in one place.

He pushed his hat to the back of his head and regarded her as he might a wayward child. "You do ride, right?"

"Yes," she said. She took riding lessons at Miss Newcomb's Academy, though she never was much good at it. Living in Boston with its hansom cabs and horse-drawn streetcars made horseback riding a luxury more than a necessity.

"So what saddle did you use?" He rolled his eyes. "Don't tell me it was English."

"Oh no," she said. Miss Newcomb would never approve such a thing. "It was side-saddle."

His eyes popped open. "Are you telling

me you ain't been on a *real* saddle?"

Her heart sank. "I . . . I . . ." Miss Newcomb had strictly forbidden anyone to do anything as gauche or unladylike as to ride astride. "I'm afraid not."

"Does the boss lady know this?"

"We never discussed the saddle," she said, quickly adding, "but I'm a fast learner. I learned to type in less than two weeks and I could recite Tennyson's 'Ulysses' from memory after only two days."

Doubt settled in every crevice of his face, even the pockmark at the corner of his eye.

"Far as I know, neither one of them skills will matter much to a horse. Won't matter much to the cattle either."

He pulled a clean red bandanna from a box and tossed it to her. "Wear it at all times. Next to a hat it's the most useful article of clothin' you'll ever own."

"Does it come in any other color?" she asked, tying it around her neck.

"I reckon you can have any color you want long as it's red. If you git shot you don't want the other fella seeing blood. Puts you at a disadvantage."

Her mouth fell open. If she got shot? She studied his face for some sign of humor but he looked serious as a monk.

He walked over to an iron saddle stand.

"This here is what I call a real saddle," he said, stabbing it with his finger. "If you know what's good for you, you best get to know it like you know the back of your hand." He patted the saddle before continuing. "First thing you do is move everythin' out of the way."

He demonstrated by folding the cinches and breast collar on top of the saddle. Naming each part as he worked, he hooked the right stirrup over the horn. He tossed her a colorful blanket before lifting the saddle with both hands and starting for the door.

She followed him to a brown gelding that stood far taller than any of the Morgan horses she'd ridden back in Boston.

The horse pricked his ears at the sight of the saddle, forefoot stomping.

"This here is Decker," Ruckus said.

"After the English author, Thomas Dekker?" she asked.

Ruckus looked at her cockeyed. "Decker because it's the bottom of the deck as far as workhorses go. It's the smallest horse we have and also the slowest."

She gulped. This was the smallest horse?

Ruckus chuckled. "Don't look so worried. He's also pretty gentle. Just let him know who's boss and you'll be fine." He nodded toward the blanket in her hand.

Taking her cue she placed the blanket onto the gelding's back and ran her hand along his long slick neck.

"First you place the saddle gently on the horse like so," Ruckus drawled. "Don't thump it down or you'll startle him. Tighten up the front cinch first. Next you lower all the trimmin's, making sure everything hangs down nice and neat."

He dropped the cinches and breast collar in place. He then showed her how to lace the latigo through the cinch ring. "You gotta make sure the back cinch is buckled over the belly, like so."

When the horse was saddled, he demonstrated how to take the saddle off. "Now you try it," he said.

"You want me to saddle the horse?" she asked.

"I don't see anythin' else around here needs saddling," he said. "Do you?"

Ignoring his comment she bent to pick up the saddle. It was heavier than she imagined, weighing at least thirty or forty pounds. It took every bit of strength she had to lift it high enough to place on the horse's back. After that it was a series of missteps and errors, but she finally got all the straps connected.

"I reckon you're as ready as you're ever

gonna be," he muttered. "Just remember God forgives." He waved his outstretched hand side to side like a rocking boat. "Horses not so much." He patted Decker's rump. "Time to ride. The thing to remember is not to spook him. Let yourself into the saddle nice and easy." He mounted and dismounted the horse himself before handing her the reins.

Kate braced herself with a deep breath. The horse blew through its velvety nose but otherwise looked calm enough. She held the reins tight in her left hand and grabbed the cantle with her right. Shoving her left foot into the stirrup, she bounced off her right foot.

"Nice and easy," Ruckus repeated.

She bounced up and down several times without leaving the ground. Finally, Ruckus put his hand on her behind. *Of all the . . .*

Finding herself suddenly astride the enormous animal, she grabbed the reins tightly, heart pounding, and was afraid to breathe. Seated upon a horse clothespin-style didn't seem natural.

"Get down and try again," Ruckus said.

Getting off the horse wasn't any easier than getting on, but she was determined to prove she could do it. Once both feet were on the ground she sprang up and down to give herself momentum. Ruckus moved toward her. In her haste to keep him from touching her again, she bounced up with such force she settled into the saddle with a thud.

Startled, Decker arched his back, kicked up his back legs, and took off running.

"Ohhhhhhhhhhh," she cried. Her hat flew off and she flopped around in the saddle like a rag doll, gripping on to the reins for dear life. "He-e-e-elp!"

Chapter 6

Eleanor stared at the white pine coffin, her divided skirt flapping against the top of her boots in the early morning breeze. The first warm rays of the sun trickled down the mountain like melted butter over freshly baked rolls. Though this was her favorite time of day, she never grew tired of watching the ever-changing colors of the desert as the sun journeyed across the sky.

The only sound breaking the silence was O.T. digging her ex-husband's grave. His real name was Chip Mason, but she called him O.T. like the others did. He'd worked at the ranch for fifteen years, a record. Working on a cattle ranch was hard work and most cowmen didn't last for more than seven or eight years, ten tops.

At age twenty O.T. had managed to escape a Texas hanging for killing a man, which to this day he claimed was self-defense. For some reason Eleanor believed him. She'd given him a chance to prove himself by working hard and staying out of trouble, and he had done exactly that many times over.

A compact man with a weathered, clean-shaven face, he was the best wrangler who ever worked at the ranch. He never met a challenge he didn't like, and she had a corral of former wild horses to prove it. More than one rancher tried to steal him away by offering higher wages, but fortunately O.T. was more loyal than ambitious. Or maybe he was just grateful that she had given him a job when he was down on his luck.

Even at age thirty-five O.T.'s movements were quick and strong, whether dealing with horses or cowboys or, in this case, digging a grave. Alternating between slamming the spade of his shovel into the ground and tossing soil over his shoulder, he worked steadily. Even so, it seemed to take forever to dig through the hard, arid ground.

While he worked, Eleanor glanced at the weathered crosses that marked the graves of her parents, Harold and Mary Walker. But it was the smaller cross that gave her pause and brought a lump to her throat. After all these years it still hurt. Drat!

She'd battled droughts, floods, Indians, rustlers, and cattle fever without so much as a blink of the eye. Only four years ago she lost nearly half her cattle in that terrible drought. Five years before that she was forced to rebuild the ranch house and outbuildings after the original ones were destroyed in the '87 earthquake and subsequent fire.

Oh yes, she'd seen and done it all. So why, then, did the sight of the little white cross tear her apart after all this time? It was Ralph's fault for making her come to the little cemetery — a place she tried to avoid except on rare occasions.

Irritated that a man to whom she owed nothing, let alone a decent burial, had imposed his death upon her, she impatiently tapped her foot. She had work to do, cattle that needed tending, calves to pull, books to balance, fences to repair.

She also had to oversee the training of that new woman, though she didn't hold much hope that any of it would pay off. A writer. Great guns, what would be next?

So far six women had answered her advertisement, each progressively worse than the one before. First there was the teacher — what was her name — Marcy something, who fainted at the mere sight of a scorpion. Then the Irish girl who broke out in hives the moment she got near a horse. Of course none were as bad as the woman she found rolling in the hay with one of the cowpunchers.

Still, something about this latest candidate intrigued her. Kate Tenney let down her guard for only a moment, but Eleanor saw a little bit of herself in the flashing blue eyes and combative stance. The woman had secrets, no doubt, but she also had backbone.

A cloud of dust signaled a visitor and her thoughts scattered like frightened cattle. Who would travel way out here at this ungodly hour of the morning?

The horseman drew near and she folded her arms across her chest. She should have known. It was Wells Fargo banker Robert Stackman. On her more amicable days she considered him a friend and confidant. This was not one of those days.

He dismounted and staked his horse to a metal spike. A tall man in his early sixties, his sharp, analytical mind was hidden behind a calm, unhurried exterior. If his impeccable dark trousers, white shirt, vest, and bow tie didn't instill confidence in his banking clients, his mild, confident manner certainly did. He pulled off his black felt hat, revealing a full head of silver hair as neatly trimmed as his mustache and goatee.

"What are you doing here, Robert?" she asked, pretending not to know. "Is it the first of the month already?" Forced to take out a loan to rebuild following the earthquake, she'd gone from being relatively debt-free to owing a great deal of money, all on the whim of nature.

"I thought you might like company." He nodded toward the casket. "It's not every day that one buries a husband."

"Ex," she said. "And I wouldn't have to bury him had he not been so inconsiderate as to die on my property." Even in death the man caused her trouble. "How did you know?"

"Doc Masterson came into the bank yesterday."

Her lips puckered with annoyance. Apparently the death of an ex-spouse did not rate doctor/patient confidentiality.

He narrowed his eyes. "I thought you and your *ex* weren't on speaking terms."

"We weren't," she said. She hadn't seen Ralph since the divorce some twenty years earlier. To say that she was shocked when he showed up on her doorstep would be an understatement. She hardly recognized him. He was once the most handsome man in all of Arizona Territory, but time had not been kind to him. He'd worn his years like a soldier wore his battle wounds. He'd looked old, bent over — a mere shadow of his former dashing self.

"He came to apologize." Arizona Territory followed the Mexican "Community of Acquests and Gains" law, dividing property equally between husband and wife. Following their divorce, he'd made her buy his half at twice the amount it was worth. It was the second time she'd been forced to purchase her own property. The first time was when the United States acquired the land from Mexico and refused to acknowledge the original deed. It took her years to repay the first loan but even longer to repay the second because of the '70s depression.

Her ex-husband's apology when it finally did come was too little, too late, and she ordered him off her property. Only he never got any farther than the bottom of her verandah steps before he dropped down, dead.

"Did you forgive him?" Robert asked.

"My word!" she exclaimed, hands on her chest. "What would ever make you think such a thing?"

"I figure something must have caused his heart to stop," he replied.

She gave her head a righteous nod. "Rest

assured I'm completely blameless for his death."

"What a pity. It would have done you good to practice a little forgiveness." He reached into his saddlebags and pulled out a well-worn Bible. "Do you mind if I do the honors?"

"Oh really, Robert. Must we?"

"Everyone deserves a proper burial."

She supposed he was right. In any case he didn't wait for her approval before he began to read the Twenty-Third Psalm. "The LORD is my shepherd . . ."

No sooner had he finished the psalm and started on the "Our Father" when the galloping sound of a horse's hooves and a woman's high-pitched screams pierced the air.

"Heeee-lp!"

Eleanor spun around just in time to see Decker race by, his rider holding on with both hands and flopping around like wash on a windy day.

Irritated by the intrusion, Eleanor threw up her hands. Could the girl not even control an old nag? "For goodness' sakes, O.T. Do something."

But already her foreman had thrown down his shovel and was running toward his own horse. With one smooth move he swung into the saddle. "Gid-up!" he shouted, and horse and rider leaped forward.

Robert stared after him, his eyes rounded. "Good gracious, who is that woman?"

Eleanor shook her head. Whatever had made her believe that someone who wrote purple prose could learn ranching? "Her name is Kate Tenney, and I do believe I made a dreadful mistake."

Kate and the horse parted company before O.T. could reach her. The horse went north and Kate went south. Landing on top of a prickly pear cactus, she screamed bloody murder.

Robert groaned, "That poor girl!"

Eleanor thought of the unpleasant task ahead and sighed. Cactus run-ins were not that unusual, especially for greenies unfamiliar with the desert. Normally, the job of plucking out barbs was left to one of the ranch hands. She could well imagine how her men would love putting their hands on the likes of Kate Tenney. Eleanor would allow nothing of the sort to happen, of course, which meant she had no choice but to take on the tedious task herself.

"Robert, finish your prayer and whatever else you think befitting a funeral while I fetch my medical kit. Just don't sing. You'll scare the cattle."

■ ■ ■ ■

The door to Kate's room flew open without as much as a knock. Miss Walker breezed in all businesslike carrying a small basket.

Gasping, Kate held a towel in front of her naked body with one hand and wiped away her tears with the other. She pranced from foot to foot but nothing relieved the burning, itching, and agonizing sting. Her entire backside all the way down to her knees felt like it was on fire. A glance in the mirror earlier had revealed red welts as ugly as they were painful.

Initially, Miss Walker had pulled the longer thorns from her arms and legs. She then ordered Kate to her room to undress. Now the ranch owner lifted a large needle out of her basket and wielded it in the air. "Bend over."

Kate stared at the needle but didn't move.

"Oh, for goodness' sakes, forget your modesty. You can't remove the thorns by yourself. If I see something I haven't seen before I'll throw a boot at it."

Face ablaze, Kate turned. As humiliating as it was to stand in front of the ranch owner stark naked, she would do anything to stop the pain. She let the towel drop and leaned over the back of her wooden desk chair.

Miss Walker immediately got to work. She picked what thorns she could by hand and dug out others with the sewing needle.

Tears rolled down Kate's cheeks, and despite her best efforts to hold her tongue she couldn't help but cry out on occasion, "Ouch!"

"Do keep still," Miss Walker ordered, her voice lacking any sort of sympathy or compassion.

"It hurts."

"Of course it hurts. They don't call it the devil's tongue for nothing." Miss Walker lifted her voice. "Rosita! What's taking so long?"

The bedroom door flung open, and Rosita scurried across the room and handed a small basin to Miss Walker. Her eyes grew wide as she glanced at Kate's bare bottom. She then turned and hurried from the room as if running away from a contagious disease.

"This will get the hairy spines out," Miss Walker explained, pouring something that felt wet and cold on her back and legs.

"What horrible plants. What terrible, horrible plants," Kate wailed.

"If you think this is bad, wait till you meet

up with a jumping cholla," Miss Walker said. "I swear that thing can jump out and grab you as you pass by."

Kate groaned at the thought. Jumping plants? What would be next?

"In any case, the prickly pear is a useful plant," Miss Walker continued. Having finished plastering Kate's back and arms with some sort of paste, she walked to the washstand and poured water from the pitcher into the basin. "The juice has many medicinal qualities and Indians use it to purify water. The fruit is quite good, actually. A few prickly spines seem like a small price to pay for such a useful plant, wouldn't you say?" She washed and dried her hands.

For an answer Kate moaned. The glue on her back began to harden and her skin felt taut, but the coolness had relieved some of the itching, or at least made it bearable.

After several moments, Miss Walker peeled off the glue and tossed the papery strips into the wastebasket. She then proceeded to apply a poultice to Kate's skin.

"This is an old family recipe made from dried bread crumbs and sweet oil," she explained. After she had completed the task, she said, "That should do it. It'll feel uncomfortable for a day or two, but I think we got them all."

Kate grabbed the towel and held it up in front of her. "Thank you," she murmured. Now that the worst was over, she feared Miss Walker would tell her to pack her bags and leave.

Instead, Miss Walker gathered up her supplies and started for the door. "Get dressed. There's work to be done. We've got to get ready to start pulling calves." With that she was gone, leaving only the sound of her footsteps fading away.

Kate stared at the closed door. *That's it? Get to work? No time off to recover?* She frowned. *And what an odd term, pulling calves. What could it possibly mean? How does one pull a calf?*

CHAPTER 7

Brandon scooped a pitchfork of straw and tossed it into the wheelbarrow with one easy move. He had mucked out all thirty-five horse stalls in less than two hours. She greeted him with a smile and fell into his arms. He smelled like the sun and rain all rolled into one . . .

Horse dung! That's what she smelled like. It was in her nose and hair and even her mouth. It seeped into her pores like water in a hole, along with the horsey smell of soggy hay and stinky urine.

Her body still sore from yesterday's horrid ride, her muscles ached as she swung the last pitchfork of soiled hay into the wheelbarrow. Her skin still felt prickly from the cactus needles. Though the burning had all but disappeared, her embarrassment at having to bend over naked in front of Miss Walker remained.

The relatively tame horseback rides she'd endured at college were nothing compared to the kind of riding expected on the ranch. Certainly she'd never been on a horse as large or fast as that gelding, Decker. Ruckus said it was old and slow. A racehorse should be that slow!

She collapsed against the wooden side of the stable. Two days felt like two years.

As usual, whenever she stopped working Ruckus appeared as if able to see through the walls that divided the stalls. He glanced around and pulled out his pocket watch. "Forty-six minutes," he announced in his gravelly voice.

"That's good, isn't it?" she asked, although at the moment she was too hot to care. It had been one mishap after another. Why hadn't Ruckus told her to remove the horse *before* cleaning the stall? And how was she supposed to know to turn the wheelbarrow in the direction you wanted to go *before* filling it?

"God created the world in only seven days. *That* was good," he said, and not even his drawl could hide the sarcasm. "At the rate you're going you won't have the rest of the stalls mucked out until next month sometime."

"The rest? You mean I have to clean them *all*?"

Hat tilted over his forehead, he scratched the back of his neck. "Yep," he said cheerfully. "All thirty-four of them."

Luke Adams hunted through his scrap pile. The waist-high mound was made up mostly of discarded horseshoes, old nails, worn-out gun barrels, and other scraps of metal. Railroads had lowered the cost of transporting iron in recent years, but he enjoyed the challenge of twisting and turning old iron into something new.

Every door latch, windmill rod — even Doc Masterson's scalpels — had once been forged exclusively in his shop, first by his uncle and then by him.

Uncle Sam was fond of saying that the blacksmith was the heart and soul of the community. He and the town's former preacher had some lively disagreements over that one.

Things had changed in recent years and not necessarily for the better. Everything from kitchen utensils to farm tools could now be ordered through Montgomery Ward's catalog. The quality wasn't as good, but the novelty of ordering through a catalog and waiting for its arrival took precedence over workmanship. It was this lack of craft that had turned Adams Blacksmithing into little more than a fix-it shop. He no longer made tools; he repaired them.

Finding a piece of metal he wanted, he returned to his workbench.

Homer let out a bark, tail wagging. He put his nose to the crack beneath the door and sniffed.

"What is it, boy?" Luke asked. "Do we have company?"

Just then his two aunts walked in. Aunt Bessie stopped to pet Homer, whose entire rear end followed his tail in greeting.

"How is my nephew treating you?" she said in an unnaturally high voice reserved for babies, animals, and anyone she deemed hard of hearing.

She straightened and glanced around. She was a hefty woman with birdlike legs and arms. Her bow-shaped mouth pursed thoughtfully upon a stack of three chins, her features drawing together in a knowing frown.

"Where's Michael?"

"Running an errand," Luke said. He hated lying, but if he told her that his brother was up to his old tricks it would only worry her.

Aunt Bessie's eyes sharpened as if she picked up some signal he gave off without knowing. "Fighting again, eh?"

"I didn't say that."

"You didn't have to." She wagged her finger. "The trouble with you two is you don't talk to each other."

"We talk," Luke muttered, "but the moment he hears the word *work* he runs the other way."

Aunt Bessie heaved her ample bosom and stared at him with haughty rebuke. "There's nothing wrong with your brother that a good wife won't fix."

Luke clamped his jaw tight. According to his aunt, a wife was the cure-all for everything from gout to heart failure.

Sensing she was gearing up to deliver one of her oft-repeated lectures on brotherly love and family obligations, he quickly changed the subject.

"So what brings you two to town?" Despite his aunts' obsession with finding him a wife, he was glad to see them.

"You tell him." Aunt Lula-Belle nudged her older sister. "It was *your* idea."

The shorter of the two, she was as thin as Aunt Bessie was wide, her snowy hair wound in tight springy curls. Her red frilly hat sat atop her head like a cherry on a mound of whipped cream.

"Oh, all right," Aunt Bessie said, speaking

in her normal throaty voice that made him suspect she still smoked cheroots on occasion even though she had promised to stop.

Her habit of putting her nose where it didn't belong would try a saint, and Luke was anything but one. She meant well, of course, even though she did delve a little too deeply into his personal affairs. They both did, though Aunt Lula-Belle was more of an accomplice than an instigator.

Aunt Bessie cleared her throat. "Remember the woman we met on the day that Cactus Joe tried to rob the mercantile?" she asked.

Luke grimaced at the memory. He hadn't known his aunts were in town during the attempted holdup until two days later. It was bad enough that they interfered in his life, but he still shuddered to think they tried to take on an outlaw.

"The day my hat was ruined," Aunt Lula-Belle added with a woeful sigh.

Aunt Bessie rolled her eyes. "Would you stop complaining about your hat? Losing it was the best thing that happened to you since Murphy gave up playing the fiddle."

Aunt Bessie turned her attention back to Luke. "I'm talking about the woman you saved."

That wasn't exactly accurate, but Luke let

it slip by. Instead, he leaned against his workbench, arms crossed. "What about her?"

Was she still in town? It had been nearly two weeks. That meant she had lasted longer than any of the others. That was a surprise. A big surprise.

Aunt Bessie's hand fluttered to her chest. "You won't believe this, but she took the trouble to find out our names and wrote a lovely note inquiring as to our well-being. Wasn't that thoughtful of her?"

"Yes, it was." He still remembered how she looked sitting on this very workbench, all soft and pretty and more than anything, vulnerable. Of course she seemed more scared than vulnerable when they reached the ranch house, though she did her best to hide it. Not that he blamed her. Facing Cactus Joe *and* Miss Walker on the same day was enough to scare anyone.

"And so we were thinking" — she glanced at Aunt Lula-Belle — "that maybe we should get to know her better. Perhaps invite her to supper. And of course we think you should be there too. I'm sure she would love to see you again."

So that was the reason for their visit. He should have known they were up to their usual matchmaking tricks. "I don't think that's a good idea," he said.

Aunt Bessie feigned a wounded look. "Why not?"

"We have nothing in common. We don't even speak the same language," he said.

Aunt Bessie's mouth turned down in disappointment. "I don't remember her being foreign." She looked to her sister for confirmation. "Do you suppose she had someone write the note she sent us?"

Aunt Lula-Belle looked as perplexed as her sister. "She didn't look foreign either."

"Yes, but we only saw her for a moment before Cactus Joe dragged her outside," Aunt Bessie said.

"She's not a foreigner," Luke said. Last he heard Boston wasn't a foreign country. "She's one of those book-learning women who talks over your head."

He was a plain and simple man and he didn't need no ten-dollar words to say what he had to say. Nor did he go around naming things after Greek philosophers.

"Like Louise?" Aunt Bessie asked, her voice edged with dislike.

"No, not like her," he said gruffly. Louise had run off to Chicago to attend one of those fancy schools. It hurt like crazy when she wrote to tell him she was betrothed to a professor. He cared for Louise, had wanted

111

to marry her. Miss Tenney was little more than a stranger. Not the same thing at all.

Regretting his harshly spoken words, he leaned over and pecked Aunt Bessie on her crinkly cheek. He would always be grateful to her for taking care of him and his brother just as she promised her dying sister she would. She and Uncle Sam treated him and Michael like their own. Apparently, in his aunt's mind at least, finding wives for them was part of her responsibility to her deceased sister, and she had no intention of resting until she had fulfilled that obligation.

"I've got to get to work." He hated to rush them out the door, but orders were backed up and since Michael had taken off again, he was on his own. He really did need to hire an assistant. "See you Sunday."

Each Sunday after church he had dinner with his two aunts and uncles. "Maybe I'll ask Miss Chase to join us," he added, hoping that would please them.

Aunt Bessie's smile did not reach her eyes. "That would be wonderful, dear," she said, sounding more distracted than happy at the prospect of seeing him with the schoolmaster's daughter.

He watched them go with a fond sigh. He supposed listening to Miss Chase rattle on incessantly, as she tended to do, was a small price to pay to appease his two meddling aunts.

CHAPTER 8

"Shoot at your own peril," the ruffian
  yelled.
"Curses on you!" Brandon yelled back.
  Bang, bang, bang!

Ruckus was a slave driver. That was the only
way to describe him. Every day he greeted
Kate with that mournful face of his.

"You're still here, eh?" he asked, as if he'd
expected her to sneak away in the dead of
night.

That morning, after his usual greeting, he
made her saddle up. "Today we're riding
the range. Since you haven't fallen off your
horse for three days, it's time you did some
real ridin'."

She greeted this news with both jubilation
and dismay. Her legs were so sore she'd
barely made it down the stairs that morning. Her arms throbbed and her tailbone
ached. Even her bruises had bruises. Already

her hands were calloused, the nails broken to the quick.

The thought of getting on her horse filled her with dread. On the other hand, Ruckus wasn't big on praise. Letting her ride out on the range was about as close to a compliment as she was likely to get from him, and she intended to prove herself worthy — if it killed her.

She filled her lungs with crisp air and mounted, grimacing against the pain that spread from her inner thighs all the way down to her ankles.

With grim determination she pressed her legs against the sides of her horse and followed Ruckus out of the corral. Stretch, Moose, and Mexican Pete waited a short distance away. None of the three looked happy to see her, Moose least of all.

"Why do we have to take her?" he asked, his lip turned up. "All she does is slow us down and make a mess of things."

Kate gritted her teeth. She hated the way they talked about her as if she weren't there.

"I'm only doin' what the boss lady says," Ruckus said. "Now quit your yappin' and move it."

Moose cast a frown in her direction, pulled his hat as low as his ears would allow, and rode off.

Kate patted her horse. "Come on, Decker. Let's show them." She kicked her heels into the horse's sides and followed the four men who rode in a straight line, one after another.

Oddly enough, the past intruded less when she was in a saddle. Perhaps it was because nothing about the desert reminded her of Boston and all that had happened there.

As they rode, Stretch spun a tale of a man who fell in the Grand Canyon wearing rubber boots. "He kept bouncing up and down for days. They finally had to shoot him to keep him from starving to death."

This brought guffaws from the other three men and a chuckle from Kate. The stories told by the hoboes outside her childhood window were never as amusing as Stretch's.

"You ought to be a writer," she called to him.

Stretch glanced over his shoulder. "Nah. Writers are for people who read. My stories are for everyone."

"Yeah, but it's sure a lot easier to close a book than turn off your ears," Ruckus moaned, and Moose laughed.

"Stay behind me," Ruckus ordered when her horse wandered off the tracks made by the others. "We don't want to disturb no

116

more grass than necessary. And keep your eyes peeled lest you see somethin' strange."

"Like what?" she called. There wasn't much out here but cactus and sage. What little grass there was didn't seem worth protecting.

"Injured or sick cattle," he said. "Fire. Rustlers. Broken fences." He pointed to a rabbit hole. "Everything out here lives in a hole. So, Goldilocks, watch where you're riding."

She had grown used to his calling her Goldilocks but still grappled with the rather odd ways westerners expressed themselves. She still felt uncomfortable calling Miss Walker the boss lady, though Ruckus insisted it was a sign of respect.

"If she was male, we'd call her old man," he'd said. "That's whatcha get for bein' the biggest toad in the pond."

She learned that a hat was a lid unless you were from south of the border and then it was a sombrero. A cowboy's rope was a lariat not a lasso, one being the noun and the other a verb. It was Arizony and New Mex, though the men seemed to have too much respect for Texas to call it anything other than its rightful name.

It wasn't just the language of the West that confounded her; the desert that seemed so barren from afar actually teemed with life. Nothing was as it seemed at first glance. Sage that looked purple from a distance was actually gray. Rocks that seemed dull from afar glittered with fool's gold up close. Wildflowers grew in abundance, and what appeared to be endless flatland was actually filled with rocky gullies, rough gulches, and dry riverbeds.

The desert was like a painting whose beauty could only be uncovered upon close observation, and a thrill raced through her with each new discovery.

They rode through wild mesquite and prickly scrub brush. Ruckus had loaned her a pair of chaps to wear, but they were heavy and uncomfortable so she'd left them behind. Now she wished she hadn't.

Range mustangs looked up when they rode by, then calmly resumed grazing. "What beautiful animals," she called to Ruckus.

Grazing cattle lifted broad white faces, jaws making circular movements as they chewed. Up close the cattle, even with their short legs, looked so much larger than Kate ever imagined.

However, the animals she found most amazing were prairie dogs, which seemed to be everywhere. They stood up on hind legs and made funny little barking sounds, and she couldn't help but laugh at their antics.

Equally amusing were the roadrunners that raced frantically across the desert floor, their legs but a blur beneath their fast-moving bodies.

Ruckus slapped his rope against his chaps to chase a couple of cattle out of a gulch, his movements deliberate and unrushed. The steers scrambled up the incline with low moos.

"The quickest way to move a steer is slow," he explained. "Otherwise it'll take off in the wrong direction." After a while he added, "I reckon that's why the Forever Man sometimes takes his time answerin' prayers. He wants to make sure we ain't gonna run off and get lost once we get what we want."

Having no experience with answered prayers, Kate guided her horse around a prairie dog mound and said nothing.

Ruckus veered off in another direction and stopped to examine the remains of a campfire. He didn't look happy and Kate wondered if it meant trouble.

She was so busy watching him she didn't notice that her horse had strayed away from the trail left by the others. By the time she heard the rattling sound it was too late.

Decker reared back on his hind legs, pawing the air with a loud whinny, and Kate hit the ground.

"Oomph!"

Ruckus galloped up, pistol in hand, and shot the snake with a single bullet. "You all right?" he asked, looking down from astride his horse.

"I'm f-fine," she stammered with a wary glance at the lifeless snake. No doubt she had another batch of fresh bruises, but the rattler could no longer harm her. Moose's sneer made her face burn with humiliation.

Ruckus holstered his gun, rested his arms on his pommel, and stared at her.

She glared back at him. "Why are you looking at me like that?"

He tilted his hat away from his face. "I plumb don't know why God brought you here, but I reckon if he wanted you to be a rancher he'd have built you so you could stay in a saddle." He shook his head and blew out his breath. "If you can't even ride a horse —"

"I *can* ride a horse," she yelled. "I just can't ride *that* horse." Decker was like every other male she ever knew — one moment gentle and the next wild and unpredictable.

"Fallin' off of Decker makes as much sense as fallin' out of a rockin' chair. If you can't ride an old nag, how do you expect to ride a cuttin' horse?"

She had no idea what a cutting horse was, but it sure didn't sound too appealing.

Mexican Pete and Stretch rode back at the sound of gunfire and laughed upon seeing her on the ground.

Mouth clamped shut in annoyance, she stood and brushed herself off. She looked around for her hat, shuddering anew at the sight of the dead snake. Spotting Miss Walker on her horse a distance away, Kate's heart sank. No doubt the woman saw her hit the ground. Again.

Moose rode up with her horse in tow. He didn't laugh. Instead, his lips puckered with exasperation.

"Thank you," she said, taking Decker by the reins and ignoring Moose's reproachful expression. He shook his head and rode off without a word.

She glared after him before mounting her horse. This time she kept her eyes on the trail in front of her, careful not to stray away from the tracks left by the others.

She caught up to the men watering their horses by a windmill. Ruckus stood in the skimpy shade of the stiltlike tower, hands on his waist.

"We just oiled it last month and listen to

it. Sounds like a bunch of rattling chains."

Kate listened but it didn't sound any different from any of the other windmills they had passed.

Ruckus lifted an oilcan off his saddle. "Who's going up this time?" he called.

While Stretch, Moose, and Mexican Pete argued among themselves, Kate quickly made up her mind. Before any of the others volunteered, she snatched the oilcan from Ruckus, slung it over her shoulder, and started up the ladder.

Ruckus yelled after her, "What in blazes do you think you're doin'? Git down from there. You hear me? Now!"

Ignoring him, she kept going. Teeth gritted against the sting of calloused hands on wooden rungs, she climbed. She would show Miss Walker, Moose, and the others she could do a man's job. She would show them all. Grim determination blocked out all other thoughts as she clambered up, leaving the desert floor below. It seemed to take forever, but she kept climbing and Ruckus kept yelling for her to get down.

By the time she reached the platform she was gasping for air. Much to her surprise, a cheer rose from below. Mexican Pete waved his hat and Stretch called out, "Hee-haw!" Even Moose had a wide grin on his face.

Taking a moment to catch her breath, she glanced around for the rope used to tie down the windmill blades. She'd watched cowhands oil other windmills and knew what to do — at least she hoped she did. What she hadn't anticipated was just how far away the ground looked from twenty feet up.

CHAPTER 9

Eleanor stood a distance away from the windmill they called Job and surveyed the land. *Her* land.

She knew every square mile of it like she knew her own mind. Every crevice, every valley, every cactus and hill were etched into her memory like carvings in a rock. She trusted the men who worked for her, of course, but she trusted her instincts more. She was often the first to spot a broken fence or an ailing steer. She knew which of her fifty odd windmills needed oil even before the grind of dry gears brought her men on the run. She knew exactly how many gallons of water each pumped in an hour.

She also knew her workers and their capabilities. Knew her best riders. Knew who to depend on in the face of catastrophe like the earthquake of '87 and the torrential flash floods of '82. Knew who to trust with numbers and figures, even money.

What she didn't know was what to think of the woman named Kate Tenney. Oh, she knew a broad range of things about her. Kate was a writer, but apparently not a very successful one. She was educated, had gone to a very good school, but instead of teaching or choosing a similar profession she opted for mucking out stables and fighting with cacti.

That Tenney girl had tenacity all right. Eleanor knew that much. It had only been three weeks — a record — but still she hung on, albeit by a fine thread by the looks of her. Granted, Eleanor had instructed her men to pile it on but never had she expected them to make the woman climb twenty feet up a windmill to oil it, for goodness' sakes. Even Eleanor had never scaled a windmill. She wasn't afraid of much, but she disliked heights.

She had planned to question the woman one night at supper, but so far Kate had resisted joining her in the dining room. Instead, the woman dragged herself up the stairs at the end of each workday and wasn't heard from until morning.

Now, Eleanor shaded her eyes against the sun. Kate had made it all the way onto the platform, her slender figure barely visible from this distance. What in heaven's name was Ruckus thinking? More than one ranch hand had been injured by a windmill. One had fallen off a ladder and suffered back injuries. Another had his right arm chewed up by the expansive blades.

The air was still, but the wind could start up at any moment. If Kate failed to tie down the huge blades before oiling the gears, the smallest gust of wind could cause her to be knocked to the ground.

Eleanor held her breath until Kate waved to the men below, signaling that the blades had been properly stabilized.

This particular windmill had been nothing but trouble since Eleanor purchased it. She had replaced the old wooden windmills with new steel ones following the terrible '91–'92 drought after she had lost nearly half her cattle. It had been one thing after another ever since, which is why Ruckus called this particular troublesome one Job, after some fellow in the Bible.

Wooden windmills were so much easier to repair, but the newer steel ones required the services of Adams Blacksmithing. Not only was that an added expense, but it meant the windmill was out of service for a day or two while Luke Adams fixed it. However, Eleanor's biggest complaint about steel mills was the constant need for lubrication.

The sound of a horse's hooves drew Eleanor's attention away from the windmill.

Robert Stackman rode up on his bay and greeted her with a lift of his straw hat. Dressed in striped trousers, his one concession to the heat was the absence of a jacket, though he still wore a buttoned vest. His stark white shirt had a fashionable high collar better suited for cooler weather.

"Eleanor." He dismounted and tied his horse to a stake next to Eleanor's roan. "Your foreman told me I'd find you here."

She took her eyes off Kate just long enough to give him a sideways glance. They were a good five miles from the ranch house. "What is so urgent?" she asked. "It's not the first of the month, is it?"

He grinned at her. "Not quite. It's April tenth. I came to wish you a happy birthday."

She groaned. It seemed like the time between birthdays grew shorter each year. It was one of the drawbacks of aging.

"Let me think. How old are you?" he continued, knowing full well it was a sensitive subject with her. "Forty-eight? Fifty?"

"You know very well I'm sixty-six. Five years older than you." What a nuisance it was, growing older. Not that she felt her age, of course, or at least not that she was willing to admit. Still, there was something about birthdays that made one take stock and reflect, even if the last thing she wanted to do was think of the past. It was hard enough thinking of the future, which was shrinking at an alarming pace.

"I hope you're not holding our age difference against me," he said.

"You make it hard not to," she replied. He wore his years well. *Too well.*

"Shall we get on with it, then?"

"Oh, Robert. Must we?"

He shrugged. "It's your birthday."

He picked out a clear sandy spot and knelt on one knee. He pulled off his hat and held it to his chest. Most men his age would be at least half bald, but not him. His silver hair was just as full and lush as that of a much younger man.

She rolled her eyes and glanced at the windmill, but the ranch hands all had their backs toward them and were focused on Kate high above their heads. Still, someone might turn and look their way.

Eleanor gazed down at Robert. "Must you be so dramatic?"

"It's my proposal. I can be as dramatic as I please."

"Very well. If you insist."

He cleared his throat and his pale blue

eyes held hers. "Will you, Eleanor Walker, do me the honor of becoming my wife?"

Each year on her birthday he proposed marriage, and each year she turned him down — and for good reason. Both her father and ex-husband had put the ranch in jeopardy. Her father had mortgaged it to pay off his gambling debts. However much she was tempted to marry Robert, she would never do so. Arizona Territory community property laws would make Robert half owner of her ranch. Her painful divorce taught her the folly of shared ownership and she had no intention of making the same mistake twice.

"How long have we been doing this, Robert?"

"Fourteen, fifteen years," he said. "But like I've told you many times through those years, I'm a patient man."

"I'm not sure that *patient* is the right word," she said. "In any case, the answer is no." No surprises there.

Robert was nothing if not a shrewd businessman. Land-ownership meant profit to him, nothing more. He was a banker through and through. He had no ardor for land, no passion for anything but cold, hard cash. He knew nothing about ranching. Had never stayed up all night with a sick cow or rescued a lost calf. He had no feeling for cattle except how much per pound they would bring at market.

If he thought it financially wise to do so, he would sell his half of the ranch in a flash. Not only would that break her heart, it would make her hate him. Turning down his proposal had as much to do with preserving their friendship as protecting her property.

Her answer hung between them for several moments before he rose and brushed the sand off his trouser leg. "Same time, same place next year."

"Same answer."

He replaced his hat, his eyes shadowed by the yellow straw brim.

"Just thought I'd save you the effort," she said. It couldn't be pleasant being turned down as much as he had been.

"A lot can happen in a year. Who knows? You might even believe me when I tell you that the cattle business is past its prime."

"People will always eat beef," she said. "And mine is the best." Hereford beef with its fatty marbling was certainly more tender and tasty than the leaner longhorn beeves, which is why most Texas cattlemen had made the switch in recent years.

"I can't argue with you there." He grabbed

the reins of his horse and mounted. "Happy birthday, Eleanor," he said, touching a finger to the brim of his hat.

No sooner had Robert ridden away than Ruckus came galloping up on his horse.

"Job's workin' again. Just needed some oil, is all," he said.

"Excellent." Keeping the fifty-some windmills in good working order was a full-time job. "But really, Ruckus? Sending Miss Tenney to do the task? You know how dangerous it is even for experienced men."

"I had no say in the matter," he said. "She took it upon herself to climb it."

Eleanor raised her eyebrows. "A brave one, isn't she?"

"Foolhardy, more like it," Ruckus growled.

She didn't blame him for being irritated. The qualities Ruckus looked for in a new ranch hand were not the same as required in an heiress. Still, she trusted his judgment.

"It's been what? Three weeks. She's lasted a lot longer than any of the others. Do you think she's got a feel for the land?"

"She feels the land, all right. Every blasted time she falls off her horse."

"Hmm." Oh yes, the woman had tenacity. The question was, would it be enough? "Tell Miss Tenney I shall expect her for dinner at six."

"Yes, ma'am."

"Make certain she understands that it's an order." She sniffed. "I think it's time I got to know her better, don't you?"

"I'll tell her."

Eleanor watched him ride away. Her motive for wanting Kate to join her for dinner had to do with ranch business, nothing more. It had absolutely nothing to do with her birthday and not wanting to eat dinner alone yet again.

CHAPTER 10

Brandon pointed two guns at Miss
Hattie's tormentor.
"Touch a hair of her head and you'll
answer to me."
The man of ill fame backed away and the
grateful
woman sprang up with frenzied joy. "My
hero."

"Of all the foolhardy, idiotic, stupid" —
Ruckus sputtered so much he could hardly
get the words out — "dumb things to do."

Kate stood outside the barn while he
ranted and raved, his crooked nose practically in her face.

He had been at it for the last several
minutes and she figured sooner or later he
would run out of steam. He'd waited until
they returned to the ranch and they were
alone to voice his displeasure, first at climbing the windmill, then for almost shooting

him in the foot with a shotgun. Now he grabbed the weapon out of her hands and slid it onto his saddle.

She stood facing him, fists at her sides. Nothing she did satisfied him, and she had just about had enough. Her body ached and she was tired to the bone. All she wanted was to crawl into bed and sleep for forty-eight hours straight.

He tossed her a rope. "It's time you earned your keep."

Red flashed before her eyes. What did he think she'd been trying to do?

She threw the rope on the ground and crossed her arms. "I'm tired and I don't want to do any more!"

Ruckus leaned so close that had his nose been less crooked it would have collided with hers. "By the time I get back you better be able to nail that fence post with that there rope," he said brusquely. He turned and stalked away, then stopped. "The boss lady expects you for dinner tonight." He glanced at her over his shoulder with knitted brow. "And if you know what's good for you, you better tighten your fiddle strings. Right now you look like something the cat's dragged in and that ain't gonna score no points with Miz Walker." Shaking his head, he walked away.

Watching his retreating back, she chewed on her bottom lip and felt a sinking feeling. Why now, after all this time, did the ranch owner want to have dinner with her? Was it to send her packing?

The day had gone from bad to worse. How she regretted lashing out at Ruckus. True, he demanded much from her, but sometimes she had the distinct feeling he was secretly on her side. Of course that was before she nearly shot him in the foot.

Still, he was her only ally. If anyone could convince Miss Walker to let her stay, it was Ruckus. Somehow she had to find a way to get back in his good graces.

She snatched up the rope and heaved a sigh. She had practiced for a week solid and the only thing she'd managed to nail was thin air.

Determined not to let a length of rope get the best of her, she tied her lariat loop exactly as Ruckus had taught her. She then coiled the rope and swung the noose overhead, eyes on the fence post not ten feet in front of her. Somehow the free end of the rope got tangled around her foot and she lost control of the noose. Instead of landing on the fence post as she planned, it dropped over the head of her grazing horse.

Startled, Decker glanced around with

frenzied eyes, kicked up his heels, and bounded around the pasture, dragging her on the ground behind him.

"Ahhhhhhhhhh!" He pulled her halfway around the corral before her foot broke free of the rope and she let go. Sprawled belly-down in the mud, she gasped for air.

"I have to say, ma'am, that was some mighty fancy roping."

Startled by the male voice, she lifted her head. Luke Adams sat on his horse staring down at her from the other side of the fence.

Embarrassed to be seen like that she was momentarily tongue-tied, which only added to her dismay. She had suffered more indignities than she could imagine, but having Mr. Adams of all people see her sprawled on the ground was the worst indignity of all.

"I never saw anyone lasso a horse backward like that." When she made no reply, his forehead creased in concern. "Are you all right?"

No, she was not all right. She was covered in mud and felt like a fool. She wanted to cry. She wanted to scream. She sat up and, holding her arms out, stared down at her muddied clothes.

"I quit!"

"I didn't figure you as a quitter." His

mouth twitched with amusement. "I figured you'd get fired, but I didn't figure you'd quit."

She glared at him. "You thought I'd get fired?"

He dismounted and tied his horse to the fence. Telling Homer to stay, he then climbed over the wooden barrier and knelt by her side. Pulling the bandanna from around his neck, he leaned toward her.

She jerked back so quickly mud splashed all over his trousers. Before she had a chance to apologize, he splashed her back and laughed.

"So you think this is funny, do you?" She picked up a handful of dirt, but before she could throw it at him, he waved his bandanna in surrender.

"I give up," he said, his eyes filled with humor.

"Chicken." She tossed the dirt down and brushed her hands together.

He gave her a lopsided grin that made her heart turn over. "You'd better smile when you say that."

She *was* smiling. She couldn't help it. "I'm sorry. I didn't mean to mess up your clothes. I've had a hard morning. It's been one disaster after another."

"It can't be all that bad. It looks to me

like you're gainin' ground," he said, referring to her mud-covered clothes.

Laughing at his joke, she shook her head.
"I don't know that Ruckus sees it that way."

She tilted her head to the side. "I never
got a chance to thank you for your kindness
on the day I arrived." She had meant to
write him a note, but for some reason could
never figure out quite what to say.

"No need to thank me, ma'am. I reckon
anyone would have done the same."

He moved closer and she tensed, her play-
ful mood evaporating as quickly as a soap
bubble.

His forehead creased in a frown. "I'm not
going to hurt you, if that's what you're worried about."

"I know that," she said. It was a lie, of
course. She knew nothing of the sort. Every
man she'd ever known had given her reason
not to trust him, the sole exceptions being
fictional men, the ones she'd written about
— men who sprang from her imagination
or maybe from the depths of her heart.

He dabbed her nose gently before moving
his cloth down to her chin. The nearness of
him made her heart pound and she closed
her eyes. Perhaps if she didn't look at him,
his presence wouldn't seem so overwhelm-
ing.

Wrong. She could still feel his nearness, sense his gaze on her, and breathe in his essence. His gentle touch sent currents of warmth through her. Worse, he made her feel things she didn't want to feel. She'd vowed never to be like her mother, never to depend on a man, never to be ruled by love, and she meant to keep that pledge. To do otherwise would jeopardize any chance of proving herself a worthy heiress to the ranch.

Miss Walker's advertisement in the newspaper, shortly after her publisher dropped her, couldn't have come at a better time. Whether it was serendipity or just plain luck, Kate didn't know, but she was convinced her problems were over. If she could prove to Miss Walker she was capable of learning the ranching business, her future was secure. She wouldn't have to depend on anyone but herself. Nor would she ever again have to watch a man walk out of her life, tossing her aside like yesterday's newspaper. She would win the respect of all who knew her and never again be made to feel inferior.

He completed the task and she opened her eyes. "Thank you."

He studied her. "You aren't really gonna quit, are you?"

"Absolutely not," she said, though after today the choice may no longer be hers to make.

"There you go," he said, standing.

He offered her his hand and she let him pull her to her feet. To refuse his help would be rude, especially since he had shown her such kindness.

"What are you doing here?" she asked, pulling her hand out of his as one would pull away from a fire.

"Had to deliver a bunch of new horseshoes. They go through them like penny candy around here."

Aware of how awful she must look, she backed away. "I . . . I better go and change."

He nodded. "Like I said, that was some mighty fancy roping."

He held her gaze and much to her dismay she felt herself blush. With a quick farewell she whirled around and marched to the ranch house. Only when she had reached the security of the porch did she dare look back.

Luke Adams hadn't moved from where she'd left him, his face shaded by his hat. She couldn't say for sure, but she had the feeling that he was still watching her, and the very thought made her already-pounding heart beat that much faster.

■ ■ ■ ■

Later that afternoon, Kate dipped her hand into the tank and splashed water on her heated face. It felt cool and refreshing. Her body was still sore from her unfortunate roping accident earlier in the day. Now she ducked in the shade of the windmill to take a break.

Laughter drifted from the direction of the ranch house. Some of the other ranch hands were relaxing on the verandah. Mexican Pete leaned against a post, arms folded, straw hat shading his face. Stretch was telling one of his tall tales, this one about the winter he spent on a cattle ranch in Montana.

"It was so cold that your words froze soon as they left your mouth. It took two weeks for the words to thaw out enough to be heard." This brought more laughter.

How she longed to join them and sit in the shade away from the heat, but she didn't dare. Feedbag, Wishbone, and the others considered her an outsider and, for that reason, she knew they would not welcome her company. Sighing, she splashed more water on her face. *Just wait till I'm the boss lady. They won't be so eager to discount me then!*

She walked around the barn looking for Ruckus. Normally, she would ask for a longer break, but she was already in his bad graces and didn't want to rile him any more than she already had.

Ruckus rounded the corner. "Where's Decker?"

"In the barnyard," she replied.

His lips puckered as they tended to do whenever she called something by the wrong name. "After you brush the *chicken* feathers off your horse, have Luke check his shoes."

She grimaced. "I meant corral. Decker is in the corral."

He spun around and walked away and she hurried to get her horse. A short while later she led Decker around the barn to where Luke and Ruckus stood talking.

Ruckus was discussing a paint horse that had been giving him trouble all week. "Normally, he's so gentle I could stake him to a hatpin and he would stay put. Lately he's so ornery he practically bucked off my whiskers."

Luke examined the horse's hoof, shaking his head. Obviously he didn't like what he saw. Not wishing to interrupt their conversation she stopped and waited.

"I'm not much in favor of cold-shoeing," Luke said. "It made sense during the War Between the States. Time and equipment were limited back then, but this is peace-time." He ran his finger along the outer edge of the horse's hoof. "You can't get as good a fit. That's why your horse keeps throwin' a shoe. See this? This should be smooth and it's not."

"I knew that greenhorn farrier didn't know what he was doin'. The horses just didn't cotton to him. Soon as they saw him comin' they took off on the run, leaving their shadows twenty minutes behind. All he done is make the horses ornery."

Luke set the hoof down gently and straightened to stroke the horse's neck. The black-and-white horse had refused to let anyone ride him in recent days but seemed to welcome Luke's touch. "I reckon you'd be ornery, too, if you were wearing ill-fitting boots."

"O.T. sent him packing and now we don't have a farrier. The job's yours if you want it." He pointed to the open door of the ranch's blacksmith shop. "As you can see we're fully equipped and the boss lady pays well."

Kate held her breath. Luke working here?

At the ranch? Finding the prospect vaguely disturbing, she waited for Luke's reply, but before he had a chance to respond, Ruckus motioned for her to join them.

Luke greeted her with a smile. "Your horse givin' you trouble too?" he asked. He said nothing about their earlier encounter, but his eyes sent a private message.

"I suspect it's the other way around," Ruckus muttered.

"Let's take a look." After running his hand along Decker's flank, Luke lifted a back leg and rested it upon his leather-aproned knee to examine it. She marveled that a man able to bend iron was capable of such a gentle touch.

"Got a loose shoe here," he said. Locking the horse's leg between his knees, Luke pulled a rasp from his apron pocket and began working on the clinches. Decker twisted his head to look behind him, ears straight up, but didn't move.

Ruckus watched for a moment before nodding in approval. "We'll talk later. Let me know what you decide." He walked away, leaving her alone with Luke.

"Did . . . did I do that?" she asked. "The loose shoe?"

"I doubt it. Nails come out. It happens." He glanced at her. "You know what they say. For want of a nail the shoe was lost . . ."

Recognizing the childhood ditty, she joined in: "For want of a shoe the horse was lost."

His mouth spread into a lazy grin. "For want of a horse the rider was lost."

She tried to think of the next line. "The kingdom was lost?" she asked.

"Battle," he said. "For want of a rider the battle was lost."

"Of course," she said, feeling as if she was losing some sort of battle herself. She studied him while he worked. "Thank you for not mentioning my earlier mishap in the corral."

Luke glanced up at her, his eyes warm with humor. "I still think that was a mighty fine rope trick. I reckon Buffalo Bill could use someone like you in his Wild West show."

The idea was so absurd she couldn't help but laugh. "I'll keep that in mind."

For a moment they stared at each other and her heart fluttered. His gaze settled on her mouth and warmth rushed to her cheeks. As if to suddenly catch himself, he bent his head down and continued working on Decker's shoe with firm but careful movements.

Shaken, she was unable to find her voice. What was the matter with her? One smile from him and all good intentions flew out the window.

"You're lucky your horse isn't lame," he said, his voice husky. "I'll replace all four shoes."

She swallowed hard. "Is that why he keeps throwing me off? Because of his shoes?"

"Hard to tell. There's no injury that I can see. Looks like we caught it in time."

She moistened her lips. "Ruckus said that when a rider eats gravel it's seldom the horse's fault."

Luke glanced up at her. "That's true most times. Except when the rider is a lady. Then it's always the horse's fault."

"It would be just my luck to have a misogynistic horse," she said lightly.

His square jaw tensed and some unreadable emotion flashed in his eyes. Without a word he straightened, walked to the workbench, and exchanged the rasp for a long-handled pull-off.

Did she imagine the sudden chill in the air? Or had she simply imagined their earlier rapport as they recited that silly rhyme? "I heard Ruckus ask you to work here. Do . . . do you plan to accept his offer?"

" 'Fraid not." He checked one front foot and then the other before returning to the one he started working on. "People in town depend on me. If I worked here at the ranch I'd have to close my shop. Can't do both."

Kate let out her breath, surprised at the mixed feelings of disappointment and relief that surged through her.

"I'll trim him up and give him new shoes and he'll be rarin' to go. Shouldn't take more than an hour."

"There's no hurry," she said. Still sore from the morning's spills, she looked forward to keeping both feet on the ground for a while. How she longed to take the afternoon off and sit in the shade with a nice cold drink. The thought burst like a bubble the moment Ruckus rounded the corner of the barn and beckoned to her.

"Come on, Goldilocks, let's get to work," he called.

She gave an inward groan. Would the day never end? And why didn't the heat bother Ruckus like it bothered the rest of them?

She thanked Luke and followed Ruckus to the barn.

CHAPTER 11

Brandon stole a glance at her sweet countenance. The slight stain of tears upon her cheeks added to her innocent beauty and stole his heart.

The day before, Kate had helped clean the calving barn, and now the scent of fresh hay tickled her nose. A loud moo greeted them as they stepped inside and rounded a corner. A pregnant cow in obvious distress was strapped inside a chute. Restlessly stomping her hooves, the bovine bellowed and thrashed from side to side trying to pull free from her restraints.

Ruckus led the way to the back of the cow. "This lady's ready and you're gonna learn how to pull a calf."

Kate's eyes widened. She never dreamed the term was meant literally. For all the stories she'd heard about working on a ranch, never once had she heard about delivering calves.

Ruckus wrapped twine around the cow's tail and tied it to her neck. After rolling up his sleeves he picked up a bucket of clean water and splashed it onto the cow's backside.

"You're about to witness God's work at his finest," he said, lowering the empty bucket to the ground.

Kate clamped her mouth shut and said nothing. If it was God's work, then why was the cow in such terrible pain? She pushed the thought away and rolled up her sleeves.

The cow's deep bellows were almost constant. Her hide rippled from head to tail with strained muscles.

Ruckus nodded. "She's pushing. If we're lucky, she'll complete the job herself."

He talked to the cow in soothing tones. He was equally at ease no matter what he was doing, whether chasing a steer, calming a cow about to give birth, or reciting the Bible.

"How long have you worked on the ranch, Ruckus?"

"I've been here 'bout nine, ten years," he said. "Prior to that I drifted from ranch to ranch, which was hard on the family. Most ranches can't afford to hire people year-round. When the boss lady offered me a permanent job I grabbed it. She gave my wife and me a place to live and a way to make an honest livin'."

"You're married?" That was a surprise. In all the time she'd worked at the ranch, Ruckus had never spoken of his private life and she simply assumed he had none.

"Yep, goin' on twenty years."

"That long?" Her voice rose in surprise.

He studied her for a moment before replying. "I don't know how it is where you came from, but out here *for better or worse* means for *good.*"

"Miss Walker's marriage wasn't for good," she said.

He shrugged. "Miss Walker ain't like normal folks."

She bit her lip. No argument there. "So where is your wife?"

"We live in a cabin on the northern part of the property. That's where us married folks live. The good Lord blessed us with three children, two sons and a daughter. One's in law school and another's studying to be a preacher." He chuckled. "A preacher. Imagine that? Soon as he finishes seminary he plans to come back and preach right here in Cactus Patch. After hearing me preach to him all these years, he's gonna make me sit

150

in church every week so he can return the favor."

Kate laughed. "What about your daughter?"

He flashed a fatherly smile. "Our daughter got hitched and she and her husband started their own ranch west of Tucson."

He was obviously proud of his family and she couldn't help but envy his offspring. Could they possibly know how lucky they were to have such a caring father?

"And you've been happy all these years?" she asked. "Some people might even say this is godforsaken land."

Ruckus's eyebrows rose as if the thought were inconceivable. "And they would be wrong." He pointed at the pen. "What do you see?"

She followed his finger. "I see a miserable cow."

"What I see is God's amazing handiwork. Man has figured out how to build trains and send messages through wires, but there ain't no man on earth figured out how to turn grass into milk."

"I never thought about it that way," she said.

Ruckus's faith in an almighty God never failed to amaze her. Growing up, she'd never attended church. Her mama seldom mentioned God except in a drunken stupor and that was to curse, not worship him. So Kate had a hard time believing in the loving and caring God Ruckus so often talked about. She wanted to, oh, how she wanted to. She just didn't know how to make herself believe that God could be as good or trustworthy as Ruckus insisted.

"Get ready," Ruckus said. "You're about to witness more of God's handiwork."

One hoof popped out and Kate gasped in delight. Just as quickly another hoof showed.

Ruckus grinned. "Two front legs. See that?" He pointed to the hoof. "The soles are pointing down. Pointing any other way and we're in a heap o' trouble. Today, we're in luck."

No sooner had he said it than the young cow popped free, dropping upon the pile of clean straw. Ruckus quickly grabbed the not-so-little calf by its hind legs and dragged it to a clean bed of straw.

Fearing the calf was dead or had been injured in the fall, Kate fell to her knees by its side.

"Come on, little fella, you can do it." She patted the calf's wet hide. "Breathe!"

Ruckus pushed a strand of straw into the calf's nostrils. "This helps the calf cough up anythin' plugging up its breathing tube," he explained. It worked. The calf made a funny sound and opened its eyes.

Kate exhaled with relief, her own eyes moist with tears. "It's alive."

Ruckus's grin practically reached his ears. He looked like a proud rooster and Kate couldn't help but laugh. He scooped the calf in his arms, his body bent backward to accommodate the weight, and laid it down on a pile of fresh hay in front of its mother.

"Whooeee. That baby gotta weigh at least a hundred pounds." He stepped back and wiped off his hands with a clean towel.

The cow stared at the calf before nuzzling it with her nose and, finally, licking it clean with gentle strokes of her large gray and pink tongue.

"That . . . that was incredible," Kate said. All the weeks of torturous work were forgotten in the wonder of the moment. She was exhausted, but she couldn't take her eyes off the little calf. She felt some odd sense of maternal pride when later the little fellow struggled up on wobbly legs and probed its mother's udder with its mouth.

"Do you normally help with the birthing?" In all her ranch stories, never once had she written a birthing scene. "I thought cattle had their babies naturally out on the range."

"They do most times," he said. "But this

one lost a calf last year and had been acting strange for a couple of days. We decided to bring her in."

"How do you know her history?" she asked.

"What?"

"All the cattle look alike. How do you know this one lost a calf?"

He laughed. "A cattleman ain't worth his salt if he don't know his cattle," he said. "We only have to keep track of a thousand or so cattle, whereas God the Father has to keep track of millions of his people. Kind of makes you feel humble just thinkin' about it."

"Miss Walker owns a thousand head of cattle?" she asked. She hadn't seen more than a few cattle at any one time.

"Yep. Used to be two thousand but that was before the drought. It's getting harder. More ranchers are fighting for grazin' rights on public land and there's only so much grass to go around." He shrugged. "But, God willing, we'll get the numbers up again. Done it before and we'll do it again."

She never met a man like Ruckus, a man so comfortable with his faith that it seemed as much a part of him as his crooked nose and relaxed, easy manner.

"Are we finished here?" She was anxious

to clean up. More than that, she didn't want to hear any more references to God the Father. The very word *father* turned her blood cold. The term *Forever Man* didn't help much either. Nothing was forever, except perhaps land.

"For now. One down and only fifty-five more calves to go."

Her mouth dropped open and he laughed at her expression. She followed him outside and together they washed in a wooden barrel.

"Don't worry. The boss lady figured out that if we feed the cattle at night, they're more likely to drop their calves durin' the day. Since we switched feedin' times, we've gotten a whole lot more shut-eye." He studied her. "Speakin' of the boss lady, it's late. You better go and get ready for supper."

In all the excitement Kate had almost forgotten that she'd been summoned by the ranch owner. "I hope she's not going to send me packing," she said, rinsing off the soap lather. "If that's what she plans to do, I'd rather she tell me now and get it over with."

Ruckus lifted a bushy brow. "If she was gonna send you packin', she'd have told me first." He wiped his hands dry and then

155

tossed her the towel. "That's not why she invited you to have supper with her. She just wants to get to know you better. Can't blame her for that."

Kate hoped Ruckus was right. Miss Walker did make her nervous. She'd lost count of the number of times she caught Miss Walker watching from a distance. Kate was certain the woman could see more than humanly possible. Would anyone else have noticed that feeding times affected birthing? She doubted it, and it was Miss Walker's uncanny insight that worried Kate.

She finished drying her hands and hung the towel up on a hook to dry.

"I reckon you don't much like the boss lady."

What Ruckus said was true, but she hadn't wanted to admit it even to herself.

"I don't really know her," Kate said, hedging.

Ruckus chuckled. "See that cactus over there?" He pointed to a barrel cactus that grew by the side of the barn. "Outside it's covered in thorns. Inside it's all soft and mushy."

She arched an eyebrow. "Are you saying that Miss Walker has a soft spot somewhere?"

It didn't seem possible.

"I'm saying that nothing is what it seems. Some people think God is harsh and cruel. That's 'cause they don't take the time to get to know him."

She let her gaze wander across the land all the way to the distant mountains. Even as she watched, the colors, shapes, and shadows of the desert shifted and changed, blended and blurred — a canvas at the whim of an artist's brush.

"Have supper and make it your business to get to know the boss lady. You may be surprised."

"I hope you're right." She started for the ranch house, then stopped. "Ruckus, about what happened earlier. I didn't mean to give you a bad time and I had no intention of shooting you."

"I ain't got no idea what you're talkin' about," he said. He shooed her away with a wave of his hands. "Go!"

She stared at him a moment, wishing she could be more like him. Ruckus saw only the good in people, saw only the good in God. She saw the good but looked for the bad. It was a survival skill that had served her well in the past and kept her from making mistakes she would later regret.

She turned with a sigh and headed for the ranch house. Ruckus was right about a lot of things. She hoped he was right about Miss Walker.

CHAPTER 12

The villain banged on the door. She was doomed, doomed, doomed! Just when she thought her life over she heard Brandon call to her from outside. She ran to the balcony, hands clasped to her chest. "Quick, my love," he beckoned. "Jump and I shall catch you."

Kate groaned at the balcony scene in her head. Shakespeare would surely turn over in his grave. Not that it mattered. Right now all she could think about was how exhausted she was, how every muscle in her body ached.

Her calloused hands were sore and it took a hard scrubbing to rid her fingernails of dirt. Still, she was on shaky ground. Disobeying Miss Walker's order — and Ruckus had made a point of telling her it was, indeed, an order — would be a mistake.

Each day spent at the ranch had been

tough, but this day had been especially difficult. Even so she felt a sense of exhilaration never before experienced. Not even her dread of having supper with Miss Walker could dampen her spirits. All the days and weeks of hard work were forgotten in light of watching the birth of a single baby cow.

Smiling at the memory of the little fellow struggling to its feet, she brushed her hair and wound the unruly locks on top of her head, letting curls cascade down her back.

She stared in the mirror and hardly recognized herself. She wore a blue skirt and white shirtwaist but, oddly enough, after wearing the divided skirts and shirts provided by Miss Walker these past couple of weeks, her own clothes felt awkward and confining. She'd lost weight, which was hard to believe. All that manual labor gave her a ravenous appetite, and she ate nearly as much as the ranch hands.

Though she took care never to go outside without her wide-brimmed hat, it kept flying off. Consequently, her skin had lost its paleness and her pink cheeks glowed beneath a golden-brown tan. The Arizona sun had a unifying effect as it was almost impossible to tell Mexicans and whites apart from skin color alone. Only her hair gave her away. Having turned a few shades lighter, it was now more sunshine yellow than honey.

No one in Boston would recognize her. Certainly no one at Miss Newcomb's Academy for Young Women. With this thought came an onslaught of memories. She'd only been sixteen when the school hired her to clean the premises. The pay was small but it provided for her and her mama's few meager needs. More importantly it opened doors that she never knew existed.

The college held classes in social skills, morals, piano, and oil painting, but she had no interest in such feminine pursuits. Instead, she timed her chores so she could listen to lectures on science, history, and philosophy. As she polished brass railings and scrubbed floors, a whole new world opened up to her. It was two years before she grew brave enough to slip one of her short stories onto the English instructor Mr. Abbott's desk.

A short time later she was called into the school office. She naturally feared she'd lost her job. Instead, the headmistress offered her the opportunity to attend classes, based on Mr. Abbott's recommendation, providing of course she didn't let her duties slip. And she didn't. It took her six years to do what most women did in four, but at last she graduated and it felt as if she'd conquered the world. People came and went but an education was forever. No one could take that away from her.

Within six months of earning her diploma, she sold her first novel. She didn't get much money, but sales increased with each subsequent book and eventually she was able to purchase a Remington typing machine and rent an apartment with heat. By then her mama's lungs had deteriorated and she'd died soon after, but she lived her last few months in relative comfort, and for that Kate was grateful.

If only she hadn't written that last book. Her editor wanted to call the book *The Hay Dilemma* instead of *Miss Hattie's Dilemma.* The term *grass* was given to works of minor value, which is why Walt Whitman titled his controversial book of poetry *Leaves of Grass,* which he meant as a pun. The word *hay* was her editor's way of saying her work was less than trivial.

Still, nothing prepared her for what happened once the book was published. She'd written a simple love story, revealing the inner longings of a woman's heart. The Watch and Ward Society didn't see it that way. Instead, they read between the lines and banned her book on immoral grounds. No one could have been more shocked than she was.

Pushing the memories away, she stared at her image. What did Luke see when he looked at her? Startled by the unbidden thought, Kate ripped open the door and hurried out to the balcony. Trembling, she ran her hands up and down her arms, wishing the sudden pounding of her heart would stop. *Mustn't think of Luke.* The ranch — that was all she could think about. All she wanted to think about.

The sun dipped beneath the horizon in a blaze of red and orange, taking the heat of the day with it. Never had she witnessed such magnificent sunsets. It was the thing she liked best about the desert. That and the wide-open spaces.

Along with the thought came another. What if Miss Walker sent her packing? The thought nearly crushed her. Where would she go? What would she do? How would she support herself? With the banning of her latest book, she doubted she could even get a tutoring job. She had an education, but what good was it if no one would hire her? She'd put her stock in her education only to find that it deserted her when she most needed it.

She tried to recall what Miss Walker had

said on that first day. *"Nothing in this world is permanent except for land. It will always be there for you."* Kate sighed. The question was, would it be there for her after tonight?

A knock on her bedroom door chased away her thoughts.

"Miss Tenney, supper is served," Rosita called.

"I'm coming," Kate replied, stepping into her room and closing the balcony door. Pulling herself together, she mentally donned her protective armor and took one last look in the mirror. No one could ever guess her poverty-ridden background and failures by appearances alone, and she meant to keep it that way.

With a bracing breath she exited her room and walked unhurriedly downstairs to the dining room, determined to prove to Miss Walker once and for all that she was serious about ranching.

Eleanor Walker sat at the end of the dining table and greeted Kate with a businesslike nod.

"There you are." She pointed to the only other place setting on the opposite end of the long polished oak table and waited for Kate to be seated before ringing a bell.

Kate clasped her hands tight in her lap. It

never occurred to her there would only be two of them dining. She was more convinced than ever that Miss Walker planned to dismiss her. Ruckus insisted not, but what if he was wrong? She fought the panic that began to rise.

Rosita appeared and Kate forced herself to breathe.

"We're ready," Eleanor said.

Rosita vanished again, and Eleanor picked up her linen napkin, flapped it open, and settled it on her lap. "So have you fully recovered from your unfortunate brush with the Devil's Tongue?"

"Yes, thank you," Kate replied, hoping that her flaming cheeks were hidden by the flickering candlelight. The sheer size of the table intimidated her, and she had the strangest feeling she was on stage and expected to perform.

Soft and mushy? Hardly. Miss Walker's rigid exterior looked as formidable as Boston's Deer Island Prison and just as difficult to penetrate.

"Excellent." After a beat she said, "I commend you for climbing Job. Those new steel windmills are more trouble than they're worth. I much prefer the older wooden models. Now I'm going to have to hire a full-time windmiller just to take care of them." She gave a sigh of disgust before leveling her gray eyes on Kate. "Obviously, you have no fear of heights."

"I believe everyone fears heights." The truth was she had been terrified.

"Hmmm. So tell me, what else did you do today?"

"Ruckus and I helped deliver a calf." Kate smiled at the memory.

"Ah. I trust all went well."

Kate nodded. "Yes, perfect." She didn't want to think about her shooting or lariat mishaps. She'd learned to ride a horse and she was determined to learn the other skills too.

"Good. We've lost more calves this year than we've gained. If we don't get some rain soon, I fear things will get worse."

Rosita entered the dining room pushing a cart and set a dinner plate in front of Kate piled high with beef, gravy, potatoes, and string beans. The menu varied little from day to day, but the food was always cooked to perfection. Instead of bemoaning the size of the portions as she once did, she now welcomed it. She was famished.

Miss Walker spread butter on a hot roll. "So, tell me, what do you think of ranching?"

Kate placed the linen napkin on her lap.

The meat was still sizzling and it smelled delicious.

"Speak up, girl. Don't be shy."

"The work is rather arduous," she said, choosing her words with care. She stole a glance at the older woman while cutting her meat. "But I don't think there's anything else I'd rather do."

Miss Walker studied her. "You've lasted for three weeks." She laid her butter knife across her bread plate. "That's longer than any of the others."

"Ruckus is a good teacher," Kate replied. "I've learned a lot from him."

"I daresay you have a lot more to learn."

"I can't wait," Kate said. She was especially eager to learn the business side of ranching, but it would probably be awhile before Miss Walker trusted her with the books.

The ranch owner measured her for a moment. "Tell me about your family. Are your parents still alive?"

Kate's mouth went dry. The question caught her off guard and she immediately marshaled her defenses. Miss Walker didn't strike her as someone to ask questions out of idle curiosity. For this reason Kate gave her answer full consideration. She could easily have concocted a story about her family, but writing fiction was one thing, lying quite another.

"My mother died three years ago," she said in a clipped voice.

"And your father?"

"He left when I was five."

Kate expected a word of sympathy — at the least a look of pity — but none came. Instead, Miss Walker shrugged and said, "He probably did you a kindness."

Kate stared at her, momentarily speechless. The woman was even more coldhearted than she'd thought. Mushy, indeed! Not knowing how to respond, Kate concentrated on her meal.

"I've never tasted such tender meat," she said after several bites. "Is it your beef?"

"I wouldn't eat any other," Miss Walker replied. "I don't like the way the other ranchers around here raise cattle. Some of them are too lazy to move their herds around and allow them to overgraze down to the nubs. That means the cattle are taking in more sand than nutrition. You can't get a good steak from a gritty diet."

"You've been ranching a long time," Kate said.

"My family came here in the '50s. I remember when Tucson was but a mud village and Tombstone a canvas city."

"I had no idea cattle ranches had been around that long in the territory."

"The Spanish established cattle ranches long before white men came, but the Indians pretty much ran them off. My family was on the way to the California gold mines when our wagon wheel broke. That was way back when this was still part of New Mexico Territory."

"Your whole family was going to California?" Kate had heard that the lure of gold pulled men away, but she thought women and children had stayed home.

"Mother refused to be a California widow. She also didn't trust that my father would come home."

Kate's hand tightened around her fork. She understood all too well how a woman might distrust a man.

"My father got a job with a Mexican hauling company, but by the time we'd saved enough money to continue our journey, the California gold rush was over — so we stayed." Between bites Miss Walker continued.

"We started out with a little land and a small adobe hut, and my mother planted vegetables and raised chickens. One day she found an injured Englishman on her property taking a small herd of cattle to California. Mother nursed him back to health. To show his gratitude he gave her one of his steers, which he claimed was sired by a bull belonging to Queen Victoria. He told her to slaughter it to feed her family, but Mother was too smart for that. Instead, she decided to go into the cattle business."

"With only one cow?"

"Steer," Miss Walker said. "Ah, but you see it had *royal* blood. Of course every Englishman claims nobility either for himself or his livestock. I guess it's some sort of status symbol like the *Mayflower.* With the number of people claiming ancestors aboard, it's a wonder the ship didn't sink before it left the harbor."

Kate laughed, and for the first time since entering the dining room felt herself relaxing. If Miss Walker had intended to fire her, surely she would have done so by now.

"By the time my father was killed in an Indian attack, we had a hundred cattle," Miss Walker continued. "Some we bought from a Mexican rancher. Most were feral steer left over from the Spanish."

Kate lowered her fork. "Your father was killed by Indians?"

"That was Mother's version. He actually drank himself to death."

Kate's mouth dropped open, but she

quickly smacked her lips together. People in Boston were so much more circumspect than they were out here in the West. Never would such words as *drunk* be heard in polite company.

She searched for something to say to break the sudden silence that made the elongated table seem even longer.

"It's rather remarkable that she would think to start a cattle ranch here in the desert," she said at last.

"Mother could make pie out of thin air. Come to think of it, I believe she did. But enough about the past. Right now I'm concerned about the present. We'll soon be ready for spring roundup. There's something invigorating about putting my brand on a new generation of cattle."

"Isn't . . . isn't that painful?"

"Oh, posh. Spoken like a true greenhorn. A cattle's hide is many times thicker than human skin. Trust me, any pain is minimal."

Kate bit her lip and looked away. It seemed like everything she'd written about cattle and ranch life had been incorrect. Perhaps her last book had been banned for the wrong reason.

She yawned and quickly drew her napkin to her mouth, hoping Miss Walker had not noticed.

"I hope it's not the company," Miss Walker said in her usual forthright way.

"Oh no! I . . . I can't tell you how much I'm enjoying this." She smiled. "What better way to celebrate a birth?"

Miss Walker stiffened. "How did you know it was my birthday?" Her brusque voice snapped through the air like a whip. "No one knows that except for my banker."

"I . . . I didn't know," Kate stammered. Had she said something wrong? "I was referring to the calf we delivered."

"I see." Miss Walker tapped her fingers on the table. "Now that you know, I trust you'll keep the knowledge to yourself."

"If that's what you wish." Kate hesitated before holding her glass aloft. Surely Miss Walker wouldn't fire her for showing common courtesy. "Happy birthday."

Miss Walker failed to lift her glass in return but she did give a curt nod. "Do you have any questions regarding ranching?"

Kate set her glass down and hesitated. Dare she push her luck? "I haven't had a day off since my arrival."

"You want a day off? Goodness, girl, this is a cattle ranch — not a girls' school. This is our busiest month. No one gets time off except to go to church and even that's hardly possible during calving season."

172

"I won't be long. I just need to purchase some toiletries."

Before Miss Walker could reply, O.T. entered the dining room. He glanced at Kate before turning his attention to Miss Walker. "Sorry to bother you, ma'am, but I need to have a word with you. It's most urgent."

Miss Walker pushed her chair back and stood. "Of course it's urgent. I wouldn't expect you to enter the house wearing spurs unless it *was* urgent." To Kate she said, "When I come back we'll have dessert."

With that she ushered O.T. out of the dining room and into her office, closing the door.

Curious, Kate stared at the door and yawned. Whatever the urgent business was, she hoped it didn't take long. All she wanted to do was climb into bed and go to sleep.

The flickering light of the candle only added to her drowsiness. Muffled voices carried into the dining room from behind the closed door of Miss Walker's office, but Kate couldn't make out what was said. She yawned and shook her head in an effort to stay awake. Maybe if she laid her head down for just a moment . . .

He carried her upstairs in his arms and laid her gently on the bed, covering her with a blanket. *"Sleep tight, my love,"* he whispered. *"Sleep tight."*

Even in her dreamlike state she knew it wasn't Brandon. The man who filled the pages of her books and occupied her dreams now had another man's face.

CHAPTER 13

Eleanor leaned against her desk, arms crossed. "Are you sure about this?"

O.T. nodded. "That's a big drop from the number of calves branded last year."

Yes, she had noticed that, no question. Her ranch averaged sixty new calves per hundred cattle. If what O.T. said was true, this year the same number of cattle would produce closer to forty calves and that meant a big drop financially when it came marketing time.

"We had less rain this year than last." Less rain meant less grass. Though it wasn't just lack of water that was the problem. There was a limit to the number of cattle the land could support, but some ranchers insisted upon overstocking the range. Even the Tombstone Stock Growers had called for a halt in importing more cattle.

"We've still managed to maintain the herd's weight," O.T. argued. "Drillin' that new well on the south side helped. Besides, the count doesn't match up."

"So what do you think the problem is?" Eleanor asked.

"I doubt there're any less calves. I think someone already branded them. Our men only counted the unbranded ones."

Eleanor touched her forehead. "Not again." Five years ago a quarter of their calves had been rustled from beneath their very noses.

"Sorry, ma'am, but I think the Dunne gang is back."

Eleanor grimaced. The gang had a unique way of operating, which is why it took so long to nail them. They hair-branded calves with the Last Chance brand to prevent them from being counted. Since the iron burned through the hair and not the hide, the rustlers could afford to wait until the calves were weaned before cutting them out of the herd. By then, the hair had grown out and the unbranded calves were easy to spot. No one had been the wiser — at least not at first.

Now, O.T. made it his business to count pregnant cattle and record the number along with live births. If he said the Dunne gang was back, Eleanor had every reason to believe he was right.

"So how do you wish to handle this?" she asked.

"We need to inform the marshal. We've got some time before the calves are weaned, but the sooner he knows the better. I just hate having to give up one of my hands to ride into town right now."

"You don't have to. I'll send Miss Tenney instead." The girl wanted a day off and now she would get it.

"That'll be a help," O.T. said. "Sorry to bother you during supper, but I thought you'd want to know." He turned to leave.

"O.T." Hand on the doorknob, he looked back at her. "Be careful out there," she said. "Don't try to take the law into your own hands."

He nodded. "I sure won't, ma'am."

After he left, Eleanor remained where she was. Calving season always came with a new set of challenges, but cattle rustling was the worst. It had caused more headaches through the years than all that Indian trouble put together.

The Texas Cattlemen's Association had clamped down on cattle rustling in the Lone Star State. Unfortunately, all that did was drive the rustlers out of Texas and into New Mexico and Arizona territories.

Arizona had its own cattle association, of

course, but it was neither as strong nor as organized as the one in Texas. She blamed that partly on the marshal. Morris had been in town for three years and crime had gone up, not down. Outlaws like Cactus Joe pretty much had the run of the town. Informing the marshal of this latest threat was the right thing to do, but she had little faith it would do any good.

Recalling with a start that she had left Kate waiting in the dining room, she sighed. The girl had spirit and tenacity, but none of that would do a bit of good if she didn't learn the ranching business.

Twenty-nine. The girl was twenty-nine years old. Not much older than Eleanor's daughter would have been had she lived. Rebecca had been blonde and blue-eyed too. Was that why Eleanor had been more accepting of Kate's lack of horsemanship? Shown her more tolerance than she'd given the others? Because of the resemblance to her long-dead daughter?

If that were true, then either Kate Tenney was the answer to a prayer — or a cruel twist of fate.

"What better way to celebrate a birth?"

Hmmm. Well, why not? The cat's out of the bag, as they say. May as well make the most of it.

She turned off the fringed parlor lamp in her office and walked down the hall to the kitchen. Bo Spencer, the cook, was putting the finishing touches on one of his marvelous angel cakes. He stood six feet tall, had black kinky hair and skin the color of dark oak.

A former slave, Bo had been with the ranch for ten years now, after she found him trying to steal a horse. He claimed he was returning it after it wandered off, but she didn't believe him. When she ordered him off her property at gunpoint, he sneaked into the ranch house kitchen instead and prepared the best meal she'd ever tasted. No one cooked a steak or roast beef as good as he did.

"Do you still believe I'm guilty?" he'd asked at the time.

What cooking had to do with his guilt or innocence she couldn't imagine, but she liked his gall. The whole thing was so ridiculous she laughed and hired him on the spot, and never once had she regretted it. Not even when he introduced her to grits, which tasted like mushy cornbread.

Now he looked up. "Ready for dessert, Miz Walker?"

"Yes, we are." She turned to leave but thought of something. "Bo, would you mind putting a candle on the cake?"

Bo's syrupy brown eyes regarded her from beneath his floppy white hat. "A candle?"

"Yes. A lit one."

"It someone's birthday?" he asked.

"Yes, as a matter of fact it is. Miss Tenney helped deliver her first calf today."

She walked from the kitchen to the dining room and stopped in the doorway. Kate was sound asleep, her blond head resting on the table.

Eleanor stepped back into the kitchen, surprised and irritated at the disappointment that washed over her. "Never mind, Bo. Forget the dessert. I'm going to bed."

CHAPTER 14

She was ruined! Her character had
  suffered a blemish.
Never again would Brandon believe she
  had purity of soul.

Kate was horrified. How could she have
fallen asleep at the table? How rude. How
humiliating. How absolutely inexcusable.

She might have slept in the dining room
all night had Rosita not wakened her. Oh,
what must Miss Walker think?

That morning she hurriedly dressed and
rushed downstairs at a little after 4:00 a.m.
to apologize, but she never got a chance.
Miss Walker's place setting was cleared,
which meant she'd already left the house.
According to José it had something to do
with the calf count.

Kate slapped her hand on her forehead
and groaned. Four a.m. and already she was

late. What was wrong with these people?

She shook her fist. "Would the world end if we slept in until, say, five o'clock? Do they not know that the early worm gets eaten?" That would be the first thing she'd change when she took over the ranch.

Sensing she wasn't alone, she turned. Rosita stood in the doorway staring at her with rounded eyes.

"Miss Walker said to give this to you." Rosita hurried across the room and thrust a single sheet of paper into Kate's hand. She then quickly ran from the room before Kate could thank her for waking her the night before.

She scanned the bold handwriting. It read, *You are to drive into town and inform the marshal that the Dunne gang has returned and are up to their old tricks.* It was signed *Eleanor Walker.*

A fluttery feeling shot through her. It would do her a world of good to spend a day in town and give her sore body much-needed time to recover.

Anticipating the hours ahead, she joined Ruckus and the other men for morning prayer at exactly 5:00 a.m. Today, there was none of the usual jostling and bantering between the men, just silence and somber faces. Even Upbeat wasn't his usual cheerful self.

"Let's pray," Ruckus said. "Dear heavenly Father, hear our prayer. Send rain and help us catch those connivin' scoundrels. Amen."

She kept her head lowered but her eyes open. Conniving scoundrels? She marveled at how Ruckus talked to God much like he might talk to a friend. And who was this gang that seemed to have everyone up in arms? Outlaws, no doubt. Whatever dastardly deed they were guilty of must be bad for Miss Walker to send her into town.

While O.T. gave the men their instructions for the day, she hastened toward the barn to check on the calf she'd helped deliver.

"Hey, little fella," Kate said, kneeling in the hay. The calf's hair was dry and fluffed out and it was definitely steadier on its feet.

The mother cow bawled and started toward her. Kate scrambled backward spiderlike. Heart pounding, she jumped up and slammed the gate closed, locking mother and baby inside the cow stall. She always thought of cattle as placid but this one looked fierce. Even now the cow seemed to glare at her.

"Just 'cause she's a mother is no reason to think she's a lady," Ruckus said from behind her.

"She tried to attack me," Kate said, shuddering. "She could have injured me. Maimed me. She could have broken my bones or . . . or even killed me."

Ruckus shrugged. "The last thing you want to do is get in the way of a cow protectin' its young."

She brushed the hay off her divided skirt. *Protecting its young.* The words rattled inside her head like marbles in a bag. An animal knew instinctively to protect its young? How was that possible? Why wasn't the same true of humans? Why hadn't Mama known to protect her? The unbidden thought shook her to the core and a lump rose in her throat.

"A mother can pick her calf out of a whole herd," Ruckus continued, shaking his head. "And they say cattle are dumb."

The cow nuzzled her young, seeming to push it away from the two of them.

Ruckus grinned. "The Good Book says God cares for us folks like a mama cares for her babe."

Kate glanced at his profile. The man seemed to know a Bible verse for every occasion. This one, however, was ill chosen. If God's care was anywhere near like her mama's, Kate wanted no part of it.

Keeping her thoughts to herself she asked,

"May I name him?"

Ruckus made a face. "Never name an animal you plan to eat."

Her mouth dropped open. "I'm not planning —"

"Maybe not, but someone is. Come on," Ruckus said impatiently, as if suddenly realizing the time. "The boss lady said you're goin' into town. While you're there, I need you to take a broken windmill part to the smithy for repairs."

She hadn't planned on stopping at the blacksmith shop and was unprepared for the odd combination of anticipation and dread that assailed her. It made no sense. Confused, she lowered her gaze to hide her reddened cheeks.

"Also, I need you to stop at the post office. I'm expectin' a letter from my son."

"I'd be happy to, Ruckus."

He gave a nod. "We'll get some riding in before you leave."

Kate groaned. Ruckus insisted she learn to ride a cutting horse, and that was a whole different experience than riding Decker. She was still sore from her workout three days earlier.

"Next week we start roundup and you plumb better stay in the saddle 'cause you're gonna be dealin' with a whole bunch of protective mothers."

She followed him outside to the horses he'd already saddled. "Tell me about the Dunne gang."

"There ain't much to tell. They're a bunch of no-good cattle rustlers. They hair-brand our heifers before we get to them."

"What's a hair brand?" she asked.

"The brandin' iron only burns through the hair. It looks real enough from a distance. We figure we already branded it, so it don't get counted. Unless you're a-lookin' for it you might not notice. The brand soon grows out. That makes it easy for the culprits to cut the calves out of the herd and take off with 'em."

He checked her saddle, then stepped aside. "Come on. You're gonna have to leave for town soon. We best not waste any more time."

The horse's name was Bullet, which did nothing for Kate's confidence. Bullets were fast and deadly. Nevertheless, she shoved her booted foot in the stirrup and mounted.

"Now that you know how to fall off your horse, you're gonna learn how to ride him."

"I *do* know how to ride him," she said. "I only fell off once last time."

"Congratulations. You're the only one I know able to fall off a standin' horse. You ain't gonna be much help if you can't ride faster than a lame cow." He blew out his breath. "Okay, remember what I told you. Your horse is trained to make sudden stops and hard turns. Relax. Let your horse do the work. Otherwise he'll unseat you sure as shootin'." Without another word he mounted his own horse and galloped off.

Kate braced herself and held the reins tight. "All right now, you and I have an understanding. Remember?" The horse's ears twitched and his tail swished. "Good boy." She mounted and pressed her heels gently into the horse's sides. "Giddi-up!"

With the speed of a bullet, her horse took off running, leaving her in the dust.

CHAPTER 15

She raced along the dark, dismal road with great urgency, her horse's hooves thundering through the cold, still night. Brandon would know how to handle the villains, if only she could reach him in time . . .

The ride to Cactus Patch was uneventful and monotonous with no sign of the outlaws — and for that Kate was grateful. The sky was clear blue with not a cloud in sight, for all the good Ruckus and his praying did.

Still sore from her early morning spill, she wasn't enjoying the rutted dirt road. Dressed in her own clothes — a blue skirt and white shirtwaist trimmed with lace and tied at the neck with a blue ribbon — she'd decided against wearing her fussy feathered hat that offered little if any protection from the sun. Instead, she wore the wide-brimmed felt hat provided for her, and of which she had grown quite fond.

It was after ten by the time she reached town, but already Main Street bustled with horses, carts, and wagons. It looked and felt entirely different from the day she first stepped off the train. She slowed as she neared Luke's shop. The metal sign hanging over the door creaked as it swayed in the breeze. The sign read Adams Blacksmith Shop. The smaller print beneath a metal horseshoe promised Quality Workmanship.

Though she didn't see the owner, her pulse quickened and her sun-heated face grew another notch warmer. She sucked in her breath. All right, so he was amiable, attractive, and had a devastating smile — so what? Her mama often said those were the most dangerous kind. Now Kate knew why. No matter. Her future was the ranch and she had no intention of letting herself get sidetracked.

She drove right by the blacksmith shop with little more than a glance and pulled up in front of the marshal's office.

Deputy Marshal Morris looked up from behind his desk when she walked through the door. A craggy-faced man with scraggly black hair and mustache, he sat back in his chair, hands interlocked on his rounded belly, and frowned.

"My name is Kate Tenney and —"

He stopped her with the palm of his hand. "I know who you are." His eyes narrowed. "You're the new Walker girl. The one who let Cactus Joe get away."

She was momentarily speechless. Nothing could be further from the truth, of course, but the bluntness of his tone and manner surprised her more than his accusation. Would she ever get used to such plain talk?

Obviously the marshal didn't fully understand the circumstances. "He had a gun. I could have been shot or kidnapped or . . . or . . ."

He waved both hands at her. "Cactus Joe couldn't shoot a chicken coop if he was standin' inside."

"He shot my trunk," she said. "My clothes and books could have been ruined."

"That'll teach you to go barreling through town when I'm trying to uphold the law. I'da had him if it wasn't for your meddlin'."

Kate bristled. Meddling? *Meddling!* The nerve of him. "First of all, I had just set foot in town and had no way of knowing a robbery was in progress." She leveled an indignant glare at him. "I certainly was *not* meddling."

He grunted and continued to stare at her like it was all her fault. "So why are you here now?"

She was so incensed by his unfair accusations she'd almost forgotten her reason for coming. "I'm here on behalf of Miss Walker. The Dunne gang is back."

The marshal rubbed his forehead. "I thought we'd seen the last of 'em. How do you know they're back?"

"Some of the cattle have been hair-branded," she replied.

He nodded. "It has the markings of the Dunnes but that don't mean it's them."

"I'm only conveying Miss Walker's message."

He blew out his breath. "All right, I'll round up some boys and we'll take a ride out there. Have a look around." He didn't sound all that eager to ride out to the ranch. "Probably won't find anything."

"I'll tell Miss Walker to expect you," she said, her voice cool. Meddling, indeed! She turned to leave. Hand on the doorknob, she glanced back at him. "I do apologize for any part I might have played in Cactus Joe's escape, but I am surprised he got away. He didn't have that much of a head start."

"Oh, I coulda caught him if I put my mind to it. But anyone caught outside of town has to be hauled all the way to Tombstone."

"Why Tombstone? What's wrong with this jail?" she asked, staring at the small empty cell behind his desk.

"After the last jailbreak, the county sheriff checked it out and said it was as flimsy as a paper bandbox. Said it wasn't strong enough to keep a dead man from escapin', let alone a criminal. Said anyone captured outside of town was under county jurisdiction and had to be taken to Tombstone."

"How many jailbreaks have you had?" she asked.

"A dozen or so, but you can't go by the numbers. Some folks got themselves arrested just so they could see how long it took 'em to break out. The record is three hours and seventeen minutes."

"I see," she said, though in reality she didn't. People in Cactus Patch certainly had an apathetic regard for lawlessness.

"Now that Luke fixed the lock and reinforced the window bars the jail is sound as a cash box, but that don't make no difference to the sheriff." Hands behind his head, he leaned back and plopped his feet on the desk like he had nothing to do and all day to do it in.

She narrowed her eyes. "What time shall I tell Miss Walker to expect you?"

He looked puzzled. "What time? Oh, that's right. The Dunne gang."

It was obvious the marshal had no intention of riding out to the ranch, and that was a problem. Miss Walker had given her a simple task — a test, no doubt — and Kate couldn't afford to fail.

She turned toward the marshal and tried to think how she would write this scene for a book. Brandon would plant his feet firmly in front of the marshal's desk, look that marshal square in the face, and take no guff.

Positioning herself exactly as she pictured her protagonist doing, she hung her thumbs from the waist of her skirt and lowered her voice a full octave. "Actually, there's reason to believe it's not the Dunne gang after all." She glanced around as if to check for eavesdroppers before continuing. "There's some speculation that it might be the . . . Arizona Kid." Did such a person even exist?

Apparently the marshal thought so. His eyes widened and he snapped to attention like a soldier awaiting orders. He rose to his feet as soon as his boots hit the floor. "This *is* serious."

Surprised and even encouraged by the change that came over him, she gave an enthusiastic nod. "Yes, I believe it is."

"Capturing the Arizona Kid would make the journey to Tombstone worthwhile. The sheriff might even recommend me as town

marshal of Tucson or even Phoenix where
the real action is. Don't you worry none,
ma'am. I'll ride out to the ranch soon as I
kin get a posse together."

Kate thanked him and left, barely able to
keep a straight face. Outside his office, she
laughed and was still laughing when she
crossed the street to the post office to
inquire about Ruckus's mail.

"Sorry, ma'am," the postmaster said. The
sign on the counter read Jeb Parker. An
older man with a concave chest and a
goatee, he shook his grizzled head. "No
mail." His pallid skin seemed out of place
in Arizona. Apparently the man never
stepped foot outdoors.

Ruckus seemed anxious to hear from his
son and she hated to disappoint him.
"Would you mind checking again?" she
asked.

The postmaster gave an impatient shrug
to indicate he did indeed mind, but he
nonetheless flipped through a stack of mail
for a second time.

"Nope. Same as before."

"Thank you," she said.

Leaving the post office, she bumped into
a stoop-shouldered man with a long beard.

"I'm sorry," she said, but the man ignored
her apology. Instead, he brusquely brushed

194

past her and limped toward the post office counter.

She'd only gotten a glimpse of his face, but he seemed strangely familiar. Odd. She was almost positive she had not met the man. Stranger still was the way the fine hairs on her arms stood up.

Pushing the thought away, she quickly grabbed the broken windmill tailbone from her wagon and crossed the dirt-packed street to the blacksmith shop. The sooner she finished ranch business, the sooner she could take care of her own.

The side door was ajar and she elbowed it all the way open. Surprised and more than a little annoyed to find her knees shaking, she called, "Mr. Adams?"

The shop was empty. A fire in the forge made her hesitate before crossing to the workbench. Fire made her nervous, even after all these years. The flame of a candle or the striking of a match brought back memories she'd sooner forget.

Only eight at the time, she had been locked out of the apartment while her mama entertained a man. She fell asleep curled into a ball in the hallway outside the door, only to be awakened by her mother's cries for help. The sound of pounding fists through the thin walls sent chills through

Kate's small body. Knowing from experience that none of the other residents would interfere, she reached into the pocket of her frock and pulled out the matches kept there. All it took was one strike and a piece of loose wallpaper caught fire. No one was hurt in the inferno — and she saved her mama from further harm — but the flimsy wood building had burned to the ground.

Shaking away visions of the past, she laid the windmill parts on the workbench and dug into her drawstring purse for paper and pencil to leave a note.

A sharp, angry voice from outside startled her. It came from the side of the building. "Last night was the last time I'm bailing you out of jail. Do you hear me?" She recognized the deep baritone voice at once as belonging to Luke Adams.

Another male voice replied, "Don't do me any favors!"

"Either you take that job at the Last Chance or you're on your own. You won't get another penny from me."

The argument escalated, and not wanting to be caught eavesdropping, Kate looked around for a means of escape, but the two quarrelling men blocked both the carriage and side door, trapping her inside.

She dropped her pencil and stooped to

pick it up, accidently knocking against the workbench. Something fell to the floor with a loud clank. Startled, she practically jumped out of her skin and sent the lantern flying. Kerosene splashed into the burning forge and sparks shot out, turning the pine chips on the hearth into flames. In a flash, the blaze spread across the floor devouring all the wood shavings in its path.

Kate stared at the flames in horror. Transported to another time, another fire, she froze, her body seemingly encased in steel.

The door banged open and Luke bolted inside. He ripped off his leather apron and threw it down on the floor, smothering the flames. He then stamped out the remaining sparks with his booted foot.

He whirled to face her. "Are you all right?"

She nodded. The moment the fire was out the past lost its grip on her, but she was horrified by what she'd nearly done. "Please forgive me. I never meant to start a f-fire," she stammered, close to tears. "Your building could have burned down. The whole town could have gone up in flames, people could have been hurt and —"

He held up both hands. "Whoa. Let's not make this any worse than it was. No real damage was done."

She blew out her breath in relief, though

she still felt bad. Now he would know she overheard the argument.

Homer appeared at her side, tail wagging. Grateful for a reason not to have to look at the man, she stooped to run her hand through the dog's soft fur. Homer nudged her with his cold nose and licked her hand.

Finally, she straightened. "I was about to leave you a note."

White teeth flashed against his bronzed skin. "You must have been usin' some mighty heated words."

Disarmed by the humorous twinkle in his eyes, she smiled back at him. She couldn't help it. "So were you," she said, surprising herself with Arizona-type boldness.

His face grew somber and, hoping to lighten the mood again, she added, "Though I wasn't anywhere near as cantankerous."

"That was my brother you heard me arguing with." His frown contradicted his concerned voice. "The boy's headed for a whole peck of trouble. He has a job here if he wants it, but he'd rather gamble and rest a boot on a brass rail than do an honest day's work."

Not having any siblings of her own, she could only imagine what it was like to have a troubled one. "It must be difficult dealing with insubordination, especially with a family member."

He frowned and scratched his head as if trying to figure her out. "I don't know what's it gonna take to straighten him out." He studied her. "I see you decided not to quit after all."

She smiled at the memory of the two of them sitting in the mud. "I guess I'm too obstinate to quit. I also like the ranch too much to give up."

He studied her but said nothing. "How's Decker? He still givin' you trouble?"

"Not so much anymore. My main problem is learning to ride a cutting horse."

"Ruckus hired anyone yet to take care of the shoeing and windmills?"

She shook her head. "He's still looking."

"Glad to hear that. I want my brother to go out there and talk to him about it. Would be good for him. Keep him out of trouble in town." He picked up the two pieces of tailbone she'd set on his workbench and held them together. "Zechariah," he said.

"I beg your pardon."

"This is from the Zechariah windmill." He glanced at her. "Just like the prophet, this windmill can predict the future, or at least a coming storm."

She tilted her head. She was an educated woman with a college degree. She knew

Shakespeare's plays inside and out, and had studied the works of ancient philosophers — none of which did her any good on the ranch. The one book she had little or no knowledge of was the Bible. Yet Ruckus constantly referred to scripture, if not altogether quoting it, and she was embarrassed by her ignorance.

"The Last Chance has more than fifty windmills. Can you really look at a single piece of metal and determine its source?"

He shrugged like it was nothing. "I notch each piece so I know where it belongs. Kind of like marking the ear of a steer." He grabbed a broom and swept up the ashes. He was obviously a man who liked order. "If you hang around for a while I'll have old Zac here ready in no time."

"I do need to stop at the general store," she said.

"It'll be ready by the time you're done with your errands."

She hesitated. "I hope things work out with your brother."

He looked up from his sweeping. "Me too."

Her gaze locked with his. "About the fire . . ."

He stood the broom on end in the corner. "No harm done. I had no use for those

200

wood chips." He turned to face her.

Pulse skittering, she looked away. It sickened her to think he'd found her staring at the fire unable to move. What must he think of her? And what did it matter what he thought?

She cleared her throat. "I'll . . . I'll be back shortly," she said.

She didn't expect him to follow her outside, but he did. She walked away as quickly as she could without running, but no amount of distance could erase the worrisome hold he had over her.

The air still scented with her sweet fragrance, Luke watched her cross the street. Once she left his shop she walked toward the general merchandise store with quick, confident strides. He was taken with the way she moved, the way her hips swayed gracefully from side to side, the way she swung her arms. He liked pretty much everything about her looks.

He'd never seen anyone look so scared of fire. It was a good thing she hadn't been around in '87, the year an earthquake shook the area. The fire that followed the temblor pretty much destroyed everything in its path, including the Last Chance Ranch and most of the town.

However, it wasn't Kate's fear of fire that worried him. It was the way she stiffened whenever he came near. At times he swore he saw mistrust in her eyes. What had he done to make her so wary of him? Was it because he had seen her under-riggin's? Was that it?

Or was he simply imagining it? He wasn't good at picking up on other people's feelings. Aunt Bessie complained that a body would have to fall down dead before Luke knew anything was wrong. So why this sudden awareness? Why did he weigh Kate Tenney's every nuance as if each sigh or quick smile held some special meaning?

Whatever the reason, it bothered him. It bothered him a lot. He had no personal interest in her. Couldn't. She was an educated woman and he was a simple smithy with little book learning. So why waste so much time thinking about someone altogether in another class? It made no sense.

CHAPTER 16

Bessie grabbed her sister by her knitted shawl and yanked her back inside the general store.

"What's the matter?"

"Shh." Bessie hastened to the window and ducked behind a display of Log Cabin syrup, as if the slender stack could hide her generous proportions.

"Look over there. What do you see?"

"Oh dear, it's not Cactus Joe again is it?"

"No, no, thank heavens," Bessie assured her.

Lula-Belle craned her neck to look out the wavy paned window. Shorter than her sister, she rose on tiptoe. "I see our nephew."

Bessie folded her arms across her ample bosom and nodded in satisfaction. "And what is he doing?"

"He's standing outside his shop doing nothing."

Bessie threw up her arms. Could her sister

bury her head any deeper in the sand? How could she not understand the meaning of this momentous occasion? It's what the family hoped would happen.

"He's watching that woman," Bessie said, trying not to let her irritation with her sister show.

"What woman?"

Just then, the door of the shop opened to a chorus of jingling bells and Kate Tenney stepped inside and walked right by them. Since Bessie and her sister were now hunkered behind two large sacks of flour and a barrel of pickles, she obviously didn't see them.

"*That* woman," Aunt Bessie whispered, barely able to contain her delight. "She's the one that Cactus Joe grabbed, remember?"

She should have known. Luke *was* interested. All that talk about the woman not being his type and not speaking his language — hogwash, all of it.

Lula-Belle whispered back, "Why do you suppose he was watching her?"

"Why do you *think?*" Bessie said. Mercy. Did she have to spell out everything? "He's sweet on her."

It was about time the poor boy found a wife. The good Lord said it wasn't right for a man to be alone and, at age thirty, Luke had been alone long enough. A firm believer in order, she couldn't set to work looking for a wife for Michael until after his older brother, Luke, was married or, at the very least, betrothed.

"But he said —"

"I know very well what he said, but actions speak louder than words." Bessie straightened and moseyed on over to the counter where Miss Tenney stood waiting for Mr. Green to fill her order.

She was pretty all right, even if a mite too thin. Some good home cooking would take care of that. Her blond hair was gathered into a tight bun beneath her wide-brimmed hat. Delicate brows arched over long-lashed blue eyes. Her plain blue skirt and lace-trimmed waistcoat emphasized a small waist, narrow hips, and a pleasing bosom. Of course Luke was interested. A man would have to be blind not to be.

Mr. Green returned with several bars of Pears soap and added them to the growing pile on the counter. "Anything else?" he asked, addressing the woman.

"I'd also like a box of bonbons," she said. "Those are my favorite."

"They're everyone's favorite," Mr. Green said, reaching for a box of the foil-covered chocolates. He was a compact man whose spectacles magnified his eyes to twice their normal size. He reminded Bessie of a lizard, and his unfortunate habit of sticking his tongue in and out of his mouth did nothing to dispel that notion.

His pointy nose twitched as he began punching numbers into the National Brass cash register, a new addition to his shop and one that met with Bessie's disapproval. What a crying shame that people were too lazy to add things up in their heads like the good Lord intended.

"Do you want me to add these to Miss Walker's account, Miss Tenney?" he asked.

"No, I'll pay for them myself," Miss Tenney said, digging into her drawstring purse.

Aunt Bessie exchanged a glance with her sister. Miss Walker's name never failed to strike a chord of curiosity in Bessie even when her nephew wasn't involved. The ranch owner's antics were legendary, which made her the main topic of conversation at any and all town gatherings.

Lula-Belle whispered, "Do you suppose she's one of Miss Walker's relatives?"

Bessie rolled her eyes. Her sister was hopeless. "Miss Walker doesn't have any relatives." At least none that she was willing to acknowledge. Supposedly she had a brother, but according to rumors the two were on bad terms and hadn't spoken in years.

Imagine the nerve of the woman advertising for an heiress. Heiresses were born, not made. Everyone knew that. Of course, it was nothing more than you'd expect from a *divorced* woman who walked, talked, and — mercy — even dressed like a man.

Bessie didn't mean to be forward or nosy — heavens, not that. But with her nephew's future on the line, this was no time to restrain herself.

"Excuse me, I'm not sure you remember me, but we met briefly a short while ago."

Miss Tenney nodded. "Oh yes. The day of the holdup." Her gaze darted from Bessie to Lula-Belle. "I remember both of you." The woman smiled, revealing straight white teeth. "How lovely to meet you again. This time under less trying circumstances."

The woman had a cultured voice and spoke with a Boston accent. Obviously she was a lady, a *real* lady. No wonder Luke was put off at first. In Cactus Patch, ladies were few and far between.

No matter. Where men were concerned, appearances trumped character faults, and this particular woman was pretty enough to overcome any number of negative qualities she might have, even faults involving uppity language. Of that Bessie was certain or Luke wouldn't have been caught staring.

"I can't tell you how relieved we are that Cactus Joe brought you no harm." Bessie inched closer. How fortunate that she chose today of all days to wear her best navy blue going-to-town skirt and shirtwaist. "Thank you for your kind note. That was very thoughtful of you, Miss Tenney."

"Please, call me Kate."

"Kate it is." Bessie smiled. She liked that Kate was friendly and not stuck-up like other easterners who drifted through town from time to time and didn't seem to have a nice thing to say about Cactus Patch or even Arizona. "I believe you know my nephew Luke."

"Yes, Mr. Adams gave me a ride to the ranch my first day here."

Bessie gave a motherly nod of approval. "It was the least he could do after your unfortunate encounter with that dreadful outlaw. I can't tell you how lovely it is to see you again."

"Yes, it is," Lula-Belle said. "Especially since Luke —"

Bessie poked her sister with her elbow.

"What my sister was about to say was that our nephew has spoken highly of you."

The beginning of a smile tipped the corner of Kate's pretty pink mouth. "I'm grateful to him for his kindness to me."

Bessie grinned. Gratitude was good. At least it was a place to start. "That's our Luke. Always willing to lend a helping hand. So how do you like running a ranch?"

"I'm afraid I'm a long way from doing that," Kate replied. "I have much to learn."

Bessie felt a surge of hope. "Is there a possibility you won't be able to learn the ranching business?"

"Oh, I'll learn," Kate said. "It's just that I had no idea how much work went into caring for cows . . . eh . . . cattle. But I do so love it there. Have you been to the ranch?"

"Not recently," Bessie said.

"You must come. The cactus are all in bloom and we have these lovely little calves running around. We're getting ready for roundup and . . ."

While Kate babbled on Bessie tried to hide her impatience. It wasn't normal for a woman to carry on so about a bunch of cattle.

"I imagine it would be difficult for a woman to be both a rancher *and* a wife," Bessie said when she could get a word in edgewise. She hated to be so brash, but how else could she learn what she needed to know?

Kate looked momentarily confused by the sudden change of subject. "I imagine so, but I have no intention of getting married."

"So how long do you expect to remain *un*married?" Bessie asked.

"I don't plan on ever getting married," Kate replied.

Bessie blinked. "Really?"

"I only have a hundred days left to prove myself to Miss Walker's satisfaction. After that, my one and only concern will be the ranch."

A hundred days? Bessie did some mental calculations. That would take them to the end of July.

Bessie sidled up a notch closer, friend to friend. "If you ask me, it's a crying shame that a woman as pretty as yourself should . . . deprive some poor man of a wife."

"Running a ranch is a full-time job," Kate said. "I'm afraid a man would find me wanting as a wife."

"Running a ranch didn't stop old man Thomson over at the Lazy T from getting married," Lula-Belle said.

"I couldn't get married even if I wanted to. Miss Walker forbids it," Kate explained.

"That's one of her requirements."

Bessie had never heard anything so ridiculous in her life. "Staying single isn't so bad, I suppose, as long as it's *your* choice and no one else's."

Kate glanced at her but remained silent, which was annoying to say the least. On the other hand, Bessie had to give the girl credit for loyalty. Most people jumped at the chance to gossip or otherwise say something unpleasant about the owner of the Last Chance Ranch.

Mr. Green finished packing Kate's order. "I'll help you carry your purchases to your wagon, ma'am." He walked around the counter, lifted the wooden crate, and started for the door.

"Thank you," Kate said. "That is very kind of you." She turned from the counter. "It was nice seeing you both again. Good day." She then followed Mr. Green outside.

Bessie stood staring after her. She couldn't believe Kate planned to stay single just to appease Miss Walker. It made Bessie sick just thinking about it. Not only was the girl a looker, her speech was so polished a person could skate on it. What an utter waste. Bessie couldn't imagine anything worse than staying single. She was willing to bet that the good Lord wasn't all that in favor of it either.

Bessie tapped a finger to her chin. "Do you think she'd make a good match for Luke?"

Lula-Belle studied the label on a can of peaches. "The only thing that girl is interested in is the ranch."

It certainly appeared that way, but Bessie wasn't willing to give up so easily. Marriageable women were few and far between and she had two nephews in dire need of wives. What a pity that she only had a hundred days in which to work. Still, a lot could happen in that short time. If she played her cards right, Luke and Kate might even fall hopelessly in love.

Humming the tune of the "Yankee Wedding March," Bessie rushed her sister through her shopping and dragged her out of the store. No time to waste. A hundred days!

Nearly a week later Kate followed Ruckus's mule-drawn wagon out to the southeast corner of the ranch. Ruckus insisted she ride her horse for practice rather than ride in the wagon with him. The wagon was loaded with fencing supplies, cattle remedies, and salt licks.

She and Decker had formed an understanding — or at least she hoped so. She would refrain from hopping, bouncing, kicking his sides, or roping him, and he would refrain from bucking, kicking, taking off at a run, and otherwise trying to unseat her.

Ruckus brought the wagon to a halt. He pointed to the barbed wire fence running the length of the property. "We're moving the herd out of open range for brandin'. The first thing any self-respectin' steer will do is walk the fence to check out its new paddock. It's up to us to make certain no side of beef leaks through the bobbed wire."

Kate was eager to get started. Fixing fences didn't sound that hard. After mucking out stables, cleaning the barn, and learning to ride, she looked forward to doing something that didn't involve dirty hay or falling off a horse.

Ruckus hopped to the ground and pointed to a gap in the barbed wire. "See that there?" He tossed her gloves and donned a pair himself before leaning over the back of the wagon to snip off a piece of baling wire with fencing pliers. He then showed her how to fix the fence by wrapping wire around a nail to tighten it.

"That should do it." He stepped back. "There's something satisfyin' about mendin' fences. Don't much matter if it's the wire type or the human type."

"What? No Bible verse?" she teased.

He grinned. "How about this? God says if you're holdin' a grudge you plumb better get over it or you'll be as sad as a tick-fevered dogie."

She grinned back. "I didn't know God spoke western-like."

"God speaks all languages and he don't just use words." He cocked an eyebrow. "Anyone you need to forgive, Goldilocks?"

She thought about the father who deserted her, the mother who neglected her and clamped down on her jaw. "No, no one," she said through gritted teeth.

"Hmm. Guess you can call yourself lucky then. Come on, let's get to work."

He let her fix the next gap they found. Tongue between her lips, she twisted the wire tight as she could. She was all thumbs at first, but it didn't take long to get the hang of it.

A cloud of dust signaled a horse heading in their direction, but Ruckus was able to identify the rider as Feedbag long before he reached them. "Looks like trouble."

"We found a band of sheep in the northern section," Feedbag called upon reaching them. "That's why our beeves refuse to go there."

Ruckus muttered beneath his breath, then immediately lifted his hand up to the sky in apology. "Sorry, God, but you know the trouble those four-legged underwears cause."

As if to concur, Feedbag spit out a stream of tobacco juice.

Kate looked from one grim face to the other. "What kind of trouble?" In Boston sheep were valued for their wool.

"There ain't nothing left when they leave," Feedbag growled. "They eat the grass to the roots, dig up the dirt with their sharp hooves, and leave a terrible stench. No self-respectin' steer would be caught dead on the same range as a hoofed locust."

"Can't blame 'em. Can't blame 'em a bit," Ruckus said.

"The others are pretty riled up. If Stretch and Wishbone have their way, that herder will be tradin' in his woolies for a wooden overcoat."

Ruckus glanced at Kate and hesitated.

"You go. I'll finish here," she said. She didn't want anyone dying on her account, even if he was a sheepherder.

Ruckus dropped the roll of wire and pliers in the back of the wagon. "I'll need your horse. You can drive the wagon." She nodded and he quickly mounted Decker.

"Watch out for snakes and other fiends."
He touched his hat and he and Feedbag
rode away.

Other fiends? She glanced around. Her
imaginative mind kicked into high gear.
What if she ran into Cactus Joe? Or rustlers?
Or rattlers? What then?

She scanned the ground for reptiles and
jumping cacti before looking the short,
thick-headed mule square in the face. His
name was Gus. "It's just you and me."

The animal wiggled his long, pointed ears
and let out a loud *hee-haw.*

She climbed onto the wagon seat and
grabbed hold of the reins. "Giddi-up."
Nothing. "Come on, Gus, go!" The mule
stayed put and, if anything, looked even
more stubborn.

"I guess we're going to have to do this the
hard way." She climbed out of the wagon,
grabbed hold of the bridle, and pulled.
When that didn't work, she straddled the
wagon tongue and pushed the mule from
behind, keeping her head away from his
swishing tail. Still, the mule didn't move.

Hands on her waist, she debated what to
do next. She was almost out of drinking
water so she couldn't stay there. Who knew
when Ruckus would return?

The closest windmill was only about a

quarter of a mile away. She decided to walk to it, fixing any needed repairs along the way. Her mind made up, she snipped off a length of wire, grabbed the pliers and canteen, and began walking. A slight breeze helped cool her down but it was still hot.

A short distance from the windmill she spotted a gap in the fence. She slid down a slope and crossed over a dry gully before reaching the barbed barrier. She measured off a piece of wire and wound it around the post like Ruckus showed her. She was in luck. The gap was small and required little effort to repair. Satisfied that the wire would hold, she climbed back up the incline and headed for the windmill.

A strange snorting sound startled her. She stopped in her tracks and glanced over her shoulder. A wild boar stood not more than twenty feet away. It was a strange-looking animal with salt-and-pepper hair, short skinny legs, and small beady eyes that stared at her from above a piglike snout.

Kate took a step forward. The boar didn't move. Encouraged, she took another step.

This time the animal bent its head, tusks pointed like daggers. For a moment it didn't move, then all of a sudden it grunted, wiggled its ears — and charged.

Kate dropped everything and ran.

CHAPTER 17

Was there a woman in the world so devoted as to sacrifice herself to save the
man she loved? Yes, there was but one.
She would swim the deepest sea or climb
the greatest heights to save Brandon, for
her love for him was matchless.

She barely managed to grab hold of the
windmill ladder and pull herself up before
the hog lunged, missing her leg by inches.

She scrambled halfway up the windmill
before she dared look down. The animal
grunted and rammed the ladder with its
tusks ten, twenty, thirty times and showed
no signs of stopping. The ladder shook so
hard Kate feared it would break. The wind
picked up and the windmill blades turned
faster. Climbing onto the platform was out
of the question. She had no choice but to
stay where she was.

"Go away," she yelled. "Shoo!" She pulled

off a glove with her teeth and tossed it at the hog, but the battering of the ladder continued.

Kate leaned her forehead against a rung, closed her eyes, and held on tight. *God, please make it go away.* Surprised to find herself praying, she bit down on her lower lip. It wasn't like her to turn to God as the first response to trouble. If she hung around Ruckus much longer she wouldn't recognize herself.

She glanced at the sky. Even if by some miracle God did answer prayers, she doubted he would bother with hers.

She peered downward. The wild hog had stopped butting its head against the ladder but still hadn't left. Instead, it rooted around the base of the ladder, grunting. She threw down her other glove to no avail.

Shuddering, she forced herself to think, but that only gave her imagination full rein. What if the hog remained there all night? Or she fainted from dehydration? What if the dreadful beast battered the ladder until it broke? Every possible scenario raced through her mind, each more frightening than the previous one.

After crying herself to sleep for the first sixteen years of her life, she'd vowed never to shed another tear. Any failings to adhere to her vow had been due to physical pain, not emotional. But today she was hot and scared and tired and confused and . . .

Brandon heard the woman's cry for help and urged his horse to go faster. Ahead a windmill rose high above the ground, the tail turning toward the wind. At last he spotted her halfway up the tower, her long curls tumbling from beneath her felt hat. On the ground below was the meanest-looking critter this side of the Gila River. He pulled out his gun and fired. Bang, bang, bang!

Dismounting, he looked up at the woman still clinging to the ladder. "You can come down now," he said. "It's safe."

Kate blinked. Surely she was hearing things. That wasn't Brandon's voice; it was . . .

Her eyelids flew up and she peered at the ground. Ruckus stood at the bottom of the ladder beckoning to her. "You can come down now," he repeated.

She almost collapsed with relief. She couldn't believe her eyes! God did answer prayers!

"Am I ever glad to see you," she cried. Legs trembling, she slowly descended the ladder.

Ruckus laughed. "Now that's what I call being high on the hog."

She stepped off the lower rung of the ladder and glared at him, hands at her waist. "It's not funny. That . . . that beast tried to attack me. If you hadn't come along I could have been eaten alive. Or died of thirst. Or been carried away by vultures or . . ."

"I don't think vultures generally carry folks away. Least not that I heard."

"There's a first time for everything," she said with a stubborn nod of her head.

"Come along," he said. "I think you've had enough fence mending for today."

Later that afternoon she walked out of the barn and bumped into Luke — literally. The impact made her drop the rope she was carrying and they both stooped to pick it up, their hands meeting on the braided twine.

She pulled her hand away and quickly rose. He gave her a quizzical look before gathering the rope, coiling it, and handing it back to her.

"Thank you," she said.

He grinned. "Heard about your run-in this morning."

"Everyone in Cochise County has heard about my run-in with that hog," she muttered. The ranch hands hadn't stopped joshing her since she returned to the ranch. She bumped against Luke's arm and she quickly lengthened the distance between them.

"It was a *javelina*," he said, as if that made a difference. He stared at her with a puzzled frown. "Do I make you nervous?"

The question surprised her. "No, of course not. Why do you ask?"

He shrugged. "You always act like I'm gonna grab you and kiss you."

Her mouth dropped open. "The . . . the thought never occurred to me."

"Oh?" He looked genuinely perplexed. "Why not?"

She stared at him. "Why . . . not?" Did he really expect her to answer such an outrageous question?

"The thought occurred to me. I just wonder why it never occurred to you," he said.

He thought about kissing her? That meant she hadn't imagined the heated glances that passed between them. They had been real. Her heart thudded against her ribs. Her mouth went dry.

"I . . . I can assure you I'm not the kind of woman who goes around thinking such things." Her voice sounded haughty even to her own ears, but it couldn't be helped. There could be no misunderstanding between them.

"I'm mighty sorry to hear that, ma'am.

Mighty sorry."

She straightened her shirt. "Yes, well . . ."

"If you don't think about kissing me, then I guess there's no reason for you to be so jumpy around me. 'Less you're worried about makin' that Brandon fellow jealous."

She stared at him for a moment before recovering from her surprise. "How . . . how do you know about Brandon?"

"That day you arrived and I carried you into my shop. You were half out of your wits and you mistook me for Brandon. Is he a beau or something?"

She shook her head. "He's . . . nobody. I made him up for one of my stories. He doesn't exist."

Luke scratched his head. "You made him up?"

"It's what writers do," she said. "Haven't you ever made up anyone? Even as a child? An imaginary playmate, perhaps?"

"No, ma'am. I figure the world's crowded enough without makin' up people."

"Yes, well . . ."

"So if this Brandon fella doesn't exist, and you don't think about kissing me, I reckon that means you have no reason to be nervous around me, right?"

"Right," she said.

He hesitated and she feared he would

223

pursue the subject. "I'm not much of a reader but I sure would like to read somethin' you wrote. Maybe somethin' with that Brandon fella."

Relieved to talk about something else, she said, "I'm afraid it wouldn't be to your liking." Secretly, it pleased her that he'd asked.

"Because it's literary?" he asked, his voice oddly distant and taut.

She laughed. "Not according to my critics."

His eyebrows shot up. "It's a good thing critics weren't around when God created the world."

"I agree." Her gaze bounced off his lips and she felt her cheeks grow warm. Why did he have to mention kissing? Glancing past him she spotted Miss Walker watching from a distance.

"I . . . I better get back to work." She turned and walked away as fast as she could without running, but it was a long time before she could breathe normally again.

Luke beat the red-hot metal with a hammer, the sound ringing in his ears. *Twe-rink, twe-rink, twank.* Blacksmithing was physically demanding work and normally he welcomed the manual labor required to shape iron into something usable. Today no amount of pounding relieved his tension. Nor did it get his mind off Kate Tenney.

Flipping the metal over with his tongs he tapped the end. Behind him the forge burned brightly and the mechanical fan emitted a steady hum. Homer was outside but kept poking his nose through the open door as if sensing his master's ill temper.

A vision of blue eyes came to mind and Luke pounded harder. She didn't think about kissing him — least that's what she said. Could've fooled him. He never could figure out the way a woman's mind worked, but she sure did *look* like she wanted to be kissed.

She also said her writing wouldn't be to his liking. Why didn't she just come out and say what she really meant? He didn't have enough book learning to understand what she wrote.

He pounded harder still.

Not that he cared. It was probably some scholarly tome filled with ten-dollar words that only college professors and Greek scholars could understand.

This time he pounded so hard that pieces of hot iron flew off his anvil.

CHAPTER 18

Many a form bit the dust and a gasp of horror rose to her lips. Then, thinking that Brandon was among the wounded, she fell back in a dead faint.

Kate sat on her horse watching what looked like sheer chaos. It was the first day of branding and Ruckus didn't mince words. "Once the action begins, stay out of the way!"

It wasn't what Kate wanted to hear. "How am I going to learn if I don't practice?"

Ruckus made a face. "Practicin' brandin' makes as much sense as practicin' for a hangin'. You either do it or you don't."

The air vibrated with expectation. Men on horses, some from neighboring ranches, waited for the signal to start. Ruckus called some of the older men "use-ta wases." The younger men he called green hands.

O.T. and Miss Walker had their heads

together, their expressions serious.

"What are they waiting for?" Kate had to lift her voice to be heard above the bawling calves separated from their mothers.

Ruckus pointed to the north where dark clouds rolled over distant mountains. Already a few clouds had broken away from the pack to blot out the overhead sun.

"They're worried about rain. You can't brand a wet calf. Not if you want to read the brand."

"You've been praying too hard, Ruckus," she called.

Feedbag and Upbeat laughed and Ruckus chuckled.

"Next time I'll be more specific about the timing."

Stretch said, "At least it's not as hot as it was last year at this time. It was so hot, the hens laid hard-boiled eggs."

Kate shook her head and grinned. Stretch never ran out of tall tales.

O.T. and Miss Walker moved away from each other and mounted their horses.

"Is it time to start?" Kate asked.

"Not yet," Ruckus said. "The boss lady gets to down the first calf. It's a Last Chance tradition."

Kate could feel the tension in the air as all eyes remained on the boss lady.

Miss Walker sat tall in her saddle. From a distance she looked like one of the cowhands, giving no clue to gender or age. She rode her roan around the corral once before racing to the center, rope coiled over her head. Arm circling, she whipped her rope through the air with amazing speed and force, catching a calf by both hind feet. Twisting her lariat around the horn of her saddle, Miss Walker dragged the bawling calf up to the blazing bonfire.

Kate's mouth dropped open in admiration. "I never would have believed that a sexagenarian could do such a thing."

Feedbag's eyes widened. "The boss lady's a sex . . . ?" He sputtered and his face got all red. He glanced at Miss Walker with awe. "I always knew she was a force to be reckoned with."

"Oh, I didn't mean . . ."

A loud bawling drowned out the rest of her sentence. The roped calf struggled fiercely, its cries answered by its anxious mother on the opposite side of the fence.

One of the cowpunchers looked between the calf's legs and yelled, "Bull!"

The red-hot branding iron was pressed into the animal's side, leaving a distinctive mark only three inches high. "That smells awful," she cried, waving her hand in front of her nose.

Ruckus grinned. "That's what we call branding smoke. You'll get used to it."

It was all done in a blink of the eye.

She leaned over her saddle horn. "The brand is so small. I can hardly read it."

"By the time the little fella's full-grown, it'll be a foot high," Ruckus explained. "We used to brand the entire side of a steer, but then we got complaints from leather makers. I guess there was no call for Last Chance boots or saddles."

Wishbone was the tally keeper. He made a mark on his tally sheet and called out, "One calf."

The instant Miss Walker's honorary calf had been counted and let go, O.T. yelled, "Let's get rolling." He waved his hat over his head. "Last year we branded three hundred calves in four hours. Let's see what we can do this year."

"Here we go," Ruckus called. "Go!"

Kate was mesmerized by the thunderous mass of horns and hooves in front of her. The smell of hot branding irons, sweaty horseflesh, heated cowhide, and dust made it hard to breathe, and her eyes watered. The air rang with bleating calves, bellowing steer, and exuberant shouts of men.

At first it seemed like chaos but, like

everything in the desert, nothing was as it seemed. Branding required precision and timing — like a carefully choreographed dance.

Feedbag ran by her on foot. He threw his right arm around a steer's neck and seized the animal's left horn with his left hand. The beast ran and Feedbag's legs touched the ground in flying leaps — and at one point his legs even flew straight out. It looked like the steer was about to claim victory when at last the animal lost its balance and fell on its side.

Feedbag was the only bulldogger of the bunch. The other ranch hands preferred to rope the calves from atop their horses.

After nearly three hours, Ruckus called out to her, "Let's see what you can do."

Surprised, Kate sucked in her breath. She had practiced for days, but roping a single calf in an otherwise empty corral was a whole lot different from working in a chaotic pen of thundering horses, panicked calves, and shouting men. Still, she was too caught up in the excitement not to try. Just as long as she didn't fall off her horse.

She tied the end of her rope to the horn of her saddle, just as Ruckus had taught her. Failing to do so could result in the loss of a thumb. Picking out her target she pressed her heels into her horse's sides and took off. Lariat circling overhead, she timed her toss but still came up empty. She yanked the rope back and tried again.

On the fourth or fifth — or maybe it was the tenth or twelfth — try she caught a calf by a hind leg, or heel as Ruckus called it.

"I did it!" she yelled in astonishment.

"Ride your rope!" Ruckus yelled back, the urgency in his voice telling her there was no time for celebration.

She rode toward the calf, taking the slack out of the rope so that Ruckus could wrestle the struggling critter to the ground, pin it on its back, and wrap the calf's legs with pigging rope.

Ruckus looked up at her. "I'd never thought to hear myself say this, but congratulations. You're now officially one of the boys."

She grinned back at him, surprised at how good those words made her feel. After weeks of hard work her efforts had finally begun to pay off. She might just make it as a rancher after all.

Bessie barged into Lula-Belle's house without so much as a knock on the door. Mercy, she didn't have time for such amenities, not this of all days.

She found Lula-Belle in the kitchen pulling a pie out of the oven. Bessie threw up her hands in disgust. On a day that was clearly about to break ninety degrees even with the threat of rain, the woman was not only baking, she wore a knitted wool shawl. It made Bessie hot just looking at her.

"What are you doing here so early?" Lula-Belle asked, though it was well past noon. She set the pie on the counter to cool. "What is it? Are you ill? Is something wrong with Sam?"

"No, nothing is wrong with Sam. At least nothing that can't be fixed."

Lula-Belle ran her hands down her gingham apron and frowned. "Are you sure? It's not his heart, is it?"

Bessie touched her head and groaned. "Mercy, why do you always think the worst?"

Lula-Belle took Bessie by the arm and dragged her out of the kitchen and made her sit. "If it's not Sam, who is it? Do tell me." Lula-Belle sank onto the cushion by her side.

Bessie lowered her voice, though it was not necessary since they were the only two in the house. "Two weeks ago I bumped into José in town and he told me the most amazing thing." She glanced around to

make sure they were still alone. "He overheard Kate Tenney say that she once wrote
dime novels."

A houseboy at the ranch, José provided an
endless source of juicy gossip, but none
quite as delicious as this latest tidbit.

Lula-Belle sat back and looked confused
or, at the very least, unimpressed. "Kate is a
writer?"

"Apparently not a successful one. However, I thought it my duty to read one of
her books. You know, to see what kind of
woman she really is. Picking out a wife for
Luke is too important to go by appearances
alone. Fortunately, I was lucky to get hold
of the one banned in Boston."

Lula-Belle gasped. "Her books were
banned?" Eyes rounded, she covered her
open mouth with her fingertips.

"Only in Boston," Bessie assured her.
"You know how prudish they are there."

Lula-Belle's eyes practically popped out
of her head. "You read a banned potboiler?"

Her sister's shocked expression came as
no surprise. It was a well-known fact that
no decent Christian woman would read
such trash.

"It was my *duty*," Bessie explained. She
looked toward heaven. "God forgive me, but
there's nothing I wouldn't do for Luke. Mi-

chael too."

She pulled a paperback book out of her pocketbook. *Miss Hattie's Dilemma* was written across the cover in big bold letters.

Lula-Belle leaned back as if the mere presence of the book could corrupt her fine sensibilities.

Bessie riffled through the book until she found the right page. "Listen to this."

"Oh my stars," Lula-Belle gasped. Her springy curls were practically doing handstands. "You're not going to read it *aloud*."

Bessie gave her a stern look. "Only the good part." She cleared her voice and began to read like she was auditioning for a part in a play. " 'Brandon took her in his arms and captured her trembling lips. Ripples of desire shot through her body and' " — Bessie paused for effect — " 'curled her toes.' " She snapped the book shut. It was hard to believe that the mere mention of something as commonplace as toes could cause an entire book to be banned.

Lula-Belle obviously was not of the same mind. Indeed, she couldn't have looked more incredulous had Bessie sprouted orange and black spots and turned into a gila monster.

"Now I ask you. Did Murphy ever make your toes curl during a kiss?"

Lula-Belle's face turned scarlet and her hand fluttered nervously to her lap. "For goodness' sakes, Bessie, what are you talking about? Curling toes?"

Bessie gave a self-righteous nod. "I thought so."

"I'm not even sure I want my toes to curl. I'm ticklish. Besides, what has this got to do with Luke and Kate Tenney? Are you saying that she's not the right woman for him?"

"Oh, she's the right woman for him, all right." Bessie waved the book as if it were absolute proof. "Make no mistake about that, but I'm not talking about Luke or even Michael."

"Then what *are* you talking about?"

"Us. You and me. It's time we lit a fire under our husbands. There's got to be more to life than loose skin and bald heads. Just because passion hadn't been invented when we were young is no reason we can't enjoy it now. Why should the young have all the fun?"

Lula-Belle made a funny choking sound. "Passion was invented?"

"Of course it was. How else can you explain its sudden appearance? Did you ever hear about it when we were young?"

"No, but . . . but who would invent such a thing?"

"How am I supposed to know? Howe, Edison, Bell . . . What difference does it make? If they can send words through miles of high-strung wires who's to say what else they can do?"

"Oh my!" Lula-Belle pressed her fingertips against her mouth again. "Maybe we should stay away from the telegraph."

"Nonsense. A little passion would do you a world of good. Maybe then you wouldn't need to wear that tiresome shawl all the time."

"I don't know, Bessie. This don't sound right to me. Sam and Murphy are set in their ways. They're not gonna take kindly to having to worry about our toes."

"Oh, they'll worry about them all right. We'll make certain of that." She stabbed *Miss Hattie's Dilemma* with her finger. "We have this to guide us. It tells us everything we need to know about capturing a man's heart. For example" — she thumbed through the book — "on page ninety-nine it says, 'She brushed her hair until it shone and it fell down her back in glorious waves.' "

Bessie peered at her sister's tight corkscrew curls and grimaced. "Never mind that. There are other ways we can make ourselves appear more attractive."

"What you're planning on doing don't sound normal. There's a reason why men's hair and women's assets fall when they reach a certain age. God don't want us worrying about our toes in our twilight years."

"Poppycock. Why do you think God invented night? It's so we older folks can enjoy the benefits of youth without seeing how awful we look." Bessie closed the potboiler and stood. "According to this book, perfume and satin unmentionables will do the trick. Green's General Store won't have what we need, so we'll have to order from Montgomery Ward."

"I don't know, Bessie. I don't want anyone to think I'm one of those . . . you know . . . painted ladies."

Bessie rolled her eyes. "You should be so lucky." She argued with her sister for the better part of an hour, but Lula-Belle refused to even consider changing her ways.

At last Bessie threw up her hands in disgust. If Lula-Belle chose to live a passionless life, that was her business. Bessie had no intention of letting her sister hold her back. She stood and took her leave. If she hurried, she could mail in her order to Montgomery Ward before the post office closed.

CHAPTER 19

What could they possibly do to her should she dare set foot in their den? Take advantage of her helplessness? Surely not!

Kate stood on the verandah of the ranch house, too wound up to sleep. Already Miss Walker and the house staff had retired for the night and the house was dark. It had been an exhausting but satisfying week. O.T. had been right about the Dunne gang. Some calves had been hair-branded, but Ruckus ordered everyone to "pick 'em out and brand 'em right." And that's what they'd done.

Now that the Last Chance "LC" brand had been seared into every calf's hide, the rustlers' plan had been halted, if not altogether stopped. No thanks to the marshal, who nosed around but lost interest upon discovering it was the Dunne gang and not the "Arizona Kid" responsible for the misdeeds.

Time had gone fast and already it was May. Kate couldn't believe that nearly six weeks had shot by since she'd first arrived on the ranch. She'd actually helped with the branding, though the other ranch hands had lassoed dozens if not hundreds of calves to her scant one.

She gazed at the sky, the stars hidden by clouds. The air felt thick with the promise of rain. She still felt a rosy glow from roping her first calf. The ranch that had once seemed so bleak was now filled with endless possibilities and, for the first time ever, her future seemed bright. Maybe Ruckus would make a rancher out of her yet.

Laughter exploded from the bunkhouse. The men were in good spirits. No doubt Stretch was regaling them with another tall tale.

Kate envied the camaraderie they shared, and though she tried her best to fit in she longed for female companionship. Of course, that didn't mean she was anxious to join Miss Walker again for supper anytime soon. The woman made her nervous. Kate couldn't begin to guess what thoughts prevailed behind Miss Walker's steady gray eyes.

"You're one of the boys."

She smiled at the memory. She left the verandah and hurried through the darkened courtyard to the bunkhouse. A flash of lightning pranced along the distant mountains, but still no rain.

The bunkhouse door ajar, the ranch hands were gathered around a long wooden table, all eyes on Stretch who sat at the head.

Mexican Pete held both hands to his chest, a lovesick expression on his broad face. He acted like Romeo declaring his love to Juliet. His antics were met with jovial laughter.

"Read more," Feedbag begged.

Stretch looked down at the book in his hands. "It gets better. Listen to this. 'Her lips quivered with anticipation as Brandon brushed a gentle kiss along her forehead.' "

Recognizing her own writing, Kate's mouth dropped open and heat flooded her face. How did they get hold of her book? She would have left right then and there had the Englishman Dook not tossed a nod in her direction, signaling her presence to the others.

Stretch fell silent and all eyes turned toward the door where she stood. No one moved or said a word. *You're one of the boys.*

She threw back her shoulders and forced

a smile. If she really was one of the boys then she best start acting like it. She marched over to Stretch and took the book out of his hand.

"Allow me."

She opened the book to the first page and began to read. If they wanted a K. Matson book, she would give them one. Only she would read the book from the very beginning. Random paragraphs sounded absurd when taken out of context. Let them laugh if they must, but at least they would do it to her face and not behind her back.

And so she read.

No one moved, although Feedbag tittered at one point. She lifted her gaze and he immediately sank lower in his chair, the face behind his squared black beard all serious.

Mexican Pete's brown eyes grew bigger as she read. Several times he stopped her to ask the meaning of a word.

"What does *remuneration* mean?" he asked at one point.

"It means payment for work done," she explained, pausing only long enough to answer his question.

Wishbone sat with hands clasped on the table, head bent. Next to her Stretch was hunched over. The new man they called Greenie leaned against the doorjamb that separated the sleeping quarters from the living space and quietly smoked a cheroot. He looked slightly familiar but Kate couldn't place him.

"I say that's bloody marvelous," Dook exclaimed at one point. Another time he yelled out, "Rubbish!"

Ignoring his outbursts Kate kept reading. " 'Miss Hattie was in a quandary. She didn't know whether to give her heart to the dashing Brandon or to stay true to the dull but safe Mr. Booker.' "

Stretch thumped the table with his fist. "To Brandon!"

Wishbone shook his head. "That's ridiculous. Brandon sounds like a saint or somethin'. No man worth his salt is that good."

"Speak for yourself," Stretch said.

Wishbone glared at him, his steer horn mustache twitching. "So what are you? God's gift to women?"

Stretch leaned his body over the table. "Are you saying I ain't?"

Fearing a fight was about to erupt, Kate cleared her throat. "Gentlemen." The instant she had their attention she continued to read and didn't stop until she reached chapter five.

"I think that's all for tonight," she said, and the men groaned.

Feedbag frowned. "But we don't know who the lady will snag."

"Or what happened to the gold," added Wishbone.

She'd hoped to make them pay for making fun of her writing. Consequently, she was surprised — shocked really — by their interest in the story. She bit back a smile. Normally, most males wouldn't be caught dead reading a love story. Instead, these rough-and-tumble men were practically begging for more.

If she wasn't so tired she might have been tempted to keep reading, but it was late and dawn came early.

"That's for another time," she said, rising. "Good night, gentlemen."

Book in hand, she walked out of the bunkhouse and headed toward the ranch house. A drop of rain fell on her forehead and she quickened her pace.

"I like your writing."

Startled by the male voice, she turned. The owner of the voice was silhouetted by the light from the open door of the bunkhouse, and she knew from his unkempt shoulder-length hair it was the new man, Greenie.

"Thank you," she said. "Do . . . do I know you from somewhere?"

He moved toward her, stopping a few feet away. "Name's Michael. Michael Adams."

Now she knew why he looked familiar. "You're Luke's brother."

"Yeah, but don't hold that against me."

She'd heard Luke and his brother argue, and the rancor in Michael's voice told her that the two were still at odds with one another.

He struck a match on the heel of his boot. The flame flared briefly over his whiskered face as he lit his cheroot. He took a generous puff on the slim cigar before removing it from his mouth.

"You best watch where you're walking," he said. "Never know if a rattler is waiting in ambush."

She brushed his smoke away from her face and turned her gaze downward, though it was too dark to see the ground.

"Are you a permanent hire?" she asked.

"Where work is concerned I'm what you might call a drifter," he said. "They hired me as a cattle guard and I'll do it until I can't stand the boredom any longer."

"I see. By the way, my name is Kate Tenney."

"I know who you are."

The nearby windmill squeaked and the tail turned to follow the wind. Another drop of water fell, this time on her arm. It looked like Ruckus's prayers were about to be answered.

"I gotta go," he said. "Get me some shut-eye."

He turned and she called after him, "What is the best way to walk back to the ranch house? I don't want to step on . . . anything."

He continued walking. "You could make a lot of noise. Let 'em know you're coming."

She stared after him. He walked and even sounded like his brother, which did nothing for her peace of mind. The last thing she needed was a daily reminder of Luke.

A lot of noise. She could do that. She clapped her hands and stomped her feet as she headed for the ranch house. Something moved in the courtyard — a shadow big enough to be human.

She stopped. "Hello. Anyone there?"

Silence greeted her, but she sensed someone hiding in the dark. The fine hairs on her arms stood up and she shivered. *Here I go again, imagining things.* Still, just to be on the safe side, she flew up the steps and into the house, slamming the door behind her.

CHAPTER 20

He gasped in horror. "You write dime novels?" the stranger asked.

"Certainly not!" she replied with cool regard. "Can't you see that the cover price is clearly marked twenty-five cents?"

Two days later Kate joined the circle of men outside the barn.

It had rained solid since Thursday night and the ground was still wet, puddles of water dotting the area. Work on the ranch had come to a standstill except for watching for flash floods and checking the herd. Now the sky was clear and the air smelled fresh.

Stretch, Feedbag, Mexican Pete, and all the other ranch hands grinned at her like they shared some sort of secret. At the men's insistence she had finished reading her book to them the night before. The men had taken bets as to which man the heroine would marry at the end, Brandon or Mr.

Booker. Feedbag had put his money on Mr. Booker and didn't take kindly to having to pay out a week's salary to those wise enough to bet on Brandon.

O.T. arrived and the good-natured teasing stopped, but not soon enough. O.T. walked around the circle, looking each person square in the face. "Must be a reason why you're all in such a jovial mood at this hour. Something I need to know?"

All eyes turned to Kate. Taking the hint, O.T. walked up to her. "Goldilocks?"

Kate tried to think what to say. She wasn't about to admit to reading the cowhands a dime novel. O.T. looked about to press her but Michael Adams joined the circle, late, and the foreman was immediately distracted.

Luke's brother looked like he hadn't slept a wink. Even in the dim light of dawn, his eyes looked glazed and his clothes rumpled. His tan Stetson failed to hide his unkempt hair. Today he looked nothing like his brother.

"Look what we have here," O.T. said. "Sleeping Beauty." He walked up to Michael and barked in his face. "Is there something about 5:00 a.m. that you don't understand?"

Michael gave a sheepish grin. "Nope."

Belatedly he added, "Sir."

"Good." O.T. backed away. "Ruckus, it's all yours."

"Let's pray." Ruckus lowered his head. "Dear heavenly Father, hear our prayer. Thank you for the rain. If you ain't too busy, we can use more."

At that moment the sun rose over the distant mountains revealing a carpet of grass that spread outward from the horse corral for as far as the eye could see.

"Look at that!" Kate squealed in amazement.

Ruckus laughed at her enthusiasm. "Just takes a little rain."

"But it's only been a couple of days." One short rainstorm and the dry land had turned into a luminous carpet of green. Even the nearby barrel cactus looked fuller as if bursting with pride.

"Grass roots grow close to the surface," Ruckus explained. "The desert is probably the most efficient place on earth. It don't waste nothin'."

Kate rubbed her nose. "What's that funny smell?" It was a strong musty odor, stronger even than the smell of cattle.

"What you smell is the creosote bush," Ruckus said. "You'll smell them after every rain. You best be careful of those bushes.

248

That's where rattlers like to hide." He turned, his arm held high. "Come, men, let's get to work."

The circle broke up, the others took off in different directions, and Kate grabbed a pitchfork leaning against the barn. She could hear Ruckus yelling before she even entered the building. Curious as to who got his dander up so early in the morning, she peered through the door and spotted Luke's brother, Michael.

Ruckus continued in a loud voice, "How many times have you heard me say to lock the gates? Do you have any idea how many hours it'll take to round up those horses? We might never get them all rounded up. If I didn't like your brother so much I would have sent your hide the way of the wind long ago. This is the very last straw."

Kate stepped inside the barn. "I left the gate open," she said, lifting her voice to be heard.

Ruckus spun around. "You did that?" His voice was every bit as disbelieving as his expression.

"I . . . I'm sorry."

Ruckus opened his mouth to say something, changed his mind, and stormed past her.

Kate regretted the lie, but she didn't know

how else to keep him from firing Luke's brother. She turned and walked outside. Michael caught up with her, but she was in no mood to talk to him. She tried to ignore him, but he stayed by her side.

"Why did you do that?" he asked. "Why did you take the blame for me?"

She kept walking. "I didn't do it for you. I did it for your brother who is concerned about you."

"Thank you," he said.

She spun around to face him. He looked every bit as sincere as he sounded. "You're welcome." She tilted her head. "You do know what you did was pretty serious, right?"

"I know." Hands at his waist he stared at the ground a moment before settling his gaze on her. "I guess I'm not cut out to be a ranch hand."

"So what are you cut out for?" she asked.

He blew out his breath and drew a line in the ground with the toe of his boot. "I want to be a writer like you." He looked up and in a quieter voice added, "Not quite like you. I mean I don't want to write about that man and woman stuff."

"So what do you write?" she asked.

"Adventure stories," he replied. "Like *Treasure Island.*"

"You want to write about pirates?"

"Not just pirates. I want to write about explorers and inventors and people doin' amazin' things." His eyes shone as he spoke and she couldn't help but smile at his enthusiasm.

"So what's stopping you?" she asked.

The question seemed to surprise him. "I haven't got me a fancy education. Not like you."

"You don't need a fancy education," she said. "You just need to write."

"I've been doing that." He gave her a sheepish look. "I spend most of my nights writing. If I'd gotten more sleep I probably wouldn't have forgotten to close the gate."

She couldn't help but sympathize. She'd had her share of absent-mindedness when working on a book. "Does your brother know you want to be a writer?" she asked.

"He knows." He shrugged. "Luke knows how to make things out of iron. He don't cotton to making things out of words."

"Hammering out words is not so different from pounding out iron," she said. Sometimes the words came easy, but more often than not a writer had to work at them.

"I don't think Luke sees it that way." He cleared his throat. "I was wondering, ma'am, if you'd be kind enough to look at something I wrote?"

Flattered by what he asked of her, she nonetheless hesitated. "You do know I'm not writing anymore."

He looked surprised. "If I could write like you I would never give up."

"I'm not that good." Since working at the ranch she now cringed at the errors she'd made. In one of her books she described a herd of *bulls.* In another, she had her heroine feed her horse *straw.* Then there was that lariat/lasso mix-up. Even now she had to think which one was the noun.

"You're good," he said. "And I'm not just sayin' that to be nice or anything."

He sounded so earnest she couldn't help but smile. "I'd be honored to read your work."

He looked pleased and then skeptical. "Are you sure it won't be too much trouble? I'm not much of a speller and my punctuation gave my old teacher Miss Gimble conniptions."

He cited more reasons why she might not wish to help him, but never mentioned what she suspected was the real one. Each word on a page was like a little window opening up the secrets of a writer's heart. Writing was the easy part. The hard part was releasing it to the prying eyes of others.

". . . and I'm not sure the ending is right and you may not even like that kind of story and . . ."

Head askance, she waited for him to either pause for breath or run out of excuses. "Are you finished?" she asked at last.

"Eh. I think so."

"Good. I'll read your writing. But right now we better get to work before we're both in trouble."

He grinned, gave a nod, and, clutching his hat to his chest, took off running. Envying his exuberance, she couldn't help but smile as she headed for the tack room. Her encounter with Luke's brother got her thinking.

As much as she enjoyed writing, she got more satisfaction from working on the ranch. She loved riding the range and racing the wind. Nothing pleased her as much as the wide-open spaces and the feeling of camaraderie when herding cattle with the other cowpunchers. She loved the idea that one day the Last Chance Ranch would be hers, and her mind fairly danced with new ideas on how she would run it.

Miss Walker's aloof managing style was not what she envisioned for herself. She dreamed of filling the ranch house with guests. She might even extend an invitation to that annoying classmate of hers who looked down her nose at anyone not owning property.

On Declaration Day and the Fourth of July she would plan picnics. At Christmas she would invite ranch workers and their families to the main house for roast beef and all the trimmings.

Ah, yes. When Miss Kate Tenney took over the Last Chance Ranch, things would be different.

Ruckus called to her from atop his horse. "We got a fire over yonder. Stay here and start muckin' out the stables." He jerked his thumb over his shoulder to the north. A column of smoke spiraled from the ground to the sky.

He took off after Stretch, Feedbag, and the rest of the ranch hands. No sooner had he ridden away than Miss Walker mounted her horse and chased after them. Hands on her waist, Kate watched her. She envied the ease with which Miss Walker and her horse moved as one.

Sighing, Kate stared at the black smoke in the distance. A fire? After all that rain? It didn't seem possible but smoke didn't lie.

She chewed on her bottom lip. What if they didn't put it out in time? What if it burned a path to the ranch house? Or even started a stampede? It might even burn all the way to town and . . . Worried now, she headed for the tack room for her saddle. The stables could wait. Her job was putting out the fire with the rest of them, and as the future owner of the Last Chance Ranch, that's what she intended to do.

The thought terrified her, but it was high time she faced her foe — just like the windmill faced the wind in Longfellow's poem. Ruckus had said she was one of the men — and she intended to prove him right. With grim determination she ran the rest of the way.

The tack room was dark except for a stream of sunlight from the single window.

A strange feeling came over her. Goose bumps traveled along her arms and she almost lost her nerve. Berating herself, she balled her hands and gritted her teeth, determined to conquer her fear of fire.

She reached for her saddle. Something — a sound. She spun around and gasped.

The outlaw Cactus Joe stood behind her, blocking the door, a wide grin on his swarthy face. "We meet again."

CHAPTER 21

When Luke opened for business that morning, Uncle Sam was waiting outside the shop. Homer greeted Luke's uncle with wagging tail.

"Hello, boy." Uncle Sam leaned sideways to pet the dog so as not to bend his bad back.

Luke eyed him with more than a little concern. Not only was it unusual for Uncle Sam to drive into town this early since his retirement, his face looked drawn as if he'd not been sleeping well.

Luke thought the world of the man. Everything Luke knew about the blacksmithing trade he learned from his uncle. It was a bittersweet day when Uncle Sam turned over the business to him. Said he wanted to try his hand at wood carving, but Luke knew his uncle simply couldn't adjust to the changing times. He considered ready-made tools, door hinges, and other household necessities an affront to his blacksmithing skills, and had even gone so far as to ban mail-order catalogs from his household.

"What brings you here so early?" Luke asked. "Is Aunt Bessie all right?"

Uncle Sam straightened. "Depends what you mean by all right." He pointed to the mug in Luke's hand. "You don't happen to have any more Arbuckle's, do you?"

"Upstairs. I'll get you some."

Luke returned from his upstairs dwelling a few moments later with a steaming cup of coffee. Uncle Sam had his hand on the anvil. "I remember the day I found this meteor," he said. "A couple nights earlier we saw this light streak across the sky and some of us boys decided to hunt for it. It took me three days but I found it. You ain't gonna find a better anvil than this, not anywhere."

Luke handed his uncle the cup of the steaming brew and listened patiently to the story that had been told perhaps a hundred, two hundred times through the years. He knew his uncle would eventually get around to telling him the real reason for his early morning visit and he was willing to wait. It was the least he could do for the man who had treated him more like a son than a nephew and had even given him his name.

Uncle Sam blew on the hot coffee and

took a sip. "Just what I needed," he said. He glanced at the broken handle of a water pump. "They don't make things like they used to, do they?"

" 'Fraid not."

His uncle studied the miniature windmill centered on Luke's workbench. "How's it coming along?" Luke and his uncle had been discussing a new design for windmills.

"I still can't figure out how to make it flexible enough to lower to the ground, and strong enough to hold up to the wind."

"Hmm." His uncle glanced around the shop. He offered no thoughts on how to get around the wind problem, which further convinced Luke something was not right.

"Do you know of anyone other than a blacksmith who works with the four elements — fire, air, earth, and water?"

"I don't know. Glassblowers maybe?" Luke said. Where was his uncle heading with this?

Abruptly Uncle Sam got to the point. "Have you seen your Aunt Bessie recently?"

"A couple of days ago. Why?"

"How did she seem to you?"

Luke shrugged. "She seemed fine." Her usual meddling self. "Why? Is something wrong?"

"I don't know. Somethin's gotten into her

and it ain't right."

Alarmed, Luke set his coffee mug on his workbench. "What do you mean? Is she sickly?"

"No, nothin' like that. It's just that all of a sudden she's very demandin'. Affectionate-wise, I mean. Why, the other night she insisted I peck her on the cheek for no good reason."

Luke didn't know what to say. It wasn't like his uncle to talk about personal matters. "Is that a bad thing?"

"That's what I don't know." Uncle Sam lowered his voice. "When an animal changes its habits, it means somethin's not right. You never know what it means with a woman." He took another sip of his coffee. "She even dresses different. What do you call that slippery fabric?"

Luke scratched his head. "I don't know. Silk? Satin?"

"Satin, that's it. When she walks, her nightshirt sounds like rustling grass. I thought someone had left the front door open. But that's the least of it. The other night she was so slippery she plumb slid right out of bed. A body could get herself kilt wearin' that stuff."

"It sure don't sound like her," Luke said slowly. "So what do you figure is going on?"

Uncle Sam considered the question for a moment. "Years ago, when me and your aunt first got hitched, I saw this real purty Mexican woman in Tucson. I didn't mess up or anything, but I was tempted. I prayed to God like I never prayed before to lead me from that temptation, and he did."

"You done the right thing."

"I know, but I couldn't stop feeling guilty. So I went out and bought your aunt the best frying pan money could buy. I'm tellin' you, Luke, temptation is bad, but guilt is worse. So here's what I'm thinkin'. Your aunt feels guilty about something. Do you suppose she's got her eye on someone else?"

Luke's eyes widened. "Aunt Bessie?"

"I'm thinkin' it might be Jeb Parker."

Luke couldn't believe his uncle was serious. Far as he knew his aunt didn't even like the postmaster. "You're wrong."

"I'm not so sure 'bout that. She's always coming up with reasons to order from that snake oil catalog even though she knows how I feel about it."

Luke blinked. "Aunt Bessie's ordering from Montgomery Ward?"

Uncle Sam nodded. "Hard to believe, ain't it? She don't know that I know. The way I figure it, it gives her an excuse to keep going to the post office. Do you think that's what she's up to? Do you think she's got her sights set on Parker?"

Luke shook his head. "Aunt Bessie is a fine Christian woman. She would never look at another man."

"Stranger things have happened. The thing is, I don't know what to do about it."

Luke ran his fingers through his hair. For the life of him he couldn't imagine his aunt interested in anyone else. His uncle was mistaken. Had to be. "Maybe you should spruce yourself up a bit. Show her your good side."

Truth be told his uncle wore his clothes until they practically fell off him. He'd still be wearing the same boots he wore in the War Between the States had his aunt not put her foot down and insisted he buy another pair.

"You figure that would help?"

"Couldn't hurt," Luke said, though he was a fine one to give advice. He much preferred his old clothes to new.

His uncle ran his hands over his bristly chin. "Maybe I'll stop at the barber for a haircut and shave on the way home."

"Good idea. Have you thought about giving her a geegaw?" Luke didn't know a lot about women, but he knew they liked flowers and trinkets and such.

"A present? You mean like it's her birthday or somethin'?"

"I don't know of any law that says gift giving is only for special occasions."

His uncle thought for a moment. "Maybe you're right. Maybe a gift would get her mind off Parker. I bet she'd like a saucepan to go along with that frying pan I bought her." He set his coffee mug down. "I can't tell you how much I appreciate our little talk."

"Glad to help," Luke said. He rested an arm around his uncle's shoulder and walked him outside. "You take care of yourself, you hear?"

Uncle Sam nodded. "See you Sunday?"

"You know you will."

"I'm sure Aunt Bessie will whip up something good in that new saucepan I plan to give her."

"Can't wait," Luke said.

The sound of a galloping horse made both men turn.

Michael thundered up on a heaving pinto waving his hat and yelling, "Miss Tenney has been kidnapped!"

Luke's blood turned cold. "What are you talking about?"

Michael battled his horse in a circle. "Cactus Joe has Miss Tenney." He jammed his heels into his horse's sides and took off hollering for volunteers to search for her.

No sooner had Michael taken off than Luke was on the run. Whistling to Homer, he raced to the livery for his horse.

CHAPTER 22

"Stay away from her, you scoundrel!"

"Curses!" The bandit's hand flew to his side to grab his weapon but Brandon was quicker. With a single bullet to the chest the outlaw met his doom.

Kate battled her way through the fog. What happened? Where was she? Her head ached and nothing made sense. Was she dreaming? Maybe this was her imagination. Or simply a scene from one of her books?

Her eyelids heavy as lead, she blinked against the glowing light. She tried to move but her arms and legs felt as if they were shackled.

She opened her eyes again, but it took several tries before she could keep them open long enough to take in her surroundings. Hands and feet bound, she occupied a cot in a corner of a small, windowless adobe brick cabin. An apple-bellied stove stood in the center of the room. A plain wood table and two ladder-back chairs took up what little space was left.

She realized suddenly that she wasn't alone. The man she recognized as Cactus Joe sat watching her with his one good eye.

Fear knotted inside, but she refused to look away or let him know how scared she was. She pressed an elbow against the narrow cot and forced herself into a sitting position.

He sat between her and the only door in the place, his chair balancing on the back two legs.

"What . . . ?" Her mouth was so dry she could barely form the words. Moistening her lips she tried again. "What do you want?"

A slow grin inched across his face. "At last she awakes." Lowering the front legs of his chair to the floor he rose to his feet, his bulky form seeming to fill the room.

Nerves tensed, she flattened her back against the rough surface of the adobe brick wall.

"Let me go," she pleaded. "I have to help put out a fire."

His grin widened. "There is no fire. I just created some smoke to get everyone out of the way." He made a face. "I took a chance

they'd leave you behind. Now don't go looking at me like that." He sounded offended.
"You and me, we're friends."

She glared at him. "You kidnapped me
and tied me up!"

"I only do that to people I like." He waved
his hand. "Sorry I can't offer you better accommodations. Crime doesn't pay much
but at least you get to work your own
hours."

She frowned. "What do you want with
me?"

"I've been tryin' for years to get people
around here to take me seriously. But no,
they think I'm a joke. The marshal chases
me a mile out of town and gives up. He
doesn't even bother forming a posse. The
way this town treats its criminals, it don't
deserve none."

His one good eye watered and Kate stared
at him, not sure what to think. Was the man
crying?

"When you think of outlaws, what name
comes to mind?" He sniffed. "Not Cactus
Joe. Oh no. It's Jesse James." He pulled a
handkerchief from his pocket and blew his
nose. "The man is dead but he still gets all
the respect. That's where you come in.
You're gonna help me get some of what he
has. I want respect too."

Brushing away a single tear that rolled down his cheek he stuffed his handkerchief back in his pocket. He picked up a book from the table and she immediately recognized it as her own. She groaned inwardly. Did everyone in Cactus Patch own her book?

"Miss Hattie's Dilemma," he read aloud. He studied the cover of a man and woman in an embrace. The man was supposed to be Brandon, though the cartoon rendition bore no resemblance to the man she envisioned.

"Not bad. But I need a title that's a bit more catchy. I read your story from beginning to end. Every page. And you know what? You ain't half bad. None of them other books have heart. Not like yours. You're even better than that fellow Dickens."

She gaped at him. *Dickens?* The man obviously didn't know anything about literature. Critics had torn her stories apart and called her last book a "hapless piece of flapdoodle." The highest praise her editor ever paid her was to say that her stories were "interesting."

Such criticism was especially painful since the only reason she became a writer was to earn respect. Unfortunately, writing earned her no such esteem. In Boston, people were judged by their circumstances and hers were found wanting. Those who knew her never saw her as anything more than the daughter of a deserting father and an alcoholic mother. Her classmates still referred to her as "the girl who cleaned latrines to pay her way." It was as if her diploma had less value, somehow, because of what she had to do to get it.

It was just her luck that one of the few people outside of a few bored cowhands to appreciate her writing talent was an outlaw.

"How . . . how did you know I was a writer?"

He grinned. "People talk and I listen." He pulled off his eye patch and tossed it into a box with others. He then lifted off his mustache and black wig and her mouth dropped open. He was completely bald, his head as shiny as a newly laid egg. He looked like a completely different man.

"The day you and I bumped into each other at the post office was the day your book arrived in the mail."

"Bumped into —" She thought back to how her hair had stood on end. No wonder. "The bearded old man I ran into that day. That was you." She was willing to bet it was also him in the courtyard the other night.

He nodded and tossed her book on the

table. He then reached for a stack of dime novels by several other authors, holding them up one by one. "Kit Carson. Wild Bill Hickok." He scoffed. "What's good for Kit and Bill is good enough for Cactus Joe."

With a sweep of his arm, he brushed the books off the table and they scattered upon the dirt floor.

"That's why you're here. You're gonna write a book about *me.*"

She shook her head. Luke said the man was short a couple of hat sizes and apparently he was right. "I've given up writing. I'm a rancher now."

"That's plain loco. Why would anyone in their right mind trade books for beeves?"

"It's none of your business why." She didn't owe him an explanation.

He shrugged and pointed to a Remington writing machine on the table. "I take it you know how to use one of those."

"I do but —"

"Excellent." He rubbed his hands together. "You're gonna write about the life and times of Cactus Joe — the Master of Disguise." He pulled a lethal-looking knife from his waist and moved toward the cot.

Thinking he meant to do her harm, she cried out, "I'll write your s-story!"

He grinned. "As if you got a choice." He

cut the ropes off her feet and hands. Replacing the knife at his waist, he gestured toward the table. "Have a seat and we'll get to work."

When she didn't move, he whipped the gun out of his holster and blew in the barrel before pointing it in her direction.

Since his vision was no longer hampered by his eye patch, she figured she better do as she was told. For now. Who knew what kind of shot he was when using *both* eyes?

Swallowing hard, she slid off the tick mattress and he smiled with approval. "Good. Now set your carcass in that chair and do what I tell you."

Her legs stiff, she felt slightly woozy. The room spun around and she reached for the table to steady herself.

"Chloroform will do that to you," he said.

"You chloroformed me?" she gasped.

"Now don't get yourself all in a snit. You'll be good as new when it wears off. At least that's what the bottle says." He pulled out the chair and gestured with his arm. "I'll get you some coffee."

Holding on to the chairs she circled the table to avoid contact with him and sat in front of the typing machine. He holstered his gun and handed her a sheet of paper. He then poured coffee from the pot on the stove and set the chipped cup next to the typewriter.

Sitting opposite her, he poured himself a shot of whiskey. He lifted his glass, swallowed the contents in one gulp, and wiped his mouth with the back of his arm.

She took a sip of the strong, cold brew and immediately wished she hadn't. Never had she tasted anything so bitter. Hands shaking, she set the cup down with a clatter. "Do you have any water?"

He handed her a canteen of water and she wiped off the top before raising it to her lips.

After quenching her thirst, she fed a sheet of paper into the machine and rested her fingers on the keyboard.

"What are you waiting for?" he demanded.

"I . . . I don't know what to type." She'd never written a book about an outlaw. Her stories were fantasy and held no resemblance to real life. She wrote about true love.

"Don't you normally start by writing 'Chapter One'?"

"Yes, of course." She could type moderately fast with a minimum of errors, but today her trembling fingers made it necessary to go slow or risk hitting the wrong keys.

He stood and walked behind her to peer

over her shoulder. After she finally managed to get the two words centered on the page, he nodded and rubbed his hands together. "Excellent."

He paced back and forth. While he considered how to start his story, her gaze darted around the cabin. The walls were bare except for a Pears year calendar hanging from a nail. A few dates were circled in black ink.

She had little hope of anyone coming to her rescue. Since she hadn't taken her clothes Miss Walker would know something was wrong, but that's all she would know. That meant Kate was on her own. Keeping her wits about her might be the only chance she had of escape.

Cactus Joe stopped pacing. "I guess the best way to start is at the beginning. How about this? Joseph Smith Landers was born in Kentucky in 1850." He stopped and glared at her. "Why ain't you typing?"

"That's . . . boring." A man intent upon having his story told probably had a high opinion of himself. If she was right, then perhaps she could use his overblown ego to her advantage. First she would have to earn his trust. Let him think she was on his side.

"There's nothing boring about being born," he said, sounding peeved.

"It's just that readers want excitement. They want adventure." She forced a smile. "I suspect you're just the one to give it to them."

Her ploy seemed to work because he looked pleased and his chest puffed out. "You're right." He rubbed his whiskered chin. "So where *should* I start?"

She pretended to give the matter careful consideration. "Perhaps you should start with your first holdup. Why you became an outlaw."

"Hmm." He resumed pacing. After several moments he began again. "I held up my first stage at the age of ten."

She typed half the sentence before pausing. "No one will believe you were ten when you held up your first stage." Even fiction had to be plausible.

He thought a moment. "You're right. The truth is I was only eight when I held up my first stage."

She frowned. "Eight?"

He splayed his hands. "What can I say? My poor mama was sick and we needed money for food and medicine. I pretended that I had fallen off a horse and broke my leg." He laughed at the memory. "You should have seen the look on the driver's face when he stopped to help me and I

273

pulled out a gun."

Eight years old. It was hard to believe. She set to work typing and the more he talked the more her imagination took flight. Her fingers flew over the keyboard as if having a mind of their own.

Little Joe held the gun steady in both hands. His heart pounded with fear and sweat poured down his back. If the driver figured out the gun was empty, Joe would never get his hands on the money box, and his poor mama would not get the medical care she so desperately needed.

Words poured out of her like water from a pump. She forgot she was writing under duress, forgot, even, that she was held captive. She had no idea how much she had missed the exhilarating feeling that came with creative flow, but it was more than that. Much about Cactus Joe's early life paralleled her own experiences. His father deserted the family, forcing him to take over as breadwinner at a very young age, and the inner pain she'd carried around for so long now found a place to light.

Hour after hour Cactus Joe dictated his story and she typed. She typed until she was no longer certain whose story she wrote, his or hers.

His language was crude and his thoughts

fragmented, but there was something compelling about a young boy's determination to save his sick mother — just as she had tried to save her own. Though she had no pity for the man, her heart ached for the child.

From time to time he peered over her shoulder to read what she wrote. "Yes, yes," he'd shout with glee. Or, "Wait till they read about that!"

The cabin had no windows and it grew hot and stuffy. Sweat beaded her forehead and her shirtwaist stuck to her back, but the stack of typed pages kept growing.

In the past, when she wrote her own books, she held back for fear of giving away too much of herself. But in telling Joe's story she could tell her own without holding back. As a consequence, she wrote like she had never before written, wrote even better than she knew how to write.

How such a thing was possible she didn't know and didn't care. At that moment all that mattered was getting the words out and releasing her pain. Oh yes, and earning Cactus Joe's trust.

CHAPTER 23

Eleanor stood next to the horse corral while O.T. gave her a rundown on the search efforts. He finished with a frustrated shrug.

Foot resting on the weathered fence, he pressed down his hat to keep the wind from blowing it off. "Sorry, Miz Walker, but me and the boys will keep lookin'. All hands and the cook are on the task."

"How could this have happened?" she fumed. Five days. Five days Kate had been gone, and nothing. The wind softened her voice, but not the frustration and worry. She'd asked herself that very same question countless times since Kate disappeared. She now asked it of her foreman. "How could we have fallen for such a ruse?"

There was no fire. The smoke had been created from saltpeter and sugar. It was an old but effective trick that succeeded in getting Eleanor and her men away from the ranch.

Had Ruckus not found that eye patch in the tack room, they might never have known what happened to Kate. Several saddles had been turned over and it looked like the girl had put up quite a fight.

"I dunno, Miz Walker. That man is sneaky as they come."

"Sneaky, yes, but he's never been more than a nuisance." Postmaster Parker was more of a crook than Cactus Joe. "The marshal has never considered him a serious threat." No one had, for that matter.

"I dunno what to say, Miz Walker."

Eleanor sighed. She was used to trouble. Running a ranch meant dealing with trials and tribulations. Thieves had been stealing Last Chance cattle for years, but this was different. This was personal. Losing Kate was like losing her daughter all over again.

Poor girl. She must be scared out of her wits. That is, if she was still . . . Eleanor quickly banished the thought. No sense thinking the worst. Not yet.

Following Kate's run-in with the javelina, Eleanor had issued an order that Kate was not to be left alone on the range. The desert was a dangerous place for even the most experienced cowhand, but it could be deadly for a greenhorn like Kate.

It never occurred to Eleanor that the real

danger lay closer to home — in the tack room of all places. She scanned the distance, turning to take in all four directions. With the high mountains, hidden canyons, abandoned mines — not to mention the Mexican border and vast desert — Eleanor didn't hold much hope that Kate would be found.

"Where is he keeping her?" And for what purpose? So far they'd received no ransom note — nothing!

O.T. lowered his foot and grabbed the reins of his horse. He was obviously exhausted, dark shadows skirting his watery eyes, but he looked no worse than Eleanor felt.

"I don't know, Miz Walker. Me and the boys are doin' everything possible to find her."

"What about the marshal? What is he doing?" *What does that man ever do about anything?*

"He's searching like the rest of us. Everyone in town is helping."

"Everyone?"

"Even the church ladies. They've been providing meals for the searchers. And the widow White made a generous donation to up the reward for capturing Cactus Joe."

"That old gossip Mrs. White did that?"

"That she did, ma'am. That she did."

Eleanor pursed her lips. It was hard to believe. She hadn't spoken to the woman in a good twenty years. Not since Mrs. White led the boycott of Last Chance beef following Eleanor's divorce. Eleanor hadn't stepped foot in the church since and only went into Cactus Patch on rare occasions, preferring to conduct her business in the county seat of Tombstone.

The wind picked up and Adam's spinning blades clanked and creaked. Eleanor didn't like the sound of it because it signaled trouble. June was the start of monsoon season, and the strong wind was a sure sign that one was on the way. Even the horses in the corral seemed to sense it. One bay kept nodding his head and pawing the ground, and the newly broken pinto paced nervously.

As if she needed further proof of an impending storm, a funnel of reddish-brown sand rose from the distant desert floor.

A dust storm, or Arizona duster as the locals called them, would slow down the search, if not altogether bring it to a halt. Still, there was no beating the weather. All one could hope for was to outlast it.

"Find her," Eleanor snapped.

O.T. nodded. "I'll do my best."

He mounted his horse and rode away,

lowering his head against the wind. Her divided skirt whipping her legs, Eleanor tightened the rawhide straps beneath her chin. Then she closed her eyes and prayed.

It had been a long time since she'd turned to God. Not since she sat at her young daughter's bedside. God hadn't seen fit to answer her prayers then. Why this time should be any different she didn't know, but what else was there to do but pray?

During the day, Cactus Joe made Kate work nonstop on his story. She typed until her hands ached and her eyes grew weary. She typed until her brain turned to mush. She was exhausted and the body that once ached from too much exercise now ached from lack of it. Her irritability increased and she was less cautious around her captor and more confrontational.

"I'm not writing that," she said, her voice as irritable as she felt. It had been five days and she'd had enough. She wanted to go home in the worst possible way. Though she'd only been in Arizona for a short while the ranch felt more like home than Boston ever did.

She pushed away from the typewriter and folded her arms across her chest. "It makes you sound like a victim."

"I *am* a victim."

"You're a thief, a crook, and a kidnapper!"

"That's what makes me interestin'." He pulled out his six-shooter as he did on such occasions and brandished it. "Now write."

The gun no longer scared her. He wasn't likely to do her harm until after she had finished writing his story. As far as she could tell, she wasn't even halfway through.

Nonetheless she set to work again and the steady *tap, tap, tap* of the typewriter keys accompanied his voice. From time to time he ranted about other outlaws — or rather one specific outlaw.

"Jesse James!" He practically spit out the man's name. "He needed a gang to do what I do alone."

Kate raised an eyebrow but said nothing. They worked for hours on end stopping only to eat. He served her three meals a day and the menu of cheese, beef jerky, and crackers never varied.

He watched her like a hawk. Every morning he stepped outside to allow her time to attend to her ablutions in private while he guarded the door. At night, he tied her to the cot and stretched out on the floor in front of the door.

He seemed interested only in her writing ability, and never took advantage of her physically. Oddly enough, she no longer feared him. His overblown opinion of himself made her laugh. He took offense but she couldn't help it. By his own admission he'd never hurt anyone, and his most successful holdup was for a little less than thirty dollars.

"It's not the money. It's the thought that counts," he hastened to explain.

Kate clamped her mouth shut. What he said may be true for most things, but he would never be compared to Jesse James unless he thought a whole lot bigger. Of course, she had no intention of saying as much.

The few times she was unable to keep her opinions to herself they argued, but mostly he talked about his life and she wrote.

At night she stared up at the dark ceiling unable to sleep, trying to think of a plan to escape. At such times the memory of Luke would come unbidden.

"Do you think I'm going to grab you and kiss you?"

Such recollections only made her ordeal that much harder to bear and she quickly turned her thoughts in another direction. Better to use her time to think of a way to outsmart her captor than to waste it with foolish memories.

She was allowed outside only to use the privy. At such times, Cactus Joe stood guard, gun in hand. Not that escape was possible. It wasn't. Except for a small barn where Cactus Joe kept his horse and wagon and a windmill that provided water, his adobe hut was surrounded by flat desert land, with no place to hide.

She didn't often turn to God. Instead, whenever she was in trouble her fertile mind concocted possible scenarios that would work in a book but seldom in real life. But by the fifth night of her captivity she was desperate enough to try anything, even prayer.

Dear God, the Father. Send rain. She wondered if she would ever be able to start a prayer without repeating Ruckus's refrain. Tears slid down her cheeks as she thought of him and the others. What they must think of her, taking off like that.

Once again she turned to prayer, but this time it was her words, not Ruckus's, she sent to heaven. *God, Ruckus said you care about your people. If that's true, I need your help. I really, really want to go home.*

Even as she pleaded with God, she doubted it did any good. God had deserted her long ago, just like her father. Just like her mother. Just like Luke would if she gave him the chance.

And that she would never do.

But not the ranch. The ranch would always be there for her.

On the morning of the sixth day she awoke from an uneasy sleep to the sound of the howling wind. It had blown all night long and at times she feared it would rip off the roof.

On occasion Cactus Joe peered outside but quickly slammed the door shut. Sand filtered through cracks and soon even the keys of the typewriter felt gritty.

"I need to use the privy," she said after a couple of hours of working nonstop.

Cactus Joe made a face. "I'm not going outside in this weather."

"And I'm not writing until you do."

He pulled out his gun. "You'll do what I say."

She glared at him and read aloud as she typed. " 'Cactus Joe is an ugly mean outlaw who can't even steal gold from a dead man's purse!' "

She pulled out the paper and tossed it at him. That was a far cry from how he wanted to be portrayed. Predictably, her ploy worked, for though he glared at her, hand on his gun, he relented.

"Have it your way. But you better not keep

me waiting long in this weather or I'll drag you out of the privy by your hair."

Switching the gun from his right to his left hand, he reached behind his back for the door handle. The door flew open and slammed against the wall with a bang, ripping the calendar off the wall.

Head lowered against the wind and grinding sand, Kate ducked outside before Cactus Joe could change his mind.

The wind practically knocked her off her feet, the sand nearly blinding her. She held a hand in front of her watery eyes and squinted between her fingers. It was impossible to see more than a foot in front of her. She glanced around, but Cactus Joe had vanished behind a thick cloud of churning sand.

Arms held out in front, she stumbled forward blindly and hit the ground on all fours. She tried standing, but the wind forced her to crawl on hands and knees. She could hardly breathe. Grit entered her mouth and nose and lashed at her flesh. She pulled the bandanna from around her neck and covered the lower part of her face. She still couldn't see, but at least now she could breathe without swallowing sand. The wind at her back, she lost all sense of direction. Where was Cactus Joe? Behind her? In front of her? Where for that matter was the cabin? *Please, God, help me.*

Was she crawling in circles? Was that Cactus Joe calling her? It was hard to tell over the loud whooshing sound of the wind.

If things weren't bad enough her imagination took flight and she began to imagine the worst. What if she was buried alive? What if all that was ever found of her was bleached white bones? Torn between escape and the safety of the cabin, she mindlessly and frantically crawled.

She forced herself to concentrate. *Mustn't stop. Got to keep going.* Her knees and palms stung and her eyes burned. *Right hand, left knee. Must keep going.*

Time and place held no meaning. She crawled for hours, or was it minutes? She couldn't be sure. She crawled for miles, or was it only a few feet? Any moment Cactus Joe could pluck her out of the grinding sand. The thought surged through her like fire, urging her onward, ever onward.

Was that someone calling her name? Was she dreaming? Was that Brandon? And why did he sound like . . . Luke?

She moved blindly ahead, heart pounding, mouth dry as cotton. *Right hand, left knee . . . got to keep going.* Panting breathlessly, she crawled on hands and knees until she could crawl no more.

CHAPTER 24

Luke set out again the instant the wind died down. Desert sandstorms generally lasted only a short time, but this one had started the day before and had blown all night.

The air still smelled of dust and the sky showed more gray than blue. Visibility was still poor, but at least he could see for a good twenty feet or more — a blessing. He narrowed his eyes to see the moving dot up ahead that was Homer.

He'd searched for days, ever since his brother first broke the news of Kate's disappearance. Even when the wind started and the sand whipped around like bits of metal, he searched. He'd checked every mine shaft, deserted cabin, and old Spanish ruin he could find and so far, nothing. Any tracks that Cactus Joe might have left had long been covered by shifting sands.

Where is she, Lord? Where is she?

Visions of her hampered his search. He

imagined her in the distance waving to him, calling to him, beckoning him, and he kept chasing down ghosts. Exhaustion affected his thinking, his vision, his hearing.

The only real sleep he'd had was last night during the height of the sandstorm when visibility was zero, but even then he'd only gotten an hour or two of shut-eye. His body ached from the hours in the saddle and although he didn't normally carry a gun, he carried one now. He'd borrowed the weapon from Uncle Murphy. He hoped to God he wouldn't have to use it, but he felt better having it.

He wasn't a vengeful man, not by any means. He was more likely to turn the other cheek than fight back — except for when family was involved. For that reason he was completely unprepared for the anger — the absolute outrage — that coiled inside like a snake ready to strike. If Cactus Joe hurt a single hair on Kate's head, Luke wouldn't be responsible for his actions. God help him.

He told himself he would feel no different had someone else been kidnapped — a stranger even. He told himself that the searing pain in his chest was nothing more than natural concern he would feel for anyone. He told himself a lot of nonsense during the long hours in the saddle. Finally he had no choice but to acknowledge the corn. He felt something for Kate — some kind of hankering. Didn't know what exactly. Wasn't love. Couldn't be love. A man like him and an educated woman like her.

She didn't even belong in Cactus Patch — and certainly not on a ranch. Eventually she'd figure that out for herself. She would then go back to Boston, go back to her books and Greek philosophers. Go back where she belonged. The thought drove through him like a knife. He reined in his horse and took a moment to calm himself. Mustn't think about Kate leaving. The only thing that mattered was finding her.

Homer let out a series of short barks. Leveling his gaze toward the dog he could see no sign of a cabin or shack. Homer had probably found another prairie dog town or tortoise hole. Or perhaps a dead steer. They'd passed several already that morning, all done in by sand suffocation.

Homer's barks grew more intense, and Luke yanked his bandanna away from his mouth and whistled. Normally Homer would come running upon hearing Luke's call but not today. Instead, he continued to bark.

Spotting something ahead, Luke urged his horse into a gallop.

The odd shape turned out to be an over-turned wagon probably left behind by some hapless traveler. Since Homer kept barking and wagging his tail, Luke slid off his horse to have a look, hand on the weapon by his side.

He spotted a boot beneath the partly buried wagon. Heart pounding, he quickly flipped over the wagon, not knowing what he would find until he saw a flash of blond hair.

"Kate!" He dropped to his knees and shook her.

She groaned and her lashes fluttered, and he let out a cry of relief. Praise God she was alive. Had it not been for Homer he might well have missed her. After a moment, big blue eyes peered at him from over a red bandanna and he thought never to see a more beautiful sight.

"Luke? Is that you?" She sat up, her back against a wagon wheel, and gazed at him in disbelief.

He grinned. "It's me." Her voice was hoarse but nothing had ever sounded sweeter to his ears. At least this time she didn't call him the name of that imaginary fellow, Brandon.

He removed her bandanna and, after fetching his canteen from his saddle, dropped down on one knee to hold it to her parched lips. Though the wagon provided shade, heat rose from the desert floor.

She drank thirstily before pushing the canteen away. Homer was suddenly all over her, licking her face and hands.

"Down, boy," Luke ordered. Homer sat, panting, his wagging tail whipping up a cloud of sand.

Luke searched Kate's face for some clue as to her condition. He still couldn't believe he found her. It was nothing short of a miracle.

"Are you all right?" he asked. Her hands and face were reddened by the sand and wind, but otherwise he could see no signs of injury.

Her mouth curved slightly. "Now I am."

He smiled back at her and he thought his chest would burst with relief. His prayers had been answered. God was good.

"He didn't hurt you, did he?" He couldn't bear the thought of the man putting his grubby hands on her.

"No," she whispered. "He didn't hurt me."

"Why did he take you? I don't understand."

"He wanted me to write the story of his life," she said. "Somehow he found out I was a writer."

"That's it?" he asked, astonished. "That's the reason he kidnapped you?"

She nodded. "That's it."

Luke shook his head. "I was so worried." Half out of his mind more like it. "The entire town has been searchin'."

"How . . . how did you know Cactus Joe kidnapped me?"

"They found an eye patch in the saddle room." He grinned. "From what I heard you put up quite a fight."

"For all the good it did me." She stared at him from pools of liquid blue. "I can't believe it's you. I thought I'd never see you or the ranch again," she whispered. "I thought I would be buried alive. Or hopelessly lost. Or mauled by a pack of tarantulas or —"

He laughed. "I don't think tarantulas travel in packs."

"It's not funny," she said. "I could have been attacked by a band of javelinas."

He shook his head. "I don't know what's worse. The things that happen to you or the things you think might happen."

She gave him a sheepish look. "It's a writer's curse."

"Ah, that explains it." He poured a little water on his bandanna. "You have sand on your nose."

She flinched when he touched her but whether from pain or something else he didn't know. She said Cactus Joe hadn't harmed her and he hoped to God that was true. The thought of her being hurt or compromised in some way filled him with horror.

Knees in the sand, he dabbed her face gently while gazing into her eyes. Now, as always, he could see sadness in their depths and he wondered what it would take to make that sadness go away.

"I don't have a very good way with words. If Michael was here he'd know what to say. I just want you to know I'm not gonna hurt you," he said.

She studied him, a thoughtful shadow at her brow. "I'd say you have a very good way with words."

He knew it wasn't true, but he liked that she said it. Ever so gently he ran his bandanna over her brow, nose, and cheeks in an effort to soothe her sand-burned skin and clean off the tiny grains of sand. He felt her tremble beneath his touch, but she didn't move away and for that he was grateful.

"There you go," he said, his voice hoarse with emotion.

Her lashes flew up and she smiled. "Thank

you." Then all at once her eyes filled with tears. "I'm sorry . . . It's just I thought I was lost and no one would find me."

Something tugged in his chest and a lump rose in his throat. The need to protect her was like a fire burning deep inside. "It's all right," he said. He ran a knuckle down her damp cheek. When she offered no resistance he wrapped a protective arm around her and cradled her. "You forgot about Homer. His nose can sniff out a pretty woman any-where."

Hearing his name, Homer barked and wagged his tail, and Kate laughed even as tears rolled down her face.

Luke smoothed her hair away from her face. Hugging her close, he sat and rocked her, murmuring sweet words of comfort in her ear. She buried her head against his chest and sobbed quietly, her tears leaving a damp spot on his shirt.

He worked with steel and iron and knew the strength that each required. This tender, gentle side of him was something new, requiring strength of another kind.

Gradually her sobs subsided and she peered up at him, the first glimmers of trust shimmering in the depths of her eyes.

"You're safe now," he whispered. He

tightened his hold and she clung to him like she was never going to let him go.

CHAPTER 25

Offering her hand to Brandon, she fervently prayed that her power of duplicity was such that she could hide her all-consuming passion.

No one had ever held Kate the way Luke held her.

He was gentle, soft-spoken, and kind, his concern for her sincere. He was all the things she never thought she'd see in a man. All the things she'd dared not hope for. All the things that, at the moment, she so desperately needed.

Cradled in his arms, she lifted a hand to his face, absorbing the sweet essence of his flesh against her open palm. His gaze met hers and a warm shiver flowed through her. Words escaped her but none were needed. Tension left her body, and for the first time in her life she felt she could completely and wholeheartedly trust a man, that she could trust *this* man.

His steady gaze bored into her as if he sensed she had given him permission to proceed, to claim more of her heart.

He pressed his lips tenderly on her forehead. It felt so good to be kissed by him, held by him. Oddly enough, she felt safe. More than that, she felt cherished — respected — and no one had ever made her feel that way.

She lifted her chin and his gaze settled on her lips. He hesitated before covering her mouth with his own. Even with his lips pressed against hers she hesitated to kiss him back. Startled, she realized how little she'd given of herself to people through the years. How that must have frustrated him, frustrated others. Cheated her readers, even. How would it feel to give her heart fully and completely to someone without fear of being hurt or disappointed?

Shyly at first, she worked her hands up his chest and around his neck. He gazed at her tenderly and waited, allowing her to set the pace. His patience broke through her last reserve and she rose up to kiss him full on the lips.

With a soft groan he crushed her against his chest. Nothing had prepared her for the taste, the feel, and the heat of him. Nothing she had written in her books could compare.

"Love isn't kind. Men can't be trusted."

Desperate to shut out the echoes of the past, she gave herself freely to the full pleasure of his kiss. He pulled back, his eyes warm with approval, before reclaiming her lips. Soft currents rushed through her, chased by the chilling words she tried so hard to forget.

"No man is forever. He will use you and discard you like yesterday's newspaper."

Go away, go away, go away. But her mama's words welled up from the past, clamoring in her head. Mocking her. *"Nothing good happens to people like us."*

She tore away from him with a choking sob. He looked all at once worried, puzzled, and concerned. "Kate?"

She tried to speak but her voice caught in her throat. Her tears veiled his face but not the pain in his eyes. His kisses were more wonderful than anything she ever could have imagined. But rather than satisfy, he made her want more and this made her cry harder. There could never be more.

"I can't," she whispered. "I can't do this." *I won't.* She knew what she wanted and it wasn't Luke. Her future was the ranch and she refused to settle for anything less.

He stared at her, his face a mask of confusion. Sensing his master's bewilderment, Homer barked and the tension snapped.

She pulled away and brushed off her skirt with shaking hands. She then palmed away her tears. "Would you mind taking me home?"

"Look at me, Kate. Please."

Looking at him was out of the question. She needed to put as much distance between them as possible. She must forget his kisses, forget being in his arms. What she couldn't forget — must never again forget — was that no man could be trusted. Not even a man like Luke Adams.

It was late, but Kate was too wound up to sleep. Instead, she stood on the balcony off her room and stared at what seemed like an endless night. The scent of cattle was especially potent — or maybe it was simply that her nose hadn't yet adjusted to being back at the ranch.

Ruckus had been the first to rush out to greet her the moment she and Luke rode up on his horse, but the others, even Wishbone and Stretch, hadn't been far behind. Ruckus, of course, couldn't let the occasion pass without reciting from the Bible.

"I'm gonna have to start callin' you Moses," he said. "Even though you didn't roam the desert for no forty years."

"It felt like it," she said.

Bo made his special cactus pie to celebrate the occasion, and Rosita filled her bath with three inches of water instead of the usual two. Miss Walker didn't say much, but she insisted that Kate take the following day off.

O.T. gave strict instructions that Kate was to be watched at all times until Cactus Joe's capture. Kate wasn't allowed to leave the house without an escort.

The excitement of returning to the ranch had nothing to do with her inability to sleep. It was Luke, pure and simple, and she didn't know what to do about it.

It had been hours since he kissed her, almost a full day, and yet her lips still burned with the memory, and her body still ached with the need he had awakened.

His kisses had been tender, his touch gentle, and so different from anything she had known, even in her imagination.

Never before had she allowed herself to be tempted by a man. Having an education helped, for many men shied away from a woman with a college degree. Writing helped, too, for she could live vicariously through her characters without opening herself up to harm.

"I'm not a fancy man. I don't have a way with words."

Oh, but what a way he had with his lips, his touch. She squeezed her eyes shut. *Mustn't think of that, mustn't think of his kisses.* He was a man, which meant nothing about him was permanent. He could walk away and never look back, just like the others. The only difference was she had no intention of giving him the chance.

Kate was late for breakfast and so she was surprised to find Miss Walker sitting at the dining room table. Usually by this time, the ranch owner was already in the saddle checking out her cattle or windmills or fences or the hundred and one little details that cropped up on any given day.

"I'm sorry . . . I slept in."

Miss Walker waved away her apology. "I told you to take the day off."

Kate went to the buffet and poured herself a cup of coffee. She then took her place at the opposite end of the table.

Miss Walker regarded her with analytical eyes. "Has your unfortunate experience with Cactus Joe changed your mind about the ranch?"

The question surprised her. "No, of course not," she said, alarmed. What would ever make Miss Walker think such a thing?

"And you still wish to proceed as planned?" Miss Walker asked.

"Yes," Kate replied. "Nothing has changed." She hesitated a beat before asking, "You're not . . . having second thoughts about me, are you?"

"I've had second thoughts about you from the moment you arrived at the ranch," Miss Walker said in her usual forthright manner. "But this isn't about what I think. Now that you've been kidnapped I wouldn't blame you for wanting to return to Boston."

"I have no intention of returning to Boston," Kate said. Arizona was her home and she meant to stay.

Miss Walker's eyebrows rose. "Even though Cactus Joe is still out there God knows where?"

"He doesn't frighten me. He simply wanted me to write his biography."

"He kidnapped you to write?" Miss Walker sat back in her chair. "That's all he wanted?"

Before Kate could answer Rosita appeared. "Marshal Morris is here. He wishes to speak to Señorita Tenney."

Miss Walker made a face. "For all the good it will do. The man couldn't find a bull in a chicken coop," she muttered. In a louder voice she said, "Show him in."

The marshal walked into the room a moment later, hat in hand. He greeted Miss Walker with a respectful nod of his head. "I'm sorry to bother you so early, ma'am, but I need to ask Miss Tenney a few questions."

A shadow of annoyance crossed Miss Walker's face. "Can't this wait? Miss Tenney has had a terrible ordeal."

"It won't take long," he assured her.

"It's all right," Kate said, though she was touched by Miss Walker's concern for her welfare.

Miss Walker gestured toward the buffet. "Then pour yourself some coffee and have a seat."

"Much obliged but I've had my belly wash for the day." He sat on a chair and set his hat on the table. He wasted no time on formalities. "Where exactly did Cactus Joe keep you captive?"

"All I can tell you is that it was an adobe hut. It had no windows and only one door and a flat roof. There was a windmill outside and a privy." She glanced at Miss Walker, who listened attentively. "I can't think of anything else."

The marshal cleared his voice and looked away. "Did . . . he hurt you?"

"He chloroformed me," she replied. "But

otherwise, no. He didn't compromise me in any way."

The marshal nodded as if relieved. "How far away would you say the hut is?"

She shook her head. "I have no memory of how I got there. As I told you, he chloroformed me."

The marshal studied her. "What about when you escaped?"

"The wind was blowing and visibility was low. I could barely see my hand in front of my face. I'm sorry."

The marshal scratched the back of his head. "You spent more than five days with him. What did you do all that time?"

She moistened her lower lip. "I wrote."

"Wrote?"

Miss Walker drummed her fingers on the table and regarded the marshal with a look of impatience. "Miss Tenney is a writer. Cactus Joe kidnapped her to write his biography."

The marshal's eyes widened in disbelief. "That's all? I came all the way out here and that's all the man wanted? To have his biography written?"

Kate frowned. Apparently the marshal didn't care that she had been kept against her will. "That's not all. He . . . he tied me up. Fed me horrible food."

The marshal scratched his neck. "You said you were writing his biography. Do you know anything about him? His real name? Where he's from?"

She quickly filled him in on the few actual details she knew about the man. "He calls himself the master of disguise."

"So you think he comes to town in one of his disguises?" the marshal asked.

"He's actually bald and clean shaven and there's nothing wrong with his eye. If he came to town looking like that or dressed in one of his other disguises, no one would ever guess his true identity. In fact, I saw him at the post office dressed as an old man. I didn't know at the time it was him. I suspect he may have been spying on me at the ranch. The night I was reading to the . . . eh, the night I was reading."

The marshal stroked his chin. "It's hard to believe he's been under our noses all this time."

He looked so doubtful that Kate added, "How else would he have known I was a writer?"

Miss Walker nodded in agreement. "How, indeed?"

The marshal frowned. "What else did he tell you?"

"I suspect most of what he told me was

exaggerated, if not altogether untrue. He has a very high opinion of himself."

Miss Walker scoffed. "Which only proves he's a dreadful judge of character."

The marshal reached for his hat. "It doesn't look like any real harm was done."

Kate stared at him, incredulous. "Aren't you going to do something? Track him down? Form a posse?"

He shrugged. "It's a big desert out there."

Kate's temper flared. "The man is dangerous. Evil. He had a gun and a knife and he threatened to use them. He likens himself to the bandit Jesse James." On and on she went, making Cactus Joe sound worse than he actually was.

Nothing she said seemed to convince the marshal to take her kidnapping seriously. Seething, she glared at him, but then an idea occurred to her. The marshal had at least one thing in common with Cactus Joe — his ego.

Elbows on the table she rested her chin on folded hands. "When I finish Cactus Joe's story I will naturally devote a full chapter to the man who brings him to justice." She gave the marshal a meaningful look. "I hope that man is you."

Her ploy seemed to work because suddenly he seemed more interested. "Well now, ma'am. That would be mighty nice of you." He donned his hat. "I'll get a posse together and we'll see what we can find. I'll let you know if I have good news."

"We won't hold our breaths, Marshal," Miss Walker muttered.

Seeming not to hear Miss Walker, he leaned toward Kate. "Just be sure you spell my name right. That's Morris with two *r*'s."

He left and Kate rested her hands on her lap. A posse. She smiled. Cactus Joe would be so pleased.

Miss Walker cast a probing look Kate's way. "You have no idea how I've tried to make the marshal do something besides sit on his endgate." She shrugged and took a sip of coffee, setting the cup down with a clatter. "Hmm." She rose and walked to the doorway and stopped, her back to Kate. "Never thought I'd say this, but someone with the imagination of a fiction writer might be just what this ranch needs to take it into the next century." With that she was gone, her hurried footsteps fading away.

For the longest while Kate didn't move except to smile. At last she had earned Miss Walker's approval, maybe even her respect. It's what she wanted. It's what she'd worked for all these weeks. The Last Chance Ranch was her chance for a long and happy future, and she had no intention of letting anyone or anything ruin it for her.

And that went double for Luke Adams.

CHAPTER 26

With solidity of strength acquired from weeks of drudgery, she banished Brandon from her life, if not her heart.

A week later Kate paused outside the blacksmith shop. Luke had ridden out to the ranch several times to see her, but each time she was either on the range or had Rosita send him away with apologies.

She wasn't certain she was ready to see him even now, but she couldn't keep avoiding him. Still, she had just about made up her mind to leave when Homer appeared by her side. She stooped to pet him and he licked her cheek. She drew back and laughed.

Following Miss Walker's orders, Ruckus had driven her to town. He waited for her now in his parked wagon across the street. She was grateful for his protection, but she regretted not having time alone. Even on the ranch she was constantly watched and guarded.

She no longer feared Cactus Joe, but she wouldn't put it past him to kidnap her again to finish his book. She glanced in both directions. A man crossing the street was similar in height to Cactus Joe, but when he looked her way she realized it was the owner of the mercantile store, Mr. Green. Another figure gave her pause, this one a Mexican with a limp, but a glimpse of the man's broad face convinced her it was not Cactus Joe.

She walked into the blacksmith shop. She felt guilty for keeping Ruckus waiting. The sooner she finished what she had come to do, the sooner they could return to the ranch.

The clanging sound of iron upon iron greeted her as she stepped into the shop, her gaze freezing upon Luke's long, lean form. His shirtsleeves were rolled up to the elbow beneath his brown leather apron. Each downward swing of his arm was swift and powerful. The anvil rang with the heavy blows of his hammer, sending sparks darting about like little fireflies.

Homer brushed against her, reminding her with a start why she had come. "Luke?"

Arm frozen over his head, he glanced over

his shoulder and his mouth curved upward. He gave the piece of steel he was working on one final whack before setting his hammer down and turning to face her.

"I didn't mean to disturb you," she said, feeling oddly out of breath.

"Your timing is perfect. I'm done here." He picked up a towel and wiped the sweat off his forehead. "I stopped by yesterday, but Rosita said you were out on the range."

She nodded and took a deep breath, an uneasy silence filling the air. "Your aunts came to see me and brought my favorite bonbons." A steady parade of well-wishers had streamed to the ranch to see how she was.

Kate was touched, even though Miss Walker insisted everyone was just being nosy. Kate couldn't imagine people stopping what they were doing in Boston just to check on a neighbor, especially if they lived a distance away.

He tossed the towel on the workbench. "Leave it to my two aunts."

Her gaze fell upon a miniature windmill on his workbench. "What a lovely windmill," she exclaimed. "It's perfect." She leaned in for a closer look. "It looks so real. Is it a toy?"

Her interest seemed to please him. "Not a

toy, a working model. I'm trying to design one that can be oiled from the ground." He demonstrated and the top of the windmill tilted downward.

"That's amazing." The fine craftsmanship took her breath away. "Just think of all the time that will save. The lives and limbs. When will it be ready to market?"

"Whoa! That's gonna be awhile. It's too flimsy. It won't stand up to the wind. I'm working on another design."

She met his gaze and yet more silence stretched between them. She felt oddly shy, awkward, like a schoolgirl talking to a boy alone for the first time.

"About last week. What happened . . ." She spoke slowly, pronouncing each word carefully as if learning to speak a foreign language. "You saved my life." She never would have been able to find her way back to the ranch by herself. "I don't know how to thank you."

"No need to thank me." White teeth flashed against his tanned skin. "Come, I have something to show you." He motioned her out the door and around back.

Homer raced ahead and waited for them in front of the small wooden shed attached to the back of Luke's shop.

Luke patted Homer. "What do you say,

boy?" he asked in a conspirator's voice. "Is it okay if I show Kate what you have?"

Homer barked.

"I think that's a *yes*. Come on." He grabbed her hand and pulled her inside before she could protest.

It took a moment before her eyes adjusted to the dim light. A collie lay in a corner nursing three tiny pups.

"Ohhhh, they're adorable," she said softly.

As if agreeing, Homer barked twice. "Woof, woof."

Luke laughed. "Have you ever seen such a proud pa?" He dropped onto his haunches and scooped up the smallest pup in a single hand. Even as the young canine was held aloft, he made little sucking sounds. Luke rose to his feet and placed the pup in her arms.

The puppy was so young he hadn't yet opened his eyes. "He feels so soft." She glanced at Luke with a broad smile and found him watching her with a smile of his own.

"Soon as he's weaned he's yours, if you want him."

Kate's mouth dropped open. "Mine?" She'd never owned a dog or any animal, for that matter, and didn't know what to say.

"His name is Locker."

She held the puppy in front of her with both hands, his curling tail dangling between her wrists. "Locker?"

"After John Locke. Some philosopher Michael told me about."

Her eyes met his and she felt a well of emotion rise inside. She handed the puppy back to him and practically stumbled out of the shed. Once outside, she quickened her pace.

Chasing her down, he grabbed her by the arm and swung her around. "Why did you take off like that?"

"You don't have to do that, Luke."

He looked genuinely puzzled. "Do what? What don't I have to do?"

"Name dogs after philosophers."

"I thought you'd be pleased."

"You don't have to please me!" She shook her head and remembered her original reason for coming. "I'm afraid I led you on and I didn't mean to."

A muscle tightened at his jaw and his gaze sharpened. "Led me on, how?"

"I was upset when you found me. I wasn't myself. Even so, that does not justify" — she couldn't say *kiss* because that sounded far too intimate — "what we did, and for that, I apologize."

"Are you saying you're sorry you kissed

me?" he asked, his voice curt.

She sucked in her breath. "There's no room in my life for anything but the ranch."

Kissing Luke had been surprisingly pleasant but that was because she had been half out of her mind when he found her. The soft, caressing kisses she wrote about were a figment of her imagination. They promised love everlasting, and no such thing existed between a man and a woman in real life. Men weren't dependable. Kisses held no meaning. Love wasn't kind. She wanted no part of it except for the fantasies she weaved and the stories she once wrote.

"The ranch." His lip curled upward. "It's always the ranch. Nothing else matters to you."

"I'm sorry, Luke." She counted on Miss Walker's spinster pact to protect her from all future heartache and disappointment. She'd had enough of both to last a lifetime. Unfortunately, she hadn't counted on meeting a man like Luke. A man so intent on pleasing her, he'd resorted to naming a dog after some historical figure he'd probably never heard of.

"I don't know what else to say . . ." She wanted to erase the pain on his face, the disbelief in his eyes, but she didn't know how. "I have obligations and responsibilities

316

and —"

"Drat, Kate!" His voice snapped through the air like a whip. "Whenever you feel cornered you hide behind some fancy words. Say what you mean plain and simple."

"All right," she yelled back, more angry at herself than at him. She never should have let him kiss her, but her biggest failing was kissing him back. "I want you to forget we ever met!"

His hard eyes bore down on her. "Is that what you want? Really?"

"Yes," she whispered, flinching inwardly at the sharp pain that sliced through her.

He took a step back, a closed look on his face. "Then consider it done."

The finality of his words affected her like a slamming door. It was what she wanted, of course. She only wished he hadn't made it so difficult. She quickly turned away and practically ran all the way to the wagon where Ruckus waited for her.

Climbing onto the wagon seat, she swallowed the lump in her throat and kept her head down.

Ruckus acted like he didn't notice, but he'd have to be blind not to know she was upset. "Mind if we stop at the post office?" he asked. "Expecting a letter from my son."

She swiped at a tear. "I don't mind." She folded her arms and stared straight ahead, blowing a wayward tendril from her face. It was done. She did what she had to do. From this moment forward nothing or no one would be allowed to distract her from the ranch.

"I'm ready for a faster horse," she said. "Decker's too slow."

Ruckus glanced at her from the corner of his eyes but said nothing.

"I also want to carry my own weapon. I'm ready to go full hog as a rancher," she said, using a term Ruckus often used. If she was going to be a rancher she might as well start talking like one. "And spurs. I want spurs."

Ruckus moved his jaw up and down like a cow chewing its cud. "Nothing wrong with that," he said at last. "As long as you ain't chasing after no wind."

Forgetting to hide her face she stared at him. "What's that supposed to mean?"

He pulled up in front of the post office, reached into his pocket, and drew out a small Bible. "Look it up yourself," he said. "Ecclesiastes chapters 1 and 2. By the way. It's yours. The Bible. I reckon you'll be needin' it."

Hands at his waist, feet apart, Luke watched

the wagon carrying Kate roll down the street.

Good riddance! What did he need a woman like that for, anyway? Her and her fancy schooling. What did he have to offer someone like that?

So she wanted him to forget that they'd ever met, did she? That's exactly what he intended to do — God give him strength.

Drat! Life had been so simple before she came to town. Now he acted like a plain fool. Didn't sleep. Didn't eat. All he could do was think about the memory of her sweet lips on his. No more!

He spun around and walked into his shop with Homer at his heel. He had work to do and no time to think about Kate. He picked up a piece of iron and set it down again. He grabbed a wagon wheel and tossed it aside. Who was he kidding?

He couldn't work. He couldn't even look at his workbench without remembering her lying there, looking at him with her big blue eyes.

Those same eyes had often been guarded when they looked at him, but not on the day he held her in his arms and kissed her. Then he saw longing — at least for a while — and it was a longing that matched his own. She'd pushed him away in the desert, but he hadn't taken it seriously. She'd just come through a difficult ordeal. Any woman would react similarly after being kidnapped — or so he thought. Today, he knew better. She wanted no part of him.

With a sweep of his arm he sent his carefully constructed windmill flying, and poor Homer seeking cover.

It was his own fault. He'd known from the start that she wasn't the woman for him. He was a blacksmith plain and simple. She was a college-educated woman, a writer. It was plumb crazy to think she would be interested in someone like him.

No matter. He'd made a mistake and it wouldn't happen again. He had simple needs and they certainly didn't include the likes of Miss Kate Tenney.

Bessie sat in the seat next to her husband, Sam. It occurred to her how handsome he looked dressed in his dark pants, boiled white shirt, and spiffy bow tie. It was hard to believe they'd been married nearly forty years. He'd brought her to Arizona Territory as a young bride shortly after the area had been taken over by the United States. In all that time, she'd never felt as insecure about their marriage as she did today.

He was up to something, she knew it. She

could feel it in her bones.

It was the fourth Sunday in June, which meant the circuit preacher was in town. In honor of the occasion she and the other churchgoers dressed to the tees in their Sunday go-to-meeting best and, for the most part, were occupied with pious thoughts.

Cactus Patch had a proper church with a skyscraping steeple, large wooden cross, and stained glass windows. What they didn't have was a full-time preacher, though heaven knew they could use one. Since Reverend Johns ran away with the offering five years earlier, they had to make do with a saddlebag preacher who rode into town every other Sunday spreading the Word as one might spread flower seeds, hoping that one or two would take root.

Sam parked behind a long line of wagons and buckboards. Before Bessie had time to leave her seat, he lowered himself to the ground with the enthusiasm — if not vitality — of a much younger man. He then shuffled around their dapple gray horse and appeared at her side. A crooked grin made its way from ear to ear as he offered his hand for assistance.

He hadn't shown her that much courtesy when they were courting. Oh yes, he was up to something, all right, and she intended to find out exactly what it was. Keeping her suspicions to herself, she let him assist her to the ground. He surprised her by offering his bent elbow, and she slipped her arm through his.

Upon seeing her sister, she waved. "Sam, save me a seat. I'll be there in a minute." She broke loose from him and hurried to greet Lula-Belle and her husband, Murphy.

She grabbed her sister's arm. "I need to talk to you. In private. You don't mind, do you, Murphy? It'll only take a short while."

Murphy shrugged. A compact man with bushy eyebrows, sideburns, and mustache, he hung his thumbs from his suspenders and gave the kind of resigned look husbands were prone to give on such occasions.

"I'll go on ahead," he said.

Bessie waited for Murphy to walk away before pulling Lula-Belle aside. "Sam's up to something."

Lula-Belle stared at her from behind an outlandish veiled hat topped with an over-sized black ostrich feather. Since the ostrich farm opened in Phoenix, almost everyone could afford the previously rare feathers, which in Bessie's opinion was a detriment to good taste.

Had it not been for Lula-Belle's white

woolen shawl, onlookers might have mistaken her floral print dress and feathered hat for an overgrown flower box. Bessie quickly banished the uncharitable image from her mind. This was Sunday and she was in church. *Pious thoughts, pious thoughts.*

"What do you mean he's up to something?"

"He bought me a saucepan to go with the frying pan he gave me forty years ago. Don't ask me how he was able to find one to match after all this time."

He bought the first pan out of guilt. Oh yes, she saw him gape at that young Mexican woman, saw the way his gaze followed her every move. He didn't know she saw — he was too busy lollygagging. Forgiving and dutiful wife that she was, she'd not uttered a word about the incident until now.

Lula-Belle inclined her head. "Isn't that nice?"

"Nice?" Bessie glanced around and lowered her voice. "There's nothing nice about it. I think he's interested in someone else."

Lula-Belle's mouth dropped open. "No!"

Bessie forced herself to put on a brave front. "Why else would he buy me a saucepan?"

"I have to admit that does sound

rather . . . odd. But we're talking about Sam. He wouldn't part with his old army boots until you put your foot down. Even with the War Between the States over for thirty years."

Bessie tapped her foot. "What does that have to do with my pots and pans?"

"I'm just saying that Sam prefers old things to new." Lula-Belle patted her on the arm. "So you haven't a thing to worry about."

Bessie only wished it was that simple. "I'm telling you he's up to something, and I intend to find out who she is!" *And then I'll kill her.*

Shocked that she would consider such a thing in church of all places, she rolled her eyes to the cross overhead. *Pious thoughts, pious thoughts.*

"Find out who *who* is?"

"Mercy, Lula-Belle. Who do you think I'm talking about? The *other* woman, of course." She tapped her chin with the tip of her finger. "We haven't had a social event since Christmas. Maybe it's time we had another one."

Lula-Belle pulled a lace handkerchief from a mutton-legged sleeve. "You think Sam's interested in another woman and you're going to throw a party?"

"Not a party. A barn dance. And I will invite every woman in town. You'll let me use your barn, won't you?" Lula-Belle's barn was larger than the one she and Sam had, and seldom used. "Knowing Sam, he'll give himself away and I'll know exactly what he's been up to."

"I don't know, Bess." Lula-Belle dabbed at her nose with a corner of her handkerchief and shook her head, the feather and flowers on her hat bopping up and down. "I don't have a good feeling about this."

"Oh, butter corn! You never have a good feeling about anything. Trust me, this is a brilliant plan."

Upon spotting Miss Tenney walking up the steps of the church with Ruckus and his wife, Bessie nudged her sister and gave her head a slight toss. How pretty Kate Tenney looked in her rust-colored skirt and matching cape. She wore a fashionable flat hat adorned with flowers and ribbons but, thankfully, no ostrich feathers.

"That poor, poor girl. Can you imagine being held captive all that time? Yet here she is in church already." No whimpering or feeling sorry for herself. If Bessie didn't already know that Miss Tenney was the right woman for Luke, she knew it now.

"Where else would she be? It's Sunday,"

Lula-Belle said, tucking her handkerchief into her sleeve.

Bessie rolled her eyes. How could anyone be so utterly thickheaded? *Oh dear, here I go again. Pious thoughts, pious thoughts.*

"Getting back to the barn dance . . ." Something suddenly occurred to her and a smile inched across her face. Nothing was more satisfying than killing two birds with a single well-aimed stone. "I will, of course, invite Miss Tenney."

Lula-Belle gasped. "You think Sam's interested in Miss Tenney?"

Bessie threw up her hands. Her sister was absolutely hopeless. "Miss Tenney I'm inviting for Luke."

The organ let out a deep, solemn call to worship and Lula-Belle tugged on her arm. "Come on, we'll be late."

She shuffled away, but Bessie didn't move. Of all the ridiculous ideas. Sam and Miss Tenney? Why, the woman was young enough to be his daughter. And everyone knew Sam preferred the old to the new.

She frowned. At least that's what she'd always thought.

Moments later Bessie took her place in the church pew between her sister and Sam. It was a good choice, not too far in front, not too far back. Best of all, it allowed her to keep an eye on Miss Tenney, who, either by choice or good fortune, sat directly across the aisle from Luke.

The choir director stood in front of the congregation. "Please rise."

The organ groaned, voices lifted, and Luke glanced across the aisle.

Bessie elbowed her sister and nodded her head toward the couple. "He's looking at her."

Lula-Belle lifted her head to stare over her hymnal at their nephew, her voice cracking as she reached for a high note.

The hymn ended and the last gasping organ chord faded away. Feet shuffled as churchgoers took their seats, and Bessie glanced at her husband. He looked straight ahead without so much as a wandering eye, which only fueled her suspicions that much more. A restless man by nature, Sam wasn't usually so attentive. He generally fidgeted and let his gaze wander during worship.

The preacher took his place behind the lectern. Dressed in black trousers and a long duster, open to reveal a white shirt and string tie, his top hat rose above a ruddy square face.

"I'm sure you've all heard of the daring Frenchman known the world over as

Charles Blondin," he began, his voice booming.

Next to Bessie, Murphy folded his arms and muttered an unholy word beneath his breath.

Her sister jabbed her husband with her elbow and gave him a stern look.

Looking properly chastised, Murphy muttered, "Another Blondin analogy."

The preacher continued, "He walked across the Niagara Falls on a tightrope not once, not twice, but many times. He even walked blindfolded. During one crossing he carried a stove on his back. He stopped halfway across the chasm to make breakfast for himself, much to the amazement of onlookers."

Miss Tenney looked across the aisle at Luke and the two exchanged a quick glance before turning their heads to face the front of the church.

Bessie glanced at Sam, but his gaze remained glued upon the preacher. Any suspicion that Miss Tenney might possibly be the woman who had turned Sam's head was immediately put to rest.

The preacher continued to drone on about the amazing Blondin, during which time Luke glanced at Miss Tenney at least a half dozen times.

Bessie knew this because she counted. Obviously, the two were meant for each other. All they needed was a little shove in the right direction — and a barn dance seemed like the perfect place to plan some strategic moves.

She glanced up at Sam. She wasn't above shoving him too — over a cliff, if necessary. God forgive her. *Pious thoughts, pious thoughts.*

The preacher paused, indicating he was about to get to the point of his story, and a collective sigh rippled through the congregation.

"When Blondin asked the Prince of Wales if he could carry him across the Niagara Falls on his back, the prince declined. Even though Blondin had proven his ability to successfully cross the falls numerous times, the prince did not trust him." The preacher paused for effect and in a softer voice asked, "Who would you trust enough to carry you over the falls? Your wife? Your husband?"

Bessie glanced at Sam, whose gaze locked with hers. Sucking in her breath, she quickly pulled her gaze away and stared straight ahead.

The preacher closed the Bible and stared out over the congregation. "Or would you put your trust in God?"

In the past, Bessie would have answered that query with a resounding *yes*. It would never occur to her not to trust God. But knowing her husband was interested in someone else changed everything. Her entire life had been turned upside down and she no longer knew whom to trust. Her marriage on the line, she now questioned everyone and everything. As much as she hated to admit it, she even questioned the heavenly Father. *Pious thoughts, pious thoughts.*

Kate had a difficult time relating to the preacher's sermon. Trust God? She didn't trust anyone, let alone God. Knowing that Luke sat only a few feet away, she couldn't even trust herself.

I won't look at him, I won't.

But she did look — but only because she sensed him looking at her. She heaved a sigh and focused her eyes directly in front of her.

"Who do you trust?" the preacher asked again.

Not Luke, not anyone.

She hadn't wanted to come to church today, but Ruckus insisted it would do her a world of good. "You can't let Cactus Joe turn you into a hermit. Me and the boys will watch out for you. Don't you worry none about that."

As good as his word, he stuck by her side. He made Wishbone and Feedbag sit in the pew behind her. Stretch sat in front, blocking the view of the altar from anyone unfortunate enough to sit behind him.

She wouldn't be a bit surprised to find Cactus Joe in church dressed in one of his disguises. Would she be able to pick him out? She glanced over her shoulder to study the row of faces behind her. In so doing she inadvertently met Luke's eyes. Heart skipping a beat, she quickly averted her eyes. An infant wailed and was immediately carried outside. The owner of the general merchandise store, Mr. Green, sat with his arms crossed, nose on his chest, snoring.

Ruckus patted her on the arm, drawing her gaze from the back of the church to the pulpit. His concern touched her. Before coming to Cactus Patch, she'd never known anyone to worry about her welfare. Not even her mother had done that.

In many ways Ruckus was an enigma. He'd rant at her or any other ranch hand who earned his disfavor, but he was never cruel or unkind. His wife, Sylvia, seemed genuinely fond of him. A pleasant woman with a full-rounded figure and dimpled smile, she held her husband's hand and gazed at him on occasion with loving eyes. Never had Kate known a couple so devoted to each other and who had stayed together so long. Did Sylvia worry about Ruckus taking off? Abandoning her? Tossing her aside like an empty tin can?

Pushing her thoughts away, she concentrated on the sermon.

The ranch. That was all she wanted, needed. She loved working there, loved seeing the cattle thrive. Ruckus suggested she was chasing the wind but he was wrong. She chased after a dream that would one day become reality.

Miss Kate Tenney, owner of the Last Chance Ranch. She liked the sound of that. Liked knowing that no one would ever look down on her again.

She smiled. With this thought firmly in place she managed to ignore Luke for the remainder of the sermon, but it took a whole lot of effort on her part — and maybe a little help from above.

CHAPTER 27

Since her estrangement from Brandon her misery was consummate, and she struggled against the depths of despair with every bit of obstinacy she possessed.

Three days later Kate found an envelope on her desk addressed to her. Inside was an invitation to a summer barn dance. The purpose of the dance was to raise reward money for the capture of Cactus Joe. A handwritten note at the bottom of the card read, *Dear Miss Tenney, We do so hope you can attend.* It was signed *Aunt Bessie.*

Aunt? No one in Boston would dare sign an invitation to a mere acquaintance with such informality. Kate tossed the invitation aside. It was a worthy cause and Cactus Joe would be so pleased. The town finally took him seriously as an outlaw, though she doubted anyone would compare him to Jesse James.

She had no intention of going to the dance, of course. No doubt Luke would attend and the less she saw of him the better. Still, the dance did stir the muse. She couldn't help it. Since her kidnapping, she had not been able to stop writing. It wasn't that she had a compelling need to resume her writing career. Nothing could be further from the truth.

Rather, in writing Cactus Joe's story, she had inadvertently tapped into her own. Though she had never been able to write about her inner pain, she found she could easily write about his. In writing about Cactus Joe's deserting father, she was able to pour her own anger into each sentence.

"How odd that an absent parent could create both a void and a presence in one's life," she wrote. "Neither of which was possible to escape."

Sitting at the typewriter in Cactus Joe's cabin had lit a fire in her and sometimes, like now, it felt like the words in her head would consume her if she didn't put them on paper. She lived for the moment she could sneak away from her chores to jot down a note or two. At the end of each day she escaped to her room to spread her notes across her bed and plan her night's work.

Anxious to get started she opened the

door to her room and strained her ears. Miss Walker's muted voice floated up from the bottom of the stairs. Though Kate couldn't make out the words, she knew it was Miss Walker's habit to give last-minute instructions to the staff before retiring.

Heart racing with excitement, Kate closed the door. Soon the household would retire for the night, leaving her free to sit at the desk in Miss Walker's office and type her story on the Remington writing machine.

Her body still ached from long hours on horseback, but her creative mind overcame any physical exhaustion. And it would only be for a short time. Once she had completed Cactus Joe's story and put her own demons to rest, she would hang up her pen for good and concentrate solely on the ranch. For now, however, she enjoyed the process of putting words on paper and gained great satisfaction from watching a scant few pages grow into a hundred or more.

Impatient to get started, she sat at the desk in her own room and dipped her pen into the inkwell. *He gazed at her from across the crowded room and it was as if no one else existed. The fiddlers played a romantic melody and Luke started toward her . . .*

She stared at what she had written. Luke? Where did that come from? She dipped the nib of her pen into the ink and scratched out Luke and wrote Cactus Joe. She then read what she wrote and grimaced. Cactus Joe was not a romantic character by any means.

After jabbing the pen into its holder, she ripped the page from her notebook and scrunched it into a ball. Tossing it across the room, she watched it bounce off the wall before falling to the floor. That's when she noticed that someone had slipped something beneath her door.

She hurried across the room to see what it was. Several pages were clipped together and it appeared to be a story. Clutching the manuscript in her hand, she shot out of her room and ran down the hall to the stairwell just in time to see the front door close below.

She hurried down the stairs and rushed outside. "Michael!" She could barely make out his dark form, but she sensed she had his attention. "I can't wait to read what you wrote."

"You don't have to if you don't want," he said.

"I want to," she said. "I do . . ."

"I'm no good at spelling and I never figured out the difference between a colon and semicolon."

"I'll help you with those."

"You will?"

She couldn't make out his face in the dark, but she could hear the pleasure in his voice.

"Yes, but only if your story has merit."

"How will you know that?"

"Oh, I'll know," she said. "Readers always know such things." She thought for a moment. "I'll read your story, Michael, on one condition. No more being late in the morning or leaving a gate open or neglecting to put in an honest day's work."

"That's three conditions."

She grinned. "I know you can count. Now let's see if you can write."

Eleanor stood in the shadows of the dining room, listening. It was nearly eleven and the only sound that broke the late-night silence was the peck, peck, pecking of the typewriter. How the girl managed to stay up till all hours typing and still do her chores was nothing short of a miracle.

Eleanor let out a sigh of envy. Ah, the energy of youth . . .

She leaned against the wall, eyes closed, and prayed. She hadn't prayed in years and now here she was, turning to God for a second time in less than a week. *Keep this under your hat, God. I don't want my men to*

337

think I'm growing soft in my old age, but just between you and me, I'm mighty glad that you brought Kate back. You did good. Real good.

After Kate had disappeared, Robert had accused Eleanor of using the girl to replace her long-dead daughter. She'd brushed away his concerns as a bunch of hogwash, but now she wondered if he might be right. When Kate disappeared, it felt like losing Rebecca all over again.

Now she had another worry. If the passionate pounding of typewriter keys was any indication, Kate's heart and soul did not belong to the ranch, no matter how much she insisted that they did. The ranch demanded one's all, and nothing must be allowed to interfere. Not marriage, not family, and certainly not such frivolous pastimes as writing.

Something had to be done and done fast. The future of the ranch depended on it.

Luke stared at his aunt's invitation, not sure what to make of it. "Hmm."

Kate's kidnapping had been the main topic of conversation for days and the town was in an uproar. Guards had been posted outside the schoolhouse and women were never left unescorted. Some townspeople had even gone so far as to have Luke make bolts for doors that had never been locked.

As much as he approved of his aunt's fund-raising idea, Luke doubted crime fighting was her true motivation. The question was, what was she really up to? Did it have anything to do with his uncle's suspicion that she was interested in Postmaster Parker?

At first Luke had dismissed his uncle's concerns. The idea that his aunt would look at another man seemed too ridiculous to consider. But the tension between his aunt and uncle at last Sunday's dinner worried him. Now he didn't know what to think.

Luke folded the invitation and shoved it into his shirt pocket. He felt a fierce need to protect his family. On the night of the dance he'd keep an eye on things, make sure that Parker stayed away from his aunt.

He wondered if Kate would attend. He was pretty sure she would. Since the funds raised would help capture her kidnapper, it didn't seem likely that she would stay away.

The last thought raised his spirits. He didn't want it to, but it did. No matter how hard he tried not to think about her, he couldn't help himself. Trying to forget Kate was like bending steel with bare hands.

He wanted to see her again. Had actually ridden out to the Last Chance again to talk to her, but she was out on the range and he never did find her. The ranch. It was all about the ranch with her. Still, he hadn't imagined the way she kissed him or the way she looked at him in church.

"You want to see me?"

Luke had been so deep in thought he hadn't known his brother had entered the shop until he spoke.

Homer greeted Michael with a wagging tail and eagerly took the piece of dried meat from his hand.

"What have I done this time?" Michael looked worse than usual, his clothes and hair unkempt, his chin covered with a scraggly beard. He looked like he hadn't slept in a month of Sundays.

"Nothing," Luke said. If anything he was pleased that Michael had managed to hold on to his ranch job as long as he had. Maybe there was hope for him yet. "How are things going at the ranch?" He really wanted to ask about Kate, but he didn't want to rouse Michael's suspicions.

Michael shrugged. "Okay, I guess."

"Do you like working there?"

"There're worse places to work." Even before Michael's gaze flitted around the shop, his meaning was clear. He was never meant to be a smithy and Luke regretted making him his assistant, but at the time it seemed like the wise thing to do.

Prior to working at the ranch, Michael couldn't hold down a job or stay out of trouble for more than a day or two at a time. Luke had hoped that by teaching Michael the blacksmithing trade his brother would settle down. Instead, Michael fought him the entire two years he worked at the shop. Was still fighting him.

"You've been at the ranch several weeks now. That's gotta be some kind of record."

Michael shrugged. "After a while even cattle tend to grow on you."

Luke grinned. "Never figured you as a rancher."

"Steer can be as stubborn as iron, but they aren't nowhere near as dull."

"I made a mistake," Luke said quietly. "I should never have made you work here against your will."

The blacksmith shop meant the world to him. From the time he first started helping Uncle Sam at the tender age of twelve he hadn't wanted to do anything else. He naturally assumed his feelings would run in the family and Michael would feel the same way.

"The problem is I need to ask a favor of you," Luke said.

A look of curiosity crossed Michael's face. "A favor?"

"I need help with some of the horseshoeing and windmill repairs at the ranch."

"Ah, gee, Luke. You know that's not what I want to do."

"It'll only be for a short while. Miss Walker is still looking to hire someone. Meanwhile, I can't keep up with the work here and there too."

Michael made a face. "I'll think about it."

"I really need your help —"

"I said I'd think about it!" He turned to leave but Luke called to him.

"Wait."

Hands at his waist, Michael turned away from the door. Head down, he toed the metal shavings on the floor, letting his jingling spurs fill the silence. If his refusal to look Luke square in the eye wasn't clear enough, his stance certainly was. Michael had no intention of lending a helping hand.

Luke fought the frustration rising inside. His aunt's words echoed in his head. *"You just don't speak his language, is all."*

"I know you've always wanted to be a writer. You have a way with words. I swear you could make a pump believe it's a windmill." As a child, Michael never had trouble expressing himself, whereas Luke tended to get tongue-tied. It was only in recent years that Michael had stopped talking or at least saying anything that made sense.

Michael looked up. "You're just saying that. You don't mean it."

"Since when have you heard me say something I don't mean?"

Michael said nothing and Luke sucked in his breath. "I wonder if you would mind givin' me a list of words to work on. You know, so I can improve the way I express myself and all."

Michael shifted his weight from one foot to the other, disbelief flitting across his face. "You want to improve your vocabulary?"

"Not a whole lot." Nothing irked Luke more than people who sounded like a walking *Webster's.* "Just . . . a little something to decorate what I say."

Michael narrowed his eyes. "Why now? You never cared about such things before."

"No special reason." Luke wasn't about to tell his brother that he wanted to impress Kate with his newfound way with words. Maybe if he polished up his language a bit, she would stop pushing him away. His aunt's barn dance couldn't have come at a better time.

Michael scratched behind his ear. "What

kind of words are you interested in?"

Luke wiped his arm over his sweaty forehead. Here came the tricky part. "How can I express my . . . affection? To . . . say . . . Homer?" No sooner had he said it than he knew how ridiculous that sounded. Michael's eyes rounded in disbelief. "Just toss him a bone. He'll understand."

"Okay, forget Homer. Aunt Bessie and Uncle Sam are going through a rough patch right now. How can I tell them how much I" — he cleared his throat — "care for them without . . . eh . . . coming right out and saying it? You know how emotional Aunt Bessie gets."

Michael rubbed his temples with both hands. "You could say your heart pullulates with affection."

"That's good, that's good. Wait, let me write that down." He quickly searched for his writing tablet and pencil. "How do you spell it?"

Michael frowned. "Are you serious? I'm joking."

"No, no, that's good. Really it is."

Shaking his head, Michael spelled the word and Luke scribbled it into his notebook. "Now give me a word for bold or brazen."

"Audacious?"

"There you go." Luke wrote the word down in big bold print and underlined it. "What about when something causes you pain?"

"You mean like inflicted?"

"Now *there's* a word." He added it to his notes. Michael fed him several more words and he wrote them down, spelling them as best as he could. "You've been a big help."

Michael quirked an eyebrow. Lifting his Stetson he raked his fingers through his hair and set his hat back in place. "I'll help out with the horseshoeing and repairs."

Luke wasn't sure he'd heard right. "You will?"

"Yep."

"What made you change your mind?" Luke asked. He still couldn't believe his brother was serious about helping out.

"You've not been acting like yourself lately. I should have known your think box was addled when you insisted on naming that dog after a Greek philosopher."

Luke cringed at the memory. Naming the dog Locker was a mistake. All it did was push Kate further away. "I just wanted to be different," he muttered. "When Mrs. Stanton calls for her dog Rover, five dogs come running."

"That still don't explain why you're suddenly worried about your vocabulary. You know what I think? I think you're even more overworked than you know."

Luke wasn't about to argue with him. Just so long as Michael agreed to take over some of the blacksmithing chores, let him think what he wanted. "I'll be mighty grateful for your help. It won't be for long."

Michael gave him a strange look before turning to leave. He stopped and glanced at Luke from the doorway. "You better get some rest."

"I feel fine," Luke said. He stared at the list of words long after Michael had left. What was he doing? Maybe Michael was right. Maybe he was more overworked than he knew.

His feelings for Kate were real. To dress them up in fancy words was like putting a top hat on a cowboy. It didn't set right. He needed no fancy words to tell Kate Tenney how he felt. Crumbling the paper into a ball he tossed it into the burning forge.

CHAPTER 28

Two hectic blotches suffused her pale cheeks at the memory of Brandon's arms. It was an act of sheer folly to attend that dance. "Spare me from this pain," she lamented, but her forlorn prayer went unanswered.

Kate had initially turned down Ruckus's invitation to ride to the barn dance with him and his wife. She had no interest in socials or dances, but Ruckus insisted she make an appearance.

"Luke's aunt is doing this out of concern for you. And even if she weren't, it won't do for the future ranch owner to act all unfriendly-like," he'd chided her.

He was too loyal to criticize Miss Walker openly, but Kate got the distinct impression he disapproved of the ranch owner's lack of interest in community affairs.

"When I take over the ranch things will

be a lot different," she said. She had plans, big plans.

Ruckus grinned. "I reckon they will be at that."

Now Kate sat on the buckboard seat between Ruckus and his wife, Sylvia. Kate couldn't remember ever feeling this nervous. She dreaded coming face-to-face with Luke. What could she say to him? Would he even talk to her? "Ohhhhhhh . . ."

She hadn't known she'd groaned out loud until Sylvia patted her arm. She wore a lilac flower dress and a knitted purple shawl, her little bow mouth pursed with worry.

"Are you all right, dear?"

"Yes, yes, I'm fine, thank you." And because Sylvia kept looking at her, she turned to Ruckus. "You promised that if I attended the social you would tell me why Miss Walker refuses to come to town."

Ruckus heaved a sigh. "It's a long story, but it had to do with her divorce. From what I gather it created quite a stir in town."

"A dreadful scandal," Sylvia said. "The women in my quilting bee talked about it just last week."

Ruckus continued, "A group of church ladies refused to purchase Last Chance meat. Said it was tainted by the divorce, of all things. 'Course some of those same women criticized her during the war when she sold beef to both Confederate and Union armies, but she took the tainted meat thing more personal. You can say what you want about the boss lady, but you better not criticize her beef. Simple as that."

"Did you know her husband?" Kate asked.

"Ralph? Nah. He was before my time. From what I've heard, he wasn't no cattle rancher. He owned a silver mine, but when that ran dry, he tried to talk Miz Walker into moving to Colorado but she wouldn't hear none of it. When their little daughter died, supposedly that was the beginnin' of the end. I heard tell that to hide her grief the boss lady buried herself in ranch work. That didn't set too well with her husband."

"How did her daughter die?"

"Smallpox. Rebecca was only five years old when it happened. From what I heard tell, she was the prettiest little thing you ever did see."

"Mrs. White said she was the most precious child," Sylvia added. "It near broke everyone's heart to put that sweet little thing to rest."

"Miss Walker used to keep a colored daguerreotype on her desk. I remember she had blond hair and big blue eyes." He glanced at Kate. "Just like you." He shook his head. "I gather from others that Miss Walker was never the same after buryin' her little girl."

It never occurred to Kate that someone as self-possessed as Miss Walker could be hiding a broken heart. Was that what Ruckus had been trying to tell her when he said Miss Walker had a soft center, just like a cactus?

It was a little past seven by the time they pulled up in front of the barn. It was still light, but the sun was setting in a blazing red sky and the air buzzed with excitement. Ruckus parked behind a long line of wagons, shays, and carriages.

"Here we are, ladies," he said. "I've always wanted to walk into a dance with a pretty girl on each arm."

Sylvia laughed and tapped her husband fondly on the shoulder with her folded fan.

The high whine of fiddles greeted them as they walked into the barn arm in arm. The warm summer air was filled with the smell of sweet hay and the flowery fragrance of cologne.

Kerosene lanterns hung from hooks, casting a warm yellow glow over the guests. Red, white, and blue streamers dangled from the rafters, and the wooden barn floor had been dusted with corn starch for dancing.

Luke's Aunt Bessie practically tripped over herself in her hurry to join them, her sister dog-paddling behind her. Kate stared at Bessie's shocking low-cut purple gown with big puffy sleeves and a small train.

"Oh, I'm so glad you could make it," Aunt Bessie gushed with warm approval.

Compared to the ginghams and calicos of the other female guests, Kate felt overdressed. Her circular rust-colored skirt fell from her waist in graceful folds. Neither her fitted shirtwaist nor her ruffled leg-o'-mutton sleeves would pass muster in a Boston parlor, let alone a social, but both were much too frilly for Cactus Patch.

However, considering Bessie's gown, Kate stopped worrying about being overdressed.

Ruckus's mild-mannered wife stared in astonishment. "My, my, Bessie, you look . . ." Eyes rounded, she raked Luke's aunt up and down. "Lovely," she managed finally, with puckered lips.

Bessie looked pleased. Apparently she hadn't noticed the pinched expression that accompanied Sylvia's compliment. "Why, thank you, Sylvia."

"She looks like a big purple plum," Aunt Lula-Belle muttered, patting down her own plain brown frock.

Aunt Bessie either didn't hear the remark or chose to ignore it. Instead, she motioned them toward the tables against the back wall laden with all manner of cakes and pastries.

"Help yourselves to refreshments. The lemonade is nice and cold." Aunt Bessie rolled her eyes. "Mercy, would you believe I paid two cents a pound for ice?"

"Shocking," one of the women exclaimed. "I remember when Mr. Hargrove first opened up his ice plant. The price was only half a cent."

"Those days are long gone," Ruckus said before making a beeline for the punch bowl. Aunt Bessie introduced Kate to some of the other guests. After rattling off the names of several women and pointing to each one in turn, she said, "I want you to meet our guest of honor."

Startled to learn she was more than just an invited guest, Kate nonetheless managed a polite nod. "I'm pleased to meet all of you."

"Ah, you're the writer who was abducted," the woman who had been introduced as Mrs. Turnbull exclaimed. "How exciting!" A mousy woman with sallow skin, she clapped her hands as if applauding some great achievement or honor.

None of the other women seemed to share her enthusiasm. Instead, they stared at Kate with open curiosity. The youngest, a woman introduced as Charity Chase, eyed Kate's apparel, her mouth drawn in a straight line. Brown hair twisted into a coil and held in place with a jeweled comb, Miss Chase brushed a finger against the fringe of bangs on her forehead as if to point out that she alone was in style.

The widow White, an older woman, raised a lorgnette to her eye and scanned Kate from head to toe. She wore a ready-made bun that might have matched her red locks years ago but bore no resemblance to the current color of her age-faded hair.

Mrs. White lowered her eyepiece. "You're Miss Walker's new heiress," she said, and Kate detected surprise in her voice.

"That still hasn't been decided," Kate said.

"Oh, there's Luke," Aunt Lula-Belle said, effectively stopping further discussion about the ranch.

As if she had announced the appearance of Governor Hughes, active supporter of women's suffrage and temperance, all women, young and old, turned to look with equal admiration.

Kate's knees threatened to buckle beneath

her and she started to panic. What if she fainted or said something foolish or —

"Over here," Aunt Bessie called in a high-pitched voice, waving to him.

Luke flashed a brilliant smile and headed their way, ducking beneath a dangling paper streamer. Taller than practically any other man, except for Stretch, he was a commanding presence. Kate tried not to stare, but she couldn't seem to help herself.

His black trousers and boiled white shirt barely contained his muscular physique as he made his way from one end of the barn to the other.

He greeted each of them in turn, and Kate wondered if it was only her imagination that his gaze seemed to linger on her longer than it had the others. *Oh, please don't let it be true.*

He pecked both aunts on the cheek, and it was easy to see how much they adored him.

He looked Aunt Bessie up and down and grinned. "I hardly recognized you."

Aunt Bessie patted her nephew on the cheek. "Do you like it?"

"How could I not?" he said, wrapping his arms around her. Hugging his aunt close, he peered over her head at Kate and winked.

Kate's already-heated face flared another

notch hotter, and she quickly looked away.

Aunt Lula-Belle pulled her woolen shawl closer to her body, her face registering disapproval of her sister's low-cut neckline. "You better stay away from the door or you'll catch your death of cold."

"Lands' sakes, Lula-Belle. You act like we live in the arctic instead of a desert." Aunt Bessie pulled out of Luke's arms and craned her neck to peer around the room, fanning herself furiously.

"Who are you looking for?" Luke asked.

"Eh . . . Michael. Have you seen him?"

"He'll be here," Luke said. "I've never known Michael to miss out on a good time."

Miss Chase laughed a little louder than the comment called for. A pretty woman with big green eyes and a tiny waist, she shamelessly pushed her way between Aunt Bessie and Luke.

The fiddles started playing and couples moved to the center of the barn.

Miss Chase cozied up to Luke and cast a disapproving glance at the awkward couples on the dance floor. "Why don't we show them how to do it?"

Luke smiled and offered her his bent elbow. She giggled as he led her away.

Aunt Bessie stared after them with a frown. "In my day no woman would think of asking a man to dance with her."

Lula-Belle leaned over and whispered in Kate's ear, "That was before they invented passion."

Kate smiled politely, not sure she'd heard right.

Two older men joined them and Aunt Bessie introduced the taller of the two as her husband, Sam, the other as Lula-Belle's husband, Murphy.

Sam inclined his silver head. "Would you excuse us? I would like to take my purty missus for a whirl." Aunt Bessie gave her husband a rather odd look before she took his offered hand.

Lula-Belle and Murphy followed their lead. This left Kate on the sidelines next to the row of matronly chaperones seated by the barn's back wall. The ladies obviously took their task seriously. Sitting on the edge of their ladder-back chairs they looked ready to pounce at the first sign of impropriety between the openly flirting singles.

Kate watched the dance floor with equal attentiveness, but for a different reason. She wouldn't put it past Cactus Joe to don one of his disguises and make an appearance. No doubt he would be delighted to know that this shindig had been planned for his benefit — or rather his capture. Not even

Jesse James had warranted such a grand affair.

The marshal wandered over. "Miss Tenney," he said, touching his hat with his finger.

"Marshal."

"I was kind of hoping Cactus Joe would show his face tonight," Morris said.

"I don't see him," Kate replied.

The marshal glanced around. "We'll get him." He took his leave with a tip of his hat. "Just remember two *r*'s."

"Two . . . oh, you mean your name in the book. I'll remember."

He headed for the refreshments and Kate scanned the crowd yet again. Finding no sign of Cactus Joe, she relaxed, her foot keeping time to the music. The only dance she'd attended previously was during the last year of school just before graduation. It had been a formal affair with none of tonight's boot-stomping gaiety. Here in Arizona whatever you couldn't do well you did loud, and that went double for musicians. The fiddles screeched and harmonicas whined, but no one seemed to care.

Aunt Lula-Belle's husband, Murphy, danced with the grace of a bear fighting off a swarm of bees. Sam and Aunt Bessie simply stood in the same spot, swaying back and forth like the pendulum of a clock, but with less regularity.

Stretch bopped by with a pretty redheaded girl in his arms. He practically doubled over to accommodate his short partner and was obviously telling one of his tall tales.

"It was so windy that the hen laid the same egg three times."

A few of the other ranch hands shuffled by, feet going every which way, some leading their partners, others being led. Feedbag danced like a man on a bucking horse.

The widow White stared at the dance floor through her lorgnette, holding on to the tortoiseshell handle with a delicately posed gloved hand, her magnified gaze riveted upon Luke and Miss Chase.

Kate followed her gaze, hands curling into fists by her sides. Not that it mattered who Luke danced with. Of course it didn't matter. He could dance with whomever he pleased. It was Miss Chase who irritated her. Never had she witnessed such unseemly behavior from a woman. Why, her laughter could be heard even above the whiny music.

The woman wasn't only brazen, she was downright shameless. Luke wasn't *that* funny. And did he have to look like he was enjoying himself so much? Why didn't the chaperones do something?

"Looks like something's got your dander up," Michael said by her side.

"What?" She had been so engrossed in what was going on in plain sight of God and everyone that she hadn't seen Luke's brother enter the barn.

"You look like you're ready to stretch someone's neck."

Embarrassed to be caught staring at Luke and his dance partner, she pulled her gaze away from the couple and focused on Michael. He had shaved and combed his hair, but instead of wearing his Sunday best like the other men, he wore his usual blue denim pants, checkered shirt, and mule-ear boots.

"I didn't expect to see you here," she said. Michael didn't strike her as the social type, no matter what Luke said. He kept pretty much to himself at the ranch and she thought of him as a loner.

"Gotta do something to relieve the boredom. Been busy shoeing horses and they aren't much company."

From the dance floor came the sound of Miss Chase's laugh and Michael narrowed his gaze in her direction, his face grim.

Kate studied him. "I read your story and really liked it."

His head swiveled in her direction, his eyes wide. "Really?" His astonished expression

359

gradually faded into wariness. "You're not just saying that?"

"I mean it, Michael." His story of a young crippled boy and his dog traveling around the world brought a tear to her eye. "You're a very talented writer."

Michael turned red, but he looked pleased. "That means a lot. Coming from you."

"I made a few suggestions and corrected spelling and grammar, but those things are easy to fix. The writing itself . . . Michael, it's beautiful. I think you should send it to the *Saturday Evening Post*."

She'd sold a few stories to the magazine through the years. Founded in 1821, the *Post* was reportedly in dire financial straits, but it still paid writers more than most publications and was a good place to start.

Michael's face lit up like a bonfire. Grinning, he grabbed her by the waist and brazenly kissed her on the cheek. By the time she recovered from the shock, he had already pulled away.

All eight chaperones sat staring at them. Michael either didn't notice or didn't care. Instead, he indicated the dance floor with a nod of his head.

"Do you think I can pull Miss Chase away from my brother?"

She glanced at him askew. "I know you can write, but can you dance?"

"Not very well."

"Then you should fit right in."

Miss Chase's constant laughter had the same effect on Kate as fingernails on a blackboard. Gritting her teeth, she gave Michael a shove. "What are you waiting for?"

Smoothing down the sides of his hair with both hands, he stalked away, looking a whole lot more self-confident than he ever looked with cattle. Moments later Miss Chase had a new dance partner, and judging by her pouty mouth she was none too pleased about it.

Luke made a beeline for Kate. She looked around for a means of escape, but he blocked her way.

"Dance with me." He held out his hand and waited. His determined stance made it clear that turning him down was not an option. He cocked his head to the side. "Don't worry. I'm not going to grab you and kiss you."

Her mouth snapped shut. She didn't want to dance with him, didn't want to be that close, but with Aunt Bessie staring at them and the chaperones looking on, denying his request would only create a spectacle. Nevertheless, she hesitated before placing her hand in his. *Just don't let my legs buckle.*

Their last encounter was very much on her mind and, judging by his serious expression, it was very much on his mind too. The kiss she had tried so hard to forget now seemed to stretch between them as if no time had passed since his lips touched hers.

He led her to the center of the barn, and she forced herself to breathe. It was only a dance. She was just being silly. She had nothing to fear from Luke Adams.

Hand on her waist, he waited a beat before pulling her close. She rested a palm on his shoulder and his eyes darkened as he held her gaze. He led her around the floor, his two-step even more graceful than it had looked from a distance. Nothing else seemed to exist. Not the music and certainly not the other couples.

The world was suddenly all about him — the breadth and scent of him, the nearness, warmth, and scope of him. She tried to concentrate on the other couples, but nothing banished the hold he had over her.

In spite of her best intentions, she soon relaxed and enjoyed herself. For now, she just wanted to embrace the moment and pretend it was simply a scene in one of her books.

He twirled her smoothly around the dance

floor, in and out of the other couples like ribbons around a maypole. For a man so strong and powerful, he was surprisingly light on his feet.

Her own feet so buoyant they barely touched the floor, she felt weightless and grounded all at the same time. It was as if she and Luke now shared a common breath. But how was that possible? How could two hearts beat as one?

"You look mighty pretty," he said, his rich, smooth voice a sweet melody in her ear.

Any protagonist worth her salt would think of something charming or witty to say in response, but all she could manage was a murmured, "Thank you." She quickly added, "It's a lovely party."

He nodded in agreement. "My aunt knows how to show people a good time." After a moment he said, "I looked for you after church Sunday, but you'd already left."

Her heart took an unexpected lurch. He had looked for her? "It's a b-busy time at the ranch," she stammered. "We had to rush back."

His gaze sharpened and heat rose up her neck to her face. Desperate to change the subject, she said, "How are the puppies?"

His infectious smile melted away her defenses and she grinned back at him.

"Growing by leaps and bounds," he said. "You should feel honored. Homer allows very few people near his pups."

She didn't want to think about a dog protecting its family. That only brought back painful memories of her childhood and how no one thought to protect her. Her mind scrambled for a way to fill in the sudden silence.

"Your brother looks like he's having a good time." When Luke made no comment she added, "Ruckus is pleased with the way he shoes horses. He even fixed one of the windmills."

"He doesn't much like smithing, but he's got a knack for it," Luke said. "He's been a real help."

On safer ground now, she spoke freely. "He's a gifted writer."

"Writing don't seem like a very good way to make a living," Luke said.

His comment came as no surprise. Luke worked with iron and steel, tangibles that could be molded by heat and shaped by an anvil. Words could be shaped, too, but not with fire or hammer. A writer's skill was so much more subtle, requiring prudent choices and careful arrangement of sentences and ideas.

"I can think of several writers who would

disagree with you," she said. Robert Louis Stevenson and Stephen Crane came to mind, as did Mark Twain. She never thought to come close to that kind of success. Few women authors ever did.

"Do you really think he's that good?" As if to make sure they were talking about the same person, he added, "Michael?"

"I do."

He pulled her a tad closer, his breath in her hair sending warm shivers racing down her spine. She closed her eyes and, for several turns around the dance floor, unspoken words seemed to flow between them as meaningful as if they'd been given voice.

The fiddlers finished their lively tune and immediately launched into a mournful song about lost love. Some couples left the dance floor, but she and Luke kept dancing, although at a slower pace.

He looked deep into her eyes. "What you said . . . about not seein' each other."

She swallowed hard. "I can't think about anything but the ranch." She then went on at great length about the ranch and all that she'd learned in recent weeks. "I don't know anything about the business side yet, but Miss Walker is expecting some eastern buyers next month and said I can sit in on the meeting."

He listened intently with knitted brow. "Does the ranch really mean that much to you?"

His question was not too surprising. Most men had a hard time understanding why a woman might wish to pursue a profession. "Of course it does."

"Why?" He studied her. "Why take on that much responsibility? It's hard work even for a man."

It was hard, harder than she'd ever thought possible. "Miss Walker seems to manage."

"Miss Walker doesn't strike me as a very happy woman."

She'd once held a similar opinion, but that was before she came to know the woman. "I don't think she sees it that way. The ranch is her life."

He rested his chin on her head and she swallowed the lump that suddenly rose to her throat. How did he always manage to do this to her? To confuse her and make her question her own heart?

By the time he drew back to look at her, she'd regained control enough to smile up at him.

"And is it yours?" he asked, looking straight at her. "The ranch? Is it your life?"

She refused to look away. "It is," she said.

Land was forever, and at this point in her life, she needed something that was lasting. Something she could count on.

He studied her for a moment. "I aim to make you change your mind."

"Not possible." *Just don't look at me like that. Stop tempting and confusing me. Stop making me wish things were different. Stop being you.*

"Maybe not, but I have to try. It's gonna be in my language, not yours."

She frowned. "My language?"

He nodded. "I never had much schooling. There was no school in Cactus Patch when we moved here from Texas. My aunt tried to get me to practice readin', but I was more interested in hangin' out with my uncle at the shop. I'm not much good with fancy words."

"I don't imagine you have much need for fancy words in your line of work."

The music stopped and so did they. "My line of work?"

Confused by his sudden withdrawal, arms to his sides, she explained, "I don't imagine that linguistics is required for blacksmithing."

"Drat, Kate, why do you always make everything so difficult? I'm trying to tell you that I . . . I . . . fancy you."

"I don't think we should —"

Her words were cut off by a high-pitched squeal and the sudden appearance of Miss Chase, who shamelessly grabbed Luke's arm. "Come on, Lukey, they're playing my favorite song."

Sure enough, the fiddlers played again and couples poured back onto the dance floor like ants at a picnic.

" 'Ta-ra-ra Boom-de-ay!' is your favorite song?" Kate asked. As much as she tried to sound pleasant, her voice was thin with dislike.

Miss Chase's smile failed to reach her eyes. "Better that than the '*Spinster* Polka.' "

She walked off with Luke, and once again Kate was left to keep company with the chaperones.

CHAPTER 29

Eleanor sat on the porch of the ranch house at dusk enjoying the end of another long day. Nighthawks swooped overhead on outspread wings, weaving invisible patterns in the near-dark sky. Bats flitted around a nearby saguaro, drinking sweet nectar from its night-blooming flowers.

Stars winked as if privy to earth's innermost secrets. A full moon cast a silvery light across the desert floor. A horse whinnied from a nearby corral, setting off a chorus of barks from restless cow dogs.

Nearly everyone had gone to the barn dance and Eleanor enjoyed the solitude. She could sit outside to her heart's content without O.T. or Ruckus suggesting she needed a wrap or risked catching her death of cold. In the desert, no less.

The sound of rumbling wheels made her groan. Surely the dance wasn't over this early? A shay drove up to the ranch house and she touched a hand to her forehead. It was Robert. She should have known.

Certain he couldn't see her in the dark, she waited until he'd walked up the verandah steps before revealing herself. "It's not my birthday. Nor is it the first of the month."

She couldn't make out much more than his form, but she sensed him searching for her in the shadows.

"I came to escort you to the social," he said, moving toward her. Light from the window angled upon him. His silver hair was neatly combed to the side, his mustache waxed. He wore a three-piece suit and dark bow tie as befitting a banker. The cane tucked beneath his arm was more for appearance than need, and it made him look even more distinguished than usual, more debonair. If she were in mind for a love interest — which of course she wasn't — Robert would fit the bill quite nicely.

"You've known me how many years now? Twenty?" she asked. "And you thought I would consider going to a barn dance?"

"Since the money collected will go toward a reward for capturing Miss Tenney's kidnapper, I thought you might let down your hair just this once."

"I rather like my hair the way it is, thank

you very much. Besides, I sent a check. Money is a very handy implement for avoiding social obligations. You might try it sometime."

He laughed. "You don't think a banker knows that? For your information, I've already made a generous donation to the cause."

She rocked back and forth. "In any case, I'm sure Rebecca will do the ranch proud."

"Rebecca?"

She stilled. "What?"

"You said Rebecca."

Drat! Knowing Robert, he would read all sorts of things into a simple slip of the tongue. "I meant Miss Tenney, of course."

He fell silent for a minute. "May I ask you something?"

She let out a sigh. "When have you ever needed my approval?"

His finger followed the line of his mustache. "Are you looking for an heiress or a daughter?"

Eleanor stiffened. "For goodness' sakes, Robert. You know my only interest is the ranch and its future."

"You referred to Miss Tenney as Rebecca. Your daughter's been dead for a good many years."

She grimaced. It wasn't in her nature to

think of the past, but lately it seemed it was all that she did. Worse, she even questioned some of the choices she had made, though she didn't regret fighting for the ranch. Never that. Even so, thoughts of her daughter had sent her to the attic to scrounge in the dust for the daguerreotypes stored there, along with Rebecca's clothes and toys.

She had long come to terms with the death of her only child, which made constant thoughts of her recently even more puzzling. Perhaps it was because of the sudden and unexpected death of Rebecca's father. Or maybe it was simply that Kate had similar coloring and was almost the same age Rebecca would have been had she lived.

"I'm an old lady," she said slowly. "Can you not excuse a mental hiccup or two on occasion?"

He laughed. "You old? You can still ride circles around any of your ranch hands."

She wasn't sure that was true anymore, but it was nice that he still thought so.

"I can also still fire a mean shot," she said.

At least that part was accurate. Learning to shoot had been a dire necessity during the early years when Apaches still ran rampant and liked nothing better than to raid isolated ranches, hers included.

"Is that a warning?" he asked.

"Only if you continue to harp on the subject of my daughter."

"Very well. I'll not mention her again." He paused for a moment. "On one condition."

"Oh dear. You aren't going to propose marriage again, are you?"

"I have no reason to believe that you've changed your mind about marrying me. But I am going to ask you to dance with me."

"I'm not leaving the ranch."

"You don't have to. We can dance right here to the music of the stars."

"Oh, Robert. You're such a romantic."

She almost turned his offer down but changed her mind. Something about the night made her feel that life was slipping away. Or maybe she simply took pity on him for driving all the way out here for nothing.

"Oh, what can it hurt?" she said, rising to her feet. "Just don't step on my toes."

I fancy you.

The words were still running through Kate's head while she crossed to the back of the barn to join Ruckus by the punch bowl.

Ladle in hand, he greeted her with a nod of his head. "Want some punch?"

She shook her head. "I just want to ask you something. People back east express themselves differently than they do here."

Ruckus dumped a ladleful of punch into a glass. "I reckon so."

"Here in Arizona, if someone uses the word *fancy,* what exactly does it mean?"

Ruckus arched an eyebrow. "What does it mean?"

She blushed. It did seem like a rather foolish question. "In Boston the word is used as an adjective to describe something ornamental such as a *fancy* dress. It's also an unflattering term for a loose woman. Sometimes it means simply that you like someone. As a friend, perhaps. Or that you want something. You could say that you fancy that hat, for example."

Ladle frozen in midair, Ruckus stared at her like she'd taken leave of her senses. "Far as I know *fancy* means the same here."

"That's . . . that's what I thought. I just wanted to make certain."

Smelling smoke, she glanced around and spotted a smoldering cigar butt next to a bale of hay. A flame shot up like an enormous tongue licking one side of the bundle. Without thinking Kate grabbed the punch bowl and dumped punch on the hay. The splash of liquid extinguished the fire and sent chunks of ice skidding across the floor.

"Oh dear, dear, dear." Aunt Bessie rushed up to the refreshment table, the train of her dress sweeping back and forth with a whishing sound. She stared at the charred bale.

"I'm sorry I made a mess," Kate said. Gratified that for once she'd acted quickly and without fear in the face of fire, she set the empty bowl on the table. Even Ruckus looked impressed by her quick action. Strangely enough, after all that she'd gone through these last few weeks, a simple little fire no longer terrified her.

"Nonsense. You saved the day." Picking up her train before a trickle of liquid reached it, Aunt Bessie gave an anxious glance around the barn, but few guests seemed to have noticed the near disaster. The musicians kept playing and couples continued to dance and Aunt Bessie let out a sigh of relief.

Mrs. White came rushing over. "I'll take care of it," she said, and immediately set to work mopping up the floor with a rag.

Aunt Bessie thanked her and turned to Kate. "Would you mind walking to the house and helping me fetch more ice?"

"I'd be happy to," Kate replied, grateful for a reason to escape the festivities. She followed the older woman outside and along a narrow path toward the small adobe house, a full moon lighting their way. She took in a breath of fresh air, hoping to clear her head.

Aunt Bessie stopped halfway between the barn and house to point to a couple a short distance away. "That's the marshal and Miss Watson. I've been nagging him for months to get to know her better and it looks as if he's finally taken my advice." With a sigh of satisfaction she continued along the path to the back entryway. "I'm so glad you could come tonight," she said, holding the door for Kate.

"It was very kind of you to go to all this trouble," Kate said.

"It was no trouble. I just hope the reward helps put Cactus Joe behind bars where he belongs."

They entered a small but tidy kitchen. A lit parlor lamp on the kitchen table cast a yellow glow over the cabinets and clay-tiled floor.

"Now where does Lula-Belle keep the ice pick? Ah, there it is." Aunt Bessie reached across the counter for the long pointed spike and metal bowl and opened the top of the wood icebox. Stabbing the frozen block with the pick, she chipped away.

"Would you like me to do that for you?"

Kate asked.

"No, that's quite all right. I just wanted the company." She glanced over her shoulder. "I hope you don't take anything Miss Chase says to heart."

"Of course not."

"She's got her sights set on Luke, but she's all wrong for him. She's far too flighty and Luke is more serious-minded. You know what I mean?"

Kate didn't want to talk about Luke but couldn't think of another subject. "I believe so."

"Marriage is hard enough without marrying the wrong person. He needs someone like you."

Irked by the woman's interfering ways, Kate bit back her annoyance. Aunt Bessie no doubt meant well. "I hope I haven't given you the wrong impression. I'm committed to the ranch and that leaves no room for . . . marriage."

"What a pity." Aunt Bessie gave the ice a hard jab. "Trust me, the ranch will do nothing for your toes."

"My toes?" Goodness! Had everyone in Cactus Patch read her book? Her cheeks flared and she waved her hand in front of her face to cool herself down. "I know you're just being kind but —"

"Nonsense. Kindness has nothing to do with it. I'm simply being practical. I've been married for forty years and know a good match when I see it. You and Luke are perfect for each other."

A chip of ice flew onto Kate's shirtwaist and she brushed it off. "Forty years is a long time. Were you ever concerned that your husband would . . . desert you?"

Aunt Bessie's hand froze in midair and she spun around to face Kate. The ghastly white color of her face made her purple dress look even more garish. "What do you mean by that? Did . . . did you hear something?"

Startled by the woman's reaction Kate quickly explained, "I didn't mean to imply . . . It's just that my father left when I was very young. It's hard for me to trust . . . anyone. A man."

Aunt Bessie's face softened even as it registered relief. "You poor, poor child. No wonder . . . But if you're thinking that Luke would take off, you couldn't be more wrong. Why, he's as faithful as an old hound. And trustworthy too. He's the only one in town knows how to open every safe, even the one at the bank. That's because those mail-order safes never work right and Luke has had to repair them all. But no one worries about their money because Luke is an honest, upstanding Christian."

Aunt Bessie turned back to the icebox and continued stabbing at the frozen block. She talked nonstop about the couples she had matched over the years. "Twenty-three couples," she said with a note of pride. "And in all that time I only made one error. Although I still think the marriage would have worked had she not shot her husband."

Kate listened politely, or at least tried to, but her mind kept wandering to something Aunt Bessie had said earlier. *"Faithful as an old hound. And trustworthy. Honest."* Hadn't she once used words to that effect to describe Brandon, the hero in her novel? Was it possible for a real flesh-and-blood man to possess such qualities? If only that were true . . .

Luke led Miss Chase around the dance floor but he was hardly aware of her. He was as polite and friendly as he knew how, but she wasn't the one he wanted in his arms. He counted the moments until the music stopped and he could take his leave.

He'd told Kate how he felt and she stared at him like . . . like he'd said nothing, like he hadn't poured out his heart.

Miss Chase's constant chatter and high-pitched laughter ground on his nerves, but that was the least of it.

What a fool to think he had a chance with someone like Kate. A college-educated woman. A *writer*. She'd done everything in her power to push him away, to tell him she wasn't interested. And yet . . . at times she looked at him with those big blue eyes and he swore she felt what he felt, wanted what he wanted. Fancied him every bit as much as he fancied her.

"So what do you think, Lukey?" Miss Chase said with a flirtatious smile.

He bit back his irritation. "What do I think about what?"

She pushed her lips out in a pout. "What is wrong with you tonight? You seem so . . . distant."

"Sorry. I have a lot on my mind." But even as he apologized to Miss Chase, his gaze swept from one end of the barn to the other. Where was Kate? Had she left? Skedaddled?

"You two-timing, double-crossing, bull-headed rat!"

Startled by his uncle's angry voice, Luke pulled his arms away from his dance partner and spun around. "What the . . ."

Uncle Sam and the postmaster, Jeb Parker, stood glaring at each other in the middle of the dance floor, fists clenched.

Without so much as taking his leave, Luke left his dance partner's side and hurried to his uncle.

"You ain't got no right to make such accusations," the postmaster said. A pasty-faced man with a long, lean face anchored by a goatee, he towered over Uncle Sam's five-foot-five height by a good six inches. If height didn't intimidate his uncle, the look on Parker's face should have.

"I got every right in the world," his uncle said, showing no sign of backing down.

"Oh yeah?"

"Yeah!"

The music stopped and all eyes turned to the two men.

Parker pulled back his fist and Luke quickly stepped in front of his uncle. Things were out of hand and he meant to put a stop to it.

"Now see here, both of —"

Parker's fist shot out in a high arc, catching Luke on the jaw and snapping his head back. Ears buzzing from the blow, Luke saw stars. He didn't want to fight, but the older man kept coming, his hand shooting toward Luke's throat.

Luke grabbed Parker's arm before it reached its target and twisted it around his back.

"Calm down," Luke cajoled.

He released Parker — big mistake. The man came at Luke with both arms flailing. Luke ducked the first blow, but the second one bounced off his nose.

Somehow Luke managed to wrap his arms around Parker, pinning his fists to his sides. Parker kicked Luke in the shins and the two fell to the floor, Parker's contorted face inches away from his.

Michael surprised Luke by rushing to his defense. Unfortunately, this signaled others to join in the fray. Fists flew in every direction and grunts and groans filled the air. Some men were gallant enough to escort their dance partners to safety before throwing a punch. Most, however, chose to let the women fend for themselves.

Uncle Sam grabbed hold of Parker's leg and tried to drag him away from Luke. He might have succeeded had Aunt Bessie not intervened. She grabbed Uncle Sam by the ear and pulled him out of harm's way with a thorough tongue-lashing.

"Shame on you, Samuel!" she scolded. "You're nothing but an old fool."

By the time Marshal Morris was able to instill order, chairs and tables had been overturned, and some combatants had even taken the fight outside.

The marshal grabbed Luke by the collar. "You're going to jail. All of you!"

Luke staggered to his feet, hand on his sore jaw. That's when he saw Kate watching, disapproval written all over her face. He wanted to go to her, explain, but the marshal had already handcuffed him to Parker and was leading the two of them away.

CHAPTER 30

Bessie's feet were killing her. She wanted to go home in the worst possible way and kick off her toe-pinching shoes. The dance had ended abruptly and all because of that unfortunate fight. If only she hadn't left the barn to fetch more ice from the house. All she wanted was to talk to Kate alone and now look what happened.

It was as much the marshal's fault as it was her own. Had he not been outside with Miss Watson he could have stepped in before things got out of hand.

What was Luke thinking? Getting his uncle involved in a fight, of all things. Sam could have been seriously hurt. And where was the fool man? How long could it possibly take to bail their nephew out of jail?

She should have accepted Murphy's offer to drive her home. But no, thoughtful woman that she was, she stayed to apologize to the last departing guests and make certain her sister's barn was left as she found it.

What a dreadful mess, food and decorations scattered everywhere. It took forever to clean it up.

She groaned. Not only did her feet hurt but also her head. What she wouldn't give for a cheroot. If only she hadn't promised Luke to give up her smoking habit. Sometimes a woman needed to blow off steam or, in this case, smoke. God forgive her.

She swiped a strand of hair away from her face. The night had not been a complete disaster, but close enough. She'd collected a healthy amount of reward money. No complaints there. Surely it would only be a matter of time before Cactus Joe was captured and put under lock and key. But she failed miserably in her plan to bring Kate and Luke together, thanks to that flirtatious hussy Miss Chase.

Luke getting into a fight didn't help. Not only did Kate look positively devastated, she took off like her hair was on fire. Bessie shook with irritation. Just wait till she got her hands on her errant nephew.

Just as upsetting, she had failed to identify the *other* woman and she had no one to blame but herself. She never should have gone to all the bother of looking so absolutely marvelous, for it only defeated her purposes. Instead of looking at the *other* woman, Sam hadn't been able to take his eyes off her all night. Had she not been so intent on finding out the name of his love interest, Bessie would have enjoyed his undivided attention.

The purple taffeta dress brought out all her best features. Although, to be perfectly honest, she doubted the dress color was responsible for Sam's admiring glances as much as the plunging neckline.

The youthful pink glow of her skin was no doubt caused by her tight, pinching corset, but it had been worth every excruciating moment just to see the look on Sam's face when he first caught sight of her.

Sam certainly wasn't himself. He acted as nervous as a long-tailed cat in a room full of rocking chairs. Of course, wearing a new shirt and bow tie probably explained some of his discomfort, but not all. He'd even donned those brown leather boots she had given him last Christmas and that he claimed hurt his feet.

If his odd behavior in recent weeks hadn't already roused her suspicions, the way he doted on her at the dance surely would have. Waiting on her hand and foot. Plying her with glasses of lemonade and plates piled high with all her favorite desserts.

He hadn't even waited on her all those years ago when she broke her leg. Such solicitous behavior could only be a sign of guilt. Had to be. No other explanation made sense.

Mercy, did her heart ever pound when he took her in his arms on the dance floor. It gave her goose bumps just to think about it. Normally, nothing would please her more, but not now. Not with his motives in question.

So who was she? Certainly not widow White. Sam would never act as gauche as to eye a woman whose husband had been in the grave for a mere six months.

But who else was there? Certainly not that awful Mrs. Spinnaker who couldn't say a kind word about anyone. One by one she considered every woman she could think of and came up empty.

She couldn't imagine it was any of the numerous women she knew at church or her quilting bee. None could match her in housekeeping skills, and certainly not in cooking.

That meant it had to be someone younger, and this scared the life out of her. There simply was no way she could compete with youth. Not even in her purple gown.

■ ■ ■ ■

It was after two in the morning and still
Kate couldn't sleep. The bedding tied in
hopeless knots from all the twisting and
turning, she finally gave up. She climbed
out of bed and paced the floor. She was
consumed with thoughts of Luke — the two
sides of him — the gentle, caring side that
almost had her fooled, the dark, angry side
confirming her opinion that no man could
be trusted.

He may be faithful as an old dog, but
obviously he had another side. Picking on
an old man like that. What was he thinking?
The postmaster could have been seriously
injured.

Sickened by the memory of Luke fighting,
his nose bloodied and face dark, she flung
herself across the bed. Her stomach churned
in protest as she traveled back in time to
another night, another fight — the night she
started a fire to save her mama from the
pounding of brutal fists.

As much as she hated comparing Luke to
the men in her past, experience taught her
that it was man's nature to be violent.
Luke's dark side didn't surprise her, but it
was still a crushing blow. She wanted so

much to believe he was unlike other men, to know that the gentleness and concern he'd shown her were real and not merely a guise covering a sinister nature.

She hated to admit it even to herself, but she'd been so close — so very close — to believing in him, trusting him. What a fool! What an utter, utter fool. Had she not learned anything in all her years? A handsome man tells her he fancies her and she practically loses her head. What was wrong with her?

Her heart belonged to the ranch. It was what she'd wanted and worked for these last couple of months. It was in her blood and she was convinced it was what she was born to do.

So why the confusion? Why did Luke affect her so?

She grabbed a pillow off the bed and tossed it across the room. Going to that dance had been a mistake. Any and all future social invitations would be politely but firmly declined. Certainly she would never allow herself to be in Luke's arms again.

The moment she finished Cactus Joe's book, she would hang up her pen, this time for good. Writing his story was like lifting a rock and seeing her childhood with new clarity. His mother's illness made her realize that her own mother had been ill, too, not of the flesh, but of the spirit. It was easier to stay angry at a weak person, but when illness was involved — even one exacerbated by alcohol — feelings became more complicated. She no longer knew how she felt about her mother.

That's why completing Cactus Joe's story was so important to her — she didn't know what she would discover next about her own past. Would it help her understand why her father left? Why her mother drank? Help her come to terms with her parents' flaws, maybe even to the point of forgiveness? Maybe not, but at least it gave her a place to dump her bottled-up feelings.

The ranch required every bit of energy she had and then some. Her painful past had become a distraction and she needed to put it to rest. It was time to wipe the slate clean. Her future depended on it. Perhaps taming the past would even help to resolve her confusion over Luke.

With this thought in mind, she quietly left her room. Creeping downstairs, she felt her way in the dark. She wouldn't write for long, just an hour or so. She couldn't sleep anyway, so what could it hurt? A rush of excitement raced through her as she anticipated the thrill of running her fingers over the Remington typing machine again and writing another chapter.

Having reconstructed the chapters written at Cactus Joe's cabin she would now have to depend on her creative skills to write the rest. That meant digging deeper into her own childhood. Perhaps even uncovering long-buried memories.

Reaching Miss Walker's office, she lit the parlor lamp and turned to the desk.

The typewriter was gone! Shocked, she stood perfectly still for several moments before bursting into tears and running back to her room.

Luke groaned. It wasn't a hangover, but it sure did feel like one. Or at least what he imagined a hangover felt like. His head pounded, his jaw was sore, and one eye was swollen shut. Even Homer couldn't bring him out of his misery, though the poor dog did everything but dance on his hind legs trying to get Luke's attention.

"Woof!"

"You're a dog of few words. Let's keep it that way."

"Woof, woof!"

"Okay, I get the message," Luke said at last. Homer could be such a nuisance at times. He rose from his stool and reached for the jar of jerky. He tossed a piece on the floor. Homer barked and wouldn't stop until Luke tossed him another piece. Satisfied at last, the dog picked up both pieces and ran outside, presumably to share the meat with his lady friend.

Alone, Luke surveyed the work stacked up on his workbench. What he needed was a day off. He needed to go back to bed. Maybe this time he'd actually sleep. Then again, maybe not.

For some reason everyone blamed him for the fight. Certainly his aunt did. If spending half the night in jail wasn't bad enough, he'd had to listen to her read him the riot act. Aunt Bessie had apparently gone to the house to fetch something and had missed the start of the fight. She had no idea what started it and he had no intention of saying anything about his uncle's suspicions. Not yet, anyway.

Then there was Kate. He would never forget the look on her face as the marshal dragged him away. Obviously she blamed him. The memory didn't just make his head throb — it felt ready to explode.

A sad-looking group gathered at dawn that Monday for the usual morning prayer. O.T.

and Ruckus were the only two men not sporting a black eye or bruised chin.

Ruckus whipped off his hat and held it to his chest. "Dear heavenly Father, send rain."

The others took off, although with less energy than usual, and Kate fell in step by Ruckus's side. "Rain? Is that all you ever think about?"

She was in a bad mood and didn't care who knew it. She'd had little if any sleep, but that wasn't the only reason for her ill temper. For two days she had tried to talk to Miss Walker about the missing typewriter, but the woman had been impossible to track down.

"What about your men? Don't they deserve a prayer?"

Ruckus stopped in his tracks, his eyes wide with surprise. "I did pray for them. I always pray for them."

"You prayed for rain," she argued. "Same as always." Oh, she really was in a foul mood.

Fortunately, Ruckus didn't seem to take offense. "Rain is just another word for blessings," he said. "It grows, it quenches, and it heals."

"You talk in riddles," she snapped.

He laughed at her expression. "Us western folks are easy to understand. You ought to know that by now. We may not always say what we mean but we always mean what we say."

When she failed to appreciate his humor, he eyed her from beneath a creased forehead. "What's the matter with you today? You look madder than a wet rooster."

She bit her lip and sighed. She felt guilty for taking out her bad mood on him. "I could use some of God's blessings myself right now."

"Yeah, and those horses could use some fresh hay. Nothing cures what ails you faster than work. Now get to work." He gave her a cockeyed look. "So what are you waiting for?"

"A Bible quote," she said.

"I gave you one. Exodus 5:18. It says *get to work.*"

Kate groaned. She should have known. Ruckus really did have a Bible verse for every occasion.

During the next hour she helped unload two wagons of hay. Although still early, it was already blazing hot and her clothes clung to her body. After the empty wagons left to be reloaded, she walked over to the windmill and drenched herself with water.

Someone rode up on a black-and-white pinto, an Indian. Her heart pounding nervously, she glanced around. Ruckus had disappeared into the barn. Though he was still within earshot, she would have felt a whole lot better had he been visible. Since her kidnapping, strangers made her nervous, even ones she knew couldn't possibly be Cactus Joe in disguise.

The Indian reared his horse in front of her and lifted an arm, palm outward, to show her he meant no harm. He pointed to the water tank and she nodded.

He slid off the bare back of the pinto, and while the horse drank from the trough, he cupped his hands and helped himself to water from the tank.

Never having met an Indian face-to-face, she couldn't help but stare. He seemed normal and nothing like the savages she'd read about in Boston's newspaper. Nor was he like the wild tomahawk-wielding Indians she'd written about in her novels who wore breechcloths and war paint and said "How."

Dressed in an odd combination of Indian and white man's clothes, he wore moccasins, Levi pants, and a poncho-style shirt. Dark skin stretched over high cheekbones, his black glossy hair arranged in a figure eight bun with a colorful band across his forehead.

He wiped his mouth dry with the back of

his hand and regarded her with intelligent brown eyes. She guessed he was in his late twenties or early thirties.

"I came to see Miss Walker," he said. He spoke good English, pronouncing each word precisely.

"Miss Walker is out on the range," she said. "May I help you?"

"Tell her Sky Runner send gratitude." Hand on his chest he inclined his head slightly as he spoke.

Sky Runner. Did Indians have barn names too? And how did he come to be called such an intriguing name? "You want to thank her?"

He gave a single nod of his head. "She give family two goats, chickens, and milk cow." He stuck out his chest as if showing off a medal. "Now we have farm."

"Miss Walker did that?"

He nodded again and thumped his broad chest with his fist. "You tell her Sky Runner heart big with gratitude."

"I'll tell her," Kate promised.

Thanking her, he mounted his horse and rode away so quickly, his horse's hooves barely seemed to touch the ground.

Ruckus walked out of the barn, pitchfork in hand. "We have company?" he called.

"Yes," she hollered back as she hurried

across the yard to join him. "Do you know a man named Sky Runner?"

Ruckus stood his pitchfork against the wall. "Yep. He's part Navajo. Lives north of here. Was that him?"

She nodded. "Did you know that Miss Walker helped him start a farm?"

" 'Course I knew it. I helped ready the animals myself." He studied her. "Don't look so surprised."

"It just seems like a kind thing to do."

"The boss lady does a lot of kind things. Not too many people know it. That's how she wants it."

Kate recalled the steer and other animals carted away her first day at the ranch. Now she knew why José had been so secretive.

"Every year the boss lady picks out a family or two to help. She gave my daughter a heifer for a wedding present. That's so my daughter and her new husband could start their own ranch. It's a Last Chance tradition and goes way back to when Miz Walker's ma received a steer from an Englishman."

"Miss Walker told me about that. She said her mother saved the man's life."

"That's what I heard. One heifer and now look what we have." He gestured with his arm. "Like the Good Book says, cast your bread upon the waters and it'll come galloping back with a whole gang."

Kate laughed, her earlier bad mood forgotten. "I expect it's a whole lot easier to cast bread than a steer."

His mouth twisted wryly. "I reckon you'll find out once you take over the ranch."

Once she took over? Was that a vote of confidence? Sure did sound that way.

She stared out over the land. She could no longer see Sky Runner, but the mirage of a lake shimmered in the distance.

"Nothing is what it seems," she said. Miss Walker certainly wasn't. Nor, for that matter, was Luke. He seemed honest and kind, but she now knew he also had another side.

"That's the way God planned it," Ruckus said. "It forces us to give the world — and each other — a closer look-see."

Chapter 31

Five days after the barn dance, Bessie found a box on the kitchen table. It was a plain white box wrapped with a red ribbon and tied with a big fat bow. A card read, *A good old gal if there ever was one. Always, Sam.*

Old gal? Is that what he thought of her? And why was he giving her a present? Her birthday and Christmas were still months away. That could only mean one thing. Sam was still acting out of guilt.

She quickly pulled off the ribbon and opened the box. It was a pudding pan that matched the skillet and saucepan that Sam had previously given her. Tears sprang to her eyes. After the dance, she had almost convinced herself that Sam had lost interest in the other woman, but this latest enamelware gift proved her wrong.

Mercy, what would be next? A matching teakettle? Anger soon replaced her hurt. After giving Sam the best years of her life, this was how he treated her.

She slammed the pan back into the box, walked into the kitchen, gathered up her skillet and saucepan, and dropped the whole kit and caboodle into the trash. Brushing her hands together, she threw back her shoulders. She would not play second fiddle to some husband-stealing tramp. She had her pride. Granted, she didn't have much left at this point, but what little she did have she intended to keep.

She stormed through the house and into the bedroom. Pulling a battered valise out of the closet, she stuffed it full of her old clothes. She left her new satin unmentionables behind, for all the good they'd done her.

She would not spend another moment under the same roof with that two-timing husband of hers.

In no time at all, she finished packing and harnessed the horse to the wagon. Lula-Belle pulled up in her buggy just as Bessie drove away.

"Where are you going?" Lula-Belle called.

"I'm leaving Sam. I'm going to Marion's." Their older widowed sister lived in Tucson.

Lula-Belle's eyes grew as wide as the discarded pudding pan, but Bessie had no time to argue with her or spell everything out.

Just then Sam returned from his daily walk. He called to her but Bessie drove right by him like he didn't exist.

She followed the stagecoach road to Tucson, which cut through miles of desert. She would have to spend the night at Mescal, of course, and maybe even a night at Wilmot. She would also have to telegraph Marion to let her know she was coming.

It was hot, but Bessie was too angry and hurt to give it much mind. Forty years she'd given that man. Forty of the best years of her life. She had washed and cleaned and cooked for him. Laughed at his dreadful jokes. Listened to his endless war stories. Picked up after him. And what did she have to show for it? A pudding pan!

So deep were her thoughts that it took her awhile to notice she was being followed. Thinking it was her fool sister, she slowed down, but after spotting Sam in the driver's seat of her sister's buggy, Bessie slapped the reins against her horse's rump, forcing the startled animal to pick up speed.

A few miles later she glanced back, but Sam was still on her tail. "Gid-up!" she yelled. She had nothing to say to him, and at that moment she didn't care if she ever saw him again. God help her.

The road rose over a hill, twisting and turning around outcrops of huge boulders. She didn't chance looking back until she reached the summit. Sam had apparently given up the chase for there was no sign of him. She rested her horse in the shade and let him drink from a natural spring. She dipped her handkerchief in the water and mopped the sweat off her forehead.

Ha! Give up, did he? He chased her long enough to appease his conscience, but he obviously had no intention or interest in catching up with her. Not that she cared. Of course she didn't care. Why would she? After the way he treated her. Still, the least he could have done was try a little harder to catch her. After all the years she'd given him, he could have *acted* like he didn't want her to leave.

She hoisted her skirt and climbed on the rocks to view the road below. In the far distance the eastbound train from Tucson looked like a metal snake, but there was no sign of Sam. Strange. If he wasn't on the way home and he wasn't on the road behind her, then where in tarnation was he?

Worried now, she walked back until she could see the road leading up to where she stood. Nothing. Heart pounding, she ran to her wagon, turned it around, and started back down to the valley below. She then spotted a spinning wheel off the side of the road.

Crying out in alarm, she yanked on the hand brake of her wagon and jumped to the ground. Sam was sprawled in a ditch a few feet from the overturned buggy. Lula-Belle's horse, Jordan, was on his side, squirming. Spotting Bessie, he let out a frantic whinny.

Ignoring the horse, Bessie slid down the embankment and rushed to Sam's side.

"Are you all right?"

He grimaced. "It's just my leg. Take care of Jordan."

"But —" Torn between seeing to Sam and helping the horse, Bessie tried to think what to do.

"I'm fine." Sam sounded more annoyed at himself than hurt. "I should have watched where I was going."

She gave Sam's leg a worried look before scampering toward the distressed animal. "You're all right," she said soothingly, stroking Jordan's neck.

Once she got the gelding to calm down, she unbuckled the back strap and undid the traces. She moved slowly so as not to startle the fallen animal.

"Be careful," Sam called. "I don't want

you getting yourself hurt."

Touched by his concern, she stepped back as the horse struggled to his feet. This was the dangerous part. The horse could easily stomp on her with flailing hooves. His eyes looked wild, but fortunately he showed no sign of injury. She led him out of the ditch and tied him to the overturned wagon before returning to Sam's side.

"Let me look at your leg."

"It's just a twisted ankle," he said.

She shook her head. "You're an old fool."

He stared at her from beneath knitted eyebrows. "I'm a fool? What about you? You're the one who's all hung up on that Parker fella."

Bessie sat back on her heels. "What are you talkin' about? What about Parker?"

"Don't look so innocent," he charged. "I know you've been seeing him on the sly."

Shocked by his accusation, it took her a moment to gather her thoughts. "Is that what the fight was about?"

Sam had refused to tell her what caused the fight that ruined the dance, and her annoying nephew was equally closemouthed.

"I couldn't help myself. Knowing that you and him was dilly dallying behind my back made me see red."

Bessie's temper snapped. How dare he try

to wiggle out of this one by placing the blame on her! "Don't you go accusin' me of fooling around when you're the one lolly-gagging with some other woman."

Sam's eyes widened in astonishment. "What are you talkin' about? Lollygagging?"

"You don't think I know why you bought me that pudding pan? It's to ease your guilty conscience, that's why. Just like you bought that skillet forty years ago after making eyes at that Mexican woman."

He frowned. "You knew about that?"

"Yes, I knew about that."

"I was a young fool back then. But I swear to you I've never looked at another woman since." He shook his head. "And I sure didn't expect you to go lookin' at another man."

Bessie stared at him. He actually seemed to believe his own ridiculous accusations. "Why in the world would you think such a thing?"

"You're the one who's been acting all strange. Wearing those slippery undergarments and fancy dresses cut down to your knees."

"I did that for you. I . . . eh . . . have it on good authority that men like silky things." She didn't want to admit she'd read one of Kate's dime novels.

"For me? You mean you and Parker ain't
—"

"Can't stand the man. Why, the last time I mailed a letter, he tried to overcharge me."

A smile as wide as the Grand Canyon suffused Sam's face. "I can't tell you how happy it makes me to hear you say that. I don't need you to wear no fancy garments. I like you just the way you are. I love you, Bessie Sue, and there's no other woman I'd rather be with."

"You . . . you still love me," she stammered. "After all this time?"

"Of course I love you. Do you think I'd waste my money on pots and pans if I didn't?"

"Oh." Tears sprang to her eyes and his face turned all buttery.

"Come here," he said and held out his arms. She melted next to him and he groaned in pain. "Are you all right?" she asked anxiously.

"I'm fine," he said. "Just be careful of my shoulder and leg and arms and . . ."

She leaned over and kissed him square on the mouth. Fortunately there was nothing wrong with his lips. Not one single thing.

Mercy. Her body didn't just tingle. It shivered and quivered like Lula-Belle's homemade jelly, all the way down to her very toes.

CHAPTER 32

Luke was pleasantly surprised to find Aunt Bessie and Uncle Sam acting like a couple of lovebirds on Sunday. Good news for them, bad news for him.

Now that his aunt had worked out her problems with Uncle Sam, she obviously planned to devote all her energy to finding wives for her nephews. Since Michael wasn't able to get away from the ranch because of some windmill problem, she apparently intended to zero in on Luke. No sooner had the five of them, including both aunts and uncles, sat down to noon dinner than she started.

"So have you seen Miss Tenney since the barn dance?" she asked, reaching for a bowl of fluffy white potatoes.

"No, I haven't," Luke replied, surprised at the sharpness of his voice. He stabbed at a piece of roast beef and passed the platter to Uncle Murphy. He hadn't meant to snap at his aunt. For all her meddling, she meant well. By way of apology he gave her a sheepish smile.

"I'm happy to see the two of you are getting along," he said in an effort to get her mind off Kate.

It had cost his uncle a swollen ankle, cracked rib, dislocated shoulder, and some mean-looking bruises, but he claimed it was a small price to pay for saving his marriage.

Aunt Lula-Belle scooped a mound of potatoes onto her plate and passed the dish to Luke. "It was that book that started all the trouble."

Aunt Bessie gave her sister a meaningful look. "Now, Lula-Belle —"

Lula-Belle glared back at her. "Well, it was."

Luke shoveled up a spoonful of potatoes and looked from one aunt to the other. "What book?"

Lula-Belle ignored her sister's warning. "The book that Miss Tenney wrote. Bessie read it." She stuck up her nose and shuddered in distaste. "Every . . . single . . . word."

Luke's hand froze halfway to his plate. He had no idea Aunt Bessie read anything Kate had written. Since when had his aunt been interested in philosophy? Luke could hardly contain his curiosity. Not only was he anxious to hear more about Kate's books, he also wanted to know what was behind the dagger looks flying back and forth between his two aunts.

He turned his gaze to Aunt Bessie. "I . . . I thought she wrote for Greeks or monks or something."

"Oh no," Aunt Bessie exclaimed, glaring at her sister. "The book is in English."

Aunt Lula-Belle leaned forward, her tight curls bouncing up and down like little metal springs. "And you won't find Miss Tenney's book in a monastery. At least I hope not. Any monk reading such goings-on would be shocked into breaking his vow of silence. She writes *dime* novels."

Luke stared at his aunt in astonishment. Dime novels? Kate was so reluctant to talk about her writing, he assumed she wrote literary stuff. It never occurred to him that she wrote what some people called *cheap* fiction. Still couldn't believe it.

"Are you sure?" he asked.

"Quite sure," Lula-Belle said. She lowered her voice and glanced around as if checking for eavesdroppers. "And one of them was banned in Boston."

His eyes widened. "Did you say banned?"

Lula-Belle gave a righteous nod. "Yes,

banned. For being morally decadent." She gestured toward her sister. "Tell him, Bessie."

Bessie threw up her hands. "Mercy, what difference does it make? The poor girl was probably only trying to support herself. She's not writing them now. As for being morally decadent — that's a bunch of hogwash." She leveled her gaze at Luke. "If someone doesn't do something, she'll throw her life away on a ranch. Is that what you want?"

"It's her choice," Luke muttered. Suddenly aware he still held the serving spoon, he jammed it back into the potatoes and passed the bowl to Uncle Murphy.

He couldn't get over the fact that Kate wrote dime novels. He never would have guessed it. Not with all that talk about Greek philosophers.

Of course he'd never read one of them himself, but others, including his aunt, called the books trash. And wasn't Bill Sawyer's boy Davey recently expelled from school for reading one?

"So what do you think, Luke?" Aunt Bessie asked.

Snapping out of his thoughts, Luke looked up. "I'm sorry . . ."

"I said, do you think Miss Tenney should

411

waste her life on a ranch?"

Sam rolled his eyes and adjusted the arm still in a sling. "Drat, Bessie. Why do you keep harping on this? What the girl does is nobody's business. Pass the butter."

Lula-Belle wrinkled her nose and tugged on her shawl. "Of course it's our business. Any lady friend of Luke's is our business."

Sam took the butter dish from Lula-Belle with his one good arm. "Miss Tenney is your *lady* friend?"

Luke felt heat rise up his neck. "Not the way Aunt Lula-Belle means," Luke stammered. Since both aunts and uncles were staring at him, he added, "She's a college-educated woman and I'm . . . I'm just a smithy."

"Nonsense," Uncle Sam said. "There's no such thing as *just* a smithy."

"And no woman is really educated until she marries," Aunt Bessie added.

"Now, Bessie, don't push the boy," Uncle Sam said.

"Somebody's got to," Aunt Bessie said. "Just because she uses big words is no reason not to follow your heart."

Uncle Murphy, who usually didn't speak while eating, made a guttural sound. "Big words are a waste of everybody's time. It

412

takes longer to say 'em and longer to hear 'em."

"I agree," Aunt Lula-Belle said. "Just because you can talk like Webster's dictionary doesn't mean you should."

Aunt Bessie poured gravy over her roast beef but she looked at Luke. "Fortunately for us, God gave love a language of its own and it's a language known by every heart."

She slammed the gravy bowl on the table, splashing the tablecloth with brown spots, and much to Luke's relief, the conversation turned to Utah's recent statehood. Arizona was one of only two territories on the continental US — excluding Indian Territory — that was not a state, and it was a sore point with his uncles.

"They say we have to become Americanized before we can become a state. What in tarnation is that supposed to mean?" Uncle Murphy grumbled.

"For one thing it means we can't use silver as our legal currency," Sam explained. "The US insists we use gold and I don't see that happenin'."

For the most part Luke ignored the discussion. The shock of learning that Kate wrote dime novels had worn off, only to be replaced by perhaps an even more surprising thought. If she did, indeed, write what were commonly called potboilers, she might even be broad-minded enough to give a lowly smithy like himself a chance. If only he could figure out how to break down the barriers between them.

He could see her in his head as clearly as if she were in the same room with him. Without realizing it he had memorized her every feature, memorized the way her lashes curled, the pretty shape of her full mouth that tasted as good as it looked, memorized even the way her nose turned slightly upward.

He only wished he could forget the horrified look in her eyes following the fight at the dance. The closed expression when he last tried to talk to her.

He was a simple man. He didn't really understand how women thought or how that man and woman stuff was supposed to work. But there was one thing he did know; he sure had made a mess out of things, and if he didn't think of something fast, he would lose Kate for good.

Kate awoke with a nervous knot in her stomach. It was hard to believe that four months had passed so quickly.

It was still dark overhead when she stepped onto the balcony, but dawn had

414

broken and a thin silver line marked the eastern horizon.

Today was the day she would officially become the heiress to the Last Chance Ranch. A thrill of excitement shot through her. Of course she still had much to learn, but one day this would all be hers. Now when she gazed across the desert, she no longer saw barren land. She saw ruggedness, endurance, vastness. Everything from the smallest insect to the largest plant knew to protect itself from the harsh land, and for that reason, she saw herself.

She had a long way to go, but she was determined to secure her future as a respectable cattlewoman. Never again would she be looked upon with pity.

"You and the land must become one. Its pulse will be your pulse, its heart yours. It will require everything you have to give — and then some. No man alive can compete with such a demanding lover."

She smiled. At last she understood the power of those words. To think she'd almost thrown it away on Luke Adams. "Trust me," he'd said, but it wasn't him she didn't trust as much as her own traitorous heart. She couldn't deny her attraction to him, and like a foolish schoolgirl she'd been tempted to give in to her feelings. But like the mighty saguaro, she stood firm even while bending. And once she signed the spinster pact, she would never again be tempted by a man, not even one as handsome as Luke. She counted on it.

Luke looked up from his workbench as his brother walked into the shop, then did a double take. He dropped his hammer onto the workbench and turned, arms folded across his middle.

It was Michael, all right, though he never would have guessed it from appearances. Michael's normal scraggly beard was gone and his hair was neatly combed. And was that a shine on his well-worn boots?

Yep, it was Michael all right. Though if it hadn't been for the ever-present pencil sticking out of his shirt pocket, Luke would have sworn it was a stranger.

"You look mighty spiffy today," Luke said. He scratched the back of his head, not sure what to make of his brother. "I heard Miss Walker hired someone to help out with windmill maintenance."

Michael nodded. "Yep, but Miss Walker won't let anyone shoe her horses but me."

Luke nodded. "I don't blame her." He'd taught Michael well in that regard.

"Miss Tenney said if I worked hard at the

ranch and minded my p's and q's, she would help me with my writing."

Luke let his arms drop to his sides. "Yes, I know. She told me."

"*She* likes my writing and thinks I have talent."

Luke felt a twist of guilt. He couldn't remember a time that Michael didn't carry a notebook with him. He was always scribbling away, even as a kid. And if he wasn't writing, his head was in a book.

Luke had once sneaked a peek at something Michael had written — a poem. With only a rudimentary reading ability, Luke couldn't make hide or tail out of what it said. If Kate thought his little brother had talent, who was he to argue with her? Sooner or later Michael would figure out the futility of trying to earn a living from writing. Maybe then he'd have a more favorable regard for blacksmithing.

"So what brings you to town?" Luke asked. "Aren't you supposed to be working?"

"O.T. gave me the morning off." Michael laid a book on the workbench. "For you."

Surprised that his brother would give him a book, Luke glanced at the thick tome. "*Webster's International Dictionary of the English Language?*"

Michael shrugged. "You said you wanted to improve your vocabulary." He stuck his hand in his trouser pocket and pulled out a pendant on a gold chain. "Would you have time to repair this? The clasp is broken."

Luke took the pendant from Michael's outstretched hand and examined it. "This was Ma's." It was a platinum lace pendant that held a single white pearl.

Michael nodded. "I want to give it to Miss Tenney."

Luke narrowed his eyes. Ma had died in childbirth, so naturally Michael had no memory of her. Still, Michael's plan to give away something of Ma's surprised him.

"Why?" Surely Luke wasn't thinking of courting Kate. He stared at his brother in alarm, the thought crushing him like a boulder.

"It's a big day for her. Today she becomes the official heiress to the Last Chance Ranch."

"Already?" Had it really been four months since Kate came to town?

"That's right. She's gonna sign the papers this afternoon. I heard the boss lady is going to make her sign some sort of pact not to get married."

Luke took a quick breath. This was the first he'd heard of such a thing. He shook his head in disbelief. He knew Miss Walker well enough to know she'd insist upon the signing of a legal agreement before turning her property over to Kate. But a contract not to get married? What sense did that make?

"Me and the boys planned a get-together for her and I thought it would be nice to give her a little something. You know, to show how much I appreciate her help with my writing and . . ."

Michael said more, but Luke had traveled back in time to the memory of Kate's sweet lips.

"God gave love a language of its own and it's a language known by every heart." That was easy for Aunt Bessie to say, but when he poured out his heart to Kate and told her he fancied her, it didn't do him the least bit of good.

"So what do you say? Can you fix it?"

Luke blinked. "What?"

Michael gave him an odd look. "The necklace. Can you fix it?"

Luke stared down at the chain in his hand. "I have to fix it," he said. He didn't know how or even if he could, but he had to find a way. Or die trying.

CHAPTER 33

"It's not safe, you must go," she whispered with feverish haste. Seemingly oblivious to the dangers that could befall him, he kissed her soundly on the lips before slipping away into the wretched darkness.

Kate was shocked when Luke galloped up on his horse. He was the last person she expected to see — wanted to see. She had stepped outside to get some fresh air before facing Miss Walker and all those legal papers. Already the banker had arrived to serve as witness, along with a man she guessed was Miss Walker's lawyer.

Luke dismounted, wrapped the reins around a hitching post, and strode up to her like a soldier marching to war. He looked serious, but no less handsome, and her stomach fluttered nervously even as she protested his presence. She had nothing more to say to him.

"W-What are you doing here?" she stammered. Hadn't she made her position clear?

He pushed his leather hat back, a strand of brown hair sweeping across his forehead. "Michael said you were about to sign papers forbidding you to marry."

Hearing the words from him made them sound so final. Her breath caught in her throat but she managed to nod.

"Why?" He frowned. "Why would you do such a thing? Why would you throw away your life like that?" He moved closer and she backed away.

"I'm not throwing away my life. I love it here." And she'd worked hard to get to this point. "And one day this will all be mine."

He continued to advance and she moved back, matching him step by step in an odd sort of dance. "You still didn't answer my question. Why would you do such a thing?"

He backed her all the way to the side of the barn, allowing her no room to escape, and panic gushed inside. "I told you."

He stopped inches away from her. "I've heard a lot of dumb things in my life, but this has got to be the dumbest."

"It's not dumb." She lifted her chin in defiance. "Running a ranch is an honorable profession."

"So is teaching or writing." In a quieter

voice he added, "So is marriage."

Her stomach clenched tight. "Marriage?"

He shrugged. "Most women want to get married. Why don't you?"

"Why is that any of your concern?" she asked. "Will you tell me that?"

He looked genuinely puzzled. "I just hate to see someone throw their life away on a piece of land."

"This is not just a piece of land. It's the history of a family and I'll be part of it. I'll be helping to create a legacy."

He studied her. "I can't believe you would settle for so little."

Little? Her temper snapped. "You know nothing about me or what I want."

"I know you're a writer," he said.

"The last book I wrote was banned. Did you know that? Banned!"

"So you decided to become a rancher and sign some stupid pact not to get married?" He scratched his head. "That don't make a lick of sense."

"It doesn't have to make sense. It's what I want to do."

A muscle quivered at his jaw. "Why, Kate? Tell me why." He grabbed her by the arm and she pulled away.

"Don't touch me. You're . . . you're just like the others. I thought you were different but you're not." Lashing out at him was the only way she knew to make him leave her alone. "You're cruel and hurtful and —"

He stepped back as if she'd slapped him. "What have I done to make you think such a thing?"

"At the dance. The fight with old man Parker."

A sheepish expression crept across his face. He placed his hands at his waist. "I feel bad about that. Parker and my uncle started to argue . . ." He shook his head. "When it comes to protecting family, I don't always see straight."

She bit her lip. "You were protecting your uncle?"

"It was what you might call a misunderstandin'. I just wanted to keep Parker from sharpenin' his horns on my uncle. I can fight and shoot a gun with the best of them, but most of the time I'm as harmless as a bee in butter. What happened at the dance . . ." He shrugged. "You can't hold that against me."

Defenses weakening, she tightened her hands into fists by her sides. "It's not just the dance." For some reason it seemed necessary to make him understand why the ranch was the only life she wanted, held the only future she could trust.

"My father left when I was five and after that, every man walked out on my mama and me."

"I'm not your pa," he said, as if a simple statement would set everything right. "I'm not those other men."

She took a sharp intake of air. She wanted so much to believe him. She wanted to believe in goodness and kindness and love everlasting, but how could she? The only real happiness she'd ever known had been here on the ranch. She could now ride a horse almost as well as the cowpokes and had grown to love the desert's stark beauty. There was no place else she would rather live. So why did Luke always make her question her own motives and desires?

"Goldilocks!"

She glanced at the ranch house. Ruckus beckoned from the verandah and Kate fought for resolve. Land was her future. It offered her permanence, and that was something she'd never known. Marriage offered no such security, and neither did Luke.

She gazed at his handsome face and could hardly breathe. He was like other men, he was. She had to believe that, because to believe otherwise could put her future in jeopardy.

"I've got to go." She turned to leave, but Luke caught her by the wrist, his fingers pressed firmly into her flesh. She lifted her gaze to his beseeching eyes and she felt her last bit of control slip away.

"I'm asking you . . . pleading with you not to sign those papers."

"Goldilocks!"

She couldn't speak, couldn't think. She was pulled in two different directions. Luke could never give her the security she needed, so why did she feel tempted by him? Had he not stepped back at that moment, his face grim, she might have altogether caved in — and that would have been a terrible mistake.

"Kate, the truth is . . . I have a hankering for you."

"A . . . hankering?"

He frowned. "I guess there's no choice but to spell it out. I love you, Kate Tenney, and I plumb don't know how to say it any clearer than that."

She shook her head and backed away from him. His words were like a slap in the face. Love was not what she wanted to hear. *Love isn't gentle. Love isn't kind. Love isn't lasting.* He held out his hand and she backed away more.

"If you turn away now, that will be the

425

end, I swear."

"I'm sorry," she whispered. Hurt glittered in his eyes, but nothing could be done about that. He'd soon forget her. Maybe by tomorrow or sometime next week. That's how men were. Here today, gone tomorrow.

"Kate?"

Hand on her hat, she turned and ran. She was one signature away from a bright and happy future. It was what she wanted. It was what she'd hoped for and prayed for and worked for these past few months. So why did it feel like she was running away?

Chapter 34

"Everything in order?" Eleanor asked.

She sat behind her desk peering through her spectacles at her lawyer, Jesse Barker. Her doctor insisted she wear them for close work, but they were more trouble than they were worth. She pulled the glasses off and tossed them aside.

Barker stuck his quizzing glass in his right eye and riffled through the document in his hand. "Yes. All she has to do is sign on the dotted line."

Her lawyer's ill-chosen plaid suit and dated handlebar mustache hid a brilliant legal mind, and Eleanor trusted him implicitly with her affairs. He had an office in Tombstone between Tough Nut and Allen Streets and claimed to try more cases in the town's many saloons than the stately courthouse.

"I think you're making a big mistake," Robert said. "Turning this property over to a woman who can barely stay in a saddle makes no sense." Robert leaned against the wall, arms crossed in front, handsome as ever.

"O.T. and Ruckus say she has potential," Eleanor said. Both men did, however, express reservations regarding Kate's tendency to daydream. A problem, indeed. Working with cattle demanded one's full and undivided attention. But the girl had tenacity, and Eleanor was convinced that proper training would overcome her less desirable traits.

"Actually, she reminds me a little of myself."

The truth was — and she hadn't even admitted this to Robert — she was tired. Tired of fighting. Tired of trying to stay ahead of the competition. Ever since Geronimo's surrender nine years earlier, an alarming influx of settlers had flocked to the area. Cattle ranches had popped up like grass in the rain. Some were small and some, like the Three C Company with its thirty thousand heads of cattle, enormous. All infringing on the Last Chance financially and physically, using up precious resources.

What the Last Chance needed was young blood to carry it into the next century. Eleanor needed someone to bounce ideas off and do the heavy lifting, under her watchful eye, of course. She needed someone with the tenacity of a desert flower, willing to fight the battles, meet the challenges, and stay progressive. Someone with the imagination of a writer. Oh yes. She needed Kate.

"There will never be anyone like you," Robert said.

"I had to learn and she'll learn too."

"You could sell this property and be set for life," he persisted.

She regarded him from beneath raised eyebrows. "And then what?"

"You could travel. You live in Arizona Territory and you've never even seen the Grand Canyon."

She laughed. "At my age I try to avoid anything that resembles a hole in the ground."

"Ah, but there's always Paris," he said, his eyes aglow with teasing lights.

Eleanor grimaced. "Robert, you have no sense of posterity. My mother started this ranch and she made me promise to pass it on to my children." Her gaze dropped to the drawer where she kept a daguerreotype of her long-deceased daughter. "Unfortunately, that was not meant to be. Miss Tenney is the next best thing."

"You have a brother. Surely he has a family? Wouldn't it make more sense to leave the ranch to one of your nieces or nephews? I know a Pinkerton detective who would be happy to track down your family."

Eleanor planted the palms of both hands on her forehead. "Stop right there. I have no desire to see my brother *or* his family." Stephen was just as much a ne'er-do-well as their father, and she had no intention of tracking him down after all these years. "I have my heiress."

Robert scoffed. "Since you insist Miss Tenney not marry, who will inherit the ranch from her?"

She pointed to the papers in her lawyer's hand. "It's all written out. She will do what I have done. She will find a suitable candidate as her replacement."

"There may not be a ranch by then," he said.

"Nonsense. People will always eat beef. It's in their blood."

"Yes, but even the Babbitts have diversified."

Eleanor rolled her eyes. The so-called cattle barons of northern Arizona had invested in mercantile stores, of all things. "That's because they don't know what they're doing. Anyone foolish enough to run sheep and cattle on the same spread has no business calling himself a rancher."

"Maybe not, but even you have to admit the cattle business is on the decline. The railroad has made cattle drives obsolete. Now everyone thinks he's a rancher. Too much competition has lowered the prices. I don't need to tell you this."

"Yes, it is harder today." The depression of '93 hadn't helped. "But I've survived worse times."

It made her head swim just to think about it. The Last Chance had survived the hardest of times, but that was only because she went after business with no thought of politics or popular opinion. She sold to both the Union and Confederate armies, even though others condemned her and called her a traitor.

Now she held a lucrative contract with the US government to supply meat to Indians and forts. True, she lost business last year when Fort Bowie was abandoned, but that was only one market. Others were bound to take its place.

Fortunately, the range wars of Pleasant Valley hadn't affected her. The biggest threat was the recent surge of eastern speculators. Of course, rustlers were a constant worry, but there was talk about organizing a group of lawmen similar to the

Texas Rangers. If the Arizona Rangers became reality, then livestock thieves would no doubt go the way of cattle drives.

Oh yes, the ranch had survived despite the worst possible circumstances, and she was convinced that with her know-how and Kate's imagination, Last Chance would continue to thrive.

For several moments Robert said nothing. Instead, he stared out the window. Finally, he said, "Selling the ranch now would be your wisest course of action." He turned to face the lawyer. "Don't you agree, Barker?"

Before Barker could answer, a knock came at the door.

"I believe *this* is the wisest course of action," Eleanor said beneath her breath. She lifted her voice. "Come in." She glanced at her railroad watch. It was 4:00 p.m. on the nose. She considered Kate's promptness a good sign.

Kate entered looking grim, maybe even worried. Excellent. That could only mean that she understood the seriousness of what she was about to sign.

Eleanor quickly made the introductions. "This is Mr. Barker, my lawyer. And Mr. Stackman, my banker. I'm sure you'll get to know both of them quite well in the years ahead."

Kate offered first Mr. Barker and then Mr. Stackman her hand. Robert, ever the gentlemen, raised her hand to his mouth. "A pleasure."

Eleanor pointed to the empty chair in front of her desk. "Do sit." She was anxious to get the formalities over with as quickly as possible.

Kate ran her hands down her sides and stared at the thick document on the desk. Not that Eleanor could blame her. It took Eleanor less than five minutes to lay out the provisions she wanted in the contract, but nearly fifty pages for her lawyer to turn them into legal terms.

"It won't bite you," Eleanor said lightly, in an effort to put her at ease. "It's just my lawyer's way of trying to justify his outrageous stipend."

She made a face at Robert, signaling him to drop the dark look and be happy for her.

Robert refused to comply and his expression only grew grimmer.

Kate took her seat in front of the desk and folded her hands on her lap.

"Mr. Barker, would you be kind enough to go over the documents with Miss Tenney?" Eleanor said.

The lawyer obliged, his monotone voice seeming to hum on forever.

Eleanor impatiently tapped her fingers. All the therefores and thereons gave her a headache. Who talked like that?

"Do you have any questions?" Mr. Barker asked at last.

Kate shook her head and then changed her mind. "I do have one question." She looked directly at Eleanor. "I noticed that the typewriter has been moved."

Eleanor sat back in her chair, annoyed. She was about to turn over her ranch and all the girl could worry about was the typewriter? She glanced up at Robert, whose "I told you so" look annoyed her even more.

"It was just taking up space and I hardly had occasion to use it," she said in a voice meant to discourage further discussion of the matter.

"Would you have an objection to my ordering one of my own?" Kate persisted.

Eleanor leveled Kate with a cold stare. "I have no objection as long as it doesn't interfere with ranch business."

"It won't," Kate assured her.

"Very well, then. Let's get on with it." Eleanor gestured for her lawyer to proceed.

Barker unfolded the document and spread it on the desk in front of her. "I'll need both your signatures."

Anxious to get the tiresome business over with, Eleanor reached for her pen and dipped the nib into the inkwell. She signed the document with a flourish and blew the ink dry. She then handed the pen to Kate.

Kate took it in hand and waited until Barker had positioned the contract in front of her.

She touched the pen to paper and Eleanor held her breath and waited.

Kate stared at her name typed neatly on the document in front of her. With a mark of her pen she would eventually become known as Miss Katherine Tenney, ranch owner, landowner. *Boss* lady. Who would have ever thought such a thing possible?

"I have a hankering for you."

Her hand shook. This was what she wanted. She wanted the permanence and the respectability that only land could offer her.

"I love you, Kate Tenney, and I plumb don't know how to say it any clearer than that."

She tightened her grip on the pen and it was as if her fingers cut off her breathing.

"Is something the matter?" the lawyer asked. "Some clause you don't understand?"

She shook her head. "No." She pressed the nib of the pen onto the dotted line, but some invisible force prevented her from writing.

"Yes." She blinked back tears as she met Miss Walker's gray eyes. "I . . . I thought I was ready to do this. I want to do it but . . ."

"Go on," Miss Walker said, her voice taut.

Kate stuck the pen in the penholder, laid her hands on her lap, and willed herself to stop shaking. "You've been very kind to me. Everyone has been and I love it here, I do. But . . . you once told me that I would have to give heart and soul to the ranch and I'm not sure I can do that. I want to, I do, but . . . I'm not sure that I can." A strained silence stretched across the room and no one moved.

She leaned forward, beseeching her. "Could I have more time to think about it? Another week. Another month?"

"What makes you think you'll feel different then?" Miss Walker asked.

"I . . . I don't know how I'll feel. All I know is that it wouldn't be fair to you to sign this contract until I know for certain I can fulfill your expectations."

For several moments no one spoke. Finally, Miss Walker pulled a checkbook out of her desk drawer, opened it, and began writing. "I appreciate your honesty, but it would be better for all concerned if you leave, effective immediately." She tore out a check and handed it to her.

"This is what I owe you. Consider our business complete."

Kate's mouth dropped open. She'd never expected Miss Walker to dismiss her so quickly or so coldly and completely.

"But . . . but . . ."

Miss Walker replaced her checkbook in the drawer and slammed it shut. "There's nothing more to be said."

Stunned, Kate took the check and ran out of the office.

For several moments after Kate fled the office, no one moved. Then Barker riffled through the document as if the reason for Kate's sudden departure were hidden among its many pages.

Robert was the first to speak. "You were rather rough on the girl, don't you think?"

"Rough?"

"All she did was ask for more time," Robert said.

Eleanor wished it was as simple as that. She'd tried to ignore the warning signs. The way Kate and Adams eyed each other. How Luke never gave up looking for her when she was kidnapped. How they gazed at each other the day he brought her back to the ranch. The number of times he'd come looking for her since.

Giving Kate more time wouldn't change a thing. Eleanor was as certain of that as she was her own name. It would only make the inevitable parting more painful than it already was. She couldn't stop the hurt. The best she could do was not to prolong it. Experience had taught her to cut her losses — much like one hacked off a painful limb — and get on with it. That's what she intended to do.

"If she has to think about it, then she's not the right person for the job," Eleanor said.

Robert stroked his mustache. "It's a big decision."

"And she's had four months to make it."

Robert glanced at the lawyer before turning back to Eleanor. "May I make a suggestion?"

Eleanor stood. "No, you may not." Let Robert think what he would. What was done was done.

She walked to the door, but before leaving the room she added, "And the Grand Canyon is definitely out of the question."

Kate reached town less than an hour later. She tied her horse to the hitching post in front of Luke's blacksmith shop and took a deep breath to brace herself. She hated letting Miss Walker down, but how could she do otherwise, feeling the way she did? Did she love Luke? Was that it? Was that the source of her confusion? The reason for throwing away the chance of a lifetime?

She didn't know. She had no experience with romantic love. Had never before allowed herself to get close enough to a man to lose her heart. Still, this couldn't be love. Wasn't love supposed to make you feel giddy and silly and act like a fool? This thing with Luke had sneaked up on tiptoe and buried itself so deep inside, she hadn't even suspected it was there — until now.

The sound of Luke's laughter brought her out of her reverie. She turned the corner of his shop and stopped upon seeing him with Miss Chase, their heads so close as to nearly touch. Locker was curled up in the woman's arms, tail wagging.

Kate drew back so as not to be seen. She didn't know what hurt more, having to disappoint Miss Walker or seeing Miss Chase with the dog Luke said was hers.

"Oh, Lukey," Miss Chase squealed in her high-pitched voice. "Are you sure it's all right for me to take him home?"

"Just as soon as he's old enough to wean."

She squealed again. "I can't wait."

Locker squirmed in her arms and licked her face and Miss Chase succumbed to giggles.

Luke laughed. "It looks like he feels the same."

"Oh, Lukey, you are the kindest man I've ever known."

Kate couldn't hear what Luke said next, but whatever it was put a smile on Miss Chase's face.

A sharp pain unlike anything Kate had ever known sliced through her. Obviously, Luke had already put her out of his mind. No surprises there. What did surprise her — shocked her — was how quickly he did it. It had only been a couple of hours and already he'd found another to take her place.

Kate drew back, hot tears streaming down her cheeks. Never had she felt so wretched in her life. She'd given up everything — given up the ranch — only to find out she'd been right about men all along. Right about Luke.

She wasn't certain of her own heart before coming here, but she knew it now — and knew that it was breaking.

CHAPTER 35

Weeks passed and never had more miserable ones darkened Miss Hattie's soul. Her health became so delicate that others feared for her life.

The first thing Kate noticed about Boston was the closed-in feeling. After the wide-open spaces of Arizona Territory, the narrow streets and tall brick buildings made her feel both trapped and claustrophobic. The stomach-wrenching odors didn't help much either. The stench of sewage mingled with the smell of coal, dyes, whiskey, and fish. The hot August sun baked horse manure onto cobblestone streets and flies buzzed around in a frenzy.

She couldn't quite explain it, but the ranch smells seemed so much sweeter somehow, earthier. Even with all those cattle.

Boston even sounded different. Instead of

441

creaking windmills and the soothing sounds of rustling grass and lowing cattle, her ears were blasted by peddlers blowing fish horns to attract customers and yelling, "Here comes the fishmaaaan, bring out your dishpaaaan."

Wagon wheels and horses' hooves clamored across uneven brick roads and church bells rang from tall towers. She felt as if she was being accosted from every direction. After leaving the new Union train station she hurried down Canal Street toward Haymarket Square. She passed taverns and boardinghouses, auction halls and warehouses. The sights and sounds of a city she'd known all her life now seemed foreign and she felt like a stranger in a strange new land.

Like Lieutenant Philip Nolan in *The Man Without a Country,* she felt adrift. She was born and raised in Boston, but her heart was in Cactus Patch. Refusing to sign Miss Walker's papers was the right thing to do. She now knew why; she was hopelessly in love with Luke Adams.

She hated letting Miss Walker down, of course, but loving Luke meant she could not give her heart to the Last Chance. The old lady deserved better. The ranch required it.

Kate grimaced. Pain that started in her chest now spread throughout her body. She'd done the right thing, but oh, how it hurt. It hurt so much she could hardly breathe. She missed the ranch, missed the ranch hands, especially Ruckus. She even missed her horse, Decker. But no one left a bigger hole in her heart than Luke. She'd cried on the train all the way to Boston, and though her tears were spent, her anguish remained.

It was hot, but unlike the dry heat of Arizona, it was muggy, and this sapped what little energy remained after traveling. She'd barely walked a couple of blocks from the station before the heat and humidity took its toll. She pulled her steamer trunk out of the way of passersby and sat on top of it, sweat pouring down her face.

She wished now she'd taken a hansom cab, but what little money she had left after train fare would have to last until she found employment.

People scurried by, giving her no heed. Nannies pushing prams, bankers and merchants hurrying about their business. No one seemed to notice her save beggars thrusting tin cans in her face.

She started down the sidewalk again and crossed the street, dodging shays, cabrio-

lets, horsecars, bicycles, and omnibuses. Her
trunk bumped along the cobblestones and
scraped against the curb.

Finally she reached her destination, but
even that looked less appealing than it had
four months earlier. Had the city really
changed that much in such a short time —
or had she?

The five-story brick building was just off
Richmond Street where she'd lived before
traveling to Arizona. It was located in a less
desirable part of town and lacked an eleva-
tor, but it had an indoor privy and rent was
cheaper than the Working Girls Home on
Union Park Street.

The owner of the building was Mrs.
Potter, a sixty-year-old widow who walked
with a cane and smelled like unbaked
dough. She opened the door to Kate's
knock and peered at her from beneath a
mop of white hair.

"Oh, it's you again."

Kate smiled politely. "By any chance is
my old apartment still available?"

"No, but the one next to it is."

"I'll take it," Kate said. Digging into her
drawstring bag, she pulled out enough coins
for a month's rent and placed them into the
palm of the woman's arthritic hand.

Mrs. Potter dropped the coins into the

pocket of her grimy apron. "How long you staying this time?"

"I don't know yet," Kate said. If her plans worked out and her old publisher accepted her new book, she would then be able to afford a better apartment. It wouldn't be easy to convince Mr. Conner to publish another one of her books, but she had to try. If worse came to worst, she would travel to New York and try one of the publishers there.

Mrs. Potter lifted a key off a nail and handed it to her. "This is the last time I'm renting to you. I can't have people moving in and out on a whim. And don't you forget no men visitors and no alcohol."

"I won't forget," Kate said.

"See that you don't."

The door slammed shut and Kate heaved a sigh.

The room was on the third floor at the end of a long, dark, and musty-smelling hall. The apartment was small, dingy, and so dim it took Kate's eyes several moments to focus. Identical to her old place, the room was furnished with a sagging upholstered chair, table, lumpy bed, and small wardrobe. The kitchen was an L-shaped space with a kerosene cookstove, icebox, and running water. The plumbing didn't work in the winter months when the pipes froze. During each cold spell she would have to walk down three flights of stairs to fetch water from the old well in back or settle for a bucket of snow.

Crossing to the single window, Kate yanked open the curtains, lifted the sill, and breathed in the putrid air. Even her imagination couldn't carry her away from the realities outside.

Traffic sounds rose from the busy street and sun streamed through the open window, but nothing chased away the gloom. She tried to concentrate on her plans. She needed a typewriter but couldn't afford one. What little money was left after paying for train fare and rent would have to do for a couple of months.

Perhaps Mr. Taylor, founder and publisher of the *Boston Globe,* would let her borrow one of his typewriters. He had published several of her articles and seemed affable enough. Though the *Globe* put the banning of her book on the front page, the paper was more critical of censorship than her writing.

If all else failed, she could use the typewriter at the library. That would mean having to work during library hours, and that she didn't want to do. She did her best work in the still of night and working in public was too distracting. Mr. Taylor was definitely her best bet.

Below her window a boy called to his dog and she immediately thought of Homer. Before she knew it memories of Cactus Patch flashed in her mind. It all seemed like a dream. But not Luke; he seemed all too real. She pictured him so clearly, she could imagine him standing in the room with her. Tears chased away the vision but not the loneliness or the terrible crushing pain that threatened to consume her.

Arms crossed in front, she moved her hands up and down the sleeves of her shirtwaist to ward off a sudden chill. Little by little warmth crept back into her flesh, but nothing could be done for the bleakness of her heart and soul.

CHAPTER 36

Bessie wasn't one to interfere in other people's business unless, of course, she had good reason. And if a heartbroken nephew wasn't reason enough to get involved, then what in heaven's name was?

Luke had been in such a miserable state since Kate Tenney left town that even the annoying Miss Chase had given up on him. Now the brazen girl was zeroing in on Michael, which didn't please Bessie one whit. Of course, now that the *Saturday Evening Post* had accepted one of Michael's short stories, every unmarried woman in town had set her sights on him. Michael was turning out to be quite the celebrity.

Arms folded across her middle, Bessie gave a self-righteous nod. Yes, she was right to come today. She had every right to interfere in Luke's affairs. The rate Michael was going, he would find a wife before his older brother, and how would that look?

Her mistake was dragging Lula-Belle to town with her. Her sister wasn't happy about it, but she nonetheless insisted upon driving. Thank goodness Luke had been able to repair the buggy after Sam ran it off the road.

Now Lula-Belle held on to the reins of her slow-moving horse like one might hold on to the back of a speeding train. "I still don't understand why we have to go to town today. You know Monday is my wash day."

Bessie sat on the seat next to her and fanned herself. It was the end of October but it still felt like July, and though it wasn't yet noon already it was hot. "Would the world come to an end if you did your laundry on Tuesday? Or, heaven forbid, Wednesday?"

"I've always done my wash on Monday," Lula-Belle said.

Bessie rolled her eyes but held her tongue. The last thing she wanted was to get into a spat over soiled laundry. They didn't speak again until Lula-Belle pulled up in front of their nephew's blacksmith shop.

"Let *me* do the talking," Bessie warned, climbing down from the buggy. She straightened her hat and marched inside.

Luke greeted them with a smile, but Bessie wasn't fooled. Not one iota.

"What brings you two to town on a *Monday?*" he asked.

Bessie saw no reason to beat around the bush. "We're worried about you."

"Me?" He looked from one to the other. "Why?"

"You know why." Even today he had dark shadows under his eyes. Obviously, he wasn't sleeping well. He had also lost weight. "You hardly said a word at Sunday's dinner. Nor did you touch your meal." If anything, he became more somber and distant with each passing week.

"You didn't even taste one of my sourdough biscuits," Lula-Belle added, sounding offended.

He inclined his head. "I apologize to you both. I have a lot on my mind lately." He waved a hand at a miniature windmill he'd been working on for months. As far as Bessie could tell it looked no different from the last time she saw it weeks ago.

"Nonsense," Bessie exclaimed. "You have only one thing on your mind, and you know it. And that's Kate Tenney."

Annoyance flashed across his face and his lips puckered. "I don't want to talk about her."

"Good. Because that means you won't interrupt what I have to say."

"She doesn't like to be interrupted," Lula-Belle added. "Why, I remember that time when —"

Bessie poked her elbow into Lula-Belle's side. It was no time for one of her sister's long-winded stories. "Anyone can see that you're miserable."

"So what am I supposed to do about it?" he asked, his voice curt. "She knows how I feel but she left anyway. She didn't even bother sayin' good-bye."

"That's a good sign," Bessie said.

Lula-Belle glanced at her. "It is?"

Exasperated, Bessie threw up her hands. Didn't her sister know anything? "Of course it is. Good-bye is, well, good-bye." Okay, so maybe she *was* grasping at straws, but she didn't have a whole lot to work with. "If she didn't say good-bye, that means it's not final."

Luke grimaced as if in pain. "It felt final to me. I told her how I felt and she still left."

She gave him her best motherly look. "That's because you don't know how women think. Just because a man says he loves her doesn't mean she believes him."

"I believed it when Murphy told me he loved me," Lula-Belle said.

Bessie scoffed. "You believed *me* when I told you the moon was made of green

451

cheese."

She turned back to her nephew and heaved a sigh. If love and marriage were left to the male population, civilization would have ended with Adam and Eve. "So how did you tell her that you loved her?"

He frowned. "How did I tell her? I just blurted it right out."

Bessie felt a sinking feeling inside. "No, no, no. That would never do. Women want to be courted."

"I did court her. I told her I had a fancy for her. Then I told her I had a hankering for her. Then I zeroed in for the kill and told her I loved her. If that's not courtin' I don't know what is."

Bessie threw up her arms in exasperation. "No wonder she left."

Luke frowned. "You think I should have come right out and asked her to pair up with me?"

Bessie rolled her eyes. "No, no, no!" Where, oh where had she gone so wrong? "You only mention pairings if you plan on building an ark."

The frown lines deepened between his eyebrows. "Are you sayin' I shoulda played my hand closer to the chest?"

Bessie rolled her eyes. *Men!* "What I'm trying to say is that a woman doesn't just want words, she wants proof. She wants to *see* that you love her with her own two eyes."

Luke rubbed his chin. "It's kind of hard to prove anything when she's in Boston and I'm here."

"Yes, that is a problem," Bessie agreed. Now they were getting somewhere.

Lula-Belle sniffed. "That's why they have trains."

Bessie glanced at her sister in surprise. Maybe she wasn't so dense after all.

"Lula-Belle's right." Personally, she would never do anything so foolhardy as to travel on two thin metal rails. The sheer speed of a train terrified her. Nonetheless, she had no qualms about encouraging Luke to travel on one. She'd agree to let him go to the moon if she thought it would get him a wife.

"You must definitely go to Boston. No woman can resist a man willing to put life and limb on the line to chase after her." Recalling how Sam had chased her halfway to Tucson — practically killing himself in the process — Bessie smiled and added, "Trust me, I speak from experience. And I'll tell you another thing . . ."

While she expressed her considerable thoughts on the subject, Luke didn't say a word. Arms folded, forehead creased, he

453

stared at her in stone-faced silence and didn't move a muscle.

Bessie threw in every reason she could think of why Luke should go after the girl, but nothing she said seemed to penetrate his thick head. Stubborn, that's what he was. Just like Sam.

She paused for breath and that's when Luke finally spoke up.

"You think I should? You think I should go to Boston?"

Praise the Lord, Luke wasn't so pigheaded after all. "Absolutely," Bessie said.

"But only if you truly love her," Lula-Belle said.

"And are willing to show her how much," Bessie added.

Where is she?

It was a question that had run through Luke's head since Kate left all those months ago. Now it was followed by yet another question: *How do I find her?*

Traveling to Boston had taken seven days, three trains, and a whole lot of praying. It would have taken a day less had he not missed his connection in Chicago because of a snowstorm. As hard as it had been to travel to Boston, that was the least of it. Finding Kate in the desert after that terrible sandstorm had been a breeze compared to trying to find her in this ugly, crowded city. He didn't even know where to begin.

Boston confounded him with its narrow streets, tall buildings, and hordes of people. Where was everyone going? And why were they all in such a big hurry? Dodging traffic was worse than trying to outrun a cattle stampede. And cold. Never had he known such frigid weather. His teeth hadn't stopped chattering since he arrived.

He'd checked every hotel and boardinghouse he could find, but no one by the name of Kate Tenney was registered. He closed his eyes. Think. *Think.* Where would she be?

Walking around aimlessly, he found himself on the notorious Anne Street, which locals called the Black Sea. Hellhole would be a more accurate name. Any sort of vice could be purchased for a price. Brothels and taverns lined the street, reaching into a dark, dismal maze of alleyways. After one woman with a painted face and low-cut gown beckoned him from a doorway, he decided he needed a map.

He must have been half out of his mind to come to this strange city. It wasn't like him to act without careful planning. A blacksmith had to be prepared. Everything from a nail to farm equipment required a detailed plan. How could finding the woman he loved require any less?

He wasn't even certain it was possible to find someone in a place like this. Finding a needle in a haystack would be easier. What was he thinking? That she would be waiting for him at the train station?

He plumb better think of something fast. He couldn't keep running in circles. Where would someone like Kate Tenney spend her time? A bookstore. He pumped his fist. Of course. Why didn't he think of that before?

He found one two blocks away. The sign read Antiquarian, but newer books were displayed behind the dusty glass window. A riot of bells greeted him as he walked through the door. It smelled of old leather and dust. The proprietor looked up from behind a counter, spectacles balanced on the tip of his nose. The man's shoulder-length white hair and beard would be better suited to St. Nicholas's red attire than the frock coat he wore.

"May I help you?" he asked in a hushed voice.

Not sure why the man was whispering, Luke nonetheless followed his lead. "I'm looking for someone. Her name is Kate Tenney. She's a writer."

The man stroked his beard. "The only Kate I know is Kate Chopin." He picked up a volume. "I have a copy of her book *Bayou Folk*. It's her best book yet."

Luke shook his head. "Her name is Tenney," he said, forgetting to whisper.

"Shh." The bookstore owner pointed to a table in back where two men sat reading. "She doesn't go by a pseudonym, does she?" he said, his voice low.

"A pseudonym?"

"Some writers write under an assumed name. Women writers often choose male names."

Luke blew out his breath. Aunt Bessie never mentioned — what did the owner call it? — a pseudonym. "She's a . . . friend of mine and she writes dime novels. That's all I know. One of them was banned."

He wished now he knew more about Kate's writing. Books and literature were out of his realm. After leaving Texas, he had no formal education. Even under Aunt Bessie's patient tutorage, he never much improved his reading skills. Not like Michael, who always had his head in a book. Still, he felt guilty. Maybe if he'd shown more interest in Kate's writing, he'd have a better idea how to find her.

The shopkeeper made a face. "Lots of books have been banned. The Watch and Ward Society hasn't the slightest idea what it's doing. If it was left up to that stuffy group, the Bible would be banned." Obviously it was a sore subject with the store owner.

Frustrated, Luke thanked the man and started for the door. He stopped. "Where would a college-educated woman spend her time?" he asked, keeping his voice low.

With open curiosity the proprietor's gaze traveled down the length of him, lingering on his wrinkled trousers and well-worn boots. No doubt the bookstore owner wondered what a man like Luke wanted with a woman clearly out of his realm.

"Libraries, maybe. You might try the circulation library on Washington. There's also one at Cornhill Square and another on Hanover." He reeled off several more.

"How . . . how many libraries does Boston have?"

"I don't know. Fifty — a hundred. That's counting libraries in insane asylums, hospitals, and prisons. Your friend is probably not in any of those."

"I don't reckon so."

The shopkeeper continued, "There's the Athenaeum, of course, but I doubt she's

there. It used to charge an annual member-
ship fee of ten dollars, but then it sold
shares and now only proprietors can use it.
Is your friend a proprietor?"

Luke frowned. "I have no idea." He didn't
even know what a library proprietor was.

"Then there are church libraries, reading
rooms, universities. She won't be allowed in
the Masonic reading room, but you might
try the YWCA library. It's for women only
so they probably won't let you in, but you
can inquire at the front desk."

By the time the bookstore owner got
through listing every possible literary establishment, Luke's head was spinning. How
did people have so much time to read?

He thanked the proprietor for a second
time and left. He stood on the sidewalk
outside, shivering against the cold, and
glanced up and down the busy street. He
checked his map and started toward Cornhill Square.

What if by some chance he found her?
What then? What could he say that he
hadn't already said? How could he convince
her to go back to Cactus Patch with him?
How could he prove his love for Kate?

Three days later he still hadn't found her.
He'd inquired at libraries, reading rooms,

and bookstores to no avail. Feeling helpless as a cow in quicksand, he prayed, *God, I can use some help here. How about a little push in the right direction? If that don't do it, feel free to lay me on an anvil and give me a good hammering.*

The proprietor of the last bookstore he'd inquired at directed him to the reading room of a Presbyterian church. Spotting the old brick church on the opposite side of the street, he crossed over, dodging traffic and causing one carriage driver to curse him out. No sooner had he reached the sidewalk than the church sign over the wood-paneled doors caught his eye.

The sign read, "I will never leave you or forsake you."

He recalled Kate telling him about her pa. He thought back to his own childhood and the confusing months following his parents' deaths. A parent dying wasn't the same as being deserted by one, but to an eleven-year-old it still felt like abandonment, foolish as it seemed. Kate's pa didn't die — he walked out on her. That was a whole lot worse.

"I will never leave you or forsake you."

What was it that his aunt had once said? Something about God giving love a language of its own.

"I will never leave you or forsake you."

A feeling of triumph flooded through him. It was as if an iron bar had been lifted from his shoulders and the very heavens had opened up to smile on him. It was as if the earth itself had stopped spinning. At long last he had his answer. He knew what to do.

He might never get the hang of what his aunt called the language of love. He could barely manage the English language. But one thing he knew for sure: he now had the key to Kate's heart. All he had to do was find her.

CHAPTER 37

The placard announced a $500 reward for the capture and delivery of the itinerant woman. She was to be delivered unharmed to the undersigned — a man so desperate to find her he would gladly sail the seven seas.

Kate stepped out of the mercantile, a book on the life and times of Jesse James tucked beneath her arm. Perhaps the newly purchased tome would help her understand Cactus Joe's obsession with the outlaw. Maybe then she could finish the last chapter of her book in time to meet her deadline.

It had snowed again the night before and the skies were steely gray, the streets wet and slippery. As much as she hated Boston winters, snow did tend to blur the line between rich and poor. A pure white blanket of snow covered the rooftops of South Slope Beacon Hill mansions and west-end immigrant flophouses alike, showing no favoritism.

Kate shivered, her breath escaping in a long white plume. She had given her winter clothes away to a charity when she left for Arizona and she could not afford to replace them. She did, however, splurge on a muff and she gratefully sank her hands into the hand warmer's furry depths. Anxious to get back to her apartment before it started to snow again, she picked up speed, taking care to avoid the patches of ice that dotted the sidewalk.

A handbill on the post office door near city hall caught her eye but she ignored it. Not until she noticed the outside of buildings and doors fairly plastered with them did curiosity get the best of her. She stopped and flattened the curled edges of a handbill with her hand.

Someone had written "I ain't going nowear now or ever" in big, bold letters. It was signed simply "Luke." Below the signature was a drawing of a horseshoe. Her heart skipped a beat.

Stunned, she dropped her package. Was her mind playing tricks on her? Had her overactive imagination finally gone too far? Was it a mirage? She shook her head. This wasn't Arizona, it was Boston and there no mistaking the big, bold print. Was this *her* Luke?

Shaken, she reread the sign and traced her finger over the carefully drawn horseshoe, which was identical to the sign over Luke's shop. That sign promised quality. Was this a promise too? *"I ain't going nowear now or ever."*

The letters were so straight and perfectly spaced that at first she thought the signs had been professionally printed. Upon closer examination she realized they were handwritten. The writer had obviously taken great pains to write them.

She recalled the care with which Luke checked a horse's hooves and the detailed construction of the miniature windmill. It wasn't hard to imagine Luke bent over a handbill, forming each letter just so.

A pedestrian bumped into her. Jolted to her senses, she retrieved her package, brushed off the snow, and continued along the sidewalk, slowly at first. Fate had played a cruel trick on her. Nothing more.

She crossed Washington Street on the way to her apartment, but the handbill continued to haunt her. Was she losing her mind? Had she lost the ability to know fact from fiction?

"I ain't going nowear now or ever."

She was still questioning her sanity when she spotted another handbill, this one on a gaslight post. Farther up the street an identical sign was posted on the outside of a church bookstore. Another was hung in front of the antiquarian bookstore and still another on the door of a Methodist reading room.

No, no, it couldn't be. Still, Bostonians didn't talk that way. *"I ain't going nowear now or ever."* This time the voice was so loud and clear it was as if the speaker stood right behind her. She spun around only to find herself surrounded by strangers. She shook her head. She was losing her mind. Or was she?

Hand shaking, she ripped off the next flyer she found and glanced up and down the sidewalk. Luke was here? In Boston? Was that even possible? No, no, it wasn't. He would never travel all the way from Cactus Patch. Would he? The very thought made her heart thump, her pulse race, and her mouth go dry.

She spotted another flyer a short distance away, this one tacked to a gate. Farther ahead one hung from a watchmaker's sign. Faster, faster she ran, slipping and sliding at times on icy patches. She pulled down handbills left and right posted all along

Washington Street. Ten, twenty, thirty . . . she stopped counting at a hundred.

Tears rolled down her cheeks. "Luke!" He'd told her he loved her, but she hadn't wanted to hear it — was afraid to hear it. His promise to stay changed everything — or could if she let it. Loving Luke was the easy part; trusting him was a whole different story. It meant embracing life with the grace of a woman instead of the grief of a child. It meant letting go of the past and grabbing hold of the future. It meant facing the wind head-on. She knew what she wanted to do. What she didn't know was if she could.

She turned a full circle, shouting his name. Where was he? She called to a store clerk sweeping the step of his shoemaker shop. "Did you see the man who posted this handbill?"

The man shook his head and quickly disappeared inside.

She traveled the length of Washington from the Cathedral of the Holy Cross all the way to the Grand Opera House, then doubled back. Several times she thought she saw Luke, but each time it turned out to be a stranger who looked nothing like him.

Using money she could ill afford, she stepped on a horse-drawn street car that carried her to hotels and boardinghouses on the outer edges of town. She even stopped to inquire at the elegant Vendome that charged an outrageous four-fifty a night for a room, but Luke was nowhere to be found.

By the end of the day, all she had to show for her efforts was a stack of handbills tacked to the walls of her apartment.

Anguish welled up inside and tears rolled down her cheeks. Falling to her knees on the threadbare carpet, she hugged herself, rocking back and forth, sobs rising from the bottom of the deepest, darkest corner of her soul. She cried for the little girl who watched her father walk out the door, never to return. She cried for the disgusted grandfather who, upon turning his back on his daughter, turned his back on her. She cried for a mother who'd been absent in spirit, if not in body.

But mostly she cried for Luke. Of all the things he could have said, telling her he would never leave was the one thing she could not ignore.

By the time her tears were spent, she was too exhausted to pick herself off the floor.

God, tell me what to do. Lead my feet in the direction you wish me to go. Take my hand and show me. Send rain . . .

■ ■ ■ ■

Eleanor stood staring at the tiny cross at her feet. She found herself at the grave a lot lately, but she refused to admit it had anything to do with Kate and the need to bury that which might have been.

Robert found her in that uncanny way he had of finding her at such times. Grateful for the company, she nonetheless greeted him with a frown.

"It's not the first of the month already, is it?"

He chuckled. "As it turns out, it is, or will be tomorrow." When she made no reply, he added, "It's almost January. Can you believe it? Eighteen ninety-six."

"No, I can't." Another year gone. Economically speaking, '95 was a good year. Despite little rain, her cattle were fat and healthy, and she'd been able to get a fair amount for them at market. Not as much as she'd hoped, of course, but enough.

"She's been gone for five months," he said.

Eleanor blinked. "Who's been gone?"

He arched a brow. "Why, Miss Tenney, of course."

"Oh, really? I hadn't noticed."

For several moments they stood staring

down at the little grave without speaking. Finally, Robert broke the silence.

"What do you plan to do about the ranch?"

"Didn't I tell you? I may have found my heiress. I haven't written back to her yet, but her letter looks promising. She's from Kansas."

"Ah. At least that's closer to cattle country than Boston."

She smiled. "Yes, indeed. I think that's a good sign, don't you?"

"You just never know about these things, do you?"

Good old Robert. No matter how much they might disagree, in the end he was always there for her. "Why don't you stay for supper and I'll read you her letter."

He bowed. "I accept your invitation. That will give me a chance to show you some literature I picked up on Paris."

She threw back her head and laughed. "Oh, Robert, will you ever give up? I've never met anyone so mule-headed in my life."

"I guess that makes us two of a kind." Grinning, he offered her his bent elbow. "Shall we?"

Kate walked between the gravestones,

frozen brown grass crunching beneath her feet.

The cemetery looked especially bleak this time of year. It was the end of February and the ground was still covered with snow. The branches of bare trees, dark against the steel gray skies, showed no signs of spring.

Her woolen cloak offered little protection against the stiff wind that nipped at her nose and made her teeth chatter.

Her mother's resting place was on a hill behind a gray-stone church overlooking the bay. "Elizabeth Anne Tenney" was carved into the headstone in block letters. Her mother died of consumption at the age of thirty-nine. She died a bitter woman, old and worn-out long before her time.

Things weren't what they seemed and Ruckus called that a blessing. *It makes us give the world — and each other — a closer look-see.*

She wasn't sure how much of a blessing it was, but she now saw her mother for perhaps the first time. Children protected their parents even if it meant living in denial, and Kate had spent a lifetime making excuses for hers. At times she blamed herself for her father leaving and even the circumstances of her mother's wretched existence.

Her mother had been given to rants of

temper and drunken stupors. Even cattle knew to protect their young. Even Homer. But not Elizabeth Tenney.

"Nothing good ever happens to our kind." Her mother repeated those words as often as others might sing a lullaby and Kate believed them. Why wouldn't she? All she had to do was look and see that God favored the rich. But that was before she left for Arizona, before a whole town rallied around her following her kidnapping, before she met an old lady willing to turn over her ranch to a near stranger. Before she met Luke.

For the first time in her life, she knew how it felt to be protected and cared for, and it scared the life out of her. The only permanent thing she'd ever known was death and abandonment. Through the years she'd lost everyone and everything she'd ever cared about. Anything good that happened to her was discounted as only temporary.

"I came to say good-bye, Mama." She leaned against the wind to lay a stem of winterberries on the concrete slab. No flowers could be found at this time of year and she was lucky to find a branch covered with red berries — red for forgiveness.

She straightened, and in so doing, she felt a heavy weight lift from her shoulders. She wasn't ready to forgive — not yet — but if acceptance was the first step, then she was well on her way.

"You were wrong, Mama," she said. "Good things do happen to people like us." And maybe, just maybe, some things did last forever, even love.

Ruckus certainly thought so, and if he were there now, he'd probably recite scripture with words to that effect. Thoughts of Ruckus brought a smile to her face.

She shoved her hands in her muff and gazed at a steamer sitting in the frigid waters of the distant harbor. The icy wind blew off the bay, whipping her hair around her head and snapping at her skirt. She inhaled until her lungs felt ready to explode. She then walked into the wind and followed the path down the hill — as bravely as a woman in love.

CHAPTER 38

With a grim laugh the bushwhacker wrapped his cloak around him. "No one will ever get the best of me."

Miss Hattie bounded forward and pulled off the man's false beard. "This man is an imposter!" she cried.

"Cactus Paaaaaaaaaatch!"

Kate rose from her seat and rushed down the aisle even before the train had come to a complete stop. The moment the door opened she sprang past the dark-skinned porter and raced down the steps to the platform. There she stopped, clutching a small package in her hand. Not only did the reality of the full desert sun hit her but also the enormity of what she was about to do.

It had been raining when she left Boston, and after months of gloomy skies and bone-chilling temperatures, she welcomed the desert warmth. She took a deep breath, relishing the fragrance of sunbaked sand.

Feet firmly planted upon the platform, she felt her knees tremble. It was all she could do to keep from getting back on the train. But she had come too far to turn back now.

Had it not been for the success of her new book, she could not have afforded the trip back to Arizona. The early reviews had been glowing, and Boston's Corner Bookstore had sold out all copies the very first day.

The best news was that her book was recommended reading for truant boys, and she knew at least two youths who vowed to follow the straight and narrow after reading the sad but true story of Cactus Joe and his wicked ways.

Behind her came the thud of her trunk on the platform, but she didn't bother to retrieve it. Nothing in her trunk mattered as much as what was in her heart. Besides, there was no time to waste.

She'd finally figured out what the circles on Cactus Joe's calendar meant, and the closed telegraph office confirmed her suspicions.

She picked up her skirt and ran so fast that she almost stumbled over her feet. Sweat poured down her face and still she ran.

She stopped when she reached the outermost edge of the town. The street was deserted. Not a soul was in sight, but she wasn't fooled.

"Cactus Joe! I know you're here."

Nothing.

She ambled forward, cautious at first, but gradually picking up speed. She passed the barber, newspaper, and assay office. "Cactus Joe!"

At last a dark form stepped from the batwing doors of the Silver Moon Saloon, stopping her in her tracks. Her heart thudded and her mouth went dry, but she held her ground. This time she had a secret weapon.

Cactus Joe stood legs apart, gun in one hand and what looked like a sock in the other, probably holding stolen loot. As usual he was dressed in black with a patch over one eye and a pencil-thin mustache she now knew was false.

"Looky who's here," he drawled. "The writer who got away. Now you're gonna help *me* get away. Escaping is a whole lot harder now that there's a reward for my capture."

"I thought you'd be pleased," she said. "All that attention."

"Rewards don't make legends," he said. "Once I'm captured I'll be yesterday's news." He tilted his head. "I'm curious. How did you know you'd find me here?"

"Jesse James," she said. "I read a book about him. That's when I realized that the dates circled on your calendar corresponded to his robberies and other events in his life."

Cactus Joe frowned. "Go on."

"I first came to town on March twentieth. It just so happened that on that very same day in 1869, Jesse James stole fourteen thousand dollars from a bank in Kentucky. I can't remember the exact dates of your other holdups, but I'm willing to bet they match Jesse's."

"Very good," he said. "And today?"

"Today is April third," she said. "Jesse James died fourteen years ago today. I didn't think you'd let the day pass without doing something in remembrance."

"I'm impressed," Cactus Joe said.

"Thank you."

"It's all your fault, you know. Had you completed my book, I would have given up my life of crime for good."

"It's never too late." She held up her hand so he could see the package. "I have something for you."

She tossed the package through the air and it landed at his feet, stirring up a small cloud of dust.

He glanced down at it but made no move to pick it up. "Is this a trick?"

"Open it," she said.

"It better not be a trick." He stuffed the sock into his shirt but kept his hand on his six-shooter. He leaned over and picked up the package. He blew away the dust, and biting through the string with his teeth, he tore away the brown paper wrap.

He stared at the book in his hand with a wide grin. "Will you look at that?"

The title read *Cactus Joe: Master of Disguise.* She'd counted on his considerable ego to work in her favor and she wasn't disappointed. He was so enamored with the book he failed to notice the marshal sneaking up behind him.

"Drop the gun and put your hands over your head," Marshal Morris said, jabbing the serious end of his Peacemaker into Cactus Joe's back.

Cactus Joe did as he was told. He dropped his weapon — but not the book.

Kate smiled. This was exactly how she wrote the scene at the end of the book. Fiction had turned into reality. "I spelled your name correctly," she called. "Morris with two *r*'s."

The marshal grinned. "Wait till the sheriff hears about this. Looks like I'll be gittin' a

new assignment and you a handsome reward."

She didn't need any reward and didn't feel
right taking it. Maybe Aunt Bessie would
know how to put the reward money to good
use.

The marshal confiscated the bulging sock
and gave Cactus Joe a shove. "Move!"

Cactus Joe's outlaw days were over, but
judging by the big smile on his swarthy face,
he was too captivated by his book to care.

"Listen to this," he said and proceeded to
read out loud. " 'No man has ever gotten
the best of Cactus Joe, certainly no
lawman.' " He nodded in approval, ignoring
the irony. " 'All he needs is a peg leg and
parrot and he could easily pass as Long
John Silver.' "

He laughed. "Yes, yes," he boomed. "Even
Robert Louis Stevenson couldn't have said
it better. I always wanted to be a pirate and
rule the seven seas."

"That's too bad," the marshal said.
" 'Cause the only thing you're gonna rule is
a seven-by-seven jail cell."

Both prisoner and lawman disappeared
into the marshal's office and the door
slammed shut, cutting off the sound of
Cactus Joe's guffaws.

Kate couldn't help but laugh herself. Now

478

for the rest of her plan . . .

Luke set his bellows down. "What is it, boy? What do you want?"

Homer had been pacing back and forth for the last half hour or so. Now he scratched the floor by the door, cocked his head, and whimpered.

"You want to go out, eh? I guess that means it's safe." The gunfire he'd heard earlier had brought back more painful memories. It was during one of Cactus Joe's robberies that Kate first came to town. Memories of her flashed through his mind. He recalled how she felt in his arms as he whirled her about the dance floor, the feel of her lips on his. It seemed like only yesterday that he had carried her to his workbench, yet it seemed like a million years ago.

They say time healed all wounds, but it had been eight months since she left and it still hurt. It didn't seem possible that anything could hurt so much without an actual wound. If anything, the pain in his chest had grown worse, not better. It was all he could do to get through each day, let alone the long, lonely nights. Going to Boston had been a mistake. It only gave him false hope.

He could take iron and pound it into any shape he desired, but changing a woman's heart — that he couldn't do. No matter how much he wanted to he couldn't make Kate come back. Couldn't make her love him like he loved her.

Homer gave an impatient bark and Luke pulled off his leather apron and tossed it aside. He knew from experience that any reprieve from his painful memories would be short-lived. Might as well enjoy it while he could.

He donned a shirt, wiped his hands on a towel, and mopped his forehead. His gaze fell on the dictionary Michael had given him, now dog-eared from use. Each morning Luke picked out a word to memorize, hoping beyond hope that if Kate ever did come back he would be ready.

Today's word was *interminable*, meaning never-ending. Like his loneliness. Like the love he felt for Kate. Like the awful hurt that wouldn't go away.

He opened the door a crack and, seeing Mr. Green across the way, walked outside.

"Any news?" Luke called.

"Cactus Joe is in jail," Mr. Green called back.

That was a surprise. Maybe the marshal wasn't as incompetent as everyone thought.

Or maybe the reward money had done what it was supposed to do. Luke glanced down at Homer. "You knew that, didn't you?"

Ears pricked, Homer cocked his head, tail sweeping back and forth.

"Come on, we'll take a walk. It'll do us both good." He reached inside to pluck his hat from a hook and placed it on his head. The monsoon winds of summer were still a couple of months away, but a rain shower had passed through the night before. It was what Uncle Murphy called a six incher — one drop every six inches — but even a little moisture was better than none.

Luke started one way, but Homer refused to follow.

Luke turned and faced his dog, hands on his waist. "What's wrong with you?"

Homer walked a few steps in the other direction and sat, waiting for Luke to follow.

Luke scratched his head. "We always go this way. Why do you want to walk through town?"

"Woof!"

Luke shrugged. "I guess that's reason enough."

Word of Cactus Joe's capture began to spread, and Postmaster Parker ran up and down shouting the news. Fortunately, Parker held no ill feelings toward Luke or his uncle. The three of them had actually shared a good belly laugh over the whole affair.

Doors of the various businesses sprang open and shopkeepers and proprietors stepped outside to make sure they'd heard the news right.

"Are you sure?" Harry the barber called. "Cactus Joe is in jail?"

"Heard it with me own two ears," Parker called back.

Luke continued along Main with Homer by his side. He passed a handbill flapping on a post but didn't pay any attention to it until he noticed the town practically plastered with them.

Curious, he stopped at the next post and smoothed down the edges of the flyer so he could read it. "I don't aim on going anywhere either."

Shaking his head, he continued walking. A similar handbill hung from every post and every window and every door. His feet slowed. No, it couldn't be Kate's writing. She would use some decorative word. Besides, that wasn't how you spelled *anywear,* was it? Kate would never misspell a word.

He turned the corner and stopped. Was that . . . ? It looked like . . . No, it couldn't be. His eyes were playing tricks on him. It wouldn't be the first time. He'd chased many a woman down the streets of Boston thinking it was Kate, only to find it was someone else.

Next to him Homer barked and wagged his tail.

He stared at Homer. "Are you sure?"

"Woof!"

Luke didn't need any more convincing. He bolted forward. "Kate!"

The closer he got, the more beautiful she looked. The best part of all, she held a sign that read, "I'm here to stay."

He stopped a few feet in front of her, stopped short of taking her into his arms. Was he dreaming? Was this a mirage? A figment of his imagination? If he reached out to her, would she vanish like she had so many times before?

She searched his face. "Is that you?" she whispered.

Even now, even as she spoke, he was afraid to believe she was real. "It's me."

She dropped her sign and threw her shoulders back as he had seen her do whenever she had something important on her mind. "I love you, Luke Adams. I loved you since the first day we met, but my contumacious heart kept me from knowing my own mind."

His quick intake of breath sounded like a gasp. He cleared the distance between them, taking her hands in his. She was real. He could feel the softness of her flesh, smell the sweetness of her fragrance. He'd look up *contumacious* later, but he sure didn't need no dictionary to define the word *love*. Nor had a word ever filled him with more joy.

"Does . . . does that mean you trust that I'm not gonna walk away or desert you?" he asked, his voice a hoarse whisper. Even now, with the sweet-sounding word *love* still ringing in his ears, he was afraid to believe any of this was real.

She moistened her lips and looked up at him through tear-filled eyes. "I don't know, Luke. I'm trying. All I know is that I'm going to cherish every day we have together, no matter how many or how few."

Her honesty touched him, though it wasn't what he wanted to hear. He'd made a promise to be there for her, always — and he would die before breaking that vow. In return he wanted to know she trusted him, trusted in their future together.

The fact that she couldn't or wouldn't near broke his heart. Still, she was here and that was a start. He still had work to do — they both did — but a lot of good stuff could be forged from this thing called love. With God's help, maybe even trust.

This time he swept her in his arms and much to his delight she locked herself in his embrace — as if never to let him go.

Kate had dreamt about this moment for weeks and imagined every possible scenario. What if he had married Miss Chase? Or no longer wanted anything to do with her?

What if Luke had never been to Boston? What if a stranger had written those hand-bills? What if God had another plan for her altogether that did not involve Luke? There had been no end to what she imagined could go wrong. But the moment he took her in his arms all her worries vanished.

"I love you, Kate Tenney," he whispered. "And I swear I'm not goin' anywhere. Not unless you're by my side."

She stared up at him and the tenderness of his expression took her breath away. "Oh, Luke, I love you and want you and . . ." There was so much she wanted to say that words floated out like bubbles in the wind, but none could adequately express how she felt. "And fancy you and . . ."

She would have said more — a lot more — but his lips got in the way, searing a path all the way to her soul. At that moment, she was willing to believe anything — even that love could last a lifetime.

He pulled away, but only slightly. "Can you substantiate your declarations?" he asked.

"Substan—" She threw back her head and laughed. "Why, Luke Adams, I do believe you've been hanging around Webster."

As if to agree, Homer barked, but neither one paid him the least bit of attention.

Brandon and the brave, true, and kind-hearted Miss Hattie were joined together in holy matrimony. The author joins her many faithful readers in wishing this young, deserving couple much good fortune and wedded bliss. Long may they live!

READING GROUP GUIDE

In a desert land he found him, in a barren and howling waste. He shielded him and cared for him; he guarded him as the apple of his eye. — Deuteronomy 32:10(NIV)

1. In the Bible God used the desert to test Moses. In what ways did the desert test Kate? Describe your personal desert.
2. Change is as constant today as it was back in the 1800s. Every change brings new challenges. Uncle Sam gave up his blacksmith shop when the Montgomery Ward mail-order catalog made much of his work obsolete. Eleanor Walker braced herself for the changes that would affect her cattle business. What changes, good or bad, are you facing in your personal life? At work? In your hometown?
3. Do you face your problems head-on like the windmill faces the wind as described

in Longfellow's poem? Or do you tend to ignore or turn your back on problems?

4. Did you find yourself personally relating to any of the characters? If so, who and why?

5. Ruckus's faith had a positive effect on Kate. Name someone whose faith you admire. How did this affect your faith and/or relationship to God?

6. Kate thinks she can free herself from the past by avoiding love. For that reason the Last Chance Ranch seems like the perfect solution. How does holding on to the past keep her from realizing God's plan for her? Do you ever find yourself holding on to unpleasant memories or hurts? What is keeping you from letting go?

7. On the surface Kate and Luke seem like an unlikely couple. Kate is a college-educated woman and Luke is a fine crafts-man with little schooling. Name someone in your life who is a complete opposite. What blessings does this person bring to your life?

8. Aunt Bessie said that God gave love a language of its own and it's a language known by every heart. What does the phrase "language of love" mean to you?

9. Ruckus accused Kate of chasing the wind. It was his way of saying she was go-

ing after the wrong things in life. The same could be said for Cactus Joe and Miss Walker. Have you ever chased the wind? If so, who or what made you realize you were going down the wrong path?

10. One of Kate's survival tools is her habit of pretending everything that happens to her is a scene from a book. List the different ways that Luke, Aunt Bessie, Ruckus, and Eleanor Walker cope with their problems. Which character best depicts your coping style?

11. Kate's lack of faith in men caused her to reject love. Aunt Bessie's lack of faith in her husband almost broke up her marriage. What areas of your life could use more faith? Do you lack faith in yourself? Your loved ones? The future? God?

12. Kate was treated as an outcast by her neighbors and schoolmates. How much influence do you think this had on her wanting the ranch?

13. Kate viewed the world through the grief of a child rather than the grace of a woman. What childhood memories color your world? Are the memories mostly good or bad?

14. Kate longed for permanence in her life and was afraid to trust. For this reason she resisted taking a chance on love. Do

you think it's possible to trust anyone without first putting your trust in God? Why or why not?

15. Why do you think it was necessary for Kate to visit her mother's grave before going back to Arizona? Was there ever a time that you had to confront the past before you could embrace the future?

Dear Reader,

Save me, save me.
Bang, bang, bang.
Curses, foiled again!

Your Victorian ancestor may have had one shocking vice up her leg-o'-mutton sleeve — or tucked in her apron. Like millions of others she probably read dime novels — lots and lots of dime novels — similar to the ones Kate Tenney wrote.

The first dime novel, *Malaeska, the Indian Wife of the White Hunter,* was published in 1860 and quickly sold sixty-five thousand copies. That book started a craze that would remain popular until 1915. Melodramatic? You bet, but that was part of the fun. The stories were lurid — the purple prose outrageous — but readers couldn't seem to get enough.

A series of events led to the proliferation of dime novels. Mandatory education resulted in more literacy, and the invention of the steam printing press lowered the cost of printing. Railroads made distribution easier and books more accessible. Sales of dime novels surged during the Civil War. Confederates and Union soldiers were on opposing sides politically, but both camps shared the same passion for pirates, mountain men, adventurers, and detectives.

These formulaic stories ranged between thirty-five to fifty-five thousand words. The small four-by-six-inch, one-hundred-page format could be conveniently carried in pocket or purse. Most dime novels, like the popular *Deadwood Dick's Doom; or Calamity Jane's Last Adventure,* had two titles, probably to persuade readers that the story was too big and exciting for only one.

Though the lurid cover art and violent stories were severely criticized by moralists as having a bad influence on youth — and corrupting the delicate brains of women — the stories actually reinforced the values of patriotism, courage, and self-reliance. This, however, didn't stop critics from blaming them for everything from childish pranks to violent crimes and the women's rights movement. One man even had his wife committed for reading them.

Books based on real people such as Buffalo Bill, Kit Carson, and Jesse James were especially popular, though the stories were purely fiction. The good guys battled evil and no bad deed was left unpunished. Chaste damsels in distress needed rescuing and dashing heroes were only too happy to oblige. By today's standards the books were racist, but they reflected the times. They also helped to establish a new social order where males were judged by deeds rather than social status. For this reason the western hero became the symbol of the ideal man.

Speaking of ideal men and chaste damsels, if you liked Kate and Luke's story, then you might want to keep a lookout for book two in my Brides of Last Chance Ranch series. If Miss Walker thought Kate was a handful, wait till she meets the feisty heroine of my next book.

Until next time . . .
Margaret

ONE COW AWAY FROM HOPE

As you may remember, the Last Chance Ranch got its start when one grateful Englishman gave the Walker family a cow. This story is fiction, of course, but the reality is that Heifer International has been giving away livestock and changing lives for years. To celebrate the new series, I'm working with Heifer on a project to purchase two heifers. Would you join me in helping families in need achieve self-reliance and sustainable livelihoods by making a donation? You can access my Heifer page through margaretbrownley.com. If you make a donation here, leave me a note on Facebook for a chance to win a free book.

ACKNOWLEDGMENTS

In 1863 fifty ladies of the First Church of Milford formed a Society of Old Maids. Each woman paid five dollars to join and had to vow never to marry. The interest from the money was to be used for an annual dinner and the principal to go to the last woman to marry. Thirty years later all but fifteen had married. I've never been able to find the name of the winner — and I sincerely hope there wasn't one — but I am truly grateful for this group for inspiring the idea behind The Brides of Last Chance Ranch series.

I'm also grateful to you, my readers, for your many letters and emails, which always seem to arrive when I most need an encouraging word or two.

Heartfelt thanks go to Natasha Kern — friend, agent, mentor, and all-around amazing person!

I can't say enough good things about my

Thomas Nelson family. I'm especially grateful for my editor Natalie Hanemann for her insight and guidance; for Rachelle Gardner whose eye for detail makes me look good; and for Katie Bond and Eric Mullett for their creative talent and hard work. I'm also grateful for the privilege of knowing and working with Allen Arnold whose faith, wisdom, and love of story is an inspiration to us all.

I couldn't do what I do without my loving and patient husband by my side. It's not easy to live with a woman who talks to people he can't see and jumps out of bed at three a.m. to write something down. Finally, I thank God for bringing so many wonderful people into my life and for instilling in me the love of words and the need to write.

ABOUT THE AUTHOR

New York Times best-selling author **Margaret Brownley** has penned more than twenty-five historical and contemporary novels. Her books have won numerous awards, including Reader's Choice.

Though successful, Margaret decided to leave behind the secular publishing world to follow God's will for her: to write inspirational fiction. Since then she has published the Rocky Creek series, and *A Lady like Sarah* was a Romance Writers of America RITA® finalist.

Happily married to her real-life hero, Margaret and her husband have three grown children and live in Southern California.

The employees of Thorndike Press hope you have enjoyed this Large Print book. All our Thorndike, Wheeler, and Kennebec Large Print titles are designed for easy reading, and all our books are made to last. Other Thorndike Press Large Print books are available at your library, through selected bookstores, or directly from us.

For information about titles, please call:
  (800) 223-1244

or visit our Web site at:
  http://gale.cengage.com/thorndike

To share your comments, please write:
Publisher
Thorndike Press
10 Water St., Suite 310
Waterville, ME 04901